Holy Brotherhood

Holy Brotherhood

Romani Music in a Hungarian Pentecostal Church

Barbara Rose Lange

OXFORD
UNIVERSITY PRESS

2003

OXFORD
UNIVERSITY PRESS

Oxford   New York
Auckland   Bangkok   Buenos Aires   Cape Town   Chennai
Dar es Salaam   Delhi   Hong Kong   Istanbul   Karachi   Kolkata
Kuala Lumpur   Madrid   Melbourne   Mexico City   Mumbai   Nairobi
São Paulo   Shanghai   Taipei   Tokyo   Toronto

Copyright © 2003 by Oxford University Press, Inc.

Published by Oxford University Press, Inc.
198 Madison Avenue, New York, New York 10016

www.oup.com

Oxford is a registered trademark of Oxford University Press

Library of Congress Cataloging-in-Publication Data
Lange, Barbara Rose, 1955–
Holy brotherhood : Romani music in a Hungarian Pentecostal church / Barbara Rose Lange.
p. cm.
Includes bibliographical references (p.).
ISBN 0-19-513723-x
1. Romanies—Hungary—Pécs—Music—History and criticism.
2. Pentecostals—Hungary—Pécs—Hymns—History and criticism.
3. Isten Gyülekezet (Pécs, Hungary)   4. Pentecostals—Hungary—History.
5. Pentacostals—United States—History.   6. Romanies—Hungary—Religion.
7. Hungary—Ethnic relations.   I. Title.
ML3151 .H9 L36 2002
781.71'89—dc21   2002000693

2 4 6 8 9 7 5 3 1

Printed in the United States of America
on acid-free paper

Acknowledgments

I am grateful for financial support through grants from the International Research and Exchanges Board, Fulbright, the American Council for Collaboration and Exchange in Language Study, and the University of Houston that made my field research possible.

In Hungary, Sándor Martsa provided institutional support at Janus Pannonius University and the Martsa family welcomed me warmly on holidays. Katalin Kovalcsik of the Hungarian Academy of Sciences Musicological Institute helped me with lessons in Romani and with many informal conversations that led to a deeper understanding of traditional Romani music in Hungary as well as the ethics of Romani studies in Eastern Europe. Péter Heindl, Éva Kakas, László Wesztl, Károly Cserepes, Júlia Mezei, and the family of János Balogh all provided stimulating company and nurturing hospitality during my stays in Hungary. I am grateful to the many other people who were interested in the issues raised by this project and made the effort to explain their views about what those issues might mean for Hungarian society at large.

I thank Csaba Ökrös for first attracting me to Hungarian music. I write in tribute to Zsuzsa Horváth. Her research provided the original inspiration in my choice of a religious group for study. She gave advice on historical and sociological aspects of the subject and, most important, served as a model of truthfulness and conscience in the field situation. I thank Anna Cserei for her help in checking Hungarian language translations and transcriptions. Will Dull assisted me in preparing the photos.

Kay Sherman and Richard Alexander offered companionship and a peaceful place to work as I wrote various parts of this book. A Mellon Fellowship at Cornell University also provided me with time to write, as well as stimulating interchange with colleagues at the Center for the Humanities. I am grateful to Philip Bohlman, Linda Dégh, Esther Rothenbusch, Thomas Acton, the anonymous readers of the manuscript, and the editors at Oxford University Press for their advice on the best way to translate the concerns of living, singing people to the page.

My deepest gratitude goes to the leaders and members of the Isten Gyülekezet. They showed me hospitality, they trusted me with details of their private lives, they explained details of their music to me, and they willingly shared the most precious element of their present lives, their religious experience.

Contents

Note on Textual and Musical Transcriptions

The Pentecostals in Hungary possess written versions of nearly all the song texts that are transcribed here. In performance, congregations and individuals often varied slightly from the written sources. I have transcribed the texts as performed in a given field recording (see the appendix). Members of a group sometimes sang different versions of a text simultaneously; in such cases, I have chosen the version that seemed to be used by the most people. In cases where pronunciation was unclear, I have relied on a written text. Selected verses are included for the songs that had a large number of stanzas. Regional dialects are not transcribed.

Nearly all the songs transcribed here had instrumental accompaniment. A system of indicating approximate pitch that corresponds kinesically with the playing patterns of a given instrumental accompaniment is thus used (see Lajtha 1953). Tempo markings are approximate. Performers did not always follow regular beat cycles. Bar lines are placed where cycles were implied by accents in performance and are eliminated where the performers did not appear to feel a regular pulse.

Special symbols:

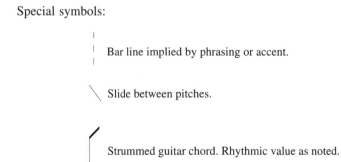

Bar line implied by phrasing or accent.

Slide between pitches.

Strummed guitar chord. Rhythmic value as noted.

Pronunciation Guide and Orthography for the Hungarian and Romani Languages

The orthographic system used for Romani follows English spelling and pronunciation rules. Interpolated vocables are indicated with the International Phonetic Alphabet.

Each sound in Hungarian has its own symbol. The sounds may be short or long. Vowel length is indicated with accents. Consonant length is indicated by doubling, and there are some alternate spellings. No consonants are aspirated.

(This guide is based on Erdős et al. [1986] and Magay and Országh [1990].)

A	a	as in w*a*s
Á	á	as in c*a*rt
B	b	as in *b*e
C	c	as in roo*ts*
Cs	cs	as in su*ch*
D	d	as in *d*oor
E	e	as in s*e*t
É	é	as in m*a*ke
F	f	as in *f*ar
G	g	as in *g*o
Gy	gy	as in *d*upe (British pron.)
H	h	as in *h*am
I	i	as in l*i*p
Í	í	as in f*ee*d
J	j	as in *y*oung
K	k	as in *k*ey
L	l	as in *l*ook
M	m	as in *m*ore

N   n   as in *n*ow

Ny   ny   as in o*n*ion

O   o   as in b*o*rn

Ó   ó   as in d*oo*r

Ö   ö   as in ch*u*rch (British pron.)

Ő   ő   as in French d*eux*

P   p   as in *p*ear

R   r   as in Spanish ca*r*o

S   s   as in *sh*eep

Sz   sz   as in *s*at

T   t   as in af*t*er

Ty   ty   as in sta*t*ue (British pron.)

U   u   as in gr*ou*p

Ú   ú   as in m*o*ve

Ü   ü   as in French t*u*

Ű   ű   as in French am*u*se

V   v   as in *v*ice

Z   z   as in *z*oo

Zs   zs   as in mea*s*ure

All translations from Hungarian and Romani are mine.

List of Abbreviations

DU   *Dicsőitlek Uram*! (I Praise You, My Lord)

GH   *Gospel Hymns Nos. 1–6* (Sankey, McGranahan, and Stebbins 1895)

HÉ   *Hitünk énekei* (Songs of Our Faith)

IG   Isten Gyülekezet (Assembly of God)

SSS   *Sacred Songs and Solos* (Sankey [1921, repr. 1972])

Holy Brotherhood

Introduction

A s I arrived early one Sunday morning in 1990 at the small meeting room of the Isten Gyülekezet (Assembly of God) in Pécs, Hungary, it was crowded with church members. Greeting each other with the word "peace" (*békesség*), a handshake, and kisses, they hung their coats in the tiny anteroom and went into the worship hall, where the congregation was already singing. The tightly ranked rows of wooden chairs with home-sewn cushions filled up with stout women and children in skirts, sweaters, and kerchiefs of neutral colors. I sat in the second row next to Sister Annus, a believer in her midsixties. A single poster hung on the whitewashed walls, depicting the message of the "narrow way" to eternal life from Christ's Sermon on the Mount. A small cross and a tiny collection box hung on the facing wall. Light streamed through white lace curtains at one end of the long, narrow room. Underneath these windows sat a row of men, the instrumental musicians with organ, synthesizer, and guitar on one side and preachers on the other. In front of them was the pulpit, holding a microphone and a small blue satin altar cloth embroidered with a cross and crown. The musicians had plugged their instruments into amplifiers and adjusted their sound volume, a tricky process because the equipment was very old.

Brother Gál, a Romani (Gypsy) preacher who was playing metal spoons, started singing the first phrase of a song, "Halleluja néked, mennyei Atyám!" (Halleluia to You, My Heavenly Father). The synthesizer player joined him, and the entire congregation began to sing in unison. Brother Rudi, a Rom who sat at the console organ, used a microphone, and I could hear his thick baritone over the rest of the group. In the middle of the singing, Sister Rózsi cried out with the rounded vowels of a rural accent, "Praise, holy king!" The congregation paused while the instrumentalists continued to play. Weeping, she called, "Dear savior king, dear Jesus, let me praise you, magnify you, my Lord." Brother Gál also began a prayer, asking: "Bless us . . . by means of your wondrous cross . . . so that enmity will stop by means of your precious spirit." Gál's voice rose gradually over the music and the prayers of other church members. "So that we can be one, as the cross is one form . . . help us, Jesus. We ask you, in your great name." The congregation members began to sing again, this time more intensely; like Sister Rózsi, many stopped sing-ing periodically to pray aloud.

At the end of this song, Brother Zoli, a Magyar, played several short runs on his synthesizer and then the individual notes of a chord. Brother Rudi began singing "Nincs olyan kis dolog" (There Is Nothing So Small), a translation of the Christian pop song "He Will Carry You," and a few people joined him. Immediately after the song faded to an end, Brother Gál announced another song that he had learned from believers in the northern part of the country. He continued, "I ask you, my brothers, give your heart to the Lord, so that he can form the Holy Spirit in our hearts," tap-ping a pattern with kitchen spoons as the whole congregation sang vigorously and began to clap. Brother Bandi, a Rom, called out "Halleluia," began to pray aloud, and then yelled a startling burst of syllables; he was speaking in "tongues."

After several more songs and a Bible reading, the entire congregation began to pray aloud. Brother Horváth, the congregation's head pastor and a Magyar, entered the worship hall. Brother Gál announced, "We will end our prayer hour with the song 'Teérted szenvedtem én, ott fent a Golgotán' [I Suffered for You up on Golgotha]." This song was contained in a small blue chapbook of texts. Then Brother Horváth announced another number from the chapbook, a translation of a nineteenth-century American gospel hymn, Fanny Crosby and William H. Doane's "Near the Cross." The congregation sang quietly and slowly; Brother Horváth's true baritone voice led the first verse. Then he stepped up to the pulpit. After a brief report on church fi-nances, to my surprise he did not begin preaching but simply talked to the congrega-tion. Earlier in the week, I had overheard one of the believers complaining to Brother Horváth that church members in a neighboring town refused to receive her as a guest at their midweek meeting. Although Brother Horváth did not refer directly to that incident, nearly everyone present on Sunday knew what had occurred.

"We are behaving dishonestly toward each other," he said to the congregation. "We don't respect each other, we are disrespectful. So we gaze over the heads of each other as [they do] out in the world. If someone feels himself to be superior, he should try to descend lower. If on the other hand someone feels himself to be very low, let him raise himself up and know that we are brothers in Jesus Christ." A young woman called out "Amen." Brother Horváth continued with some euphemistic ref-erences to the fact that there were Roma (Gypsies), Hungarians, and members of several other ethnic groups in the congregation; several weeks previously, he had mentioned to me that he tried to avoid using the term "Gypsy" and preferred to call all church members simply *testvér* (sibling or brother). He said, "I have to empha-size this here, brothers, because, well, the sum of our congregation is mixed. So there are some spiritually wounded people who, well, don't dare to be raised higher and who think, 'I'm looked down upon,' who think, 'here I can't be anyone or anything.'" Drawing out his words again, Brother Horváth said, "But let us be certain that we can be *testvérek* [pl.] in Jesus Christ." "Amen," interjected József Gál; several other people murmured "Amen" in reply.

"I'm saying this in both directions," continued Brother Horváth. "So let us not lord it over other people, let us not keep cutting against each other, but let us always first seek love, peace. Because God's word says the admonisher [should] admonish out of love." Then he humorously said, "Let us try to do this, not like they say in the world, that equality is 'What's yours is mine and what's mine you have no business with.'" The congregation members smiled at this ironic reference to how officials in the recently dissolved socialist government had exploited the citizens. Brother Horváth slowed his words for emphasis again. "But as we pay attention to the words of Jesus Christ, we are all brothers. He is our shepherd." Several of the congregation members murmured "Amen." Brother Horváth continued, "There are complaints that some people are rude, rudely admonish, and are behaving in an ugly manner—but rudeness is something of the world. . . . It is so easy to beat up a soul, but how difficult it is to bring one to the Lord and to drudge for it!" He described how during the 1960s a dispute over modest dress for women had arisen at the national level, causing a local pastor to leave his church in frustration. "So *testvérek*, no matter who it is, be he a missionary or anyone, he should always keep respect for the order and customs of the local congregation." Then with a glance at me, he made a light reference to American missionaries: "Many times it is strange to us Hungarians when American *testvérek* come. For example, they get down from the pulpit and go here and there and it is strange to us. According to Hungarian ethical rules, this is strange, isn't it? I was with them in America and there the people themselves are like that, they move around . . . but here if I try to imitate them, you would be scandalized . . . we accept it from them because it is in their temperament. But every people, every nationality has its own characteristics, don't they, like these, and they are manifested in our lives.

"So brothers, I am happy that in our vicinity, in our environment, I'm talking about those young people who have become believers, are learning rules of proper conduct." The expression "young people" was a euphemism; it actually referred to the newer Romani members of the church, a number of whom were in their twenties. Brother Horváth paused and then raised his voice. "What a huge development they have undergone. Where? At which seminary did they study?" "From Jesus Christ," interjected József Gál. Brother Horváth repeated, "From Jesus Christ, *testvérek*. Therefore I say that the highest degree of propriety, and the best ethical rule, is in Jesus Christ." Smiling, he concluded, "Then we will be believing people. The kind of people who simply want life and to meet with each other. We are happy. We are not ashamed of each other, but are happy that we can be one in Jesus Christ. So let the Lord and his Word bless everyone, and teach us—*testvérek*, let's sing a song." Immediately Brother Borovics, an elderly ethnic Serb believer dressed in a faded brown polyester suit, suggested "Oh How Dear, Oh How Beautiful," a paraphrase of Psalm 133 from the chapbook. Brother Horváth restated the first verse in a rhythmic chant: "Oh how dear, oh how beautiful / Is brotherly holy unity / In a holy brotherly circle / Praising him, him."

The members of the Isten Gyülekezet (IG), a Pentecostal church in southwestern Hungary, followed an ideal of "holy brotherhood," embracing all fellow adherents as close companions. In his talk, the congregation's head pastor outlined three major challenges to this ideal. During the sixty years of their religion's existence in Hungary, the Pentecostals had suffered persecution and social stigma. Periodically missionaries from the West promoted new dogmas, worship styles, and community structures. The greatest challenge came from the fact that the IG's membership comprised two disparate groups: Magyars, the majority national group in Hungary, and the minority Roma. Before and after the fall of socialism in Eastern Europe there was much antagonism between these two peoples.

The head pastor rejected "theology," that is, the intellectual study of Christian doctrine, as a means of resolving such tensions, instead finding solutions in "the proximity of Jesus" (*Jézus közelében*). In one way, this meant the feeling that God was physically present. In another sense, proximity meant interchange with fellow believers. At the time I was conducting fieldwork with the group in the early 1990s, the IG had the character of what Don Yoder has called a "folk church"; it was locally oriented and generated its own values, rhetoric, performance modes, and nuances of belief (1974). The dogmas, music, and histories of the believers were connected to the locality of southwest Hungary, although their religion was known worldwide. Hungarian emigrants who converted to Pentecostalism in the United States had returned to their homeland as missionaries and founded the IG in the 1920s. The name of the church translates as Assembly of God, one of the major Pentecostal denominations in the United States. Originally affiliated with each other, the two no longer have a connection. Until the 1980s, Pentecostalism had a tumultuous history in Hungary. Elderly believers had lived through decades of instability, sectarian battles, and suppression by the state. The church became multiethnic in the mid-1980s, and by 1990, the year I began participant-observation, the membership was 80 percent Roma. In the early 1990s, the IG became affiliated with a different U.S. church through some of the missionaries the head pastor mentioned in his talk.

I became interested in Pentecostal music and Roma's involvement in it for several reasons. As a classical violin player, I had been exposed to a romantic image of the Gypsy violinist. In the 1980s, I began to play East European fiddle, and I was disturbed by the clash between this image and the low status that Romani players actually had in villages. During the course of my fieldwork, this contradiction led me to pay attention to songs rather than instrumental music. Singing appeared to be personally rather than professionally significant for them; fewer and fewer Roma were playing stringed instruments, whereas every Rom I knew sang. In the United States, I learned about Evangelical church events by playing at them as a professional musician. There, the ideology of how divinity manifests in musical sound intrigued me. In Hungary, these two themes converged as my beginning study of the society revealed how religious believers had doggedly clung to their systems of thought over forty years of socialist rule. At the time I started visiting Hungary for language training in the late 1980s, the IG was almost an underground organization. I only learned about the church when press restrictions began to be loosened and I read an article about the IG in one of the new independent newspapers (Bencze 1989). When I visited the church, I heard the familiar tunes of Anglo-American gospel hymns, as well as original songs. This group seemed to offer a convergence of issues concerning Romani music, Hungarian style, and religious experience in music. At the same time, it seemed to encapsulate some of the complexities around global culture that were just reemerging in the East European societies. A further development came during a second year of research when I was living in Budapest. There I worked with Romani political activists and nonreligious Roma and researched secular popular music among Roma and working-class Hungarians (see Lange 1996b, 1997a, 1997b, 1999). The multiple interests within the IG community became clearer to me through this work on secular music.

As a Pentecostal church, the IG adhered to a special version of Christianity. Pentecostals worship in an expressive and somewhat spontaneous manner based on their interpretation of the events described in Acts 2:1–4 of the Bible. This passage relates how God became present shortly after the Resurrection on the day of Pentecost to a group of disciples and other followers of Jesus. Pentecostals believe that just as it happened to the early Christians, God materializes to them now in the form of the Holy Spirit. Among these manifestations, or "gifts of the Holy Spirit," are spontaneous healing and prophecy. To outsiders the most remarkable is glossolalia, or "speaking in tongues," words and syllables that are not intelligible in the secular language of a congregation. Pentecostals believe that these utterances are messages from God in unknown yet potentially translatable languages. Pentecostals interpret other parts of the Bible literally, and so they follow many behavioral restrictions based on their readings of Bible passages. These restrictions, combined with the ecstatic nature of their religious experience, serve as a boundary between them and secular society. Pentecostalism began in the United States at the turn of the twentieth century and, along with the related religion of evangelical Protestantism, has gained large numbers of adherents in Latin America, Africa, Southeast Asia, and other parts of the world, as well as Eastern Europe (Hollenweger 1972). At the time I was doing fieldwork with the church, the IG had adopted Oneness, a variety of Pentecostalism that recognizes all manifestations of God as aspects only of Jesus.

Pentecostals' worship forms have an intensity that is compelling not only for them but for those who study expressive culture. Pentecostals see their devotions not just as a way to praise God but also as actual manifestations of the divine as the Holy Spirit. The Holy Spirit affects preaching; it can determine the themes that are addressed and the urgency of the rhetoric and in some cases cause the preaching to resemble chant or song (Lawless 1988a; Rosenberg 1970). Believers relate many stories about their faith. As personal narratives these have unique styles of construction, often illustrating a literalist style of thinking, betraying evidence of trauma, or celebrating miracles that are fundamental to the Pentecostal belief system (Crapanzano 2000; Dégh 1990, 1994; Lawless 1988b; Stromberg 1993). Former participants have described how during the early days of Pentecostalism in the United States all forms of worship were kept flexible so that the Holy Spirit could manifest. The value on spontaneity allowed for the introduction of popular culture and modern technology, especially in songs, singing style, and musical instruments (Blumhofer 1993:170; Brumback 1961:136; Duncan 1987).

Among the aspects of Pentecostal worship, music comes across as the most flexible. Like the other worship modes, it is a type of discourse (Titon 1988), but it communicates differently. Its polysemic characteristics can generate multiple meanings and interpretations (Turino 1999). Music can be realized in different styles of performance and thus inflected with varied aspects of cultural and historical significance. By the end of the twentieth century, Pentecostal worship had many established procedures and authorities, but in the IG at least, music retained its flexibility. Many converts in Hungary told me they were attracted to the religion first by its songs; the emotionalism in elderly believers' singing attested to how music remained integral to their experiences of God. Church members embraced a variety of styles, as did the first U.S. Pentecostals, because they valued them as Holy Spirit manifestations.

I was impressed by how much pleasure IG members had from music-making, which they characterized as an infusion of divine energy. At the same time, the coexisting styles brought issues about power and authority to the foreground. Pentecostals believe that the Holy Spirit can manifest spontaneously and in any person. In small independent congregations, their flexible worship styles allow ordinary congregation members to take a prominent role. In large congregations, the worship procedures are much more codified and leadership is determined by detailed criteria extrapolated from the biblical text. The rhetoric of Pentecostalism emphasizes close community, created by rejecting the worldly and embracing mystical, ecstatic religious experience in the company of fellow believers (Clements 1976:35–40, 42–44; Hollenweger 1972). However, for the IG members at least, this communitas was intermittent. A primary tension that I observed was between two major constituencies in the church—elderly Magyars and new Romani converts.

Roma in Hungarian Society

Magyars are the majority group in Hungary. They constitute a nation (*nemzet*) as the group with whom the country of Hungary has historically been identified. However, this nation has many minority peoples who also are citizens. They include ethnic Serbs, Croats, Slovaks, and others; Roma are the largest ethnic minority. Roma have a variety of lifestyles, appearances, and even languages. Many of them are present or former speakers of Romani, an Indo-Aryan language. Migrating out of northwest India about a thousand years ago, they came into Europe by approximately the twelfth century CE (Crowe 1994:xi). Historically, many Roma engaged in special trades like metalworking, basketry, or entertainment.[1] In Western Europe they practiced what Thomas Acton has called "economic nomadism," traveling to benefit from changing regional economies (Acton 1974:254–59). In Eastern Europe, most of the Romani population is sedentary. Hungary's Roma number approximately five hundred thousand, or 5 percent of the population (Havas et al. 1995:67), forming three different major ethnic groups, the Romungro (pl. Romungre), Vlach, and Boyash. Vlach Roma are bilingual in Romani and Hungarian and migrated into present-day Hungary from the neighboring country of Romania during the last half of the nineteenth century. They specialized in trades like horse dealing and metalworking. Boyash Roma are bilingual in Romanian and Hungarian but do not speak Romani; they migrated into the southern areas of present-day Hungary from Romania in the nineteenth century. Many of them were woodworkers. Romungre speak Hungarian with Romani loan words. They settled in many Hungarian villages starting in the fourteenth century (Crowe 1994:69–71). They pursued a variety of trades, among them instrumental music; Gypsy violinists are from the Romungro ethnic group. In Hungary, Romungre comprise approximately 71 percent of the Romani population, Vlach Roma 21 percent, and Boyashes 8 percent (Erdős 1960; Kemény 1974:65). The IG drew its membership from all three Rom ethnic groups, but Romungre dominated at 70 percent, with 25 percent Boyash and 5 percent Vlach Roma.

Roma have existed at the margins of most societies in which they have lived. In modern Europe, including Hungary, they were abused in many ways. Before migrating into Hungary, Vlach and Boyash Roma had been enslaved or enserfed in Romania (see Hancock 1987:16–48). During World War II, thousands of Roma were killed in the Holocaust (*porrajmos* in Romani) and many others were impressed into labor.[2] Another strategy, forced assimilation, was damaging from a cultural standpoint. As Michel Foucault has pointed out, reforms, meant to change the nature of people, are invasive in multiple ways (1990[1976]). Many European governments attempted to reform the Roma (see Gronemeyer 1981:196–98). Empress Maria Theresa decreed a program in 1761, in effect for thirty years, that deeply affected the Romungre. She proclaimed Roma to be "new Hungarians" (*új magyarok*), officially registered them, forbade nomadism, forcibly removed children from their parents, and banned the Romani language (Crowe 1994:72–78).

The socialist state also declared the goal of assimilating the Roma. Some minorities in Hungary, for example ethnic Slovaks, Romanians, or Germans, were recognized as "nationalities" (*nemzetiségek*). The state provided funding and institutional support for many of their activities, including ethnically specific language instruction, radio programs, and folk ensembles. But the government asserted that Roma, "in spite of certain of their folkloric peculiarities . . . do not comprise a 'nationality'" (Mezey 1986:242). One of the problems for Roma lay in the fact that, unlike many other ethnic groups in Europe, they were not linked to a neighboring nation. Their material and expressive culture did not fit well into the essentialist categories used for other ethnic minorities, especially because it often differed subtly from that of surrounding groups. The state implemented programs to assimilate Roma in the areas of housing, work, and education, with the declared goal of bringing Roma into the working class. As socialism dissolved in the 1980s, activists worked to have Roma recognized equally with the other ethnic minorities in Hungary. But at the end of the socialist period, Magyar–Rom relations were in crisis. Tensions became great as all aspects of the society began changing at once.

An Orientalizing discourse has accompanied the oppressions of Roma. The very term "Gypsy," possibly associating the Roma with Egypt, places them outside Europe into the East. Another term, *tsigane/Zigeuner* (*cigány* in Hungarian), is usually translated as "Gypsy" but possibly derives from a reference to *atsinganoi*, people who lived on the margins of Greek society. Ken Lee has demonstrated that folkloristic, linguistic, and administrative documents about Gypsies are full of horror at the barbaric, attractions to the free and uninhibited, and judgments about authenticity (2000). For several centuries, such images of Gypsies were prevalent in Hungary. In his famous book on Gypsy musicians, Franz Liszt extolled their supposed freedom and closeness to the instincts with such assertions as "it is impossible to imagine an assimilation to Nature more complete than that of the Gipsy" (1881[1859] part 1:94). Even in the 1980s, when András Hegedüs analyzed images of Roma in the Hungarian press, a dual image prevailed. Overly simple, negative stereotypes emphasizing such things as criminality competed with scattered reports on outstanding artists of Romani ethnicity (Hegedüs 1989:68–70, 78–79). In her ethnographic study of Roma in Russia during the 1990s, Alaina Lemon characterizes such dual viewpoints as "misrecognitions." The Russian public thought of the characters and situations portrayed at Moscow's Romani Theater as Gypsy reality. Markets and subways represented conflicting "stages" of everyday performance; there the mainstream expected Gypsies to be "shifty" and dishonest (Lemon 2000:56–79).

These splits may be generated out of a founding fallacy of ethnic nation-states, that is, that they are constituted out of a single ethnic group (Gheorghe and Acton 1992:28–29). The East European philosopher Slavoj Žižek argues that European societies must define themselves over against something; the outcast role is given sometimes figuratively and sometimes literally to the Jew or the Gypsy (1989:128–76). Ethnographic work confirms the existence of such a viewpoint. When Zsolt Csalog surveyed the opinion of Hungarian villagers about Roma in their own environment during the 1980s, he concluded that the villagers were objecting to what they saw as the "un-bourgeois" behavior of Roma (1984). Sam Beck observed that Romanian villagers categorized others as Gypsies not according to language or by appearance but rather by where they lived at the village margins and whether they behaved in a manner that seemed uncouth to them (1985). This view even appeared to extend to a distinction between nature and culture; Mattjis van de Port concluded that the Serbs he worked with saw Roma as "pre-cultural" (Neményi 1991). A much milder version of this viewpoint was present in Hungary, with the idea that some people were lacking in high culture, education, or refinement. The Roma formed just one of the groups that were characterized this way. In Hungary, the linguist József Vekerdi asserted that the Romani language was degraded and lexically impoverished. He said that Romani folktales merely derived from those of surrounding peoples and that their material culture was characterized simply by poverty (1988).[3] As I will discuss in chapter 1, Pentecostal adherents were also labeled as being without culture.

Hungary's Roma resisted these subjugations in different ways. Michael Stewart has demonstrated how one community of Vlach Roma articulated a separate identity in part by denigrating Magyars and in part by attaching honor to behavior that connoted being Rom (1997). Irén Kertész-Wilkinson worked with Vlach Roma who appropriated Magyar songs very appreciatively; nonetheless, their musical tastes and value systems were separate (1997). Vlach and other Romani-speaking Roma often articulate endogamous family networks through tribunals, taboos characterizing non-Roma as unclean, or complicated marriage negotiations (see Liégeois 1994:70–75). The Roma of my acquaintance did not seem as autonomous as others whom ethnographers in Hungary have described. Most of them were Romungre, not Vlach Roma. Many Romungre were within an environment of misrecognitions, sometimes living in relative proximity with Magyars at the village level and other times entertaining the mainstream with instrumental music. Romungre have aspired to some aspects of the Hungarian peasant or worker's way of life (Szuhay 1999:33–36).

I believe that the Roma I knew in the IG were engaging in a mixture of strategies, in some respects to assimilate and in some ways to remain autonomous. My Romungro co-respondents did live independently in an important sphere—the family environment. Unlike Vlach Roma, they resolved disputes and made matches in somewhat informal ways. What impressed me in the Romungro households where I stayed was the intense level of communication; as I will describe, this was a crucial factor in how they adopted religious beliefs and music. Acknowledging that a group like Roma might want to assimilate contradicts an idea of ethnic autonomy that has successfully forced many European governments to cede equal rights to minorities. However, the history of ethnic change is full of cases like that of the Romungre where people have selectively suppressed aspects of their culture in order to assimilate to the mainstream. They may persist with some customs in private but consciously deploy other behaviors in the service of impression management (Banton 1981; Berreman 1975; Goffman 1959). In their dense historical accounts respectively of slavery and of the British working class, Eugene Genovese and E. P. Thompson describe how, when the power differences are great, strategies of independence are sometimes inchoate and only partially effective (Genovese 1974; Thompson 1963, 1991). As "a whole vocabulary of discourse, of legitimation and of expectation," custom, while not always verbally articulate, is at least a way that subalterns can represent their interests (Thompson 1991:2, 6). In the IG, there were several cultural vocabularies; some were more legitimate than others by virtue of their connection to the upper class or to Magyars, that is, the dominant groups in secular society. Church members sometimes conformed to dominant musical and social values, but their strategies were contingent or temporary or carried double meanings.

By contrast with Roma, many of the Magyars I knew were isolated. Elemér Hankiss has pointed out that alienation was a major effect of socialism in Hungarian society. Neighborhood, work, and religious affiliations had been broken, and even family ties were weak (1989:54–60). This was sadly evident with Magyars who were IG members; they were often single, widowed, or divorced and lived far away from their children. Since home telephones were rare in the early 1990s, the believers often had very little contact with other family members. Sister "Heléna," for example, lived by herself in a high-rise housing development, while her elderly mother lived alone in a village at the outskirts of Pécs. Her adult daughter lived elsewhere and had no interest in attending church. As a close community, the IG thus had contrasting attractions for Magyars and Roma. Magyar church members spoke of finding love, warmheartedness, and freedom in the congregation; their choices to join IG were ways to counteract isolation that was a condition of the secular society. Roma tended to join the IG along with their families and friends; they spoke appreciatively of the expressive freedom that IG allowed.

In the 1990s, terminology to refer to Roma was in flux. During the early 1990s the Roma I knew almost universally, except for those Vlach Roma who spoke the Romani language, called themselves *cigányok* (Gypsies). However, as Brother Misi, a Romani preacher from the town of Szigetvár, explained to me, depending on the context and the speaker's tone of voice, the word can have either neutral or pejorative connotations. During the 1990s many Hungarians, Romani political activists, the press, and people elsewhere in Europe began to use the term "Roma" as a general term of reference; Roma means "men" in the Romani language. By the late 1990s, I noticed many more of my co-respondents using "Roma" and *cigány* interchangeably. In this book, I use "Gypsy" in any discussion of images, and I use terms derived from the Romani language, "Rom/Roma/Romani" (sing./plur./adj.), when discussing actual people. With this choice, I also acknowledge that ethnographies cannot hope to provide "true" representations (Clifford 1986). I intend to demonstrate respect toward my co-respondents with these terms, avoiding the possible denigration—but also not achieving the intimacy—that *cigány* or "Gypsy" would convey. I use the term "Hungarian" to refer to all citizens of the state of Hungary and "Magyar" to refer to those people who are of the majority national group, including people with partial Slavic or German parentage; the latter ethnic minorities were not to my knowledge a source of tension in the IG. Although Slavs had been oppressed during the period of the Austro-Hungarian monarchy, they were not subject to a severe degree of stratification by the late twentieth century.

Pentecostals and Ethnography

Chapter 1 of this study details how the IG's different membership groups came to be involved in Pentecostalism from its U.S. origins through several periods of suppression and a recent infusion of Romani members. Chapters 2 and 3 describe how instrumental music was the site for conflicting interpretations of leadership and for initial ambivalence toward my research. Chapters 4 and 5 describe how church members experienced God. Songs and poetry came to the believers through what they perceived as the Holy Spirit; Roma enthusiastically cultivated these songs, while poetry tended to be an expressive form for the Magyar church members. Chapter 6 explores the historical resonances of the IG's other major repertoire, Anglo-American gospel hymns, and its significance for elderly Magyar believers. Chapter 7 describes the interplay of song performance styles between missionaries, Magyars, and Roma. The conclusion explores the implications of church musical dynamics for secular politics in the global and the state setting, and for the study of how divine power affects human senses of community.

In order to describe these dynamics, my study integrates historical, personal, and ethnographic material. Clifford Geertz has called ethnography a reading of the "knotted" conceptual structures of culture (1973:10). Because the membership of IG included people of different ages, genders, and ethnicity, I have paid special attention to the complex intersections of their varied musical sensibilities. These were often unverbalized, carried out as intensity of expression or a choice among song genres. The musical acts of IG members might comment on ethnic relations or partially remembered life histories, but especially their contact with the divine. Thus my study includes descriptions of the experiences of individual church members and leaders and of musical performances with the goal of expanding Geertz's observation that "social actions are comments on more than themselves" (1973:23).

Activity in Pentecostal and other small churches constitutes a type of folk drama organized in the "specially defined interpretive contexts" called frames (Bateson 1972:222; Deiros 1991:161). Within a frame, actors use speech, music, and physical movement to generate affective states. Studies on small American churches have utilized this conception to detail the sequence of ritual activities there. In the Indiana churches studied by Elaine Lawless, "traditional formulaic constructs," the options available to performers within these constructs, and the audience's evaluation of performers formed the primary categories (Lawless 1988a:55–76). In a Texas Baptist church Walter Pitts contrasted two ritual frames that accommodated the tastes of different generations and were marked by the use of musical repertoires (1991:320–21). My concern to account for how church members acted and what they experienced within ritual frames also led me to reference unframed and unstaged actions. Works like Vincent Crapanzano's depiction of a Moroccan co-respondent (1980) or Bernard Lortat-Jacob's descriptions of Sardinians making music (1995) give some feeling for the ambiguities in actual people. In addressing the contradictions that arise from comparing formal with informal interpretations and examining how the secular impinges on the sacred, I do not intend to undermine the believers' representations of themselves. It is rather my response to a wish expressed by ordinary church members for the secular world to understand them better, in particular what they feel to be the genuinely positive nature of Pentecostal religious experience and community.

Pentecostals' points of view differ considerably from those of nonbelieving ethnographers. Pentecostals attribute much to divine agency that researchers do not. Some maintain that only those people who have undergone a Christian conversion can understand their point of view (Titon 1985). Kenneth DeShane argues that Pentecostals achieve their primary sense of the divine by listening to sermons and that outsiders overemphasize dramatic manifestations of the Holy Spirit (1996:91–96). Thus the genre conventions of ethnography imperfectly address the basic concern to tell the story of Hungary's Pentecostals from their own point of view (see Tyler 1986). I faced additional challenges deriving from regional culture. Hungarian society in general has a closed character. By staying culturally discrete, Roma have gained a reputation for having very strict ethnic boundaries that an ethnographer might surmount only by a combination of perseverance and fortuitous circumstances (Sutherland 1975). This lends some mystique to a goal of moving behind the public presentation modes of one's co-respondents and being admitted to the "back" region of their society (Berreman 1962:11). In ethnomusicology, this trope has often translated as the ideal of achieving such rapport with musicians that the ethnomusicologist can experience firsthand the unique psychophysical qualities of the art. The seemingly common-sense idea that the ethnographer can obtain insight by devoting sympathetic attention to co-respondents was problematic in my fieldwork situation. Peter Stromberg has pointed out that such attention can initiate a transference whereby Evangelicals misconstrue the researcher as a fellow convert (1993:34, 89). I chose to make my nonreligious stance clear to the church members, although this sometimes brought polarization and even suspicion to the fore. The gaps of understanding between Roma, Magyars, and me were uncomfortable. Yet, as fieldwork accounts demonstrate, such rifts often illuminate essential issues (Crapanzano 1980; Rabinow 1977).

Pentecostals, Roma, and indeed most lower-class people in the former socialist countries seldom have been afforded an opportunity to speak for themselves. I have tried to compensate for this with the device of representing the subject's point of view as literally as possible through texts transcribed verbatim (see Tedlock 1983). This is additionally valuable for Pentecostals because they give a central role to interpretation, both of the Bible and of events in daily life (Crapanzano 2000; Titon 1988:11, 13). Interviews with the IG's leaders and members thus provide potentially the most direct views from the standpoint of the participants. In the hope of grasping the "radically contextual significance of public or performed actions in their social settings" (Feld 1982:227), I have also included excerpts from recordings of church events during which various believers commented on the significance of what was occurring. I needed a second methodology to investigate the IG's music as a set of vernacular idioms. I paid special attention to offhand observations about music, since they can clarify the ideas that are articulated through performances, interviews, and other deliberately designed research activities. Information about religious practice also

emerges differently in everyday contexts from through sermons or testimony. Therefore, one of my research objectives was to participate in settings that were not specifically religious or musical, where believers made casual comments. In transcribing
song texts and some other forms of speech here, I have utilized the Hungarian literary convention of *látható nyelv* (visible language) in order to transmit the vernacular
poetics of these texts in their original language. According to this convention, actual
speech can best portray a subject's point of view, even if its grammar and syntax
differs considerably from standard Hungarian.[4]

The subject position of the Pentecostals in Hungary is variegated. The experiences of older adherents contrast with those of more recent converts. There are also
differences between those believers who cooperated with government authority and
those who challenged it. Like their U.S. counterparts, Hungarian Pentecostals are
focused primarily on aspects of religious practice. However, they also reflect on the
broad forces of war, political oppression, and ethnic conflict that have affected the
entire East European region in the twentieth century. The perspectives of two people
will be highlighted throughout this book. Sándor Horváth's experience is representative of elderly Magyars; he had been a believer for over forty-five years and was
the national vice president of the IG. József Gál, a Rom in his midtwenties, had been
a convert for approximately five years. He was an ordained preacher who was involved in many types of evangelizing activities. There is a special relevance here for
Johannes Fabian's statement that "all personal experience is produced under historical conditions" (1983:89). I conducted the fieldwork for this project in the early 1990s
just after socialism dissolved in Eastern Europe. Believers, their church, and I experienced consistent, rapid, and pervasive change; thus I will use the past tense here.

The East European context generates a particular use of terminology relating to
religion. I use the term "church" (*egyház*) to refer to groups of congregations constituting one organization under a single authority structure. Like the Baptist church
and several others, the IG is one of the "small churches" (*kisegyházak*) that had come
relatively recently to Hungary. The largest churches in Hungary, historically affiliated with the state, are the mainstream or "historical" churches (*történelmi egyházak*),
the Catholic, Calvinist, Lutheran, and Unitarian. Although within Hungary's borders
its membership is barely one-third that of the Catholic Church, Calvinism dominates
the religious, moral, and national culture of Hungary.[5] Calvinism, also called the
Reformed (*református*) Church in Hungary, is a major branch of Protestantism, originating in Switzerland, that emphasized asceticism and gave rise to the values that
Max Weber called the Protestant ethic (1958[1920]). Calvinism was the religion of
nearly half the Hungarian population before the Counter-Reformation and of approximately one quarter of ethnic Magyars after that (see Walters 1988). In Hungary,
Calvinist thinkers stimulated the development of Hungarian as a literary language
and a tradition of resistance by advocating use of the vernacular and promoting the
idea of individual responsibility for salvation. Calvinist leaders contributed to Hungarian as a literary and spoken language with Bible and psalm translations, historical songs, and Hungarian grammars. This in turn inspired Hungarian nobles to take
up writing poetry, history, and drama. The leaders of the Counter-Reformation were
equally erudite (Ghezzo 1989; Sugar 1990:127; Szakály 1990:93–95). Before their influence was weakened under socialism, Calvinist preachers were major social leaders,

as village clergymen directing public attention to the conditions of the Hungarian peasantry. Currently the musical style, worship practices, and conduct of small church adherents sometimes resembles that of the Calvinists even though they react against Calvinists as part of the mainstream.

Denominations developed in the United States as "culturally accommodative religious movements" that have systematized the relationships between fairly autonomous local congregations (Wilson 1970:24). Large Pentecostal organizations that could be termed denominations sent missionaries to Eastern Europe; for example, during the 1920s when the Assemblies of God first missionized in the area, it was regularizing its organizational structure and adding local congregations (Blumhofer 1993:148–58). In the 1980s, the Oneness mission, with which the IG associated, also had a high degree of organization and a large number of branch congregations. In the United States there are many other Pentecostal churches that are independent and locally organized, so that they might be categorized as "folk churches." But the word "denomination," connoting a high degree of organization and a well-established place in American society, can be applied to the Pentecostal organizations like the Assemblies of God and others that set up missions in Eastern Europe.

Members of the IG identified themselves generally as *hívők* (believers or devout people) and specifically as "Pentecostals" (*pünkösdiek*), Christians who believe in specific manifestations of God in the form of the Holy Spirit. Several fictive kinship terms resulted from their perception of themselves as members of a single family or body under God. They addressed groups of fellow believers as *testvérek* (pl.). The word *testvér* (sing.) glosses in gender-neutral fashion as "sibling" and in context means "brother"; I translate the latter usage where relevant. A gender-marked term, *nővér*, means "sister." The term *testvér* obscures a basic distinction between leaders and followers. Here I will use the term "church members" or "ordinary church members" to distinguish them from their leaders, and "congregation" to designate both. The believers' worship style, along with that of some other non-Pentecostal churches, was "enthusiastic," in that it exhibited "a state of high emotional excitability" (Williams 1989[1980]:234). Pentecostals shared a literal interpretation of the Bible with fundamentalist Christians, forswearing activities like smoking, drinking, adultery, cutting their hair (for women), and the eating of foods made from blood. As "Holiness" believers, IG members drew a boundary between themselves and the secular world.[6] Under recent U.S. missionary influence, the IG and other small Hungarian churches also took on the character of "Evangelical" churches that stress proselytization along with biblical centrality (Williams 1989[1980]:235).

Pentecostal Worship

Worship events at the IG were very different from other services I attended in Hungary. Church members were emotionally expressive and moved somewhat freely within general sequences of action that are found in Protestant worship. The versions of U.S. worship with which IG members and their forebears had contact privileged the Holy Spirit; at the turn of the twentieth century U.S. Pentecostal events were spontaneous and communal to an extreme. There were limits to the influences from American Pentecostalism. In the United States, Pentecostalism may have begun as

African possession religion fused with Holiness practices, but the movement quickly segregated (MacRobert 1988), and it was the white variety that reached Eastern Europe. I believe that neither early nor contemporary African-American churches in the United States have relevance to this study. I observed few, if any, African cultural elements in the IG. In a study of the jazz musician Django Reinhardt, who was a Rom, Patrick Williams has commented that the two groups may share histories of being in an outcast position, but that condition is so general that comparisons cannot be usefully drawn. African Americans may look to historical origins and the shared trauma of slavery, but Roma do not evoke Indian roots. The energy of their music derives from speaking to members of the local and Romani community (1991a:14–21). In the IG, beyond the basic possession characteristic of being under the Holy Spirit, there were virtually no worship modes that could be related to the influence of African Americans.

It is not clear if the Hungarian missionaries encountered the earliest styles of Pentecostal worship when they themselves converted during the 1920s in the midwestern cities of the United States. They surely attended the large revivals that were prevalent in the Midwest at the time, but they did not organize such revivals in Hungary. Another U.S. worship style comes from the missionaries who began to proselytize in Eastern Europe during the 1980s. These missionaries came from large Evangelical and Pentecostal denominations. They brought many aspects of contemporary religion and popular culture, as well as an ideology of how the East European churches should be worked into the hierarchy of their organizations. Since I was able to observe this firsthand, I will be commenting on how IG members interpreted, appropriated, or rejected this style as well as the missionaries' practices. This directly addresses how the IG constituted itself as a community in the face of pressures with a global reach.

A third prototype of Pentecostal worship comes from independent congregations in the United States, including some that privilege the Holy Spirit but are not Pentecostal since they do not recognize spirit baptism.[7] The believers in such independent churches give priority to what they perceive the Holy Spirit is dictating. Like the earliest Pentecostals, the members of a church that Elaine Lawless studied used a varying mixture of instruments from banjos to drums. In these churches, an intense expressiveness is clear to outsiders (see Dégh 1994; Lawless 1988a). It contrasts with the plain decor of the churches; the simple altars, bare pews, and in some cases the building itself are often made by church members (see Dégh 1994; Lawless 1988a; Titon 1988). The intensity is marked with stylized physical gesture, song, or speech that incorporates rhythms, pitch, stock phrases, and special terminology. Believers see the Holy Spirit as having actual power that manifests in many practical ways (Titon 1988:7).

All these independent churches hold services on Sunday morning. They have evening services, meetings devoted to prayer, and periodic song services (Dégh 1994:113; Titon 1988:213–14). Such events last several hours. As part of their ideology that they adhere to the religion of the original Christians, many of these churches do not commemorate major holidays of the Christian calendar like Christmas. However, they may hold Sunday services with special themes that gather in members who cannot attend the church on a regular basis (Titon 1988:23–57). With their large regular attendance, Sunday services would seem to be most important, but special occasions at some of these churches appear to be more important than the regular routine. One of the major events is revival. Many U.S. Pentecostals have a sentimental attachment to this event because of their history of holding huge revivals early in the twentieth century. At revivals an outside evangelist comes to preach, extra services are held, and outside members and nonbelievers visit the church. A revival can last for weeks, as long as the intense focus to convert nonbelievers and help believers to recommit can be maintained (Clements 1976; Dégh 1994:112; DeShane 1996; Lawless 1988a:16, 86).

The expression at these events takes place mostly within well-delineated patterns of activity. The events start with individual greetings (Lawless 1988a:60). Then a sequence of interrelated activities takes place that may include scripture reading, sermons, and offerings. There can be congregational singing and what many churches call "specials," solo or small group performances by the church members. Individual believers give "testimony"; they narrate events or explain situations where they perceived God's power at work. One activity, group prayer, may have originated with the revivals of the eighteenth and nineteenth centuries (Titon 1988:260). The believers pray aloud as a congregation, each member extemporizing. Many services conclude with an "altar call," where individuals come forward to the pulpit. This may serve as an opportunity for nonbelievers to convert, for anyone to request healing, or for members to recommit or to ask for the baptism of the Holy Spirit. The group redoubles its efforts around these individuals through prayer, music, movement, or crying out (Dégh 1994:113; Lawless 1988a:60–66; Titon 1988:213–14).

Linda Dégh has observed that the sequence of activities in Pentecostal churches is similar to those for a mainstream Protestant service (1994:113), but they differ in levels of importance and in how individual members may participate. Since U.S. Pentecostals consider the sermon and study of the biblical text to be central in a service, the Sunday school can even be incorporated into a service. In many small churches of the United States, testimony is the most important activity for women. They can dominate by taking long amounts of time to testify and getting under the Holy Spirit so that spontaneous action, outcries, and intense emotion are added (Dégh 1994; Lawless 1988a; Titon 1988:359). The altar call is the most compelling and important activity for many members. Then they manifest many aspects of the Holy Spirit as well as play music, cry out, "shout" praise, and do other things to ask God to help those who are praying (see Dégh 1994; Titon 1988:277–78).

Worship Events in the Isten Gyülekezet

The styles of worship and procedures of communicating in the IG resembled the U.S. folk churches, although members of such congregations had probably never been in contact with the IG. At the time I was doing fieldwork, the IG was the most similar in ideology and community structure to these congregations. They both might be classified as folk churches, and they shared the fact of having deep connections to the local social fabric. Jeff Titon argues that the U.S. folk churches reveal continuity with past religious history and with regional socioeconomic conditions (1988). The IG congregations had similar types of connections, although to a different religious past and to the economics and politics of a different locality. Another way these congregations resembled each other was that each small church developed its own standards of discourse. These unique ways of communicating were what constituted them as a community with shared interests or history (see Lawless 1988a:58).

On a daily basis the members of the IG prayed, read the Bible, listened to religious music, and visited with fellow believers. Several times weekly they held organized meetings for worship, all in the Hungarian language. They utilized a somewhat regular order of worship activities. But because they believed that God in the form of the Holy Spirit should guide proceedings, they rejected preplanned details as *liturgia* (liturgy) that gave control to humans rather than God. IG members assembled once a week for the *istentisztelet* (worship service). According to the head pastor's estimate, the church had some two thousand members nationally.[8] In southwestern Hungary, the church had three interconnected congregations with a combined membership of approximately two hundred. The church members lived in different towns and villages scattered throughout this region. Partly because of the segregationist effects of housing policy, it was Roma who lived in outlying areas (Havas et al. 1995:74); most Magyar church members lived in the largest city of Pécs. On Sundays they traveled by public transportation for the services at the church's central location in Pécs. Sister Herceg, a believer in her seventies, arrived before dawn at the church building to sweep the floors and to stoke the wood-burning stoves that heated the worship hall and its anteroom. The church was not a freestanding building but had been remodeled from a set of joined one-story flats facing a central courtyard. Its decor was simple outside as well as inside; only an emblem with the cross and crown distinguished it from the buildings around it.

Church members gathered an hour or more before the service. After greeting one another, chatting briefly, and tending to children, they all took seats in the worship hall. In their ethnography of a Hungarian village, Edit Fél and Tamás Hofer pointed out that the seating pattern in the local Calvinist church reflected social hierarchies (1969:68–75). In the IG, there were rough differences in seating, but other than those for the preachers and musicians at the front of the church, I do not believe these indicated any status differences. Some of the most dedicated church members, young men, consulted their Bibles in small groups at the back. Older believers sat near the heating stove and knelt to pray; women seated themselves and their children at the front. The musicians plugged their instruments into the amplifiers and set up microphones. Then the congregation started singing. Church members and preachers called out the name of one song after another. Sometimes as they sang the believers felt that "the Holy Spirit descended" (*leszállt a Szentlélek*). When first feeling this *áldás* (blessing), people sang louder. They stood up and clapped to the basic beat. Then they called out to God, spoke in tongues, or wept. This period of singing, which church leaders sometimes called the *imaóra* (prayer hour), could last up to forty-five minutes. After this one of the lay preachers stepped up to the pulpit, read a Bible passage, and delivered a brief exhortation based on the passage. He then asked a member of the congregation, often an elderly female believer, to pray. "One-by-one" (*egyen-egyenként*) praying then followed, where individual members took turns praying aloud. Then at the direction of the preacher the congregation commenced group or "common" (*közös*) prayer, when all those present prayed aloud at once, for approximately five minutes. Sometimes people began to pray in tongues, lending added vigor to those praying around them. The head pastor, Brother Horváth, usually arrived during these prayers. His presence signaled the start of the worship service. The other preachers resumed their seats behind the pulpit. Brother Horváth suggested one or two songs, which the congregation sang. He then asked one of the preachers to lead a brief prayer and, consulting notes jotted on small pieces of paper, began his sermon.

After the morning service, church members who lived in the local area went home for formal Sunday dinner. Some out-of-town believers left for home. Others remained at the church. They ate cold lunches they had brought with them, chatted in the anteroom, and continued to make music. Brother Horváth and his wife arrived back at the church in the midafternoon. He had the congregation sing several songs, and then he announced a series of individual performances from a list that girls usually prepared during the lunch hour. This was the period of *bizonyság* (testimony), when individuals and small groups of believers stood in front of the congregation, sang, recited poetry, or related personal histories. After approximately one hour of testimony, Brother Horváth announced a congregational song, prayed briefly, and then delivered a sermon. The worship day ended somewhat raggedly. People from towns outside Pécs got up during Brother Horváth's sermon and left to catch the train home. Brother Horváth continued to preach to the depleted assembly, and he closed with a congregational song. A few elderly members tidied up the church and gathered money from the collection box on the wall. They chatted with each other and with the Horváths until the couple's grandson arrived to pick them up in their Volvo, which was given to Brother Horváth by American missionaries.

During the week church members gathered in other locations. In Szigetvár, approximately fifty people assembled; 90 percent of them were Roma, since many of the Romani members lived in this town. Because commuting was expensive, women with small children attended infrequently on Sunday; entire families came to these local services. The events in Szigetvár sometimes resembled those of the Sunday prayer hour, but they also included preaching by several young Romani leaders and discussions on administrative issues. In Pécs there was a midweek gathering that Brother Horváth called the *bibliaóra* (Bible hour). There a small number of believers, mostly elderly Magyars, sang songs, prayed as a group, heard a sermon or lecture given by Brother Horváth, and chatted together.

Sundays regularly included special events. Every month at the end of the morning service they held *Úrvacsora* (Lord's Supper), a symbolic commemoration of Jesus' sacrifice.[9] Then the church members washed each other's feet, also to honor the Last Supper. Immersion baptism (*bemerítkezés*) was held every few months. The new believers dressed in white and Brother Horváth held a brief, semiprivate teaching with them in the anteroom. Elderly women bustled here and there with towels and white clothing. Baptisms were held in a plastic pool filled with cold water in the courtyard outside the worship hall. The congregation crowded around the edge of the pool. Each time a believer was baptized, they sang "Halleluia" four times. Another church event was *evangelizáció* (evangelization), held at approximately two-month intervals when a West European or U.S. missionary visited the IG. At evangelizations, Brother Horváth turned the proceedings over to the visiting missionary and his translator. The missionary preached and then held an altar call, exhorting those who had not converted, those who wished the blessing of the Holy Spirit, or those who needed physical healing to come forward to the pulpit and be prayed over.

The musical life of believers developed not only within these ritual frameworks but also in secular activities. In the succeeding chapters I describe how different believers experienced power at the spiritual level, in daily interactions, as members of class or ethnic constituencies, as part of the religious organization of the IG, and as part of a global Pentecostal mission. Having asserted mutual acceptance through the ideology of spiritual brotherhood, they then had to work out the practical details of their relationships with one another. In the musical arena, they utilized a variety of performance options to negotiate the nature and scope of their song literature, singing style, and musical leadership.

The Isten Gyülekezet in Hungarian Society

Brother Horváth's Conversion

Brother Horváth, the leader of the IG congregation, became involved in Pentecostalism when the Soviet army occupied Hungary at the end of World War II. He told me was attending gymnasium in preparation to become a Lutheran pastor. His schooling ended abruptly with the occupation, and he encountered Pentecostals while he was fleeing the army.

SH: My turn toward God first happened in my historical denomination. It happened in the Lutheran church, when I was a student, in 1942. There was an evangelization at our school for the youth, and there I went forward for the first time to receive the Lord Jesus, as a youth. In 1942, I was sixteen years old.

BRL: This was in the large Lutheran gymnasium?

SH: Yes, yes. There was a big evangelization in the gymnasium for the students, three days. And there I decided that I would receive the Lord Jesus. God's mercy really penetrated my heart. At that time, the Savior's mercy touched my heart and I gave my heart to the Lord Jesus. And then I decided at the request of my mother that I would obey her, so that if I graduated, I would choose the career path of theology, of a Lutheran pastor. I prepared for this, but in 1944 when the war was raging here in our country, after graduating I went to Sopron [in western Hungary]. I was only there for three months and then the Russians came in and took us students away to work. So I was only in theology for three months and then they took us into captivity, into [forced] labor. And after two months of captivity I escaped, many of us escaped. And while fleeing, I arrived in Somogy county, in the village of Somogygeszti [in southwest Hungary] as a refugee. It was evening and I asked for lodging. My path led to a family of believers, an elderly family of believers, where I got lodging. And in the evening they went to the house of worship and I went with them to their house of worship. They were very simple people. I only thought of the Gospel as coming from the lips of clergymen, that they were the ones who were called to proclaim the Gospel. The person I saw there proclaiming the Gospel was a simple old man in clod-hoppers [*fabakkancsos bácsi*], and I looked down on him. But when he started proclaiming the Word, he evangelized wondrously and deeply. Every one of his words seemed to see into the depths of my heart, and there God's redeeming mercy and power strongly bent down to me as a refugee. I collapsed to my knees there and I prayed and they prayed for me that night. I was also sick in captivity. . . . I had gotten sick with pleurisy. During the prayer I was healed. And God's redeeming mercy filled my heart. The next day I was to travel on, but the family of believers did not allow it, because they saw that God had a plan and a goal for me. They asked that I stay with them and I stayed there as a refugee. My staying there was enough during that time for me to become spiritually strong. And this was God's truth that they represented the Isten Gyülekezet Mission. So during those three months I learned and studied their fundamental rules, their study materials, and listened to their testimonies . . . so this unfolded wondrously before me, in a way that was not unfolded by the large church's catechism that I had studied. That in our times the Holy Spirit fills [people], and the essence of baptism. And I came to understand all of this and on April 8, 1945, I was christened, baptized in the name of Lord Jesus, and one week after that, on April 14, the Lord Jesus filled me with the Holy Spirit. I had prayed for this for three months, during that time, while I studied those things, that it really would be true, that the Holy Spirit fills. That God would give it to me too.

BRL: Did you speak in tongues, was that the gift?

HS: Yes, I spoke in tongues. When the Lord filled me with the Holy Spirit, I prayed in tongues. It was beautiful. An enormous power [*erő*] went through my interior and under the influence of this strength my tongue turned and I praised God in tongues. So I experienced a wondrous rebirth by means of the Spirit. . . . I saw that what the brothers are saying here is not dogma, but truth. It was an experienced event that they testified to me about. After I was filled with the Holy Spirit, this was a Sunday morning, and since the preachers there recognized in me what I had gotten from the revival at the Lutheran church, that is being born again, revival, and the theological knowledge I had gotten in school and church history and biblical history at gymnasium, they taught all of this to us in the church school, they recognized this in me and in the afternoon they initiated me as a preacher.

The upheavals of World War II had blocked Brother Horváth's intended path toward serving as a Lutheran pastor. If he had not fled from the Soviet army, he might never have been in the small villages of southwest Hungary or heard a peasant preach. Brother Horváth acknowledged the effects of such major historical and social forces in his conversion to Pentecostalism. At the same time he believed that it was God's plan for him to be involved specifically with the IG Pentecostals. He emphasized the miraculous elements in his initiation to Pentecostal belief and leadership: in a short space of time he was healed of illness, accepted water baptism, and then received spirit baptism. Brother Horváth's attendance at gymnasium indicates that he came from a middle-class background. He had already become receptive to the Pentecostal religion's basic teachings through revival activities in the mainstream Lutheran church. But Brother Horváth's first involvement came not with the middle class or in an urban setting but with believers in southwest Hungary who by World War II were isolated into a cluster of tiny "house congregations" (*házi gyülekezetek*). They were a group of scattered rural congregations that had split in the 1930s from the main group in Budapest. But their name, Isten Gyülekezetei (Assemblies of God), revealed a connection with the first Pentecostal conversions in Hungary. Secular politics in Eastern Europe made the Pentecostal churches very unstable. In the United States,

Brother Horváth praying over a newly married couple in Szigetvár.

Pentecostal adherents have been relatively free to practice their religion, choose their own leaders, and form their own institutions. By contrast, the established churches and the political forces that controlled the countries of Eastern Europe viewed Pentecostal believers as a threat. The number of adherents grew and shrank proportionately to the degree of suppression exercised by the state and the churches affiliated with the state. The religion was simply banned in the years before World War II, and afterward socialist policies undermined its authority structures.[1]

Forerunners of the Isten Gyülekezet

The Pentecostal religion was part of a movement toward revival that had been going on since the mid–nineteenth century in Hungary. Revivalists practiced an intense religiosity with small group meetings, prayer, Bible reading, and application of biblical precepts to daily life. Some of this activity was within the Lutheran and Calvinist denominations; it also gave rise to a variety of enthusiastic and fundamentalist churches. Prior to World War I, Hungarian revivalists established Nazarene, Baptist, and Adventist churches; after the war, they introduced Pentecostalism, Jehovah's Witnesses, and the Plymouth Brethren (Szigeti 1981:16; Walters 1988:159–63). These religions came to be introduced into Hungary because several sectors of the population had a transnational orientation. Clergy and other intellectuals from the Calvinist church traveled to the British Isles for further schooling and encountered the urban revivalism there. Their activities constituted a "home mission" (*belmisszió*) within the Calvinist church (Dobos 1987; Forgács 1925). They held some large group meetings in the pattern of the Moody revivals; like the one Brother Horváth reported attending at his gymnasium, such meetings were often oriented toward youth (Révész 1943). Another constituency, tradesmen, introduced some of the fundamentalist religions. Originally from Hungarian towns and villages, these artisans were termed "wandering youths" (*vándorlegények*) because, like other skilled craftsmen in Europe, they traveled between different cities all over the continent to work. They joined the revival religions along with other new movements like trade unionism and socialism (see Polanyi 1944:173–77; Wolf 1982:361–66).[2] The founders of both the Nazarene and the Baptist churches in Hungary came from the ranks of the skilled craftsmen. The founder of the Nazarene religion was a carpenter who had encountered the religion in Switzerland. The first converts were also carpenters (Kardos and Szigeti 1988:43–64). The first Hungarian Baptists converted when they were working as cabinetmakers in Hamburg (Bereczki 1996:19–32). In the mid–nineteenth century these converts proselytized largely to German speakers, either members of the German ethnic minority in Hungary or other craftsmen like them who had some schooling and were conversant in the German language.

These religions were nativized when they connected with groups of Hungarian-speaking peasants in the southeastern part of the country. There, worship activities much like those of the revivalists, but with a puritan slant, had been functioning barely within the confines of the Calvinist and Lutheran churches. The historian Jenő Szigeti has described how in the last part of the nineteenth century, the churches were oriented toward the upper class and had no place for the devout peasant leaders or "peasant ecclesiastics" (*parasztecclesiolák*). The peasants formed their own small groups devoted to Bible reading and explication, praying, and reading of Puritan literature like the Hungarian translation of *Paradise Lost*. As Brother Horváth's experience with one of these peasant preachers attests, their leadership or, in his view, God working through them, could be gripping and powerful. Szigeti argues that the peasant groups provided a "mass foundation" for religious enthusiasm (Szigeti 1981:15–18). They split from the denominations, forming congregations of Baptists, Nazarenes, and after World War I, Jehovah's Witnesses (Csohány 1974:38–39).

Isten Gyülekezet, 1920s to 1940s

Like revival religion, Pentecostal conversions were initiated through a transnational move, this time emigration to the United States. Hungarians and other East Europeans encountered the Baptist and Pentecostal religions where they worked in the industrial cities of the Midwest. European immigrants formed a significant contingent of early Pentecostal converts in the United States (Wilson 1970). Ethnically specific conventions constitute a third stream of Pentecostalism alongside white and African-American branches. Worship proceedings were conducted in the emigrants' native languages. The ethnically separate conventions lasted only for a generation; their membership dwindled as the next generation either joined English-speaking Pentecostal churches or followed other faiths. But at the time they flourished in the 1920s, these immigrant congregations had an orientation toward their home countries.[3] A significant number of East European emigrants returned to their home countries following World War I and then again during the Great Depression, some bringing the new religion with them. As converts they adopted an "aggressive concern for recruitment" that characterizes religious movements originating in the United States (Wilson 1975:108). Some Hungarian and other East European converts in fact returned solely to proselytize.

Several Hungarian converts were named as missionaries through two Pentecostal organizations, the Apostolic Faith Church and the Russian and East European Mission at the Assemblies of God. In Hungary they began proselytizing in their home villages and also near the capital city, Budapest (Tóth et al. 1998[1978]:23–24, 30–40). Separate missionaries targeted ethnic Germans and Slovaks as well as the Hungarian-speaking majority. Until the late 1980s none evangelized consistently to Roma. The missionaries found a significant number of people receptive to the enthusiastic aspects of Pentecostalism, as well as to the independent designation of authority their beliefs implied through reliance on the Holy Spirit. One of the Assemblies of God missionaries, Imre Mihók, even followed the home mission model by urging his converts to stay with their churches of origin or to establish alliances within the Baptist church (Tóth et al. 1998[1978]:35, 45). But the practices of charismatic worship and adult baptism were antithetical to mainstream Protestant doctrines, so that even high-level members of these churches were cast out for practicing them (see Tóth et al. 1998[1978]:68). Among the missionaries, Dezső (Dávid) Rároha gained the largest numbers of converts and he instituted a centralized organizational scheme in 1927, within a year of having started missionary work in Hungary. At their first conference, the Pentecostals adopted the translated name Isten Gyülekezetei ("Assemblies of God"). Membership reached an important point when seventy congregations were registered at the fifth annual conference of the IG in 1932 (Szigeti 1987:227). Besides evangelizing, the missionaries translated much material, including organizational guidelines, tracts explaining specific beliefs, and a song booklet (Tóth et al. 1998[1978]:42).

In ecstatic religions like Pentecostalism, charisma and institutionalization conflict. As Max Weber observed, the power of charismatic leaders is perceived as having supernatural origin. The group is undifferentiated, and its bond to the leader is emotional rather than administrative or descent-based. Charismatic leadership is associated with radical change, including religious revival (1947:359–63). Routinization subsequently begins, where organizational practice is regularized and a system for approving leaders is established. Pentecostalism, because it relies on the direct manifestation of the Holy Spirit to designate leaders, could be considered a charismatic religion. However, large Pentecostal groups like the Assemblies of God or the Church of God, Cleveland, routinized their leadership structures very early in their histories (Hollenweger 1972:30–43). Some of the enthusiastic churches in Hungary have also become routinized, among them Baptists, Adventists, and Pentecostals. This has been a source of weakness as well as strength; their organized authority systems provided a means for the state to manipulate them. But some groups like the IG resisted this control and relied to a greater degree on charismatic leadership. Although he helped establish an institutional system, Dezső Rároha appears to have had much charisma. Rároha's activities strongly resemble those of healing evangelists in the United States who during the same period were incompatible with the Assemblies of God leadership structure (Hollenweger 1972:35). The evangelists organized revival events, emphasized physical healing, and embraced material prosperity. In the Pentecostal congregations that Rároha led, miraculous healings and dramatic manifestations of Holy Spirit power regularly occurred. He generated large numbers of converts in travels around Hungary.

In the early 1930s, a major split occurred among the Hungarian Pentecostals. A conflict arose between the highly organized methods of the mission and the evangelizing activities of Rároha. The Assemblies of God decided to divest Rároha of his authority as a foreign missionary because of complaints by the other missionaries that he misused church funds and had insulted government authorities. In fact, police commonly persecuted independent religious activity during the interwar period. Szigeti comments that, in spite of language in the Treaty of Trianon guaranteeing freedom of religion, "the state put the free Christian communities under general police investigation, and treated it as harmful to public morals if they attracted believers and with this put 'church peace' [*felekezeti béke*] in danger" (Szigeti 1987:207). When Rároha's visa expired, he and his wife were identified as "undesirable elements" and forced to leave the country (Tóth et al. 1998[1978]:60). Thus, Rároha's activity in Hungary came to an end in 1931 after only five years. The Assemblies of God designated a leader in Budapest who worked in government service. However, Rároha had inspired so much devotion that some converts remained faithful to him. In 1935, the congregations still faithful to Rároha and the leader he had designated split from the other Pentecostals. They retained the Assemblies of God name, Isten Gyülekezetei, but for the next fifty years these congregations had no foreign affiliation. They attracted other scattered congregations that were in conflict with the main group of

Pentecostals. The IG groups were located mostly in southwestern Hungary, where Brother Horváth encountered them approximately ten years later.

In 1939, one of the most difficult periods for Hungarian Pentecostals began. Hungary's far right political forces, who framed their ideology around national crisis, persecuted the unrecognized churches with the cooperation of the major denominations. At the beginning of World War II, the Hungarian government banned all religious activity except that of the Calvinist, Catholic, Lutheran, Methodist, and Baptist churches. Not only the police but the greatly feared Royal Guards (*csendőrök*) began to threaten Pentecostal believers and leaders with arrest, beatings, or transportation to prison camps (Tóth et al. 1998[1978]:108). In the view of Pentecostal historians, the events that occurred between 1939 and the end of World War II caused the believers to become fearful and defensive.

> Indisputably, this period left a deep impression on the lives and spiritual world of the members of the community. They could barely make ends meet, as citizens they ended up on the margins of society, and besides this they endured severe humiliation and persecution. A long time had to pass in the conditions that changed after World War II for the fear of perpetual persecution to dissolve. (Tóth et al. 1998[1978]:116)

For Pentecostals in Hungary, the legacy of fascism and World War II was thus marginalization, a sense of shame, and the fear of persecution by authorities. Pentecostal historians in Hungary have commented that this sense pervaded the IG in particular: "one of their fundamental teachings was to strive for 'perfect holiness.' Their followers strongly adhered to the conservative past and would have been happy to be martyred" (Tóth et al. 1998[1978]:130).

1945 to the Late 1980s

After the initial shock of the Soviet occupation, for several years there was relative freedom in Hungary, until Communist rule was established. Brother Horváth often commented during sermons that in spite of the material privations suffered by believers along with the rest of the Hungarian citizenry, this was a "golden age" (*aranykor*) for Pentecostalism in Hungary. Believers were free to proselytize and to assemble; the number of converts grew quickly.

> In that place [the village of Somogygeszti] we numbered twenty-five at that time. And the good God's blessing was on our work, and over the space of two years we grew to sixty members. Right at the beginning, I felt that God had chosen me for evangelism, to serve in evangelism. I evangelized. I proclaimed the Word. On the roads, by the side of the road, in the fields. Because you know it was a village and we worked in the fields. And the good God multiplied the numbers of the redeemed. And we developed nicely. We rented a house of worship, a large store building, because we didn't fit into a private dwelling any more, and there we held services.

In spite of this success in attracting new members, the IG and the other Pentecostal churches were immediately confronted with a new source of schism, the *próféta mozgalom* (prophet movement). Native to Hungarian speakers, it dispensed with adult baptism and required anyone over the age of ten to confess his sins to lay leaders designated by God. The Holy Spirit's manifestations in the form of prophecies became the central focus of the movement (Szigeti 1987:244–45). The prophet movement caused a great deal of conflict among Pentecostal leaders and may have contributed to a pattern of switching allegiances that occurred numerous times during the following four decades. Its use of public confession was exceptional in Hungarian religious life.[4] This psychodramatic feature is more characteristic of a small sect than of the somewhat open religion that Pentecostalism represented in Hungary. While the movement's participants initially had intense religious experiences, prophesying was overused. Brother Horváth scornfully recalled how even a mundane activity like a lunch break was announced as a prophecy. According to Pentecostal historians, the IG actually benefited from the prophet movement in its early days. In the ensuing disruption, the IG drew groups and leaders who had split or withdrawn from other Pentecostal churches (Tóth et al. 1998[1978]:129–30). The prophet movement was later institutionalized and connected to a British group, the Church of Ancient Christians (Őskeresztyén Gyülekezet). The Ancient Christians registered several congregations in the county where Brother Horváth led the IG (Fodor 1984:53). There was much interchange between the groups; Sándor Ungváry, the president of the national IG organization, had originally been an adherent of the prophet movement. Several IG members in Pécs, including Sister Herceg, the church's caretaker, had previously belonged to the Church of Ancient Christians. As of the 1980s Brother Horváth had harmonious relations with the local Ancient Christians, who had passed their building on to IG when they moved to a new facility.[5]

When Communism was established in 1948, another period of persecution began. A number of religious leaders, including Brother Horváth, were jailed and beaten, and one leader was even killed. This persecution may have been region-specific; the sociologist Zsuzsa Horváth (no relation to Brother Horváth), who worked with two other charismatic and Pentecostal groups, had not encountered reports of believers being jailed purely for their religious beliefs (Horváth 1990:8). Brother Horváth was reluctant to recall these events, but he sometimes commented on them in church services or to the young Romani preachers. Brother Horváth mentioned being questioned by a judge about the imminent return of Jesus, since in his jail cell he been singing verses from the spiritual song "Mi várjuk az Úr Jézust, mikor jön" (We Await the Lord Jesus When He Comes). Brother Horváth traveled a long distance to northeast Hungary, evangelized to Roma, baptized a number of converts, and was then jailed on charges of inciting them to leave their agricultural work assignments. Other leaders told me something Brother Horváth never mentioned: he suffered from tumors because of his beatings.

In 1956, there was an uprising in Hungary against the Communists. Although it failed, the subsequent government under János Kádár abandoned violent coercion and instead, in the policy called "real socialism," made pragmatic compromises with the populace. The authorities continued exercising pressure to centralize nearly every social domain. After World War II, the churches outside the major denominations formed a council. One example of real socialist practice was to approve the existence of this group, the State Council of Free Churches, but then to exercise close supervision of the member organizations (Szigeti 1987:251, 254). Some in the small churches welcomed their official connection with the Hungarian state because it gave them equal status with the Catholics, Calvinists, and Lutherans. At the same time, joining a government organization caused a great deal of controversy. One of the many obstacles was a requirement that church leaders swear primary allegiance to the Hungarian state and only secondarily to God (Tóth et al. 1998[1978]:161). The government approved leaders for the small and large churches who were willing to collaborate with them (Horváth 1990:10). In principle the Council's member churches had permission to hold worship meetings, produce publications, receive visitors from abroad, and accept foreign donations, but each venture met with bureaucratic restrictions. Several Evangelical and Pentecostal churches benefited from this arrangement. Two later combined to become the Evangéliumi Pünkösdi Közösség (Evangelical Pentecostal Fellowship), an organization that kept in contact with the Assemblies of God mission and wrote a history of the Pentecostal movement in Hungary. The mission recorded visits to Hungary throughout the socialist period, but from the Hungarian standpoint, these contacts were sporadic. Pentecostals met discreetly during the socialist years. Most of the elderly believers I knew had never lost a fear of policemen and government officials.

From the late 1950s through the 1980s, the Kafkaesque operation of the church council was a major source of friction within Hungary's Pentecostal churches. A history of conflict was built between those leaders who capitulated to the government's pressures and those like Brother Horváth who utterly refused to do so. Brother Horváth judged older leaders by whether they had resisted or cooperated with the state. He emphasized that the authorities continued to harrass him because he made decisions independently.

> SH: Under pressure from the State Office of Church Affairs, from the Free Churches, I was greatly pilloried, because I evangelized. I traveled all over the country as an independent spiritual worker [*függetlenített lelki munkás*]. Many people converted, and I baptized many of them.

> BRL: So this did not please the state.

> SH: This did not please the state, and therefore they descended on me in order to liquidate me. To put me aside. So I had police arrests and interrogations [*meghurcoltatások*] and five trials.

Conflicts within the IG combined with the church council's restrictions on operating permits to make the group disappear as an organization for nearly thirty years. The IG had become a member of the State Council of Free Churches. The IG had appeared to be at its strongest at the beginning of the 1950s, with a membership estimated by its national leader at fourteen congregations, twenty-three pastors, and 450 church members (Tóth et al. 1998[1978]:157). However, Brother Horváth told me that the IG's national leader threw the group in crisis by leaving his wife and children to marry another woman. If the church had chosen another leader, the entire group of congregations would have had to function illegally because the existing leader possessed IG's state permit. Brother Horváth switched allegiances along with the other IG congregations in southwest Hungary.

In the entire country the [IG] mission dissolved and [the leader] virtually remained by himself. But the name and the permit was with him, because he was recognized by the state . . . so I went over to the Pentecostal Community [the predecessor of the Evangelical Pentecostal Fellowship] with the whole congregation. In fact with all of our congregations in Somogy county.

Thus the IG was thought at the official level to have disappeared by the 1960s. József Fodor, who authored a government study of the Free Church Council member churches, wrote, "the group's . . . membership came to an end, having lost its believers" (Fodor 1984:39). However, the church was still officially registered with the government, and the fallen leader of the IG still possessed his organizational permit.

Several years after his switch to the Evangelical Pentecostal Fellowship, Brother Horváth was named leader of a congregation in the large town of Pécs in neighboring Baranya county. He led that church for fifteen years, from 1954 to 1969. But he resisted a state regulation that any visit by a foreign representative had to be approved (Horváth 1990:12). Brother Horváth hosted several missionaries who entered Hungary illegally. Other leaders feared that it would put them in jeopardy; Brother Horváth was sent to trial and put under police supervision. Then, after a work-related accident, Brother Horváth had to submit his passport to the government, at which time they revoked his preacher's license.[6] At the same time, Brother Horváth's eldest son defected to the United States. The state's suppression of Brother Horváth was psychologically successful for a number of years; he stopped evangelizing and met quietly with tiny prayer groups in Pécs and the neighboring town of Szigetvár. After regaining his health, Brother Horváth made contact with the original leader of the IG. Five years later, upon his death, Brother Horváth and another leader took up the church's operating permit, although it had almost no members by that time.

Brother Horváth began to evangelize again after he visited his son in the United States. He attended services at several large churches and visited the headquarters of the Apostolic Faith Church, the Pentecostal organization that had proselytized to the Slovaks in Hungary in the 1920s. He reports that his experiences in mass church gatherings and special prayers with U.S. preachers on his behalf endowed him with the spiritual strength to evangelize.

The air which was there, that sanctified [*megszentelt*] atmosphere! You didn't have to be afraid that—Oh, is the policemen coming in? . . . [The pastor] is such an important person to them! They respect him so much, they regard him so highly . . . all this really made an impression on me, and, I emphasize, only after I came home did I start this congregation.

In 1981, Brother Horváth and his coleader made contact with an American denomination that adhered to the Oneness or "Jesus only" doctrine. Oneness Pentecostals believe that Jesus is the only form of God, and they baptize in the name of Jesus.[7] In the United States, Oneness Pentecostals are often more literalist than their Trinitarian counterparts, observing more restrictions on dress and avoiding secular media to a greater degree. They express a very intense connection with Jesus, possibly showing continuity with the sentimentalism of evangelical movements from the nineteenth century (see Dégh 1994:116, 121–22; De Jong 1986; Lawless 1988a:32–

39). In the United States, Oneness pentecostals form independent churches that ethnographers have studied (Dégh 1994; Lawless 1988a), but they also have established large institutions. The IG resembled the Oneness churches in that it was more conservative during the 1990s than other Hungarian Pentecostal groups. But in all the Pentecostal and Evangelical services I visited in Hungary, the believers expressed intense devotion to Jesus. The IG's leaders brought up Oneness theology when they compared themselves to other churches in Hungary; Brother Horváth and the lay leaders distinguished themselves from the local branch of the Evangelical Pentecostal Fellowship with the comment that they were of "three Gods" (*három isteni*), a reference to baptizing in the name of the Father, the Son, and the Holy Ghost. However, church members did not mention this, focusing instead on the closeness of the people in the IG and the freedom to manifest the Holy Spirit that they found there. In southwest Hungary, Oneness was well established, but it does not appear to have been a uniform belief throughout the IG congregations until possibly the late 1980s. Brother Horváth and his fellow national leader applied for official registration with the new government in 1990. Oneness distinguished IG's existence as a church with a dogma that was separate from other Pentecostals. Should the state church council ever try to force the small churches to merge again, the IG would be able to stay separate because it adhered to a unique theology. The U.S. mission of the Oneness denomination increased its activities after socialism dissolved in the late 1980s, and in 1990, the IG joined the U.S. denomination exclusively. In 1993, the IG officially registered with the Hungarian state, changing its name to show both its original and its new affiliations.

The repressions of the 1950s and 1960s established in Brother Horváth a defiant attitude toward state authorities that persisted even after the end of the socialist period. Brother Horváth was responsible for initiating the IG's resurrection in the 1980s after its virtual disappearance as an institution. During his forty-year history as a Pentecostal, he appears to have preferred independence to the comforts of institutional or state affiliation. One illustration of this was how he reconstituted the IG as a multiethnic church by accepting Romani converts. Brother Horváth related to me how during the 1950s he had attempted to baptize some Roma far away in northeast Hungary. This was a rebellious act; the police charged him with "interrupting work discipline" and put him in jail. Thirty years later, he attempted this again, accepting Romani converts into the IG. A new group of Romani leaders fostered by Brother Horváth then expanded the membership of the church to include large numbers of Roma.

In Szigetvár, a town neighboring Pécs, a few elderly Romani women had been attending the tiny prayer meetings of the IG for nearly a decade. One of them, Sister Annus, maintained close relationships with her unconverted relatives. Sister Annus asked Brother Horváth to preach at the funerals and wakes first of her husband and then of a brother of hers who had repented on his deathbed. Brother Horváth recalled that God, working through him, effected a mass conversion.

It was the wish of Sister Annus that I preach by the grave when the Catholic priest had gone, because the funeral was held according to Catholic rites. He left and afterward I served with the Word. And the good God blessed the word so that it really seized the Gypsies. So they requested that I hold an evangelization that evening at the house. So I had an evangelization at the house. I asked everyone who was there, relatives, to come forward if they wanted to accept the Lord Jesus, and I would pray for them, because I saw that God's word had gripped them. But they couldn't come forward, because everyone knelt down. So I went out to each person, and laid my hands on them and prayed and asked for God to bless them and for the pardon of sinners, that God be merciful to the Gypsies.

Brother Gál's Conversion

Brother Horváth viewed the funeral of Annus's husband as the point when God miraculously transformed an entire group of Roma into believers. A contrasting view came from József Gál, a Rom and the son-in-law of Sister Annus. He attended the evangelization, underwent a process of conversion a short time thereafter, and was ordained the next year as a preacher. Gál's history is important because of his strength as a leader, first from a spiritual standpoint and then among Roma. Gál saw the funeral evangelization as the beginning of a gradual process whereby the expressive culture of Pentecostal services began to attract him individually, while God impressed him ever more strongly that his secular life was wrong. At the time he converted, he was a migrant worker in his early twenties, returning occasionally to Szigetvár for major family events like the funeral at which Brother Horváth officiated.

> They buried my father-in-law on August 21, 1984. That was the first time in my life I was with church members, in the house of my mother-in-law that she had inherited. There was a wake there, as is the custom with our Gypsy people— after the burial they gather and the group of guests are served lunch or dinner. There I heard very beautiful believers' songs [*hívő énekek*]. During my worldly time [*a világi koromban*] I loved to party and sing; these [songs] seized me. I promised that I would go to the next church service, and I did. I went to the church service. There I heard beautiful songs again and I decided that I would start going there to listen to the beautiful songs. I would live my worldly life out in the country, just as I had until then. . . . God spoke to my heart by means of the preacher. Seemingly as many times as I went to church services, the preacher always knew those sins I had committed in the countryside. And then a consciousness of sin came into my heart—who is this, who knows my life? I looked around the congregation. Who was there who would watch me or pay attention to me, since I was working three or four hundred kilometers away from them? They couldn't know. But God knew, and he used Brother Horváth, by means of the Holy Spirit, who always predicted my life, and preached about how the Lord Jesus is there and stands at the door of my heart out of the Book of Revelation, and he wants to give pardon, he wants to give joy and happiness.

Gál's interchanges with me, including the conversion narrative extracted here, were phrased in more personal terms than were Brother Horváth's. Whereas Brother Horváth referred to larger church organizations and the effects of state policy, Brother Gál's context was that of his home community and of fellow Roma. His personal tone may be due to the fact that he was a relatively recent convert and also that he

Brother Gál, left, singing with other Roma on an evangelization trip to northeast Hungary.

was accustomed to relating the circumstances of his conversion to a wide array of nonbelievers, from reporters to fellow Roma. Linda Dégh has proposed reading some types of personal narratives, including Pentecostal miracle stories, as legends that emerge through a process of "conflicting opinions" (Dégh 1990:76–78). Through his readings of religious tracts by English commoners of the eighteenth century, E. P. Thompson has demonstrated that although they are intended as religious apologetics, their metaphors and imagery also represent opinions about the establishment of the modern class system (Thompson 1963:350–400). Gál's narrative operates similarly: at the same time that it highlights the effects of the Holy Spirit, it demonstrates how the social conditions of being Rom in 1980s Hungary contributed to his involvement in Pentecostalism.

Gál's narrative conforms to the broad before/after structure of many conversion stories, where a life of evil is seen as being completely transformed by God (Crapanzano 2000; Stromberg 1993). Brother Horváth had begun pastoral schooling before he converted to Pentecostalism; Brother Gál described his own past as one filled with personal trauma and instability.

> I came from a family that was full of demonic and devilish powers. We were full of fear, we were full of trembling, and minority feeling [*kisebbségi érzés*]. And when my parents divorced, we were full of lovelessness. And I desired something—something—wondrous appreciation, to be taken care of. And I can say this to every person that only God can guarantee this. My relatives, my grandparents, tried to guarantee it but—they were able to take care of me physically, but spiritually they could not heal me . . . since my parents divorced when I was very young, my grandfather and grandmother raised me; my grandmother died

in '80. That year I went into the eighth grade, my grandfather continued to raise me, and after I completed the eighth grade, I went to trade school. During that year of trade school, I was in a tradition-preserving [*hagyományőrző*] dance group, a solo dancer, and I loved that with a large pure heart because—I found myself, I was with my brothers [ethnically]. There we danced together performing and we felt as if it was everything to us. We discovered the goal of our lives and our happiness. After this, much tragedy surrounded me. My grandfather got sick, my grandmother had already died, and during this time, I got to know my wife. . . . I came from a very poor family. In Szigetvár terms, they [my wife's family] were a well-to-do family. Therefore, there was enmity and feuding between the two families, which is pretty frequent among Gypsies. They didn't allow us in essence to go together. Because my mother-in-law was a believer, and I was a very good friend of her sons, I visited them many times. Whenever we were there, she always offered me food. A love for guests was in her, as one must protect orphans and widows, and if someone goes to her, she should give them food.

Brother Gál's description of his existence before conversion illustrates how several social problems affected Roma. Although members of his extended family raised Gál, he continued to feel the loss of his parents; he sometimes commented to the Szigetvár congregation in an anguished tone that he was an orphan. Gál found self-definition and identity in a youth folk dance group that was like a family, but it was only temporary because of the way educators and the state limited participation. Many performing groups like Gál's were designed only for youth and functioned as educational programs. Once a young person left the educational system almost all arts groups oriented around ethnicity also ceased; Gál and other young Roma joined the work force as early as age fifteen. In the early 1960s, the state had acted to prevent Romani performing groups from operating because they contradicted a policy of assimilation. By the early 1980s activists in Budapest had made Romani folk groups a legitimate activity (Lange 1997a). A few of the ensembles were multigenerational and in fact centered in urban hostels for migrant workers. However, in many other parts of the country, as in Szigetvár, the membership was still limited to students. Therefore, Gál and other young Roma could not make folklore performance and its feeling of ethnic community a permanent part of their lives. Gál mentioned that during the same period his future mother-in-law, Sister Annus, took special care to offer him hospitality. Gál linked this with her religious beliefs rather than with personal inclination. Although he was a friend of her sons, Gál and Sister Annus both recalled that she was very unhappy when he, yet unconverted, succeeded in marrying her daughter. Gál's family does seem to have imparted to him a heightened awareness of being in an ethnic minority. One acquaintance explained the term *kisebbségi érzés*, also used by Gál in his interview, as anger that he constantly felt about how he and other Roma were being treated. This acquaintance described feeling relieved of *kisebbségi érzés* when he converted. Gál indicated that *kisebbségi érzés* was part of a whole complex of negative feelings that belonged to his secular past. Although he was now converted, Gál did retain interest in Roma as a group within Hungarian society.

State labor policies contributed to Gál's alienation from his family and community. The government, in line with its programs to centralize industry, operated a number of huge construction projects in different parts of the country for which they recruited Roma and lower-class Hungarians as migrant workers. Gál worked in the oil sector; other IG members had worked on a major highway project in central Hungary. Under migrant conditions, groups of young men were freed from monetary and behavioral constraints that parents, girlfriends, or wives might impose. Gál related to me that he and his friends in the work brigades indulged in excessive behavior. These conditions contributed to a crisis that made him receptive to the Pentecostal religion.

> I continued to live my life as a worldly young man. I worked at geophysical plants . . . and at the oil wells as a surveyor's assistant. And there we could live out the different bodily desires and joys of life. We lived in an IBUSZ [state-owned] apartment. In the society of that time we earned good money, and it went for partying, clothes, and food, but many times we drank up our last money; many times we went home [to Szigetvár] on foot, hitchhiking. I'm telling you all this because now with my transformed heart I can distinguish between my old life and my present life. . . . I kept going to the disco, but a fear always gripped my heart. That I had already given my life to God. The congregation didn't even know about this. I kept feeling that my place was not there. My place was not there, and I always feared that one day a voice would sound, and say, "My child, my son, your place is not here. I want to accomplish something else with you." I decided one day that I would choose. With my worldly life, my drunkenness, fornication, and with everything that keeps me far from God's path. I gave up my job and took up hard manual labor at the National Monument Supervisors [in Szigetvár], where many times we had to dig out rocks and mortar. This really wears a person down physically. In Hungary it's the lowest form of work because people look down on these workers both physically and spiritually. But I did it because I did not want to live in sin.

In order to follow a believer's way of life, then, Gál abandoned the migrant way of life that led to excessive spending, drinking, and womanizing, even as it offered him the chance to earn good wages at a skilled occupation. Taking a ditch-digging job at home in Szigetvár, he was not tempted to indulge in these excesses, but he had to endure shame about his profession, take financial penalty, and even risk his health. These were the untenable conditions that most Roma, believers or not, had to face if they decided to work in their home communities. In addition to the economic disadvantage, Gál faced a social challenge that remains crucial for Roma who become converts: how to continue secular friendships and family connections. Some Roma in fact risk being ostracized after they convert (Sato 1988), but the Romani believers whom I know were not abandoned by their friends or families. They continued to live with them, conduct daily business, and to maintain friendships, but in this environment, it was difficult to follow even the most basic of Pentecostalist behavioral strictures. Gál found a way to do this through the psychophysical experiences of God that come with the Pentecostal religion. He made a crucial decision when his first child was born. His brothers-in-law and friends wanted him to celebrate with them, but Gál chose instead to go to an evangelization that day. Gál experienced an infusion of energy that was common when believers made the choice to abandon an aspect of the secular world.

> When we stepped in [the worship hall], a special strength [*erő*], it was as though I had stepped into an atmosphere as though something wanted to squeeze something together. That is, my sins that I couldn't be cleansed of until then weighed on me, and I collapsed on my knees during the church service, when I was praying. The *testvérek* were in tongues and the Holy Ghost [*Szentszellem*] of God was wondrously present. I did not know what this was, I just felt a wondrous love, heat, ardor. And there in my life almost—the first time in my life, I prayed. So this was the choice that God gave me of a gift of the kind of strength with which I could then stand against those attempts that followed in my life, when my friends wanted to tempt me back to the disco, to balls, to go womanizing in Germany. They wanted to tempt me back to my old life, but the good God knew that he had plans and a goal for me and therefore he didn't allow me. Therefore he blessed me with this strength very early so that I would be able not to do these things. I was not [yet] filled with the Holy Spirit, I just won a strength from God so that I could stand firm among people.

Gál's choice not to celebrate with his relatives and friends violated some essential Romani values. Most Roma I know feel that connections with family and friends are so important that when a new family member is born, they reaffirm such ties with celebration. In the secular situation, this involves drinking and possibly some uncontrolled behavior. Other Romani components in Gál's account are implicit; for example, he mentioned German women, who seem to have taken up only with Roma in the Szigetvár area and who even invited them back to Germany. Gál's choice to align with the IG instead of celebrating with his friends is startling. Along with this decisive turn toward the spiritual community came an infusion of spiritual energy and a reorientation toward Roma, this time belonging to a very general category of unconverted and downtrodden Gypsies. In Gál's view, Pentecostalism spread gradually among the Roma of southwest Hungary. This resulted from the work he and a few other new converts did to convince a core of young Romani believers. He began to tell his friends and relatives about the experiences he was having. During this time both he and Brother Misi, who had also converted recently, got the Holy Spirit. Several weeks afterward, brothers Misi and Gál were among thirteen new believers baptized in Szigetvár. Gál related that in the evenings after work, he went to the houses of his fellow Romani converts and preached the Gospel. He told me that he felt directed toward fellow Roma by a miraculous dream that occurred near the time of his baptism.

> JG: In my dream, God led me to a plowed field. As I went on the road to get to the field, very far in the distance a tractor was plowing . . . as I looked further out onto the field, I saw there was corn on three or four rows. It was completely crushed down, as though the tractor had run over it. . . . I lifted up the corn-stem and on it, there were beautiful big ears of corn. I pulled them down. As I shucked them, and was about to put them in the basket, a—light from heaven shone down.

By the time I put them from the ground into the basket, the ears of corn had turned into pure gold. When I woke up, God gave me the meaning of this dream by means of the Holy Ghost. The field is the world. The harvest is the end of the world. The end of the world has arrived. . . . God has shown mercy to many peoples and many nations. As the Book of Luke says, "God [sent] his servants last to the hedges" in every country.[8] He reaches down in every people and nationality to the most despised and humiliated people. And here in Hungary, in the surrounding countries and almost everywhere in the world the Gypsies are like this. And I understood from God that he has sent me into the world to seek them out, those people, those of my brothers, who are looked down upon.

BRL: Before that was there a feeling of community with regard to the Gypsy nationality?

JG: By means of the dance, I always maintained a connection with the Gypsies, since we performed in different places with the dance group. And I was always attracted to the Gypsies. That is, I never denied that I am a Gypsy, and there was never a reason for doing it, because I can say that I come from a prominent Gypsy family who made music for the nobility in the last century. So there was no reason to be ashamed of being a Gypsy. I have not denied that I am a Gypsy, but I would always have liked to help the Gypsy people in some way, and God gave the best [possibility] for this.

Gál revealed from a personal standpoint how Romani conversions to evangelical Christianity were taking place. The experience of conversion, according to his narrative, contrasted with unsatisfactory sociopolitical ties. In the 1970s and 1980s, Roma could not organize from an ethnic standpoint. The stage performance that enabled Gál to find a sense of community was limited only to young adolescents. Such activity was afterward superseded by the demands of the state for a mobile labor force, which in turn weakened the community supervision that might have reduced Gál's and other young men's excesses. Although he drew clear distinctions between his old worldly life and his new converted state, there was not a complete break. Gál continued to be involved with friends and family, whether or not they were believers. He also acted as a spokesman for Romani converts to outsiders, among them foreign missionaries, newspaper reporters, and me.

Roma and Pentecostalism

Conversions of Roma in Hungary parallel the rise of Pentecostalism as a major religion for Roma worldwide. In central and eastern Europe, including Hungary, most citizens are nominally Christian. Roma there observe major rites like christenings and funerals primarily through the Catholic Church. However, Roma have become alienated from the Catholic Church and other major religions. Local clergy have insisted on the payment of taxes and sometimes refused to perform sacraments at all for Roma, who felt these offenses keenly because these mark crucial points in the life cycle. One Rom acquaintance told me that when he took his infant daughter to be christened by the local Catholic priest, he said scornfully, "I don't concern myself with your kind." This was a serious rejection, since according to the Catholic belief system it meant that the girl would remain a pagan and not go to heaven. Some Protestant churches also have rejected Roma because of values placed on order and disciplined work. Aspects of Romani culture like common-law marriage, their occupations as entertainers, their other flexible trades, nomadism, and their loyalty to unconverted family members threaten such values (see [Acton] 1979:290–91). Because most enthusiastic religions in Hungary and other parts of Eastern Europe have a puritan orientation, they have also rejected Roma. IG members frequently contrasted the inclusive atmosphere of their own congregation with other small churches in the area. They reported how one very popular Evangelical church turned away Roma. Another church member who had been raised as a Pentecostal was the only one of his family to attend the IG, because the others disliked the fact that the congregation included Roma.

Possibly because they perceive Roma as sinful, evangelists have also regarded them as ideal targets for conversion. Since the eighteenth century, non-Roma have made consistent attempts to evangelize to Roma all over the world. Ken Lee argues that historically this "missionizing urge" was devoted to reforming Roma into suitable subjects for the state (2000:135). A change occurred when evangelists accommodated aspects of secular Romani culture. A Pentecostal movement among Roma appears to have started when Clement le Cossec, a pastor in the French Assemblies of God, started the first Pentecostal mission to Roma in the mid-1950s. Le Cossec did not preach radical changes in occupations or living habits. He encouraged an indigenous leadership to develop, and between 1958 and 1963, Roma established many independent congregations. The Gypsy Evangelical Church is now an autonomous organization in France, although in other countries Romani Pentecostals are affiliated with the Assemblies of God ([Acton] 1979:292–94). In the mid-1980s the anthropologist Patrick Williams estimated that there were 30,000 baptized church members and 60,000 other believers in France out of a total Romani population of 200,000 (Williams 1987:325). Gitanos adopted Pentecostalism in southern France and Spain, where there are an estimated 25,000 adherents (Anderson 1987:233). There are also many Romani adherents in the United States and in Scandinavia (Sato 1988).

In Hungary, some individual pastors in the mainstream denominations gained a sizable number of Romani congregation members because they treated them seriously. They held masses in Romani, recruited them for church choirs, or taught them catechism. But precisely because they were so effective, the state restricted their activities, using the church authority structure to assign such popular clergymen to tiny and remote parishes (Gyurkovics 1981; Hadházy 1983). The charismatic basis for authority aided Evangelical and Pentecostal churches that decided to include Roma. Roma in Hungary started converting simply when evangelizers began to treat them as equals, especially when they invited them to take leadership. Evangelizing efforts to Hungarian Roma came primarily from within the country; West European and Hungarian Romani believers did not contact each other directly until the mid-1990s. In the 1970s the Free Christian Church (Szabadkeresztyén Gyülekezet), a charismatic group that had split from another fundamentalist church, was the first to attract a core of Romani believers who then successfully converted other Roma. One of the Free Christians circumvented the state's ban on evangelization that had punished Brother Horváth; he was a supplier of grocery stores who began to proselytize among Roma in the villages of northeast Hungary he visited for his work (Hegyi and Kovalik 1981:687; Horváth 1984). The Romani revival spread to other areas where the Free Christians were already strong. Roma served as lay preachers at village gatherings. They attended the services of large Free Christian congregations in the cities of Debrecen and Budapest, and Rom-only congregations grew in many villages of eastern Hungary. The government did not suppress this revival, but it remained mostly in the eastern part of the country.[9] The Free Christians had won membership in the Council of Free Churches, and their work with Roma was regarded as progress on a severe social problem. In some localities, however, Magyars viewed Romani conversions to the Free Christians antagonistically, asserting that they did so in order to get donations of food and clothing (Hegyi and Kovalik 1981).

As shown in France, non-Roma may initiate Christian revivals. However, the situation in the IG during the late 1980s demonstrated to me that one of the main reasons why Roma may convert to Pentecostalism is that they can have an indigenous leadership. In the IG, it was Roma who led larger-scale conversions and, more significant, the forming of a believer's community, where people changed their behaviors, learned the Pentecostal interpretations of the biblical text, and then described their experiences to other potential converts. Proselytizing among relatives and friends, brothers Gál and Misi generated enough believers within two years to form a congregation with regular meetings, a worship hall, a treasury, and an official leader in the person of Brother Misi. Brother Gál asserted that he and other Romani evangelizers had also been the ones to spread Oneness theology throughout the country. The IG's congregations in central and southeast Hungary remained like other Pentecostal groups around the country in that they were chiefly Magyar. But in the early 1990s, in addition to its Romani membership of approximately one hundred in southwest Hungary, the IG had many Romani adherents in the north. In the late 1980s, Romani congregations in the northeast switched their allegiance to the IG from the Free Christians. In Hungary during the 1990s, a small number of Roma, about a thousand, were Pentecostals.[10] Until the late 1990s, almost none of the Romani congregations in Hungary were autonomous; like the IG they were ethnically mixed, or were part of church organizations led by Magyars.

Views of Pentecostalism in Hungarian Society

Enthusiastic religions, among them Pentecostalism, have maintained a consistent presence in Hungary ever since their introduction. Brother Horváth commented that whenever there were short periods of time when people in Hungary were free to practice religious choice, there were "awakenings" (*ébredések*), and many new converts were gained. But it is difficult for nonbelievers to understand the appeal of these religions. This is much more the case in Eastern Europe than in the United States. The multiple dissent religions in the United States are essential forms of the voluntary association that de Tocqueville saw as pervading American life. However, in the Hungarian and sometimes even the European context, such association around religious experience is exceptional. Considering the marginal status of these religions, conversion seems not to convey any type of rational advantage. Many explanations have been offered for why people convert to enthusiastic religions. But such explanations say as much about the social position of the theorist as about religious adherents.

Ecstatic religions are sometimes thought to rebel against and compensate for a deprived state (Lewis 1989; Niebuhr 1929:30). Elderly believers' recollections of why Pentecostalism spread after World War II are congruent with this idea. Brother Horváth commented in his sermons that during the immediate postwar period people were so deprived of material necessities that they turned to the spiritual arena for hope. The church caretaker, Sister Herceg, commented that her religious faith gave her the strength to endure physical hunger during a famine after World War II. In addition to believers, social critics in Hungary also thought that deprivation could explain conversions to enthusiastic religions. It appears to be a clear reason why poor peasants in southeast Hungary turned to the small churches. A number of Hungarian writers in the 1920s and 1930s studied this area, called the Alföld or Great Plain, which had retained a virtually feudal system of large landholdings. They wrote that the peasants, or *agrárproletárok* (agricultural proletarians), in this area were suffering economically and had no political means to change their condition. In a variety of essays and books, practicing the descriptive reportage called "sociography" (*szociográfia*) in Hungary, Péter Veres and György Oláh argued that the peasant religious leaders could have mobilized the agrarian sector politically. Imre Kovács described how the peasants had converted to the small churches, characterizing it as a "silent revolution" (*néma forradalom*), one that destroyed the poor people but not the authorities (Kovács 1989 [1937]; Némedi 1985:199, 282).[11] Pentecostal historians in Hungary attribute the emergence of their own religion to the same conditions. Like Kovács, they note that deprivation and the failure to effect change were an impetus for emigration, commenting that in the United States the emigrants became an "exploitable work force." The original intent of the emigrants was to return with money to buy land, but the converts returned instead to evangelize (Tóth et al. 1998[1978]:25–26).

The sociologist László Kardos, who studied small churches in central Hungary, proposed several reasons why the emigrants may have converted in the United States. He wrote that the growth of "sects" in Hungary came out of "societal and natural conditions . . . out of the social-psychological atmosphere that came from misery, uncertainty of existence, lack of a way out of this existence, [and] impediments to human success" (1969:250). Kardos interviewed emigrants who had converted in the United States and then returned to their home villages. In the mining and industrial cities of the U.S. Midwest, they had become acquainted with the Baptist religion and its different variants. The care and warmth with which the small U.S. congregations treated their countrymen attracted these newcomers. Kardos hints at another reason why the Pentecostal religion might have appealed to the emigrants: it had an aura of wealth, and the believers led a "churchlike life" resembling the mainstream religions, as opposed to a closed existence (1969:184–85).

The assessment of Kardos, the sociographers, and the Pentecostal historians is partly true. However, by the 1960s and 1970s a considerable number of members had joined who by then had a relatively comfortable existence. Material privation or lack of a political outlet to change material conditions cannot explain the conversions of the 1980s. Zsuzsa Horváth's survey of a congregation in the early 1970s revealed that a substantial portion of the membership consisted of lower-middle-class factory workers and miners (Horváth 1977:381–82). My interviews and conversations with IG members showed a similar background for them. By comparison with the general population, the IG's Magyar members were thus somewhat poor, but not desperately so. The IG's Romani members generally had lower incomes than the Magyar members did. They were roughly middle income in relation to other Roma in the area, with the exception of the Vlach Rom members, who were extremely poor. Nearly all IG members could do skilled labor, but as the career trajectories of Brother Horváth and Brother Gál show, they often made the choice out of their religious beliefs to take jobs with lower pay and skill requirements. Brother Horváth sometimes commented that his parents had been disappointed because rather than returning to seminary he harvested in the fields of Somogy county and then married the daughter of the peasant whose preaching had converted him. Brother Misi had a secure but somewhat low-status position as a maintenance person on swing shift at the city utilities plant. At the beginning of my fieldwork in 1990 most male members of the IG worked in local industries and transportation networks; women were primarily unskilled laborers. Housing conditions for Magyars were relatively satisfactory from a material standpoint. The IG's Romani members lived mostly in the segregated and substandard housing districts of the two cities where the IG's subsidiary congregations were located.

IG members suffered much stigma. The case of Brother István, a Vlach Rom, is not unusual. When he began to speak in tongues, his parents thought of putting him in an insane asylum. He told me that acquaintances had called him a "fag" (*buzi*), probably because he forswore activities like smoking, drinking, and military service, which are associated with masculine behavior. His experience demonstrates the way that many Hungarians thought that only people who fall outside social norms would join the enthusiastic religions. In a layman's application of the church-sect theory articulated by Ernst Troeltsch (1931), mainstream Hungarians tended to stigmatize all but the Catholic, Calvinist, and Lutheran churches as "sects" (*szekták*; see Horváth 1990:11).[12] In contrast to what seems to be a rational basis for the mainstream institutions, the word *szekta* implies that members are fanatical, closed to the outside world, restricted to a single leader, and geographically isolated. Believers and humanistically oriented Hungarian writers have attempted to counter these negative associations with two alternate terms, "small churches" (*kisegyházak*) and "free churches" (*szabad egyházak*). The coalition of groups in the State Council of Free Churches worked out the latter as an administrative designation at the beginning of the socialist period (Szigeti 1987; Horváth 1990).

Early in the twentieth century, one explanation for the spread of sects was tautological: adherents were attracted to these religions, with their emphasis on the nonrational divinity, because they were not well enough educated to know better. Richard Niebuhr, writing in the 1920s, argued that religious enthusiasm occurred "where the power of abstract thought has not been highly developed" (Niebuhr 1929:30). Many Hungarians believed that only "simple" people would be drawn to enthusiastic religion. Hungarians of my acquaintance made a general contrast between "cultured" (*művelt*) and "simple" (*egyszerű*) people. The *művelt* person had some education and refined manners.[13] The *egyszerű* person had very little education, behaved crudely, and spoke Hungarian with a dialect or accent. Ethnicity was almost a side effect of these norms; villagers, people with little education, or those who were not ethnic Magyars might all be considered *egyszerű*.

The idea that Roma were uncultured people was prevalent in Hungarian society. Even Magyars of my acquaintance with benign intentions sometimes commented on how Roma behaved in an unrefined way. Not only did Roma contradict the norms of Hungarian high culture, but also their pronunciation of Hungarian differed from that of educated Magyars. Many Magyars explained the appeal of Pentecostalism for Roma with the idea that they were ignorant. When Roma preached or gave testimony eloquently, some of my Magyar acquaintances assumed that they did not fully understand the theology behind their own words but were only repeating formulas. Even the sympathetic writer Ágnes Diósi bemoaned the binary thinking that Romani converts seemed to adopt and the level of fear it engendered (Diósi 1990a:20). IG members thought of themselves as uncultured. One young Romani believer asked me: "Why do you want to concern yourself with us *egyszerű* people?" Nearly all of the IG members might be considered *egyszerű* either by virtue of Romani ethnicity or because they had a low level of education. The members and leaders in their mid-twenties and -thirties, mostly Roma, had achieved an eighth-grade education with some subsequent vocational training. Elderly Magyar women in the church usually had a grade school education. The elderly Romani believers, on the other hand, were often illiterate. Only Brother Horváth and two Magyar women had received a high school education.

Another tautological explanation for the occurrence of enthusiastic religions in Hungary was that their adherents were deviant. Religious authorities took this point of view, objecting to such activities as speaking in tongues as "an incomprehensible chaos of language" (Kovács 1975:51) or asserting that Pentecostals "credit their condition, which may stem from sickness or susceptibility to ecstasy, to the Holy Spirit" (Pákozdy 1972:14). Pentecostal and other revival religions seemed deviant because they did not originate on Hungarian soil. By contrast, the IG members utilized the idea of deviance as a rhetorical device in order to publicize the power of the Holy Spirit. A few of the IG's members actually had engaged in illegal activities before converting; they mentioned this to reporters whenever they visited the congregation and also to me during my first few weeks of fieldwork. Romani members emphasized musically to American missionaries that Jesus had saved them from a life of sin. However, criminal deviance was not a matter of great importance within the church. Brother Horváth's sermons reiterated the theme of an evil former life but only with general references in order to show the believers that they could have the strength of will to keep obeying the IG's behavioral strictures. In local congregation meetings, the conversation centered on community matters, messages from God, and specific fundamentalist behavioral precepts—all details of believers' daily lives, not their former existence as "sinners."

In contrast to these hostile explanations, a number of U.S. theorists have argued that enthusiastic religions have an appeal because they are close to mainstream society; they socialize dominant values with regard to work, obedience to authority, optimism, practicality, and patriotism. Their sensational styles of worship actually motivate adherents to change their behavior and conform to the mainstream values of the Protestant ethic (Dearman 1974; Johnson 1961; Pope 1942). In the Hungarian context, Pentecostalism stood out from the other small churches as a form of American popular culture. One of the benefits that Pentecostalism appeared to offer was the possibility of upward mobility; Zsuzsa Horváth commented that as first generation workers, the Pentecostals she studied "believed that faith eased . . . the change in lifestyle and acted as an aid in their further upward rise" (1977:382). Protestant ethic values like individual striving toward a goal, independent community organization, and thrift were already present in Hungarian society because of the Calvinist church and were even part of the orientation of the older enthusiastic churches like the Nazarenes. In the IG, diligent work and obedience to authority were stressed more than in Hungarian society at large. However, the IG's leaders did not emphasize optimism or patriotism. In fact, they were bitter about many things in the past and suspicious of and opposed to the state in general. IG leaders usually stressed perfectionism in their rhetoric, but they often acted pragmatically. One example of this was how they emphasized to the press that some of their members were reformed criminals, as a practical way of demonstrating the IG's value to local nonbelievers. As I will describe in the next chapters, accepting me as a researcher also involved a practical strategy to change church music.

It is possible that pragmatism in fact explains the worldwide appeal of Pentecostalism for Roma. Pragmatism has been very familiar to Roma. Carol Silverman observed in her studies of American Kalderash Roma that many of their actions have flexible and bricolage qualities. These arise out of their practical approaches to making a living while at the same time they strive to keep a large family group intact (Silverman 1982, 1988). Patrick Williams has argued that it is a fallacy to view the Roma he worked with in France as marginal to mainstream society, since they themselves focus on everyday living (1993). This practicality finds a parallel in the Roma's new religion. Paloma Gay y Blasco has described how Gitano Evangelicals in Madrid reinforced traditional gender roles by asserting that their conversions made them ideal models in the marriage relationship (1999:119–24). Other studies in Spain and France suggest that Roma continue their own leadership structures when they convert to Pentecostalism and that the religion makes them inclined to have much closer interaction with Roma of other ethnic groups (Wang 1989; Williams 1984, 1991b). As believers, Roma can make changes where necessary to maintain a commitment to their faith and to rise in Pentecostal institutions, while they retain other cultural elements that appear to be congruent with church teachings. In Hungary, some of these choices had to do with advancement in mainstream society. In the secular context many Roma judged a basic level of reading and calculation all that was necessary to pursue mercantile and craft occupations, but in order to take leadership in a Christian church, it is necessary to read the biblical text thoroughly and interpret it eloquently. Changes made by the IG's Romani leaders illustrate a pragmatic approach; within the space of a few years, they had gone from a basic reading level to becoming persuasive explicators of Bible passages. This in turn caused mainstream society to see them as less *egyszerű*. Local Magyars commented on how once they converted, Romani believers became "well-spoken" (*szépen beszélnek*) and became "proper people" (*rendes emberek*). Subsequent chapters will illustrate how in the musical sphere the IG's Romani members achieved other practical goals, balancing their religious lives with secular relationships, meeting leadership demands, accommodating the customs of elderly Magyar believers, and attracting missionaries.

The occurrence of many religious movements worldwide has been correlated with socioeconomic upheavals. Ralph Linton and Anthony Wallace argued that a new religion means a new form of social organization that is created when a previous system breaks down (Linton 1943; Wallace 1956). Socioeconomic displacement was one consistent factor in the life stories of Pentecostal believers in Hungary. This displacement had many causes, including war, the reorganization of labor under socialism, and specific socialist policies to assimilate Roma. One elderly couple in the IG had been resettled twice as refugees during the course of World War II. Brother Horváth was uprooted from his school and family when he was forced into labor and then escaped. Roma were once again displaced at the end of the socialist period. Starting in 1990, the major state-owned firms in southwest Hungary were closed. Over the course of that year, nearly all of the IG's Romani members were fired from their jobs (most of the IG's Magyar members had reached retirement age). By 1992, only a fraction of them had found new employment, reflecting a national trend of discrimination in hiring and inadequate retraining.

Since displacement was a general fact of existence in socialist Hungary, this alone does not explain Magyars' and Roma's choice to join the IG. But almost all believers mentioned in conjunction with conversion how their family, occupational, or housing situations had undergone radical change. This may indicate that in viewing the trajectory of their lives from their present status of believers they attached importance to these changes. Sister Herceg mentioned that the Holy Spirit provided comfort not only when she was hungry but also when she encountered unfriendly neighbors after moving far away from her home village. Brother Misi and his family, as well as several other Romungre, mentioned to me that they were pleased when the government resettled them from a *putri* (a district of shacks and earthen huts) into apartment complexes and houses, most of which had running water and electricity. But resettlement can also function as "ethnocide"; communal ties are broken, and a destructive form of individualism takes their place (Jaulin 1970). Members of the Vlach Rom community to which Brother István and other believers belonged were not particularly happy about resettlement they underwent in the 1960s. Authorities had closed a large camp that they had in a forest south of Szigetvár and moved them into houses in several nearby villages. Brother István's relatives and Brother Bandi remembered their previous lifestyle positively with its orientation toward nature, living in the present, and community cooperation. Bitter feuds within their community occurred when the authorities separated them by nuclear family and they stopped sharing property. These Roma flocked to evangelizations held by Brother István some thirty years later in the 1990s, but tension remained great in the resettlement villages. Non-Rom authorities viewed the gathering of so many Roma with fear and withdrew their permission for use of the village meetinghouse.

Charles Glock proposed "psychic deprivation" as an idea that goes beyond the determinist explanations of new religious movements. It occurs "when persons find themselves without a meaningful system of values by which to interpret and organize their lives" (Glock 1973[1964]:212). Several studies in Hungary during the late 1970s applied a similar idea. Zsuzsa Horváth and Magda Matolay demonstrated that both the Catholic base community movement and small charismatic churches had great appeal in Hungary because they provided a sense of close community (Horváth 1984:6; Horváth and Matolay 1980). The state had a specific tactic to alienate church authorities from their congregations so that the churches would not have such independently organized memberships. In addition to transferring popular clergymen to rural districts, the authorities discouraged small group activities like classes and prayer groups. At times the state arrested the most rebellious leaders, and the church organizations excommunicated them (Polgar 1984; Walters 1988). Many IG members were alienated from the mainstream churches. Some had simply been nonreligious. Others turned to Pentecostalism because mainstream religious authorities had offended them.

The excessive emphasis on the rational in modern society, including in Europe's mainstream churches, is also alienating (see Wilson 1975).[14] For IG members, qualities of the religious experience that defied rationality actually attracted them and enabled them to stay committed. This is the case for Brother Gál in the initial stages of his conversion; he was gripped by the fact that God through the preaching of Brother Horváth seemed to be aware of the sins he had been committing. Pentecostals credit divine agency for the emergence of their religion. Most believers emphasized to me that they believed that God had reached out specifically to save them from lives of sin; a common phrase in sermons, that God has "wondrously bent down to us" (*csodálatosan lehajolt ránk*), drew vigorous responses of "Halleluia." In their view, enthusiastic Christianity has existed from the very beginning. The Pentecostal historians in Hungary detail charismatic revivals from the second century CE onward and connect their religion with the revival currents inside Hungary's two main Protestant churches (Tóth et al. 1998[1978]:10–30). In a sermon, Brother Horváth once outlined a trajectory of reform movements from Luther's birthday through Pentecostalism to the Day of Judgment. In Europe, one of the appeals of Pentecostalism has been its use as a means of physical healing. Many members joined the IG for this reason; they had been diagnosed with serious illnesses that had gone into remission after they converted and other believers had prayed over them.

The theory that Pentecostals and charismatics are responding to alienation and excessive emphasis on the rational in modern society is apolitical in the West, but it threatened the socialist orientation toward progress and centralized control of information in Hungary. In the late 1980s, when society began to reorganize itself from below, after being directed from above for forty years, Hungary's independent churches became significant components of civil society. One Evangelical group, the Hit Gyülekezet (Congregation of Faith), became the country's fastest-growing church; from 1988 to 1992, its membership increased from 3,000 to 20,000. Zsuzsa Horváth saw a reaction against established beliefs in Hungary, a forum for political engagement, a flexible form of church organization, and opportunities to be part of an emerging authority structure as major factors in this church's popularity (1992). During this time the IG also experienced its most significant growth since the late 1940s, evolving from tiny scattered prayer groups to its national membership of approximately 2,000. The number of Romani believers increased generally, but they stayed within separate denominations headed at a national level by Magyars and affiliated with different American missions.

Luther Gerlach and Virginia Hine have proposed viewing Pentecostalism as a type of social movement analogous to Black Power in the 1960s. They observe that a movement is not just a passive reflection of societal pressure but also can serve as "a mechanism through which . . . social change is shaped and directed." This change is effected by creating structures that function alongside and compete with established institutions. These parallel structures may never evolve into major organizations, but they are capable of stimulating change in their counterparts. Such movements embody the flexible response needed to create institutions with vitality at times when society is undergoing rapid change (1970: xiv–xvi, 207, 217–18). The IG and other Magyar-Rom churches functioned like social movements by reorganizing ethnic stratification. Several competing notions of power resulted from the mixture. An old model of Hungarian social structure as constituted in the mainstream churches persisted; the head pastor, as a member of the intelligentsia, felt the duty and the right to impart *műveltség* (refinement), as well as religious teachings. American missionary organizations had the goal of directing the IG into the detailed hierarchy of a denominational system. Roma and ordinary Magyar believers had a contrasting ideal of egalitarian community. In this they reinforced the mostly charismatic basis that had characterized the IG's leadership for over sixty years.

Instrumental Music, Charisma, and Church Leadership

During one of the first services I attended at the IG, Brother Horváth declared, "We have a healthy, unified congregation. Now there are more of us . . . there is the problem of an assistant [*helyettes*]." Commenting that "the Holy Spirit is not a municipal official," he read Acts 13:1–5, which describes how God had distinguished Barnabas and Paul out of the Antioch congregation. Then he proposed naming a number of Romani and Magyar members as leaders for the IG congregation. He suggested that Brother Misi lead the Szigetvár group. Brother Gál, he said, could serve as a countrywide missionary and lead gatherings in the neighboring town of Barcs. He suggested that some, like Brother István, simply be pastors. He also asked some Magyars to serve: the elderly brothers Borovics and Illi and the young Brother Feri. Only one person, a synthesizer player, Brother Zoli, refused this offer. After each suggestion, Brother Horváth asked the congregation: "Do you agree?" They seemed enthusiastic and happy. With their heads up and their shoulders relaxed, many of them called out "Amen," "Halleluia," and "Yes" (*igen*) just as they did during sermons when Brother Horváth had made a point they agreed with.

This event demonstrated to me how in the early 1990s the IG combined charisma and systematization in its designation of leaders. The national president of the IG, Brother Ungváry, and the vice president, Brother Horváth, officially nominated and approved leaders of local congregations as pastors. This occupation could then be notated in their passports. However, the congregation's affectionate agreement with Brother Horváth, and his own initiative in proposing new leaders, shows how he functioned as the IG's national leader from a charismatic standpoint. The IG's president was not very active; he served only one small congregation in central Hungary, and Brother Horváth ratified official decisions with him. When member congregations had problems, they turned to Brother Horváth. I witnessed a number of times how the congregation members in southwest Hungary and other regions asked him to resolve disagreements. When entire congregations of Roma switched their allegiances to the IG, it was Brother Horváth they contacted.

Brother Horváth made some comments to me later indicating that he had weighed a combination of Holy Spirit recognition and systematized learning in his decisions to designate new pastors, just as the IG leaders some forty years ago had done when they ordained him. The IG did not have a formal method for preparing its leaders. Brother Horváth explained to me that he had based his decision to ordain the young leaders on their abilities and levels of commitment. He wanted to counteract the unequal treatment of Roma in the school system. Brother Horváth believed that while they only had eighth-grade educations, young men like brothers István, Gál, and Misi had shown extraordinary motivation and ability to study and understand the Bible. His own experience of religious oppression also played a part. His wife commented that he felt it was important to bring young people into the church to make up for the fact that under socialism there had been almost no opportunity to train new leaders. Brother Horváth felt a sense of urgency about recognizing them because he feared that the current period of democracy would not last long.

The basic format of leadership by a preacher was the standard for the IG. On the day Brother Horváth designated the new leaders he summarized their roles only in a general way. Some Evangelicals believe that leaders should have very specific responsibilities based on the activities of the Apostles in the Acts. Among these are the authority and gift to prophesy, to interpret tongues, or to lay hands on others while praying. The believers in the IG did not often talk about these distinctions and instead simply used the term *szolgálat* (service). On the Sunday that he named the group of leaders, Brother Horváth did not specify what constituted *szolgálat* or cite any of the Bible passages that use this term. Some Pentecostal and Evangelical denominations in the United States have created an institutional structure that in their view replicates the leadership roles taken in the early church as described in the First Letter of Paul to Timothy and elsewhere in the letters of Paul, establishing different levels of presbyters, bishops, and deacons. But I only witnessed IG members using a general two-tier system. They called the men who were heads of congregations *prédikátorok* (preachers). They talked about other men performing *szolgálat*. These men sat in the same area of the church as the *prédikátorok* and preached for short periods during the worship hour. More men did *szolgálat* than those Brother Horváth had named. Church members referred to instrumental music performance as *szolgálat*, thus seeming to conceive of the musicians as leaders; in fact, several preachers were also musicians. The blurring of leadership categories to include music demonstrates how charisma formed a major basis for authority in the IG. The men who were designated for general *szolgálat* preached and prayed over others just like ordained preachers. Church members endowed leadership with a basis in the supernatural by valuing musicians for their ability to facilitate connection with the Holy Spirit. The Holy Spirit might manifest in preachers with prophecy, tongue-speaking, or laying on of hands; the musicians could augment this force for the whole congregation.

Instrumental Music in the Isten Gyülekezet

In the IG, instrumental music was exclusively used to accompany singing. The ensemble could include console organ, several synthesizers, electric bass, guitars, spoons, drum kit, tambourine, or accordion. There was no set number or combination of musicians; without guests, the orchestra numbered at most six but often only one or two. Most of the musicians switched functions by playing various instruments, leading congregational singing, and holding microphones for other performers. Brother Rudi, who sang and played organ, accordion, or synthesizer, also preached on occasion to the congregation in Szigetvár. When he was not preaching, Brother Gál led singing, played various percussion instruments, and occasionally performed a buzzing vocable part he called "mouth trumpet" (*szájtrombita*). Women also played instruments, but they almost never performed with the ensemble during services. Church members called this ensemble the *zenekar* (orchestra). The term reflects both the nature of the group's instrumentation and its use for sacred music. In Hungarian the word *zenekar* means a symphony orchestra, but it also refers to a rock band. Church members deliberately avoided using the term *banda* (band) for this group because of its secular connotations; the *banda* was a Romani string band that played for wedding festivities, at cafes, and for parties. Like rock or string band musicians, the instrumentalists in the IG used no musical scores. Their ensemble utilized homophonic texture; within this basic format, the musicians rendered chords, bass, rhythm, and timbre in a blend of Romani, Hungarian folk, Western pop, and Christian religious styles.

Instrumental musicians led the congregation one Saturday afternoon when they invited me to the worship hall in the town of Szigetvár to celebrate Géza's official marriage. Like many Roma, Géza had been in a common-law marriage for a number of years. Brother Horváth was unusual among the small church leaders in Hungary for accepting such people as converts. But he then taught them that what they had done was sinful and they should officially marry. After Brother Horváth finished blessing the couple and delivered a sermon, the church members called out song requests to the instrumental musicians, who on this day were playing synthesizer, bongo drums, and accordion. Géza asked for the song "Jertek, ünnepeljünk!" (Come

The IG's instrumental musicians. Brother Zoli, left, was at the synthesizer as Brother Rudi, right, prepared to sing.

Let Us Celebrate). Brother Zoli set his synthesizer to an organ timbre with moderate vibrato and turned on a percussion pattern with woodblocks and cymbals. After a few beats Brother Gál joined with bongos, and Brother Rudi started playing a single major triad in a staccato offbeat pattern on a small accordion. He continued this as he began singing the aeolian-mode melody, and the congregation joined him. Brother Zoli doubled the congregation at the upper octave, adding chords downward in a minor key harmonization. Then he connected a bass option that interspersed a silent beat with pitches a fourth and fifth apart. Brother Gál, playing the bongos with sticks, doubled and quadrupled the song's basic pulse (ex. 2.1).

The instrumentation of the IG's ensemble, with its electric instruments and drum set timbres, might seem to support the idea that Western popular music pervades every corner of the world, obliterating or "greying out" unique local styles (see Nettl 1983:345–61). The instrumentalists seemed to render that idiom clumsily, without full functional harmony in either chords or bass, and applying the most hackneyed of programmed rhythms. In fact, most of the IG's musicians were self-taught, and they did not practice or hold rehearsals. But as musicians, they invested the sounds with meanings that applied to their particular time, place, and social position. The music's use in the public sphere of church services was one key element. In addition, the players' ways of using instrumental music symbolically and of talking about music revealed that they were combining Western popular music with two major vernacular idioms in Hungary: Romani string music and Hungarian folk music.[1]

The group's volume level seemed to be directly related to popular music. The amplified voices of the musicians were very loud, and the bass often boomed out into the congregation at a level that I found physically uncomfortable. These sound volumes were common for rock bands in bars and stadiums. In the 1960s, Hungarian critics of rock (*beat*) objected to its loudness. They complained that high volume lowered musical quality because texts could not be understood; *beat* put the audience in ecstasy rather than inspiring intelligent evaluation (Biernaczky 1982[1970]):118–19). In the IG, the loudness of the instruments was not designed to produce such a reaction in the congregation but was a response to their level of spiritual involvement. The musicians linked volume with the music's tempo in order to lead the congregation spiritually. The instrumental musicians supported and intensified the directions that the Holy Spirit seemed to be taking at a given moment. The synthesizer player, Brother Zoli, described himself as having both a practical and a spiritual role. Like an organist in a mainstream church, he played introductory phrases or passages to set tempo and pitch for the congregation, but they were very brief. He led the congregation, but he also followed the direction of the Holy Spirit as indicated by the intensity of the singing. Brother Zoli was particularly careful to adjust his synthesizer's rhythm and bass programs to the mood set by the congregation. Because the congregation or the leaders chose songs on the spot, Brother Zoli had to be able to make his choices quickly and be prepared to alter them.

BRL: I've noticed that when a song begins you play softly and then you do something.

ZK: At first there is a song; they say for us to play a certain song and I turn it [the synthesizer] on softly; I turn the volume all the way down. I turn on one [rhythm setting] which I think would be about right for that beat. But if it is not good, then I try to listen to how it sounds. Then among these dance types I choose the one that is most appropriate to the music.

Brother Zoli explained that it was important to change the music smoothly and almost imperceptibly. The primary problem was to find the appropriate tempo. He emphasized that on these occasions his amplified singing was just as important as his instrument.

BRL: When the congregation begins singing, and doesn't it happen sometimes, when they sing and clap a bit slower—

ZK: When they sing more slowly it's possible to adjust this tempo control after them. For example if it's a bit fast, I take it down a little bit and it's almost un-noticeable. I take it down smoothly, and it is unnoticeable that the beat slows down. If they sing faster than my organ's beat then I can speed it up to catch up with them. But if there is no microphone for me to sing into and lead the whole congregation with, then there is no point in speeding up after them. It reaches the beat, but they don't hold the level of the beat. Then I have to sing into the microphone, so that the beat will always stay the same, because we have to keep pausing. Either we rush or we get behind.

Although he preferred to keep the accompaniment somewhat soft, Brother Zoli said that he used the bass option as a last resort to keep the congregation's tempo steady: "So that the beat won't fall out, so that the beat will be satisfactory, then I have to amplify the bass, so that at least they will hear the sound of the drum." The performance of "Come Let Us Celebrate" illustrates this; Brother Rudi began sing-ing somewhat faster than the tempo indicated by Brother Gál's bongos and the syn-thesizer percussion patterns. Then the congregation entered energetically but a bit more slowly. Just at this moment, Brother Zoli turned on the synthesizer's bass op-tion in a quarter-note pulse and steadied the whole group with a feeling of the beat hierarchy. Brother Zoli's concern with keeping everyone at an even tempo, while at the same time he adjusted to them, reflects his orientation toward being guided by the Holy Spirit. His ultimate goal was to follow the Holy Spirit direction indicated by the intensity of the congregation's singing.

In the major Christian denominations, congregations have received instrumen-tal music sound more passively. Some Pentecostal denominations of the United States follow their model. Delton Alford, an official in the Church of God, Cleveland, ad-vises that the organ should play preludes, postludes, and offertories at the points in the service that are similar to those of mainline Protestant churches (Alford 1967:62–64). In the IG, rather than establishing a relationship themselves with God, the mu-sicians had the role of supporting the connection once it became manifest in the congregation. The role of the music played by the IG's instrumentalists was much closer to that of the early U.S. Pentecostals. The free atmosphere of early Pentecos-tal gatherings in the United States encouraged musical participation. Brass instru-ments, guitars, and drums previously used in the secular context were introduced into the music of the revival (Duncan 1987:12, 14). Dance rhythms were reshaped for sacred use (Menzies 1971:350). The IG ensemble's relationship to congregational singing

EXAMPLE 2.1. "Jertek, ünnepeljünk!" (Come Let Us Celebrate). IG congregation, Szigetvár, November 1990.

53

thus derives from the emphasis of the church on Holy Spirit inspiration. Their concept may have originated as much in the secular context as in a charismatic orientation; in cafes and at weddings, it was important for instrumentalists to support or augment the singer's "mood" (*hangulat*).

Connections with Vernacular Music

The IG's instrumentalists combined the Western harmonic idiom with elements from two indigenous styles: Hungarian folk music and Romani string bands. One indication of this was how the ensemble played chords that were different from standard Western harmonizations. The synthesizer or accordion players used only one or two chords to accompany entire melodies. Mixed modalities were common, as with the combination of major- and minor-key triads to accompany the aeolian melody of "Come Let Us Celebrate." When I played my field recordings of this music to Magyar acquaintances of mine, they often heard it as *műveletlen* (lacking culture) and commented that Roma did not have any musical education. But as I listened to the IG musicians' comments, I wondered if they might be perceiving chordal accompaniments from the vantage point of Hungarian folk music rather than from that of Western art or popular music. In Hungarian folk music, drone, melodic embellishment, and rhythm take precedence over functional harmony. In his studies of Hungarian musical instruments, Bálint Sárosi has demonstrated that there was a widespread practice of accompanying folk songs and especially dance tunes with such instruments as bagpipes, zithers, and hurdy-gurdies that were equipped to play drones. Tonal accompaniment only entered the Hungarian folk music idiom in the eighteenth century with the advent of small string ensembles (Sárosi 1967:106–108).

Only the most elderly members of the IG congregation grew up singing folk songs. The secular music I heard in the region was either from the Western popular idiom or from the popular song genre called *magyar nóta*. Yet some of the church members' musical sensibilities appeared to relate to the Hungarian folk music idiom. Their choice of chords paralleled the tendency in folk music to privilege drone-style accompaniment. The IG musicians' talk about the mechanics of their instruments revealed that they did not think of their accompaniments as having primarily a functional harmonic purpose. Brother Rudi used the term *tekerő* for the programmed bass option on his synthesizer. *Tekerő* is a colloquial expression for the hurdy-gurdy in Hungary, referring to the wheel that makes the melody and drone strings sound together. Rudi's use of the term *tekerő* showed that he was identifying the bass option as a repetition of patterns and pitches rather than as a line that would be changed to follow the melody from a functional standpoint. As he did in "Come Let Us Celebrate," Rudi often used just one triad to accompany an entire melody (ex. 2.1). On other occasions, he alternated two triads in a technique resembling that of bagpipers' oscillating drones. Brother Zoli did play harmonies that were functional, but he talked about chords in a way that showed that he did not always think of them as having this purpose. His synthesizer had a programmed arpeggio option. Zoli called it an "ornamenting melody" (*díszítő dallam*) rather than referring to it as a style of chord playing.

The IG's music was also influenced by the style of Romani string bands. Everyone in the church knew string band music well. Until the 1950s it had been ubiquitous in villages and towns, and it could still be heard on the radio, at weddings, and in small bars. Nearly all of the musicians in the IG were from the Romungro ethnic subgroup of Roma who had served the Hungarian population as professional string musicians before World War II.[2] The IG orchestra had completely different instruments, but the musicians accompanied songs in ways similar to those of the Romungro stringed orchestras. Although Brother Zoli was a Magyar, with his synthesizer he filled a role very close to that of the *primás*, or lead violin, in a traditional Romungro orchestra. The *primás* was responsible for knowing tunes, establishing key, and setting tempo. All the musicians and congregation members had broad memories for song melodies and texts, but among the church musicians, Brother Zoli had the most extensive knowledge of tune accompaniment. Other instrumentalists added textural elements. They accented the predominately duple rhythm of the IG's songs with spoons, tambourine, or drums and devised their own harmonizations of the melody on synthesizers. The style of Brother Rudi was consistent with Romungro accompaniment principles. He played a variety of bouncy chord patterns, all emphasizing an offbeat, on the console organ, accordion, or synthesizer. Romungro string orchestras used very similar offbeat accompaniments called the *esztam*. The orchestras also used parallel thirds as a harmonizing technique. At particularly inspired church services like the one described in the introduction, Brother Rudi sang such a part in the technique that church members called *tercelés* ("third-ing"). Even the fact that the IG's musicians gave priority to other musical elements over functional harmony was similar to the practices of some Romungro string bands. László Lajtha, a contemporary of Bartók and Kodály who recorded rural instrumental ensembles, observed that the Romani string bands he recorded during the 1940s might seem inexpert to an uninformed listener. But their sound was "not by chance and not a deficiency." It was more important for the chord instruments to play with a strong rhythmic emphasis than for them to change their harmonies exactly under the melody (Lajtha 1953:171–72; Sárosi 1996:124–25).

The IG's ensemble synthesized Western pop instrumentation and the functional harmonic idiom with the textural conventions of Romani and Hungarian vernacular music, and then oriented it to enhance and support the excitement brought on by the Holy Spirit. Even as it evoked the communalism of the biblical early church and continued the practice of the early Pentecostals, the variety of short motives and timbres contributed by each member of the group was characteristic of music-making for several Romani ethnic groups in Hungary (see Kovalcsik 1987:48). The drone-style shaping of harmonic language indicated an emphasis on texture similar to that of Hungarian village dance music. These musical features served an important function in the IG as a community emphasizing holy brotherhood. Instrumental musicians could support a crucial phase of worship, the descent of the Holy Spirit.

The Significance of Instrumental Music for Roma

The fact that most of the instrumentalists in Hungary's IG congregations were from the Romungro ethnic group of Roma may be because the musical profession was historically significant to them. In the eighteenth century, it became common for Romungre to serve as professional music-makers for villagers and nobles in Hungary. At the turn of the twentieth century, Romungro string bands served nearly every village and noble household, specializing in dance music and the accompaniment of *magyar nóta*, a genre of song that was popular in the nineteenth and early twentieth centuries. Composed in a folkish style and identified with the Hungarian nation, it continues to be popular with Roma and older Hungarians today (Sárosi 1967:108; 1978[1971]:131–38, 197–215). During the late nineteenth and early twentieth century, *magyar nóta* singing was widespread. Hungarians sang *magyar nóta* to string band accompaniment in cafes and at major life cycle events like weddings. Because Romungro string players were so identified with *magyar nóta*, it came to be called "Gypsy music."[3] Not all Romungre worked as musicians at any time, but until World War II, string playing was frequently a part-time means of livelihood for them as the most respectable of many professions that they followed (Szuhay 1999). The events of World War II, followed by socialist economic reforms, decimated the ranks of string musicians. These patterns are exemplified in the musical histories of three young Romani preachers—Brothers Gál, Misi, and István. All came from families of former professional and semiprofessional string musicians.

Brother Gál regretted that as a boy he had not been interested when his grandfather had attempted to teach him the violin. In previous generations after having attained a minimum level of skill, Gál might have begun working in the family string ensemble as a young boy (see Sárosi 1996:49–50). But in the 1960s, when Brother Gál was a boy, there was no compelling financial motivation for Roma of his generation to keep ensembles together or pursue the difficult skill of string playing. Despite his lack of formal training, Brother Gál was intensely involved in the musical life of the IG congregation as a composer, player of percussion instruments, and song leader. There had also been violinists in Brother Misi's family. Brother Misi explained to me that their participation in the musical profession had come to an end after World War II because his grandfather served at the front and was thus not able to teach his children, including Misi's own father. Although Brother Misi did not play an instrument, he was very aware of issues surrounding musical expression, and he provided me with detailed explanations of the importance of music for IG members. Even Brother István's grandfathers had been string musicians. They were Vlach Roma, who normally do not play instrumental music as professionals in Hungary. Brother István's grandfather told me that their music-making activities had ended in the early 1960s at the point when state authorities had moved them into houses. Because they were charged with loans for these houses and required to work at industrial jobs given them by the state in order to pay off the debt, they gave up playing music. Brother István was not a musician, although when I visited him at his lodgings or at home, I occasionally heard him and other members of his family playing the guitar.

The grandfather's story illustrates that one of the most radical ways that the socialist state displaced Roma was to eliminate music as a profession. Freelance music-making and other Romani trades did not conform to the state's goal of establishing a general labor discipline. Ágnes Diósi has described how the government marginalized the performance of Romungro orchestras because it linked the *magyar nóta* they accompanied with bourgeois mentality.[4] The government eliminated the infrastructure of privately owned inns that were the forum for most casual music-making and singing with Romani bands. In addition, they instituted a system of licensing examinations for the musicians. Since most Romungro musicians played by ear and had no knowledge of such exam topics as music theory, they were disqualified or received far lower salary classifications than their reputation and skills warranted.

> Both those who played [the music] and those who once would have had it played became unskilled laborers. The conditions not only de-classed the ruling classes, but the Gypsy musicians as well. The ground slipped from under the very poor village musicians, who always had money-earning occupations, for example, adobe making, to fill in with. During this time, many children from musical dynasties became skilled factory workers. (Diósi 1988:85)

Members of the IG were among those Roma who became laborers rather than musicians. The gap spanned two generations, so that when they joined the IG, they had no direct experience of making music on instruments. Most expressed only slight regret to me about this, but pragmatically set about teaching themselves to play. Although they lacked the skills of the craft, IG members were very familiar with the string band idiom and *magyar nóta* songs from radio broadcasts and wedding festivities. In their choice of electric instruments they followed a pattern customary to the Romungro music trade; village bands had consistently updated their instrumentation by incorporating newly fashionable instruments—of which strings had merely been an eighteenth-century example. Romungre assigned a great deal of meaning to their histories as musicians. They shared a passion for musician lore, especially about famous performers who were related to their own families (Diósi 1988:81–110).[5] Regardless of whether they actually played instruments, Romungre called themselves "musician Gypsies" (*muzsikus cigányok*), demonstrating a widespread identification with the musician role.

The shared fascination with music-making was one vehicle IG members used in evangelizing to fellow Roma, especially those from the Romungro ethnic group. I witnessed this when I accompanied Brother Gál and Sister Annus on a trip to a village in eastern Hungary. Approximately thirty people crowded into the parlor of the private house where a gathering was to be held. The atmosphere was tense because Sister Annus, Brother Gál, and I were all strangers to them. In the kitchen, Sister Annus and I drank tea and ate the food that the hosts had offered to us. Sister Annus began talking with the women, explaining that I was a foreign visitor and that she was Gál's mother-in-law. "We are *muzsikus cigányok*," she said, and the women replied that they too were musician Gypsies. Then we crowded into the parlor and Brother Gál began to talk to the group. After saying that he was an ordained preacher in the IG, he asked a man standing near him to say a prayer. Like a Romungro string player, Brother Gál then detailed his family lineage. One relative had been a court musician and others had played in the Rajkó orchestra, a state-sponsored group for young Romani musicians of exceptional talent. Brother Gál stressed that his grandfather had intended to give him musical training on the violin and described his former career as a solo dancer with the folklore ensemble in Szigetvár. Then he asked two men with guitars, one of whom had led the prayer, to accompany him in a song. He explained to the group that the song text was from God but that they would recognize the tune. He suggested a key to the guitarists and began to sing. One guitarist immediately found a chord progression and the other played an accented bass line. Although this was the first time they had heard the song, the congregation joined in as Brother Gál repeated one of the verses. By the end of this song, the atmosphere of suspicion had completely dissolved. People in the room smiled warmly at Brother Gál; the guitarists started singing and playing another religious song that everyone knew. Then Gál began an exhortation, describing the wonders that God might achieve with the members of this group if they accepted Jesus as a savior and were baptized in the Holy Spirit.

Church authorities often see music as a way to gain converts. Delton Alford evokes Ira Sankey's singing for the Moody revivals. There soloists and small groups were important; "often the impact of words and music presented in this manner may be more powerful in touching the hearts of the unsaved than any other method of religious appeal" (Alford 1967:75). Evangelical leaders in Hungary concurred; when I talked to a leader of the Free Christians about my project, he made the comment that music was particularly effective in converting young people. But for potential Romani converts, music represented more than an emotional or spiritual attractor, and its importance extended to all ages. The historical resonances of instrumental music could help establish affiliation where none might normally exist. Brother Gál asserted his authority to talk about spiritual topics by linking it to the high status his family had achieved in terms of Romungro culture as musicians. He then engaged the entire group in expressing the message of potential salvation through song while at the same time he recognized local instrumental musicians as native leaders. His evangelizations created one of the deepest impressions of my fieldwork: for many Romani believers, music and specifically instrument playing was a vehicle for spiritual leadership.

Preaching and Instrumental Music

Brother Horváth's somewhat charismatic orientation did not extend to treating musicians as leaders. He called them "musician brothers" (*zenész testvérek*) and he did not, like the congregation members, refer to their activity as *szolgálat*. When Brother Horváth led worship proceedings, the musicians played a minor role. For Brother Horváth, the goal of church services was "teaching" (*tanítás*). Much of his time was devoted to emphasizing to the congregation how they should adhere to the IG's behavioral strictures. Brother Horváth's services consisted primarily of his sermon, which he prepared with short notes in advance and which could last up to ninety minutes. Before starting the sermon, Brother Horváth named several songs for the congregation to sing. If a keyboard player was present, he would start the song with an instrumental repetition of the first several phrases. The congregation was usually subdued when singing these songs. If they detected the presence of the Holy Spirit through slightly increased volume or quiet praying, the musicians would repeat verses and lines from the songs only once or twice. Then Brother Horváth led group prayer, announced other songs, and began his sermon. Brother Horváth's services did not include much opportunity for the Holy Spirit to manifest through music, although prayer could be intense. Nonetheless, church members viewed the atmosphere as very relaxed, spontaneous, and thus conducive to the descent of the Holy Spirit. During group prayer, congregation members could make extremely personal statements and heartfelt outpourings. As Brother Horváth preached, they interjected murmurs of "Halleluia" when he made points about redemption or salvation. By comparison with the Calvinist churches in Hungary, where congregations were absolutely still and silent, Brother Horváth's church allowed a great degree of expression.[6] These were some of the factors that led church members to say that the IG congregation was "more free" (*szabadabb*) than the other Pentecostal churches in southwest Hungary.

By contrast with Brother Horváth, the young Romani leaders stressed the charismatic aspects of Pentecostal religion and correspondingly accorded a great deal of importance to musical leadership. In Brother Misi's view at the time, the goal of a church service was to deepen or restore congregation members' connections with God. He explained to me that at the point when they entered the worship hall, they might be preoccupied with many worries and negative emotions. He believed that it was his job as a pastor to be aware of these problems and to create a situation where they would feel the presence of the Holy Spirit. The Holy Spirit would then relieve the congregation members of their burdens, at least temporarily. Brother Misi believed it was his responsibility as a pastor to notice the point at which the congregation members started to feel the Holy Spirit. It might be during a period of group prayer or during a song with a text on a certain theme. Brother Misi then had to continue this type of praying or singing so that the feeling of the Holy Spirit would intensify. Brother Misi noted that instrumental musicians had to observe a great deal of sensitivity in their playing at the beginning of services or else they would disturb the congregation and thus interfere with this process. But as the congregation felt the Holy Spirit, the musicians had the very important job of adding to the feeling by supporting the singing with their instruments.

The themes and character of the services Brother Misi led in Szigetvár were varied, but they all included much singing, praying, individual testimony, and short periods of preaching by a number of leaders. One evening, for example, Brother Rudi was the only musician present as the congregation gathered. As families entered the room, he picked up an accordion that was sitting on the heating stove. After playing a few melodic turns, he began the song "Názáreti, názáreti Jézusom" (My Jesus of Nazareth; described in chapter 5). The congregation joined in after one phrase and began clapping to the beat. Afterward Brother Rudi played the phrases of other songs on the accordion and the congregation sang them. Then, adding a tone of formality, Brother Misi announced several songs from the hymnbook and asked if there were any song requests. Brother Misi asked one of the men to pray aloud. As he did so, other men began to pray in sequence. Several women prayed, among them Sister Annus. Her praying became very emotional as she thanked God for touching and healing the group. Even to me, a nonbeliever, it was clear that an extraordinary energy was present; other congregation members started to pray quietly, but then their voices became louder and louder, as the prayer changed into one that was shared by the entire group. After the praying, which lasted for over twenty minutes, Brother Misi asked one of the other young preachers to "serve" (*szolgálni*). He read a long Bible passage and explicated it to the congregation. Brother Misi asked several other men to serve and then asked if anyone else would like to speak. Brother Rudi called his six-year-old daughter up to sing while he accompanied her. I also sang a solo to whispered responses of "Praise" (*hála*), and the congregation thanked me vigorously.

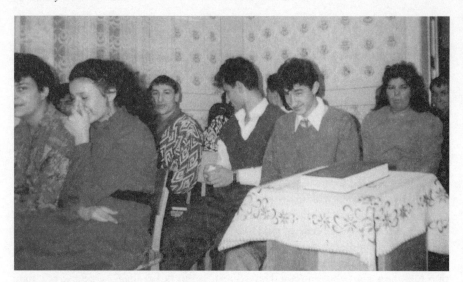

The worship hall in Szigetvár. Young church members laughed and whispered together just before the start of a service. A Bible lay on the altar.

Brother Gál was the most charismatically oriented of the IG preachers. In discussing his role as a leader, he usually referred to his miraculous dream of the corn gleanings, whereby God had directed him to spread the Pentecostal message to Roma, rather than to his official place in the IG organization. He often interrupted his own sermons or songs to say that he had received a sign, and then called up members of the audience in order to pray over them. In group prayers, his resonant voice could be heard above the others. Whereas many believers prayed about their personal problems, Brother Gál spoke for the group. He thanked God for salvation, for strength, and for blessing. He used short phrases, each begun powerfully and joined together in a continuous stream. His sermons were very straightforward; they had a conversational tone, he looked directly at the congregation, and they usually centered on a single basic aspect of Pentecostal belief. Brother Gál's musical activities also reflected his rapport with other people. He was one of the musicians who carefully changed the timbre and tempo of his percussion instruments to fit with the rest of the ensemble. When the rhythmic irregularity occurred at the beginning of "Come Let Us Celebrate," Brother Gál adjusted to the other members of the group by tapping the bongo drums more softly and interrupting his pattern briefly so that he was synchronized with the singing. During somewhat loosely structured worship proceedings (like the presermon prayer hour I described in the introduction), Gál took a key role. He increased the intense atmosphere by praying over the music or immediately following songs with prayer.

In spite of these successes, the basic format of leadership by an individual pastor contrasted deeply with the structure and values of Romani society. Roma are oriented toward egalitarian groups. The Roma of my acquaintance lived, worked, and traveled together. They organized construction or piecework projects together with relatives or friends. They constantly exchanged and borrowed material goods. The composite musical texture of the IG ensemble, where each person contributed a set of musical motives, reflects such a group orientation. But the egalitarian sense of these groups is fragile. Within such groups, Roma may perceive themselves as having uneven levels of prestige: they must compete to stay equal. According to Michael Stewart, for Vlach Roma high value on the group compensates a major tension: "a preoccupation with honour, status, and the paying of respect which is made all the sharper by the conflict between an egalitarian and a competitive individualist ethic" (Stewart 1989:83). Men from all of the Romani ethnic groups in the IG appeared to feel this type of tension. Competitiveness might explain the sheer number of Rom men who not only sat opposite the preachers as musicians but who seated themselves in the front rows near the preachers' area. This contrasted with the young Magyar men at the rear of the hall. During somewhat loosely structured worship proceedings like presermon prayer hours or midweek services in Szigetvár, a large number of men took a leadership role; a Szigetvár service might include short sermons by as many as five men. Recently converted male believers would sometimes object to not being included in leadership activities. One small congregation nearly dissolved because a man insisted that he had the right to assume preachers' responsibilities like the "laying on of hands" while praying for others.[7] Church members reported to me that during one meeting a person who had been designated for general service objected that he was not being given enough time to preach.

The church had accommodated egalitarian expectations in several ways. Brother Horváth had added a large number of young Roma to the official leadership structure. The Romani preachers organized worship services in a way that helped defuse much tension over leadership. Brother Misi demonstrated respect for other Romani preachers when he invited them to speak. Musical performance, since it functioned similarly to pastoral leadership, represented an alternate means of leadership. Brother Misi believed that performing on instruments made men more enthusiastic participants in the church. For this reason he thought that as many people as possible should play instruments. As I witnessed when I traveled with Brother Gál on missionary trips to unfamiliar Romani communities, he was masterful in divining and according leadership to fellow Roma and nearly always mediated this recognition through music. When during his evangelizations Brother Gál asked musicians from a group of people to step to the front and accompany him, he included the local Roma in a leadership role. Since many Romani religious leaders around the country were also musicians, this was a way of recognizing them even while he maintained control of the proceedings. The role of musician appeared to be satisfactory just for members of the Romungro ethnic group, who historically had been able to gain honor and prestige through the musical profession. It is significant that most challenges to leadership came from Boyash and Vlach Roma; for them music had not traditionally served as a recognized form of leadership. For a Romungro, being an instrumental musician was a way to equalize one's status, even if musicians were not formally part of the IG's institutional structure.

The blurring of leadership categories to include musicians demonstrates how in the early 1990s, IG congregations accorded leadership on a charismatic basis. This mode of leadership accommodated the egalitarian standards of Romani converts.

Roma tended to put a greater emphasis on charismatic leadership and by extension on the role of musicians in church services, whereas the head pastor, Brother Horváth, emphasized rationality to a greater degree.

Instrumental Music Ideals

In the IG, there were differences of orientation not only toward musical leadership but also toward actual musical sound. Brother Horváth and other elderly Magyar leaders valued styles that to them bore evidence of *műveltség*. The IG's musicians, Romani leaders, and the church membership in general valued playing skill. Both of these standards, though they contrast, were meant to approach the spiritual ideals manifested permanently in heaven or in the transitory state of "blessing" (*áldás*) by the Holy Spirit.

Brother Horváth frequently recalled a musical ensemble that was part of the congregation he led during the 1960s. The orchestra was made up of mandolins played by the *ifjúság* (youth or young adults). During the same period at a sister congregation in Budapest there was also a large mandolin orchestra (Búth 1991:13–14). The use of mandolins reflects the difference in ethnic and class background between the two congregations Brother Horváth had led. Before the introduction of synthesizers, mandolins and accordions were popular with Hungarian amateur musicians from the urbanized middle classes, whereas the violin was associated with professional Romani musicians. In the church setting, the mandolin orchestra appeared to carry the nineteenth-century connotations of musical culturedness, with uniform timbre, large ensemble size, and functional harmonic settings. The mandolin ensemble, through its focus on youth members, rehearsals, preparation of musical arrangements, and reading from scores, was a vehicle for education and thus for musical *műveltség*. Other elderly Magyar musical leaders shared Brother Horváth's emphasis on formal training and score reading. Sister Ungváry, the wife of the national head of the IG, stressed to me that she and her brother, a writer of hymnbook scores, had studied keyboard instruments and music theory with a Baptist music teacher in their home village. This emphasis on musical training resembled that in Hungary's mainstream churches. The three major denominations had regional education systems that came to a halt during the socialist period, although a handful of eminent choir leaders trained by Kodály still pursued their activities in the major cities. The Baptists were exceptional in that they continued musical education and training during the socialist period; they were known for the excellence of their choirs, ensembles, and composers (Bányai 1996:107–284). The fragmentation of Pentecostal communities and the IG's isolation had prevented this type of musical training.

By contrast with the older leadership, the IG's Romani converts and many of the church's Magyar members had musical ideals that emphasized directness and technical skill. The Romani members, in particular, were passionately enthusiastic about the music performed in another IG congregation in the town of Ózd, hundreds of kilometers away near the border with Slovakia, and constantly listened to home recordings sent to them from there. Every few months, members of the two congregations made a grueling train journey for weekend visits. Gál was a particular fan of the Ózd musicians, commenting often on how he would like to attain the guitarists' level of proficiency. Upon hearing that I wanted to do musical research with the IG, Brother Gál had immediately told me about the Ózd group, saying that they were "real musicians" (*igazi zenészek*). The ensemble that accompanied the Ózd congregation had balanced proportions from the standpoint of texture, rhythm, and timbre. The instrumentation consisted of electric lead, rhythm, and bass guitars, a single small synthesizer, and tambourine. The instrumentalists divided textural roles, utilized a variety of strumming techniques and other rhythmic articulations, incorporated preludes and instrumental interludes, and used largely functional harmony. The synthesizer was a background instrument in this ensemble; it played the song melody and primarily functional chords in a sustained, reedy tone. The lead guitar played syncopated versions of the song melody, sometimes adding brief improvisations. The rhythm guitar used a wide variety of strumming techniques and accompaniment patterns. Tambourine patterns emphasized syncopation and beat displacement; for example, the tambourine's version of a beguine pattern divided the quadratic cycle asymmetrically through volume changes and offbeat accents. The bass guitar played lower neighbor alternations. This part was not completely functional, frequently using a whole-step interval rather than leading tones on the dominant or tonic pitch (ex. 2.2).

Believers in southwest Hungary enthusiastically listened to the music of the Ózd group and learned their songs, but there was little performance interaction between the instrumentalists in the two congregations. One of the synthesizer players in the southwest congregations found it very difficult to synchronize with the rhythm of the Ózd guitarists. The southwest congregation members often used the synthesized percussion options as an ultimate rhythmic reference, whereas in Ózd the tempo varied because live musicians provided the rhythmic impulse. Brother Gál rarely played percussion with the Ózd ensemble; instead he improvised with vocables in *szájtrombita*. The Szigetvár believers did not change their instrumental styles to resemble that of the Ózd musicians. Brother Rudi, for example, listened closely to the Ózd tapes and was the first IG member to play one of the Ózd recordings for me. But he did not use their syncopated rhythms or their harmonies in his own playing. The IG orchestra also did not imitate the arranging style of the Ózd group. In preludes, the improvised and syncopated melody of Ózd's lead guitarist was prominent, whereas in southwest Hungary, the synthesizer prelude was an exact rendering of a song's melody in a straightforward rhythm.

There was a great difference between the musical ideals of Romani believers and elderly Magyar leaders. Brother Horváth, his wife, and other elderly Magyar leaders never commented on the music of the Ózd congregation, although they did enjoy and perform some of the songs that came from the Ózd group. Ózd figured in Brother Horváth's private comments as a congregation in need of stable pastoral guidance. During the time of my fieldwork, the congregation was in fact struggling over biblical interpretations and leadership criteria. On each occasion when I accompanied the IG leaders on missionary visits to Ózd, they spent considerable time helping to resolve tensions that had arisen in the congregation. Brother Horváth's ideal emphasized large numbers of people and uniformity. IG members and especially the Romani believers admired the practical craft of playing instruments as reflected in the guitar technique of the Ózd players. Brother Horváth's ideals were framed in terms of an elite sensibility. The musical ideals of ordinary church members were related to a

EXAMPLE 2.2. "Kopogtat egy hang" (A Voice Is Knocking). Instrumental musicians, Ózd, November 1990.

The worship hall in Ózd. The cross was made of industrial piping and lit from the back.

completely different experience, that is, the direct personal relationships they found in the IG as a group that included its distant congregations.

The direct communication with the musicians of Ózd was one aspect of the believers' community that ordinary Magyar church members valued so highly. Since Roma of my acquaintance had closer family relationships than Magyars, they idealized direct communication in a different way, looking for it in secular as well as sacred music. Nonbeliever Roma of my acquaintance, for example, admired the Hungarian pop singer Kati Kovács for how in their view she communicated directly with her audience. The fact that she wore very little makeup showed that she was not disguising herself. She also moved slightly to the music as she sang, showing that she was not just manufacturing a response in the audience but was herself affected by the music. The IG's Romani believers applied this valuing of directness to their enthusiastic contacts with the music and musicians of Ózd. Thus, two different musical ideals operated in the IG. One stressed uniformity, with a resultant valuing of large performing groups and the training needed to produce this uniformity. The other was an ideal of direct communication in small groups and the expressive idiom that individual performers worked out through their practical instrument-playing skills.

Musical Work and the Protestant Ethic

The musical ideals of Brother Horváth and other elderly Magyar leaders demonstrate one way that ascetic Protestant values permeated their belief system. The ascetic believer does not, as in Lutheranism, simply accept his social position as fate ordained; instead, he has to improve himself in the world. Through specialized labor, a "systematic, methodical character" can be achieved that leads to concrete evidence of grace (Johnson 1961; Weber 1958[1920]:159–62). Elderly Magyar leaders' views of music reflected these values. They had exercised diligence in studying with individual teachers over long periods of time. The music-reading and synchronized performances they desired to inculcate as leaders proved musical skill in concrete ways. Brother Horváth's and Sister Ungváry's experiences with musical training reflect the organized approach characteristic of several independent Protestant churches in Hungary, including the musically sophisticated Baptists, with whom Pentecostals had much interchange.

The ways that the IG's instrumental musicians worked were antithetical to the ascetic Protestant view. They stressed cooperation as a group, not performing as individuals. They never practiced together, so there was no systematic work. At Géza's wedding and almost any other time, most of the musicians just attempted to make accompaniments on the spot while the congregation sang. During the time I was doing fieldwork, several bought synthesizers. They simply brought them to church and experimented with melodies, harmonies, and keyboard fingering as the group sang. There was very little specialization, since the musicians frequently switched instruments; they learned to play by trial and error. They also learned by closely observing fellow players; Brother Rokkó, a highly skilled guitarist from Ózd, told me that he had learned his instrument by watching his neighbors play and then going home to try the chords himself. In church, this kind of ad hoc playing could happen because the members and the Romani leaders placed much value on spontaneously allowing the Holy Spirit to manifest. This religious enthusiasm in itself appears to present an obstacle to instilling Protestant values, although Benton Johnson has suggested that it motivates believers to adhere to the systematic aspect of their religion, that is, their fundamentalist behavior restrictions (Johnson 1961:313–14). The antisystematic approach to musical performance in the IG drew from an additional source—Romani values. The organization of music in the IG had the attributes of traditional Romani work practices: group participation, variety, and flexibility. These practices oppose values of individual achievement, specialization, and extensive training.

All the IG members emphasized obedience to both secular and sacred authority in their rhetoric; as Brother Misi said to a local reporter, "we accept the worldly powers as they are. We don't run after money, we don't attack anyone. We don't riot or strike" (Bencze 1989). Most believers were known by employers in their local areas as dependable workers. The state inculcated values of uniform production with its work policies, and this had provided Roma as well as Magyars with some specialized vocational training. However, one large difference between the ethnic groups became clear with the unemployment that hit the country in the early 1990s. Over twice as many Roma as Magyars lost their jobs (Havas, Kertesi, and Kemény 1995:70–73). When the Roma were laid off, most of the them organized moneymaking projects that emphasized versatility and hereditary manual skills. Carol Silverman has noted that in America "occupational flexibility has been, and continues to be, a prime strategy for *Rom* survival" (Silverman 1982:379). Following a similar pattern, the Romani members of the IG and their families took on projects of home piecework, bricklaying, construction work, and merchandising. Roma assembled work teams on short notice from among their relatives and friends. I was at a believer's household early one morning when several friends came to tell him of a construction project. Within a few moments he had changed into work clothes and left with the group. Brother Gál obtained a merchant's license, and fellow church members—as well as relatives by marriage—manned his clothing stall in the town's open-air market. It is not clear to me whether the Magyars I knew might have tried to do the same kind of flexible projects; they did not need to, since during my fieldwork nearly all of them were either retired or remained employed.

Michael Stewart found that the Vlach Roma with whom he worked were participating in the labor economy with low-paying factory jobs. At the same time, they had ways of making additional money that reversed the process of rational accumulation. Through trading, the Vlach Roma could temporarily reverse their subaltern position; not only money was gained but also a sense of superiority over their customers, the Magyar peasants (Stewart 1997:19–25, 152–62). The IG's Romani members had been far more invested in the labor economy than these Roma. Most were also from the Romungro and not the Vlach ethnic group. But as they were laid off from their jobs in the early 1990s, they searched for ways of making money that were somewhat similar to those pursued by Vlach Roma. Believers did find mercantile activity very difficult from a moral standpoint because it was so unregulated in the postsocialist setting; Brother Gál discussed his commercial venture extensively with fellow believers and with the entire IG congregation before making the decision to sell clothes.

Many Magyars react negatively to the ways Roma make money. When Zsolt Csalog discussed Hungarian villagers' attitudes toward Roma, he evoked a systematic approach to laboring. Villagers valued the accumulation of wealth and the consistent work that might produce it.

> From this viewpoint the Gypsies' un-bourgeois behavior is the basis for the charge that gives rise to rejection: inability to farm, more relaxed work morals, the lower level of orientation to production, the general disorganization of daily life. (1984:76)

Csalog hinted that the "bourgeois peasant moral system" behind this negative viewpoint had actually been exacerbated in the village setting by the socialist labor and housing reforms. Town-dwellers also viewed Roma as a problem, but from the standpoint of public security (Csalog 1984:76–77). The quality of moral judgment in these viewpoints was indicated by the outrage my Magyar and Romani acquaintances sometimes expressed about each other's behavior. Roma would angrily recall how some neighbors and proprietors of local shops did not even show them the respect of a greeting. Magyars were angry if they saw adult Roma on the street or in the market square on weekdays, assuming that they did not work but instead were collecting public assistance.

Members of the IG had some success in bridging such differences. Roma felt welcome in the IG precisely because most of the Magyar church members treated them with the respect shown to all fellow believers. Brother Horváth demonstrated much respect for Roma by recognizing them as leaders and asserting to the media that Romani believers were respectable citizens. The entire congregation agonized about and prayed together for solutions to the massive unemployment that had struck them and their families. But this mutual accommodation did not extend to music. The IG musicians' ways of organizing their performance retained many attributes of Romani work practices, whereas the elderly leaders favored an approach to music that was related to the Protestant ethic. The folk character of the IG as a church allowed no clear avenue for resolving tensions over instrumental music, since music was neither regulated by church doctrine nor by a shared secular tradition. Music was an area where change had to be attempted cautiously in order not to upset the feeling of spiritual brotherhood.

3

Mediating Moralities:
An Ethnographer's Interpretation

A few weeks after I had started to attend church meetings at the IG, Brother Horváth asked me to teach score reading to the congregation. I was surprised, since I had explained my goal of researching the church's music in a letter to him. At first I believed he simply had not understood what I intended to do as an ethnographer by interviewing church members and attending services. I later came to see his request as an indication that there were contrasting conceptions of leadership in the church community. I had anticipated a different challenge, crossing the divide between believer and nonbeliever. I tried to overcome this difference by adopting many of the believers' practices. I followed the church's behavior restrictions with regard to dress and decorum, even avoiding the nightspots that were popular with other expatriates in Pécs. I participated in Bible reading and singing during services. It felt unethical for me to engage in practices that seemed to represent direct contact with God in the form of the Holy Spirit, so I refrained from praying out loud, responding with "Amen" to points made by the pastors during church services, or expressing extreme emotions during the song and prayer even if I felt them. I did not wash believers' feet, take communion, or get baptized.[1]

I also planned to begin study with the church's musical specialists. I thought the instrumental musicians would be an obvious choice, given their prominence. But although they easily spoke with me about their conversions and religious beliefs, they seemed to avoid contact with me as musicians. I had intended to use a common way that ethnomusicologists participate in music-making: to become a student of a source musician. I hoped that way to find out about musical aesthetics and concepts as well as practical skills. But since the musicians did not teach or rehearse, I could not apprentice myself to them. I tried acting like other visiting musicians I observed and, like them, simply played in the ensemble without being specifically invited to do so. But the local musicians did not seem to react to me in the same way that they did to guest musicians. With the guests, they exchanged glances, used hand gestures, and moved their upper bodies to indicate the basic beat of the music, tempo changes, or starting and stopping points. However, when I played with the musicians, they seemed to ignore me. They did not often point microphones in my direction and they did not glance at me or even change their facial expressions when I played with them.

Advocating for Art Music

I thought one request by Brother Horváth might provide a very suitable way for me to participate: playing violin solos in church. At first, Brother Horváth asked me to perform at points in Sunday morning services where he invited visiting Hungarian preachers to address the congregation. Later I performed at afternoon *bizonyság* (testimony), where newcomers as well as church members stood before the congregation to read poetry, sing, or speak. I hoped that playing my violin during testimony periods might serve as a point from which I could start playing with the instrumentalists and talking with them about music. But my violin playing actually served as a symbolic means for Brother Horváth to advocate his ideal of musical training. He did this through his role as head pastor in directing worship proceedings. Elaine Lawless has commented that in the U.S. Pentecostal church she studied, the pastor takes a "star performance role" as he frames testimonies and other activities with interpretive comments (Lawless 1988a:75). During my performances, Brother Horváth took a similar role. As he announced my solos, he referred to me as a "music teacher" (*zenetanár*), a "cultured musician" (*művelt zenész*), or an "educated musician" (*tanult zenész*). Brother Horváth's comments introducing my performances were more than words of polite welcome; they served as an indirect yet public means of advocating a role for me in the church as a representative of high culture. One particular incident convinced me that Brother Horváth saw my level of education as a rhetorical aid to changing the congregation's music. On a Sunday when I was not present, one of the musicians brought drums and played them during the service. The following week Brother Horváth spoke sternly to the musicians in front of the whole congregation, saying that drums should give a regular "beat" (*taktus*) but "this is not a 'dance-hall' [*táncterem*]." Nodding in my direction, he said that here was a "musical artist" (*zeneművész*) who knew the purpose of an orchestra. He then mentioned the twelve-piece mandolin group of the congregation where he had previously ministered, noting that although there had been a bass in that group, it was played to accompany the singing.

Brother Horváth's comments illustrate two general concerns in Protestant thinking on instruments. The first worry is that music might have a corrupting influence. With his word "dance-hall," Brother Horváth evoked an establishment that is ubiquitous in Hungary's towns and villages—the disco. Brother Horváth had never been to a disco, but the younger church members had. I asked them about discos, and they explained that the most sinful and immoral behavior took place there; there were fights, people who met there frequently followed the impulse to have sex outside of marriage, and the discos were even frequented by young prostitutes, or *rossz lányok* ("bad girls"). Nonconverts, and my own observations when I attended discos a few times after completing fieldwork in the IG, confirmed that the church members were not exaggerating the kinds of activities that took place, although many participants seemed to enjoy simply dancing and socializing. Brother Horváth's comments on accompaniment also reflected a major concern of ascetic Protestantism: that the sound of musical instruments should not detract from the focus on the spiritual that can be accomplished through singing. Brother Horváth assumed that a classical musician like me would be aware of this issue, whereas the church instrumentalists were not. But, as I described in the previous chapter, several of the musicians were highly sensitive to this, adjusting volume, tempo, and even timbre to the singers. I felt very uncomfortable when Brother Horváth contrasted my supposed musical culturedness with the habits of the church ensemble; on the very evening he had criticized drumming, I had experimented with bringing my violin to play alongside the other musicians.

It is possible that the Romani musicians had included drums for reasons of musical taste coming from their cultural backgrounds. When I started asking them if there was anything unique about their music, several Romungro believers mentioned to me that an emphasis on rhythm and percussive effects like finger-snapping was one of the important elements of Romani music. Drums could have a presence in the IG because church members wanted to accommodate different directions given spontaneously by the Holy Spirit. The musicians reduced their drum-playing, but they did not completely stop. The same evening a brief conflict ensued among the other leaders and musicians. Brother Misi told Brother Gál to play the drums more softly, to which he replied that he was "barely breathing." He in turn told Brother Géza to stop playing the tambourine, a request that Géza ignored. I was curious about why Brother Horváth's scolding seemed to be so ineffective. He had already moderated his comments somewhat the same night by saying that the "electric organ" (synthesizer) could "nicely accompany spiritual songs." With this comment, he showed appreciation for a kind of music-making in which the musicians were already involved. After this, several musicians purchased synthesizers or brought ones they already owned to play at church services. This had the effect of suppressing the role of drums somewhat and reduced the use of the accordion.

Drum-playing in church might seem morally suspect to common sense, since it has been associated with secular dancing both in Europe and the United States. IG members did not eschew all dancing, however; even the most conservative members recounted instances where they had done "spiritual dance" (*lelki tánc*). The Pentecostal religion itself has a history of including a variety of instruments and secular dance rhythms in its music. When I asked several IG leaders about their opinion of the suitability of drums in church, they stressed that there were different attitudes between the generations. They might all abhor the secular context of the disco, but they did not share Brother Horváth's association of drums with popular dance music. When I asked one young preacher about drums in church, he commented that he respected Brother Horváth very much but that Brother Horváth did not know what kind of music was played in the disco. The IG's young converts were familiar with the deafeningly loud percussion of actual discos, and thus the unamplified playing on small bongos that musicians brought to church did not seem like popular dance music to them; in fact, the young preacher pointed out that their Bible's version of Psalm 150 called for praising the Lord with trumpets, harps, zithers, drums, and other instruments.[2] Brother Horváth had grown up during the first half of the century when in small towns and villages string bands were the primary providers of dance music, so that to him drums overemphasized the beat. Brother Misi stressed the compromise that was necessary in a church with members of different generations. He shared

Brother Horváth's opinion that the ensemble's purpose was accompaniment, but he gave a pragmatic reason for avoiding drums—they disturbed the older church members. Even then, Misi said, if those older church members were feeling joyful and singing loudly, drums could help enhance this feeling. Within a few weeks of Brother Horváth's condemnation, church musicians used drums again, but this time at Géza's wedding celebration instead of a regular church service.

As head pastor, Brother Horváth explained and recommended standards of instrumental music-making in his congregation, but he was careful not to make any direct changes. The conflict over drums illustrates that my presence as an outsider was useful for his goals. The church members, as testvérek, had to be accepted wholeheartedly if they conformed to the congregation's fundamentalist behavior restrictions. Like their ethnicity and their ages, their choice of instruments and way of playing were secondary. Brother Horváth could interpret my role in a contrasting way to advocate his own point of view about instrumental music. By praising me to the congregation, he implied to them that he did not embrace me in the same way as he did the actual church members. Introduced as a model of high culture and as someone who was musically refined, I then had to be treated with formality. At this point, so much tension seemed to surround the topic of musical refinement, or műveltség, that, although I was curious about their reactions, I avoided asking church members and other leaders if they shared Brother Horváth's opinion that they should follow my style of art music. I stopped bringing my instrument to church, and over the following six months I sat with the congregation rather than with the musicians or other church leaders.

On a night when the two of us were commuting by train back to Pécs from a midweek meeting in Szigetvár, Brother Horváth asked me if I would start teaching the adolescent church members (the "young people" or ifjúság) to read music. Over the next year, I came to realize that his request was logical in the Hungarian context. Protestant clergymen and schoolteachers have often inculcated the ideals of high culture at the same time that they documented Hungarian village folklore. The two activities were not in conflict because they focused on the folklore that in Hungary is defined as a type of high art. Bartók and other Hungarian ethnomusicologists took the position that several styles of Hungarian village song resemble art music with clear directions of melodic movement, modes presumed to be archaic, and balanced musical form. The "concentrated" and miniature nature of these forms comes from their stylistic polishing over the course of many generations (Bartók 1981[1924]:9; Vargyas 1981). The lyrics, phrase structures, melodic contours, and especially the accompaniment modes of the IG's music decidedly did not have these characteristics. When Brother Horváth introduced me to the congregation as a zenetanár (classical music teacher), I was at first pleased that he was translating my researcher role in terms the congregation might be familiar with. But after he actually asked me to begin teaching, I realized that Brother Horváth might be seeing me as a fellow religious intellectual with the skills or interest to reform the way that music was played in the church.

Brother Horváth's assumption that I was a fellow advocate of musical culturedness was probably supported by a linguistic error I made in the first months of fieldwork: I used the word for instrumental music, zene, to mean the congregation's entire musical activity. But when Mrs. Horváth commented, "We don't have any music [*zene*]" and referred to the mandolin orchestra in Brother Horváth's earlier congregation, I realized that this word must refer to purely instrumental performances. Another connotation of *zene* was art music; one indication of this was that Mrs. Horváth did not think of the IG's musicians as performing *zene*, even though they played instruments. Having been alerted to this use of music terminology, I also noticed that, except for Brother Horváth, the congregation members did not use the word "accompany" (*kísér*) in reference to the role of instruments. The concept seemed rather to be one of the whole performance. I subsequently found the most success in talking with musicians or church members about instrumental playing if I inquired about singing first and then about the actual people who played instruments like synthesizer or guitar, rather than their accompaniment roles.

In one sense, Brother Horváth's request demonstrated that he was trying to accommodate the way that ethnographic methods disrupt customary modes of activity. My wish to participate in the congregation's religious life without converting to Pentecostalism was unusual, even possibly disturbing, to the believers. The U.S. missionaries I met in the field were extremely suspicious of me. But Brother Horváth seemed to welcome me at the IG's formal church services. This might be because he viewed me as a fellow intellectual. But Brother Horváth's request that I teach the believers contradicted the method of musical apprenticeship that U.S. ethnomusicologists and folklorists treasure so much. They have agonized over the fact that if they are from a dominant social stratum or culture, they are in danger of reinforcing oppression. For an ethnomusicologist to take a student role suggests that this relationship can be equalized or reversed. Many ethnomusicologists write of having gained their deepest understanding of musical cultures at the end of their fieldwork terms as they played alongside source musicians after having studied with them for long periods of time (Berliner 1978:xii–xvi; Feld 1982:230–38; Friedson 1996:11–22). To teach score reading might impose the values and repertoire of an art tradition, and to me it implied a transfer of authority away from the musicians. As with other forms of reading instruction, the written musical text could serve as a means of social control, replacing a local style with the standard established by an elite (see Street 1984:96–97, 104–5). An incident that occurred some months after his request confirmed that for Brother Horváth score reading served exactly that purpose. Using a musical score, a visiting organist played a melody and harmonization of a song that was different from the one the IG believers were singing. Brother Horváth told the congregation that the organist's version must be the right one since it was in the score and told them to learn the new melody. But the musicians themselves had not asked me to teach music reading to them or any of their children. I later discovered that for many of the instrumentalists music reading was simply unimportant and unnecessary. Several could read music but consciously chose not to do so. Brother Zoli commented that reading a musical score complicated his operating programmed options on the synthesizer and leading of the congregation. Sister Elza, who played guitar, had also studied music reading but said that she did not use a score because it interfered with feeling the Holy Spirit.

Although it seemed unusual, Brother Horváth's request reflects a common power dynamic in ethnography. The people ethnographers work with may see them as having influence and authority, and they may ask the ethnographer to use such power in their particular interest (Shelemay 1997:201). Where there are different interests within a community, these requests can be aimed at changing power relationships that preceded the ethnographic encounter (see Dumont 1978). Teaching music in the IG might have stimulated many changes. Since I would have been teaching young people, the active role of musician might have shifted toward adolescents and away from heads of households. As my fieldwork progressed it became clear that teaching music could have disturbed the means of equalizing leadership that instrumental music represented to Romani church members. I responded to the nonmusical aspect of Brother Horváth's request by offering to teach the English language, rather than music, to the youth in the IG. This was a successful compromise. It satisfied Brother Horváth's focus on intellectual refinement, since competence in a west European language was a mark of culturedness. It offered a practical skill, since the American and European missionaries who visited the congregation needed interpreters. It appealed to all of the IG's young members because they were interested in American popular culture. Teaching English also provided a way for me to expand my participation beyond official church services.

Gender and Morality

In addition to the differences in our musical backgrounds, one reason that church instrumentalists treated me differently from other musical guests was obvious: I was female, whereas they were male. The IG granted only men the authority to preach. Church members understood this to have a scriptural basis in Paul's injunctions on silence for women in 1 Timothy 2:11–12 and elsewhere in the Bible. They also accepted this practice as natural because men were dominant in the secular context. This was true both in the village environment from which elderly believers came (see Huseby-Darvas 1989:492, 494) and for the newer Romani converts. Among nearly all the Roma I knew, men took the role of public spokesmen in both the secular and the church environment. This practice appears to be common crossculturally for Romani Pentecostals; in Spain, for example, Romani converts easily embraced the role of men as official and public leaders, since it conformed to their secular practices (Wang 1989:427, 432). There was no reason based in scripture for why only men served as musicians, and this is one reason why I first believed that I might succeed in working with them. In fact, on rare occasions during the course of my fieldwork, women did play with the other musicians during church services. But it turned out that in playing with the male musicians I was contradicting a prohibition on contact between the sexes. Although it had some secular basis, its major source of power came from the IG members' religious beliefs.

IG members saw public interactions between men and women outside of the family context as highly suspicious and defined them as "fornication" (*paráznaság*), forbidden by the Bible's seventh commandment. Brother Horváth's sermons and church members' conversations made most biblical injunctions clear. Church leaders were opposed to cigarettes and believed that when smoke issued from someone's mouth, it was a sure sign that he was close to the fires of hell. Brother Horváth said that other restrictions, like those on drinking alcohol or on women's dress, should be applied flexibly. He believed that these restrictions had caused tragic schisms; in his talk to the church members about getting along with each other, he had referred to a controversy over whether girls could use long-handled umbrellas that had shattered a large congregation. Church members believed that women should wear skirts, basing this practice on the statement in 1 Timothy 2:9 advising women to dress modestly. However, Brother Horváth asserted that health reasons could make it acceptable for women to wear pants. When I met IG believers in town during the week, some of them in fact did wear pants. American missionaries advised women not to cut their hair on the basis of their interpretation of 1 Corinthians 11, but many of the most devout IG members did have short coiffures. I found it easier than most church members to follow these restrictions, and throughout my fieldwork I wore skirts and long hair. Just as with the church members, this set me apart from secular Hungarians, Europeans, and Americans and demonstrated respect for the Pentecostals' way of life.

Church members might have been somewhat relaxed about women's dress, but they were afraid of *paráznaság*. Brother Horváth did not discuss this subject in detail from the pulpit, and for a long period, I believed that to IG members *paráznaság* only meant sex outside of marriage. But IG members understood *paráznaság* to mean a broad range of contacts between men and women. Several weeks after I began fieldwork, I came to Brother Horváth's house to interpret between him and an American missionary. A male friend brought me to the house and, as is customary in secular Hungarian society, gave me a farewell kiss on both cheeks. Brother Horváth and his wife looked at me with bitter expressions, but I did not know why. Only after four or five months of fieldwork did the believers explain to me that this kind of contact represented a severe transgression to them: *paráznaság* could include not only casual kisses of greeting but even semiprivate conversation. The threat of *paráznaság* was therefore a definite barrier to my working with the instrumental musicians. I completed a few interviews with them, always in public settings, but other musicians regularly postponed or abruptly suspended our interviews.

One Sunday after I had been attending services for about six months, I was elated when one of the synthesizer players offered to show me some playing techniques. He explained that he had been waiting to do this until a day when his wife was not in church because she was extremely jealous and would believe that we were engaging in *paráznaság*. I told him that I just intended to learn about music, but he replied that it made no difference. I realized that he must have been motivated to take this risk because he and other believers had come to trust me. After this, I was doubly careful to avoid sitting with the male musicians and I talked to them only when many other church members were present. An incident that occurred after I had ended my regular participation in the IG demonstrated how divisive mixed musical performance could be. Church members told me that a new woman convert, who had aspired to be a professional singer in her secular life, joined the musicians during services. Other church members gossiped intensely. The woman eventually stopped attending services in one town although she continued to be welcome in other IG congregations.[3]

This experience reinforces how difficult it can be for a woman ethnomusicologist to successfully work with male musicians if it contradicts a community's accepted gender roles. One solution has been to work with a fellow male scholar, who records music and participates in men-only settings. Another strategy has been to trump gender with class, offering male co-respondents the enhanced wealth or status that can come from working with an academic and a Westerner (see Friedl 1986:212). Wives and other members of the society may nonetheless see this fieldwork relationship as morally suspect. Many ethnomusicologists successfully endure this tension; I could not, because such behavior was grounds for being expelled from the church.

Women's Music-Making

One other way for me to learn about the IG's music was to focus on women's perfor-mances. This remains important in gender-segregated contexts to compensate for the lopsided understanding that comes from the massive amounts of research already done with male musicians (see Koskoff 1989[1987]:1). In the IG, women did play instrumental music. Services were held at Pécs in the morning and afternoon on Sundays. Brother Horváth and other local residents went home for a formal noon meal, but the many families who commuted from outlying villages and towns, in-cluding all of the instrumental musicians, remained at the church. They ate a cold lunch in the anteroom, strolled through the neighborhood, chatted in small groups, read and discussed Bible passages together, and played music. During these sessions, women and girls moved up to the musicians' area alongside men, played the spoons and guitar, and sang into the microphone. On one occasion, several women and one man formed a close circle in the pastors' and musicians' seating area near Sister Elza, who was singing "Áldjad lelkem, áldjad szellemem" (Bless My Spirit, Bless My Soul) and accompanying herself on the guitar. They sang along with her, adding a down-ward melodic motif on the word "praise" (*hála*), and played rhythmic patterns on the tambourine and spoons. Sister Elza accentuated the percussive quality of her instrument by using a stopped brush stroke that doubled the basic rhythmic pulse. She was one of several women who were skilled guitarists. In addition to knowing how to read music, they utilized functional harmony, and like Sister Elza they employed a variety of strumming techniques to accompany their songs.

The sessions contrasted with the music-making at church services. In addition to the fact that women, girls, and men played together, the participants performed a different literature from that used during the services, including songs that not every congregation member knew (Sister Elza's song was one of many she had learned from her cousin in the far northeast corner of Hungary). The musicians, rather than preachers or the congregation, chose the songs and did not announce them. People drifted in and out of the meeting room to listen, sometimes becoming so involved as to dance or to interject cries of "Halleluia." But the musicians did not respond as they did during church services by repeating verses or adjusting tempo and volume. They played one song after another, only stopping to try different microphone tech-niques or to change the synthesizers' timbre and percussion options. Even though they were surrounded by movement and casual conversation, musicians' lunchtime sessions had an air of concentration and intensity.

It seems paradoxical that IG members could have tolerated these sessions, given the strict guard they kept against *paráznaság*. These sessions may have flourished because it was primarily Roma who were present in the church during the noon hour. Although Roma from a wide spectrum of ethnic groups, including nearly all of those

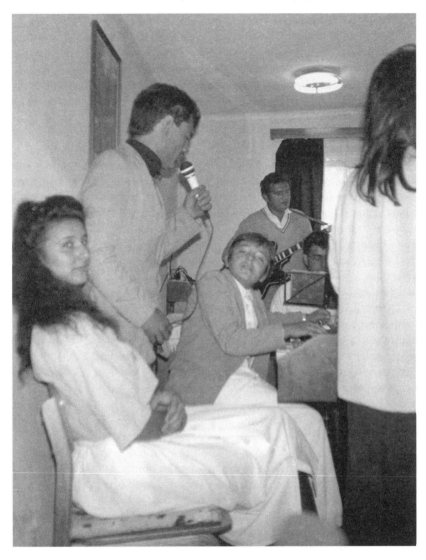

Informal music-making during the Sunday noon hour in Pécs. On this occasion, the teenaged Sister Margit waited to sing with some of the instrumental musicians.

with whom I worked in Hungary, maintain a clear division in public between men's and women's activities, they sometimes relax these separations in other contexts. With American Kalderash Roma, Carol Silverman observed that cleanliness taboos may delimit gender and ethnic boundaries, but they might be relaxed in the domestic setting (Silverman 1982:397). In the IG, "public" seemed to be represented by the formally framed worship event. The informal sessions shared the semidomestic atmosphere of the noon break. The participants' intense focus on music-making without regard to an outside audience also conveyed an atmosphere of privacy in the midst of the other lunch activities. When I joined these performances on a few occasions, I did not see the musicians make gestures that I would interpret as moves to include me. Although this paralleled my experience in church services, it seemed to have a different logic. Musicians of both sexes seemed to want to make the most of their performance time during lunch. The question of who played alongside them appeared to be secondary; in this peripheral way, I probably was welcome. Sister Elza hinted at this after a session once when she commented that she enjoyed playing with me because I was so skilled.

Playing in these sessions on a regular basis might have presented a way to participate from an ethnographic standpoint, but the difference in status between the women and me interfered. I often received invitations to eat Sunday dinner at church members' homes. Since they were gestures of welcome and friendship, it was difficult for me to refuse them. On the rare occasions when I attended the noon-hour sessions, my prestige, ironically, interfered with the entire activity. If I tried to record, the performances suddenly became public. One day I had set up my microphone and was recording a performance by Sister Elza. A church leader who was passing through the worship hall came up to me. Ignoring the fact that Sister Elza was playing, he suggested a different microphone placement, thus recording his own suggestion over the sound of her performance. This incident demonstrated to me a way in which ethnography seems bound up with hegemonic power. The subject was not just the female performer at whom my microphone was pointed but also male leadership. Michel de Certeau suggests that the ethnographer's gaze alters its object (de Certeau et al. 1986[1980]). When my gaze was turned on a woman and I tried to record her, suddenly her performance became something that others could also objectify with commentaries, and the result was that she literally could not be heard.

Some elderly believers enjoyed the music sessions, but in the view of others they disrupted the order of the worship day. Ignoring the intense study of the Bible that young men conducted in the back of the hall, one commented that church members should stop just playing music during the noon break and occupy themselves with something worship-related. In addition to finding that the music sessions were too secular, this believer expressed a general sense of worry about adolescent girls in the congregation. Although they obeyed the conventions of women's dress, the girls often drew attention to themselves by wearing rich fabrics and colors. During services, they walked in and out of the worship hall. Their attention was focused only during the lunchtime music-making and in afternoon testimony periods, where they frequently performed as singers. Most troubling was the threat that they might be alone with boys. Whereas church members told me that with adults the threat of *paráznaság* lay as much in gossip or speculation as in reality, some elderly believers thought that the young people lacked self-control and feared that contact between them might immediately lead to sex outside of marriage. Brother Horváth made a move to resolve this tension by attempting to establish institutional structure. Without repeating the worries about girls specifically to the congregation, he told the group that they needed to discuss women's health in relationship to IG doctrine. He proposed that noontime be designated a "women's hour," that only women and girls be allowed in the worship hall during that time, and that one of the congregation members, a nurse, lead the proceedings. As a side effect of this program, the musical sessions and the Bible study were stopped. However, the class was only conducted a few times. The older women attended, but in spite of being beckoned in, the adolescent girls stayed in the anteroom conversing and flirting with precisely the people they were supposed to avoid—the young men who normally would have been studying the Bible.

This incident illustrates again how mutual consensus is required, even if an existing authority aims to impose change. Church members refused to end unstructured time during the worship day, including music sessions. The adolescent girls did not regard themselves obligated to support the women Brother Horváth named as leaders. But resistance has limits that are often self-imposed. Noon events were superseded by anything the head pastor scheduled himself. If Brother Horváth conducted a special event like a lecture on baptism day, all believers quickly completed their noon meal and attended his talk.

In the IG, alternative musical repertoires, techniques, and religious ethos were generated during the lunchtime sessions. But the music sessions were not quite complementary to instrumental performance by men during worship services. Some theorists argue that although men appear to dominate in public, women in fact wield greater levels of power in private. It is their economic contributions that shore up male prestige; by creating turmoil in private, women can disrupt the smooth working of the public sphere (Rogers 1975; Sanday 1981). In the IG, the members' contrasting ages and ethnic backgrounds affected the notions of appropriate behavior. In order to account for this variety of acceptable modelings of gender, it is useful to view the performance sphere as constitutive rather than reflective; music, as a "highly symbolic" mode, has the capacity itself to shape multiple notions of gender (Sugarman 1997:30–33). Instrumental music performance during church services might shape a notion of masculinity in leadership, but between church services, it had to be kept from constituting anything so definite as gendered personas. If social consensus determines the meanings of symbols, any symbolism that obtained during the noontime sessions could not receive the consensus of all performers, for then the event would become too formal. Sherry Ortner has suggested that rather than operating in a private sphere, women simply reside out of a delimited frame: they are "simply 'there' . . . present because they are products of imagination that did not seem to threaten any particular set of arrangements" (Ortner 1989–90:45). The noontime music sessions could only stay in existence if they were amorphous. Once they were codified as musical performance by my microphone or the judgments of another church member, they faded away.[4]

Singing

I stopped most of my efforts at finding out about instrumental music and turned to two other areas: participating in the everyday lives of believers and singing. My visits to the branch congregations of the IG expanded from the formal church services into longer stays with families of believers. There I joined in running the household, including cooking, shopping, cleaning, and childcare, as well as visiting with neighbors, many of whom were not believers. As a woman I was comfortable with this orientation, and it proved invaluable in relaxing my relationships with Romani believers.[5] Contrary to the view of Romani society as closed to outsiders, I experienced an inclusionary atmosphere in the domestic setting. One reason that this could occur is that the Romungre I first visited did not appear to observe any cleanliness taboos categorizing non-Roma as unclean (see Kertész-Wilkinson 1997:107–11). Instead, it was important that I gain the necessary linguistic skills to participate in conversations. Repartee was a key part of family and neighborhood life among my Romani acquaintances. In those Romani households, the greater facility I gained in the language, the easier was my acceptance. It was important to answer questions about my own background as an American, my financial circumstances, my unmarried status, the progress of my research, or the day's plans in a light way that invited further suggestions or queries from other people who were present. It was equally important for me to put forward questions to my hosts or to visitors on similar topics, all within the very fast response time that repartee requires. I had the most success in Romungro homes, where Romani-inflected Hungarian was spoken. I gained less facility with other languages that Roma spoke in the home, and so I was not as successful in forging closer relationships with Boyash or Vlach Rom believers.

As I was beginning to establish relationships through sharing daily activities, I turned to singing. Learning the IG's songs entailed the same style of exchange that took place in Romani households. I could learn songs informally, mixed in with everyday routines. Learning songs helped in particular to deepen my relationship with Sister Annus, the church member who was Brother Gál's mother-in-law. She often sang fragments that occurred to her while we were on the train, cooking, or walking; by asking her to teach me the full texts and tunes, I learned some of the music that was not currently being sung in the church. This teaching took place orally, since Sister Annus could not read or write; and as I had then learned from my noontime experiences, formal recording procedures would probably have disrupted our exchanges. Having a closer relationship with Sister Annus helped re-

Sister Annus, center right, on an evangelization trip with Brother Gál. He consulted a road map behind her as a group said farewell by singing and raising their hands up as they prayed.

lieve the doubts of others about my not having converted. As a longtime believer, Sister Annus possessed unassailable spiritual credentials. She bridged the gap between the elderly members and young converts—and thus also between Roma and Magyars. Thanks to the company of Sister Annus, I was able to join the missionary trips to remote parts of Hungary that yielded important insights. She served as a chaperone, by her presence dispelling any potential suspicions about my conduct with the male missionaries.

Sister Annus was alert to changes in what church members saw as the power of the Holy Spirit to affect me. I did in fact have several Holy Spirit–like experiences during the intense atmosphere of the missionary trips. On one occasion during prayer, I experienced the bodily warmth of which IG members spoke and was healed of a sore throat. On another occasion, I was so shocked at the abject misery and deprivation we encountered in a district where we had gone to evangelize that I began to cry during prayer. When we returned home, Sister Annus told the others that the Holy Spirit had caused me to be on the point of repenting, although I insisted that this was not the case. In a joking way, Sister Annus and I sometimes called each other "mother" and "daughter," but establishing consistent ties of fictive kinship was not possible because of the *paráznaság* question. If I had moved into her house I would have been living communally with several of her unmarried, nonbeliever sons, and her staunch advocacy of me could not have overcome speculations about potential marriage or *paráznaság*.

I also began to sing solos in the IG during the testimony period and gave credit to Sister Annus for teaching me. The believers responded enthusiastically. Congregation members said that my singing had a deep effect on them. Only Brother Misi attributed this to musical learning; other congregation members saw my singing as both representing and effecting spiritual transformation. Sister Annus regularly added after my performances that I must be on the point of converting. Another young believer commented that my singing "breaks the heart." Brother Horváth also changed the nature of his comments about me to the congregation. Rather than introducing me as a music teacher, he used my middle name, with the diminutive "Rózsika," denoting a slight level of informality and possibly affection. He began to comment that I was learning the language well, and once near the end of my fieldwork period he commented that I was "becoming Hungarian" (*magyarosodik*). Singing thus may have enabled me to cross the gap between my orientation as a nonbeliever and the experience of the believers. Only church members had this understanding; the highest church leaders never stopped being aware that I had not converted. The positive comments of church members showed their view of the Holy Spirit as a source not only of ecstasy but also of religious knowledge. In the view of some church members, the inflections I applied to singing conveyed a deep understanding of the song's religious message rather than of the musical idiom.

This new form of participation resulted eventually in a reinterpretation of me as an instrumentalist. The musicians began to comment about my skill as an instrumental musician, mostly as a means of introducing me to Romani believers from other parts of the country. They even called me a *muzsikus*, with its connotations of one who pursues music as a trade, hinting at an affinity with themselves as Romungre. Near the end of my fieldwork, I broached the subject of our different levels of training to Brother Gál, asking him his opinion of the church ensemble's musical skills. He replied:

> Sure, we could play more beautifully and with more blessing. But nonetheless I can say that the heart is the most important thing. [When] the work started here in Szigetvár, we had a bad guitar and I could only hit it for the beat. Brother Rudi had an accordion that was almost falling apart. But when we started singing [and] if you can call it playing, God's spirit flowed down and the people collapsed and confessed their sins. I've heard congregations where they play in a professional way and there are professional musicians but it is cold there. So the spirit is not in the instrument, but in the heart of the musician who plays.

Gál himself viewed the ensemble as lacking skill, but just as important in his opinion was the fact that the group did not always have good instruments. For these believers the music was effective; their proficiency and the condition of their instruments had no bearing on the music's purpose to facilitate the presence of the Holy Spirit. Nonetheless, when I asked Brother Gál if my high level of training had made the other musicians uncomfortable, he replied that this was indeed the case.

> BRL: May I ask something? Last year, when I was here for a long time, I did not feel good when people said this person reads music, she's a trained musician, and so on. And here were the musicians who are serving the Lord and they are sitting there and I did not feel good. Do you think—I did not want them to feel bad. Did they feel bad?

> JG: Obviously when a person with greater knowledge is standing in front of us, who understands music like you, who has studied, then a feeling of lower rank comes over a person and he almost doesn't dare take up his instrument. So he's afraid that his low level of knowledge will mean shame on his part ... the *testvérek* had this kind of feeling, but you experienced how we nonetheless praise the Lord in whatever way there is. And this person, like you, can distinguish, and you did not feel good because it was as though you had to compromise. But this would put the people who are there in a difficult situation. But we have really grown to love you, Rózsika, and we know that you didn't come to cast doubt with your musical knowledge. Maybe this is why you did not play very much at all among us, and we accepted you as you were.

In these comments, Brother Gál reiterated how the instrumental musicians were keenly aware of having the distinction of unculturedness applied to them. His observations also reflect that in his view there was no way to change our differences. The original contrast between our levels of training and its implied difference in social rank could not be resolved.

Once I was involved in the vigorous singing life of the IG members, I began to see ways in which some of this activity was ethnically specific yet at the same time part of a broader popular culture. Since all of the church members sang in Hungarian, this might lead one to believe that there was an orientation toward Magyars. In Eastern Europe, where language is often equated with nationality, many scholars believe that such linguistic assimilation extends into musical style for Roma, especially the Romungre: "they do not use gypsy folk music but feel the music of the

Hungarians living around them to be their own" (Sárosi 1978[1971]:24). Yet I found that the IG's Romani members had a large repertoire of sacred songs and were continually being inspired to compose new ones. Although these songs had much in common with Hungarian popular music, the Roma's level of attention to them seemed particularly strong to me. Once attuned to this, I saw that neighbors and family members were similarly involved with certain secular songs. For Roma and for Magyar IG members, singing was a locus of personal meaning and of group identity. The remaining chapters of this book are therefore devoted to song in the lives of believers: its composition, dissemination, style, and public performance.

4

The Holy Spirit and
Song Composition

One afternoon Brother Miklós and his wife, Zsuzsa, had come to visit Pécs from their home village in the far northeast corner of the country near the Ukrainian border. Brother Miklós was deciding to switch the affiliation of the small group he led from the Free Christians to the IG because he felt that Brother Horváth had a more accepting attitude toward Roma. When Brother Miklós had visited the congregation six months before, he had declared in a short sermon that he had led a "ruined" (*romlott*) life. He said he was so moved by the music he heard the first time he visited a Pentecostal congregation that he resolved to learn it. Miklós then performed some songs for the congregation that he said he had "gotten from the Lord" (*az Úrtól kaptam*). I asked him to describe how this occurred, and he elaborated:

"O Precious Jesus"—when I got that song, you might say that I felt as though I didn't have anyone. I was sad. And meanwhile a voice came and the Lord said, "I will help you." And he said, "Take up your guitar, and sing!" I said, "My Lord, what should I sing?"—"Take up your guitar, and sing!" So I started to sing. . . . When I got these, the songs, I had begun to convert. Therefore I was saddened, and that's when I got this song from the Lord. And it made me happy. "My Lord, how could you have given me the present of such songs?" I was yelling, I sang them yelling. That is, I hadn't known that there was still mercy for me. And at a time like this, a person experiences that there is someone who loves him! You know, people hate each other. But I went to Jesus and he loves me. He said that he loves me. He said personally that he loves me. And I heard his voice, and then I got the marvelous song. I yelled every song to the end. The Lord Jesus is wondrous.

O precious Jesus, look down on me
Let me truly be your faithful servant
Because my life is with you and you are my everything
O precious Jesus, keep me safe.
I strayed for so long
When suddenly I ran into you.

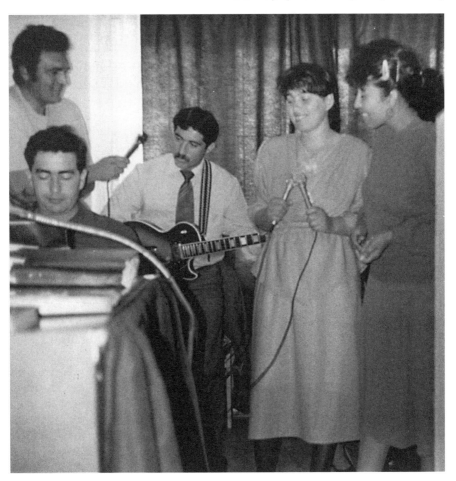

Miklós and Zsuzsa Lukács and Miklós's sister Csilla on a visit to Pécs from northeast Hungary. To give testimony, they performed songs that Brother Miklós "got from the Lord" as the church musicians accompanied them.

Joy and happiness have touched me
I did not even know that I existed.

> *Ó, drága Jézus, nézz le rám,*
> *Hadd legyek híven hű szolgád!*
> *Mert veled az én életem, és te vagy a mindenem,*
> *Ó, drága Jézus, tarts meg engemet!*
> *Oly sokáig tévelyegtem,*
> *Mikor egyszer eléd kerültem,*
> *Öröm és boldogság érintett meg engem,*
> *Én azt sem tudtam, hogy én létezem.*

Romani believers like Brother Miklós had an entire repertoire of original songs that they perceived as having come from God.[1] Song composition was part of a complex of religious experiences that these believers, like other Pentecostals, attributed to God as "the Lord" (*az Úr*), Jesus, or the Holy Spirit. Fully one-third of the IG's repertoire consisted of the music that had come to church members through divine inspiration. For IG members the newly composed songs indicated God's personal care for them. The elderly Sister Borovics explained to me that these songs were important to everyone in the IG, at the same time revealing the general concept among believers about how the songs came into existence: "I may have a favorite song and someone got it once, you know? That is my favorite song right now. But what we get is unique, more unique. As with Józsi's song, because it is very, very beautiful for him. That God was so merciful to him and reached down toward him." Here, using a song of József Gál's as an example, she distinguished between the music that came to church members through God and songs that individuals might prefer, which had come to an unknown author in the past. In her view, God's personal contact made the new repertoire meaningful to the whole community.

Many Pentecostal and Evangelical adherents in the United States also believe that music can come from God. But there, song composition appears to be more meaningful to the individual than to a group. In a study of one particular song, Jeff Titon concluded that its composition was representative of one individual's intense communion with the divinity but not extremely important as music to his fellow congregation members (Titon 1988:227–32). Gospel hymn composers wrote about their composition experiences as personal testimony. They utilized academic methods of working out songs in formal segments but reported that other compositions had come through spontaneous "inspiration" and states of deep concentration (Rothenbusch 1991:272–79).

The idea that songs could have a divine source was historically part of an enthusiastic Christian belief system in Hungary. One Romani convert commented that he was at first amazed when a song came to him, but "then I learned from the older believers that it wasn't from me, but I got this from the Lord." The believers used subjective expressions about the genesis of the songs such as "get written" (*íródik*), "come into existence" (*születik*), or "came" (*jött*). Although they were eager to tell me the experiences they and others had when they got specific songs, the believers were uninterested in my more secularly oriented efforts to discover which human was the original source for a given song. Here I use the term "composer," with the caveat that according to IG members, God was the actual composer. The church members had no specific term for the songs, but an outsiders' term for the music provides a distinction that I will apply here. Once I was visiting Brother István in his home village when he had just obtained a cassette of new songs from some other believers. As we were walking down the street, his neighbors stopped him and said, "We want to listen to those *hívő énekek* [believers' songs]."

Getting the Holy Spirit

Getting songs was just one aspect of a radical reorientation of the senses that occurred with the experience of what church members called the "Holy Spirit" (*Szentlélek*).[2] "Getting the Holy Spirit" is both a theological tenet and a subjective experience that distinguishes Pentecostal believers from other Christians. According to the biblical account in Acts 2:1–4, the Holy Spirit manifested to 120 believers on the day of Pentecost, the fortieth day after Jesus' ascension. Spontaneous healing, glossolalia, prophecies, visions, and dreams were all outpourings of the Holy Spirit, according to the words of the apostle Peter. Devout people in Jerusalem gathered when they heard that believers had spoken "with other tongues," and three thousand of them joined in fellowship with the Apostles.[3] Pentecostals believe that the descent of the Holy Spirit was not just a historical event but continues to happen to all believers who desire it. In a version of early American Pentecostal doctrine, IG members saw getting the Holy Spirit as part of a threefold process laid out by Peter in Acts 2:38: "Repent, be baptized all of you in the name of Jesus Christ for the pardon of sins, and take the gift of the Holy Spirit."[4] IG members and other Pentecostals believed that if someone converted and was baptized, that person would be saved from hell and, according to their interpretation of the book of Revelation, be "written into the Book of Life," that is, guaranteed a place in heaven (Rev. 13:8, 17:8, 21:27). IG members emphasized conversion and full-immersion baptism as the primary ways to be guaranteed a future life in heaven. Baptizing in Jesus' name was such an important part of their doctrine as Oneness Pentecostals that people like Brother Miklós and his wife who transferred from other groups had to be baptized again.

Pentecostals draw a well-defined boundary to distinguish themselves from outsiders. In its modern form, this doctrine of sanctification stems from the Holiness movements of Wesleyan pietist origin. Believers reject the worldly, which they consider evil, for an existence devoted to following God's directives as they perceive them. IG members made a sharp division between the "world" (*világ*) for an array of things they called "holy" (*szent*) or "blessed" (*áldott*)—life, brotherhood, songs, and the Bible (*szent élet, szent testvériség, szent ének, Szent Biblia*). Brother Miklós's and Sister Borovics's statements at the beginning of this chapter exemplify how church members valued getting the Holy Spirit for a somewhat different reason than the theologically based one: when they got the Holy Spirit, they felt that God had established personal contact with them.

Many IG members had experienced God as impelling their lives, habits, and physical health to change in concrete ways. Brother Babos, a Romani believer whose house served as the meeting hall in Szigetvár, described vivid physical sensations and sudden motivations upon his conversion. His own father's funeral marked the beginning of the Romani Pentecostal community in Szigetvár.

My life started to truly change when my father died. At that point, my life started and I thought about where he had ended up, how they said that there was heaven and hell and I thought about where he truly might end up. The believers said in heaven. I wasn't frightened so that on my part I thought about how I might end up in hell, but I really started to think about whether there was God or not. . . . [At the funeral service] everyone was in wonder at how beautiful the service was and how they sang there. And on that night something—so strange happened to me, it is not possible to express in human words, I felt a strange feeling inside, as though something might have passed through me, but I had no idea what it might have been. . . . Then they had a vigil [*virrasztottak*] for my father and I went to the vigil and there Brother Horváth started speaking about God and he said "Who would like to place his life with God?" . . . Somehow, I myself don't even know, I raised my hand. I don't know how, since before this I called them [the believers] everything, I absolutely did not believe in it, but somehow I raised my hand that I too [would place my life with God]. And when I prayed, again I felt the same strange thing in me, this—this—it was strange, but it was very comfortable and good. I felt a small soft warmth or something inside me.

In speaking with me, Brother Babos utilized the narrative conventions of testimony that contrast before and after, but he did not emphasize that his life before conversion was evil. Rather he stressed that his behavior was crazy and excessive. In response to a challenge from his cousin, Brother Babos vowed to stop smoking. He reported that at around this time believers prayed over him again and he experienced a sudden eloquence, praying with "beautiful words." However, he recalled that he had not yet rejected all secular pursuits.

I became very conceited, that I had converted and I was such a good person, good in this way and that way, I was very conceited. And God showed me one day what I really was. He allowed me again into the things I had formerly done. I went bowling at the bowling alley, and I lost I don't know how much money, and I tasted the same worldly life. I had taken my boy with me too. They beat me up, I got into a fight and I got drunk although I had not drunk much liquor. . . . I don't even know how I got home. The next day as I was sobering up I started wondering what this was and what had happened to me. I truly came to the realization that human action comes only to this, and I really awakened to the fact that a person needs God in order to be freed. And God freed me and I didn't go [drinking] anymore.

Brother Babos here described the change in attention and energy that occurs with the sanctification process. On baptism days, Brother Horváth often urged the congregation to reject worldly things, citing the horrific depictions from the book of Revelation of the fate that would befall people who are not converted and who do not follow Pentecostal strictures. Brother Babos did not refer to fear as a motivation but instead described how conversion changed him so that the secular world seemed to be without purpose. In sanctification, the rejection of the world simultaneously means becoming *szent*; Brother Babos remembered that with this same turn away from what he called "human action" came a greater awareness of sacred phenomena attaching to the Holy Spirit.

I lived the way God wanted me to, and I heard that many of the *testvérek* spoke in tongues and that there is such a thing as being filled with the Holy Spirit. And I started thinking about what being filled with the Holy Spirit was and I also would have liked to be filled with the Holy Spirit. Once Sister Rózsi was at our house [with other believers] and suddenly Sister Rózsi started tongues. I was startled that she prayed in another language. She didn't pray in the Gypsy language, but in another language that neither she nor I had ever studied in [our] lives. The sound went into my ears and I started to wonder how she was praying in this way since she did not know any languages. I knew her whole life, she was a Gypsy sister and we are also relatives, so she doesn't know other languages. And

I started wondering how this could be. I could hardly wait for the praying to finish and her to stop so that I could talk with her. And when the praying had stopped I said to her, Sister Rózsi, how did you pray like that? She said it was the heavenly language that God gave when someone is filled with the Holy Spirit. My mouth fell open. I was amazed about how really beautiful it was and I wanted so much—unexpectedly I had such a desire to speak like that. And I could hardly wait to be able to speak like that. And Sister Rózsi said that I should pray for it, that God could give it any time when I asked for it from my heart.

Sister Rózsi's term "heavenly language" was one that IG members commonly used to explain glossolalia. Some theories of glossolalia have concluded that it issues neurophysiologically from the trance state. Felicitas Goodman finds extraordinary speech during trance to be nearly universal, occurring in such disparate situations as shamanic cultures, the visions of Mohammed, and Pentecostal tongue-speaking. Goodman terms these situations "dissociative states," that is, "a withdrawal from external stimuli." Glossolalia is a vocalization that is "superimposed" on such states. Thus glossolalic utterances from many cultures "seemed cross-linguistically and cross-culturally identical" (Goodman 1972:viii, 119, 160, 1987:563–64).[5] But IG members saw themselves as having a type of experience that was decidedly different from the trance and possession states of other cultures. In the early 1990s, programs that depicted supernormal activities like indigenous Philippine curing ceremonies and Balinese sword dancing were just being shown on Hungarian television. Church members commented to me in shocked yet fascinated tones how such people must be possessed by the devil. Even though IG members described it to me as literally the language spoken by angels, for them the initial event of tongue-speaking was an act of association more than dissociation. Gerlach and Hine see tongue-speaking as a "commitment experience" that enables an individual to become separated from the secular world and join a specifically Pentecostal group culture (1970:120–25). One segment of this group culture in the IG consisted of Roma who were relatives and neighbors. For IG members the motivation to speak in tongues appeared to occur most often when sanctification had reoriented their energy and attention in a positive way toward their converted relatives and neighbors. Brother Babos's exposure to the alien sound of tongues was mixed with the familiarity of hearing them spoken by his relatives, and it was during a group prayer session that Brother Babos got the Holy Spirit himself.

I don't know which *testvér*, if I remember well it was Brother Misi and someone else who prayed for me. They told me to raise up my hands and confess my sins. But I had already done that, so I just said a few words, "Forgive me, my Lord, wash me with your blood, fill me up, precious Holy Spirit." After I said this, I felt as though something was coming up in my stomach. It became a lump . . . it kept coming up and it stuck in my throat. Then they told me to say "Halleluia" . . . and I felt as though that lump just kept coming up. Then I felt that the lump pressed my mouth apart and jumped out. When the lump came out of my mouth, I don't know what language I spoke, but I wasn't speaking Hungarian. I praised God in a foreign language. And when I got up, I was so happy. As though I had never been on earth. I can't say where I was.

Brother Babos and other Roma described praying along with others, thus illustrating a communal and egalitarian version of getting the Holy Spirit. In large Pentecostal denominations, tongue-speaking does seem to have a dissociative character, since it is leaders rather than family members and friends who help the aspirant. It is common for leaders to pray over people who want to get the Holy Spirit for the first time or to be "baptized" in the Holy Spirit. Since according to Pentecostal doctrine only men who have themselves received the Holy Spirit have the authority to "lay on hands," this establishes a hierarchical relationship between the leader and the individual being prayed over. The Holy Spirit came to the IG's Romani aspirants in a more undifferentiated way, in the context of intense group prayer; Brother Babos's friends gave him some basic instructions to begin with, but then he himself had the sense of undergoing a drastic physical change. Most young Magyar converts tended to have their first Holy Spirit experiences when guest missionaries from the United States conducted evangelization services, so that it was leader-initiated. Some of these missionaries had a striking gift for transmitting energy to church members, Rom or Magyar; on one occasion when being prayed over an extremely shy young women began to tremble from head to foot and to speak tongues in a chattering way. Other missionaries employed a rationalized procedure to induce the Holy Spirit. At one service, a missionary coached a woman step by step in different syllable combinations until he determined that she was speaking in tongues.

In such Pentecostal institutions, simply the fact that a believer has gotten the Holy Spirit appears to be important. But getting the Holy Spirit is somewhat different from conversion and water baptism. Those events occur only once and to an individual, whereas the Holy Spirit may come many times and be felt by an entire group of believers. With the coming of the Holy Spirit, the believer experiences a change in the nature of perception and mental processes. Walter Hollenweger comments about the Pentecostal pastor that "through the baptism of the Spirit he learns to use levels of his soul and his body hitherto unknown to him, as sense organs with which to apprehend a psychological climate" (1972:332). This is also true for Brother Babos and other ordinary believers in the IG, who described such psychophysical reorientations.

The experience of getting the Holy Spirit can be related from an outsider's standpoint to the spirit possession phenomenon. Christian believers, among them IG members, would define spirit possession as a manifestation of the devil and thus exclude the Holy Spirit from such a category of experience. In possession, there is a relationship of "container to contained" (Crapanzano 1987:13), and this is similar to what occurs when a believer gets the Holy Spirit. Spirit possession often is induced with sensory bombardment or sensory deprivation (Crapanzano 1987:14). The Holy Spirit came to IG members under both conditions. Some believers related to me how they got the Holy Spirit after fasting, a form of sensory deprivation. IG members sang many of their songs at a slow tempo and without any percussive sounds. While this contrasts greatly with the kinds of music that are described as bringing down the Holy Spirit in U.S. contexts, and with many kinds of music at possession ceremonies in other parts of the world, IG members' singing certainly resulted in sensory bombardment. The voices reverberated in multiple sound waves off the walls of the IG's tiny worship rooms and onto our bodies. Getting the Holy Spirit was also a kind of transformational exorcism. In this process, the subject takes on the character of that by which he or she is possessed (Crapanzano 1987:16). Similarly, IG members believed that they took on a divine character, becoming *szent* after they got the Holy Spirit. When I first began observing church events, I paid attention to the variety and outward intensity of Holy Spirit manifestations. But one evening when Brother Gál, Sister Annus, and I were on a visit to Ózd, they began to talk about some of the unusual feelings they had when they "obeyed" God (*engedelmeskedni*, "to obey"). I had assumed until this point that the believers were using the word "obedience" similarly to the American Evangelicals I had heard preach about following rules of dress, diet, and behavior. But Brother Gál then explained that to obey God meant to be in a state that allowed sensations vividly to come over him. If while leading a church service he got the *indítás* (impulse) that a church member needed to be prayed over, he must "obey" and act on this impulse. I asked Brother Gál if *engedelmeskedni* meant to do things that God tells you to do spontaneously in a given moment, and he replied "of course." Brother Gál seemed to mean that his whole sensory apparatus needed to follow the communications he perceived as being given by God. A further indication of this orientation is that a significant number of IG members experienced the Holy Spirit almost continuously. Brother Bandi got prophetic messages at such a constant rate that he kept a pencil and paper with him at all times. To be obedient was consciously to allow divine energy to override the sense of self as an individual; a believer had to perpetually be in a state to receive the manifestations of the Holy Spirit.

Paul's Second Letter to the Corinthians (10:5) mentions the concept of complete obedience that may be a source for the Roma's orientation. In the version of the Bible that the IG members used, Paul advises the Corinthians about "capturing every thought so that it will obey Christ" (*foglyul ejtvén minden gondolatot, hogy engedelmeskedjék a Krisztusnak*). The IG's believers favored the Bible as translated by Gáspár Károlyi, a Calvinist presbyter from the town of Göncz, and first printed in 1590. The Károlyi translation includes the terms "obedient" and "to obey" in many places where American Pentecostals' Bible translations use the words "meek" or "to submit."

The Holy Spirit as *erő*

Many of the Magyar believers expressed a sense of the Holy Spirit's physical effects that differed from that of Roma. Romani believers spoke of a "feeling" (*érzés*) and heard musical sounds; Magyar believers used a different expression, *isteni erő*, and felt surges of physical energy. *Isteni* means divine; the word *erő* in Hungarian can mean either power or strength, and believers understood the word in both of these senses. Brother Horváth felt *erő* as power entering him when he first got the Holy Spirit; tongue-speaking and healing were the results. At one of the congregation's Easter services he utilized the idea of *erő* as strength, asserting that "on the Easter holiday we gain strength in the fact that Jesus lives" and criticizing reform-oriented Christians who were "selecting commandments" to obey rather than following the full spectrum of behavioral strictures that in his view were laid out in the biblical text. Sister Herceg, an elderly Magyar, used the word *erő* to characterize how she experienced the Holy Spirit. Starting in 1972, she had belonged to the Church of Ancient Christians; she got the Holy Spirit approximately a decade later.

BRL: Sister, could you tell me again how the Holy Spirit came?

JH: I sat next to the heating stove to warm my back and began to pray. But not as I usually did, with that *erő* that I would ask for the Holy Spirit. But it might have been in there. I prayed only for a few words and the *erő* came. The Holy Spirit came, it filled me. I did not know whether to kneel or to dance. I didn't know whether I should go out into the street! Whom I'd find and whom I'd kiss. I could have kissed a Gypsy child even though he might be dirty, or anything. That was the kind of love and joy that was in me. The *erő* in me, good God's great *erő*, that I felt like going over to Agoston Square and knocking over the [Catholic] church building [*eldönteni (sic)*]. There was so much *erő* in me that I could knock it over. . . . I prayed in myself, tongues. From six o'clock until nine o'clock in tongues without stopping.

Sister Herceg used the word *erő* in several senses. She prayed with an unusual degree of *erő*, perhaps in the sense of intensity, that she associated with asking for the Holy Spirit. Upon getting it, she felt such *erő* that she could accomplish a super-human feat of strength, knocking over the most substantial building in the neighborhood, the local Catholic church. Sister Herceg recalled that the following day when she attended her church's prayer service this sense continued: "I poured the *erő* from myself, you know? The big house of worship rang." The leaders "could not stop the worship service as long as I was under the *erő*," and she continued to speak in tongues even after they left the church to go home. Here what Sister Herceg called the "Spirit" (*lélek*) created a continuous flow and a loud sound volume.

The semantic breadth of the term *erő* indicates that Magyars' Holy Spirit experiences resembled those of Roma in encompassing several domains of physical sensation. But the Hungarian expression *erő* may also show a link with the U.S. lexicon used by Pentecostal missionaries in the 1920s. The word "power" predominated in early U.S. Pentecostals' descriptions of their experiences (see MacRobert 1988:84–85). In the 1920s, one prominent U.S. evangelist associated with the Assemblies of God still utilized this concept in expressing concern that other Pentecostal adherents who identified the Holy Spirit exclusively by tongues speech were ignoring its "power"; there were many other forms of "powerful baptism" (Blumhofer 1993:136). *Pentecostal Power* was the title of the Assemblies of God songbooks, at least one edition of which Hungarian compilers used. Several songs from the gospel hymn literature that the IG members sang reinforced the perception of the Holy Spirit as power. Brother Zoli frequently led a song set to a melody resembling that of "The Old Rugged Cross." The first verse emphasizes the need for *erő*; the second, which church members repeated as a chorus, utilizes the word *erő* both in the sense of power and physical strength.

O, you precious spirit, you pentecostal *erő*, break forth with high winds roaring,
Look, those of us who are standing here are awaiting the holy *erő* to fill our hearts.

Ó, te drága lélek, te pünkösdi erő, sebes szél zúgással törj elő!
Nézd, akik itt állunk, mi, mind arra várunk, hogy szívünk töltse be a szent erő.

Trudging over stones toward you, weariness has overwhelmed your people.
Our legs are collapsing, our hands are tired, and we no longer have *erő to* raise them toward you.

Az úton haladva tefeléd köveken, fáradtság vett erőt népedben,
Lábaink roskadnak, kezeink fáradtak, hozzád felemelni nincs már erőnk.

Chorus:

Give *erő*, our God, the holy pentecostal *erő*, heal the first in our hearts,
See us standing here; we all want our hearts to be filled with holy *erő*.

Adj erőt Istenünk, pünkösdi szent erőt, gyógyítsd meg szívünkben az elsőt!
Nézd, akik itt állunk, mi, mind arra várunk, hogy szívünk töltse be a szent erő.

Some Magyar church members also interpreted the Hungarian translation of
Lewis E. Jones's gospel hymn "Power in the Blood" in a double sense. It expressed
their sensation that there was strength given by Jesus' sacrifice to redeem men from
their sins, indicated by a synecdoche with blood. This translation is faithful to the
English text, but the double meaning of the word *erő* remains.[6]

Do you want to leave your sins behind?
There is great *erő* in Jesus' blood!
Do you want to have victory over Satan?
There is wondrous *erő* in this blood.

Vágyol-e elhagyni bűneidet?
Jézus vérében van nagy erő!
Vágyol-e győzni a Sátán felett?
E vérben csodás az erő.

Chorus:

There is *erő*, wondrous *erő* in the blood of our Jesus.
There is *erő*, wondrous *erő* in Jesus' precious holy blood!

Van erő, van, csodás erő van Jézusunk vérében,
Van erő, van, csodás erő van Jézus drága szent vérében!

Sister Marika, a Magyar believer in her thirties, often requested this song. One evening
at Bible study, she exclaimed, "You know, *testvérek*, this is to me the most beautiful
song, I mean it. Because after they operated on me, I was nothing. But now, when I
vacuum I sing this. I can vacuum up both rooms [of my flat]. Until now I couldn't
even vacuum one room." Her assertions, as well as those by elderly believers, indicated that God could give strength of will as well as physical endurance. This was a
frequent theme in Brother Horváth's sermons; he emphasized that the strength of
God and of the "heavenly host" (*mennyei sereg*) was needed to combat temptation.

Song Composition as a Holy Spirit "Gift"

The Bible does not mention song composition as one of the Holy Spirit gifts. However, to IG members it shared so many characteristics with other Holy Spirit experiences that they embraced it as one. The church members evaluated all Holy Spirit
gifts critically. Glossolalia almost always seemed to be the initial manifestation of
the Holy Spirit for them, as it is for most Pentecostals. Afterward they experienced a
diverse array of phenomena. Some, like prophecy and spontaneous healing, are
mentioned in the biblical text, but many others had no direct basis in biblical scripture; these included hearing voices, musical sounds, songs, or poems and having

visions.[7] They were especially careful about deciding whether their initial experiences should be classified as Holy Spirit manifestations. One limit stemmed partly from Brother Horváth's earlier involvement in the "prophet movement" and his belief that the idea of the Holy Spirit had been carried to extremes there. The believers also expressed caution about tongues interpretation, that is, the ability to translate the divine message of tongues. It is mentioned in the Bible as a Holy Spirit gift, and is an important aspect of worship in many small Pentecostal churches of the United States (see Dégh 1994; Lawless 1988a:52). In Hungary, many had the gift of tongues interpretation in the Free Christian church, where it conferred elevated status (Horváth and Matolay 1980:78–80). But IG members did not interpret tongues. Once they even brought a recording to me of an occasion where an evangelist who they believed was a charlatan had interpreted some tongue-speaking as a message in English. I agreed with them that there were some English words in the tongue-speaking episode but that it was not completely in English. Brother Gál explained that he initially had doubts about whether his own tongue-speaking was anything more than garbled words.

> The baptism of the Holy Spirit was complicated for me, because when they taught about Holy Spirit baptism, the *testvérek* taught us that it was God's gift and we should pray in Hungarian and if the good God wants to give us the gift, then he must turn our tongues, because he is all-powerful, and we will speak in tongues at the point when God wishes it. I believed what they preached to me, and I prayed a lot in Hungarian. It reached many times into the middle of the night. I went to conferences in Ózd, Hajdúhadház, and Szeged. Everywhere I asked for God's spirit, I felt his wondrous presence, his love, in his pardoning of sins, in his giving of comfort [*vigasztalás*], that I can't say in words. But I nonetheless couldn't [speak] in tongues, which is the sign of Holy Spirit baptism, as when at the point a child is born, it means that he is alive when a sound comes from his mouth. It is the same in our spiritual life, when we believe God, then with our mouths we must give testament about our faith. And this testament is, for example, when we believe that speaking in tongues is a gift from God, we speak with our mouths and believe in the Word of God [*igében*]. In his promise [*ígéretében*]. I didn't know how the Holy Spirit comes. I wanted it and I prayed for it a lot. Once Brother Miklós Varga came [to visit], at that time he was the secretary of the national leadership, and he said to me, well it was not quite the way with the Holy Spirit that they had taught me because it is not possible to speak in Hungarian and in tongues at the same time. So this faith-based thing differs in that when I pray and ask God to give this to me I have to try to pay attention to God's spirit. And if I hear God's dear, wondrous speech that Paul says is the fruit of enlightenment [*a világosságnak gyümölcse*, Eph. 5:9] I will not understand it; it is built on the soul [*szellem*].[8] When I feel it. And I can accept it in faith, and I hear audible sounds in my soul with my own ears. If I hear foreign words out of the air, then I must say them out of faith, because I am sealing God's Word and God is sealing me.

Even after changing his method of praying and beginning to speak in tongues, Brother Gál doubted that he was having authentic Holy Spirit experiences. He became convinced of it only after receiving signs from several directions. One such sign was a vision by another church leader, but Brother Gál even asked for a second sign as an additional means of proof.

I had difficulty accepting this, because when the feeling came, then from another side thoughts attacked me in my mind: "This is just coming from you. You're speaking nonsense. What do you want? This is a child's speech, a confused stammering." Then God gave a sign by means of another *testvér* preacher, Brother István Csima. He had a vision that a huge ray of light had gone into my heart from heaven. But I still could do it only with great difficulty—I virtually forced myself to speak it. I really did not have peace or love, because I did not do it out of faith but rather did it because what else could it be? So I knelt down and I said, my God, I do not want to transgress [*vétkezni*] against you. I don't want to cheat myself about whether this is your Holy Ghost [*Szentszellem*] or not. But I also don't want to, if it is yours, I don't want to cheat you by not believing it or using it. I said, my Lord, here up in [daily] life, which we live, up here the devil can cheat us. I ask you, in dreams you can give us enough. Give the speaking of tongues to me in a dream. . . . I lay down after praying and rested. Then God gave me tongue-speaking and then I knew that this really was the work of the Holy Ghost.

Several different signs, including a dream, a vision, and the advice of two experienced believers, were thus required before Brother Gál felt certain that his Holy Spirit experiences were genuine. Believers also did not make the conclusion lightly that song composition was a manifestation of the Holy Spirit, especially since it is not one of the specific Holy Spirit "gifts" cited in the Bible. As John Blacking pointed out in his studies of the South African Venda, when musical expression occurs in unusual circumstances it has to be reconciled to a cultural norm (Blacking 1973:48–49). The believers did this by perceiving correspondences between song composition and the biblical Holy Spirit gifts: vivid engagement of the senses, sudden or unexpected manifestation, and the sense that God is in direct contact. Song composition always shared one feature with speaking in tongues—believers thought of it as manifesting divine intelligence. Church members emphasized to me that their song composition had nothing to do with formal musical training. One particular believer from Ózd expressed astonishment at the songs that came to him because although he had played the guitar seriously in his secular past, he had never composed a song until his conversion.

Composers got songs under unusual circumstances. A story circulated among believers about "Köszönöm az elmúlt éveket" (Thank You for Past Years), which was one of their favorite songs. A musician got this song so suddenly during his lunchtime meal that he rushed from the room. His wife followed him and wrote down the text on the spot as he heard it. The language style of some of the believers' exchanges with God when they got songs resembles God's speech in the Bible, giving the subsequent narratives a prophetic tone. Brother Miklós reported hearing the phrase "take up your guitar and sing" when he got the song "O Precious Jesus," paralleling Jesus' words in Matthew 9:6–7, where he instructs a man with palsy to rise, take up his bed, and walk. Vivid sensations were another feature of song composition. Brother Miklós related several instances when he woke in the middle of the night and heard music. Guitarists sometimes got songs in the form of physical chord positions or "grips" (*fogások*). Similarly to Brother Bandi's getting prophecies regularly, some composers went through phases where they got songs in a continuous stream.

Song Composition and Spiritual Transformation

Miracles are important components in the testimony of Pentecostals; many relate how they completely lost addictions or were spontaneously healed after just a single occasion of prayer (see Dégh 1990). Brother Horváth even appeared to believe that when someone converted, that person automatically gained knowledge about the church's fundamentalist rules for behavior. This ideology of immediate transformation was reflected in church members' use of the term "holy" (*szent*) rather than "sanctified" (*szentelt*). The former indicates a state, while the latter refers to a completed process. The transition from worldly to holy might occur in an instant, but it could be difficult. This was particularly true for Romani believers, who lived in close quarters with people who could be antireligious, like Brother Babos before he converted. Besides sleeping at Sister Annus's house, one of her unconverted adult sons lived periodically with Brother Gál, his wife, and children in their tiny three-room apartment. "Living for the world" (*a világnak élni*) signified the unconverted state. However, all the believers had to work or live "in the world" (*a világban*), where others around them did not focus on God. Some church members experienced intermediate states between worldly and holy; they had converted but still followed forbidden behaviors privately. These included smoking or (for women) wearing makeup and fashionable coiffures. In accepting these people, the IG differed from other Pentecostal churches; the group recruited new members, accepted casual attendees and observers like me, and reaccepted some previous members. Thus at any given time, some of the people associated with the IG were at intermediate points between the worldly and the holy.

Sanctification followed the basic three-phase structure for rites of passage outlined by Arnold van Gennep, where separation from the world was followed by a transition phase and subsequent incorporation into the sanctified existence. Ambiguity characterizes the intermediate or liminal states described by Victor Turner in his studies of ritual; the subject has no clear position with regard to established social structures (Turner 1969:95). In the IG, the rhetoric of sermons and conversion narratives often treated sanctification as a contrastive duality of worldly past and holy present, whereas intermediate states were the subject of everyday conversation, prayer, and song texts. Turner has observed that many religious groups have an almost permanent liminality since they are socially characterized with such features as rebirth, emotion, sexual continence, and communitas—a special undifferentiated group structure and rapport. Some of these religions treat the entire earthly life as a liminal phase before the "reaggregation of initiands to a higher plane of existence, such as heaven or nirvana" (Turner 1969:189). This is certainly characteristic of the IG as a group; the preachers emphasized getting to heaven and felt communitas as "holy brotherhood." However, even after having undergone sanctification, some church members were not quite sure that they would be guaranteed a place in heaven. This was partly because of difficulties they found in following the group's rules of conduct. Addiction to smoking was particularly problematic. Brother Horváth associated smoking and smokers with the devil because smoke emerged from their nostrils. But other preachers like Brother Gál reflected that if they were to get the commitment of Romani members they needed to allow time for them to change. God might transform some believers in an instant, but others needed to become gradually attracted to the IG community before making the commitment to follow the church's behavioral strictures.

Singing was one way for church members to move through ordeals of transition. Brother Misi used music this way during the Szigetvár meetings as he encouraged congregational singing to help the group stop worrying about "worldly problems" (*világi gondok*). During these meetings, as well as prayer hours, believers frequently requested the song "Halleluja néked!" (Halleluia to You) by a nationally famous Romani singer, Margit Bangó. Its text evokes water baptism with prayerlike phraseology, the image of white robes the converts wore, and references from the book of Revelation that Brother Horváth and other preachers quoted during sermons on the meaning of water baptism. The performances of this song also evoked spirit baptism. The church members sang the broad, sweeping melody very slowly. As the tessitura moved upward in the second line and reached its peak in the third line, the volume of the singing increased. Intense shouts, stamping, glossolalia, and weeping ensued throughout the repetitions of the chorus. In performance, "Halleluia to You" evoked and reinscribed church members' crucial transition experience of baptism (ex. 4.1).

EXAMPLE 4.1. "Halleluja néked!" (Halleluia to You). IG congregation, Pécs, December 1990.

Halleluia to you, my heavenly Father
I can put on snow-white clothing.
I promise you, my precious Jesus
I will stay on your path.

> *Halleluja néked, mennyei Atyám,*
> *Felölthetem én a hófehér ruhát.*
> *Ígérem tenéked, drága Jézusom,*
> *Meg fogok maradni a te utadon.*

Heavenly hosts are rejoicing
Because a sinful soul has found the right path.
Born anew by means of his holy cross
Today Jesus can go into his heart.

> *Mennyei seregek örvendeznek már,*
> *Mert egy bűnös lélek jó útra talált.*
> *Szent keresztje által újjá született,*
> *Ma már a szívébe Jézus bemehet.*

Chorus:
Halleluia to you, my heavenly Father
Hosanna in the sky, magnificent holy lamb.

> *Halleluja néked, mennyei Atyám,*
> *Hozsanna az égben, dicső szent bárány!*

The IG members who got the Holy Spirit through singing, praying, or fasting might be seen as generating what Gerard Rouget terms a "conducted" trance, one "into which the subject leads himself through his own action" (1985[1980]:286–88). Like the participants in Islamic *dhikr*, whom Rouget describes, as a group the IG members could generate an atmosphere conducive to getting the Holy Spirit. Once the Holy Spirit had descended, instrumental musicians then could help sustain the feeling. The texts of the songs in the IG were just as important as the intense way in which the church members sang, affirming Rouget's statement that "music brings about the trance as a result of the emotional power . . . of the sung poetry" (1985[1980]:316). Some of the texts, like "Halleluia to You," were doubly powerful because of their performative language. The song invokes a poignant moment of transformation, the passage between a worldly and a *szent* state.

Divine composition is associated crossculturally with transition. The Native American vision quest shares many features with the conversions of Hungarian Roma. The individual experiences a desire to become part of a special community (in the case of Plains Indians, that of grown men, and in the case of Pentecostal Christians, of those who are guaranteed a place in heaven). Sensory deprivation places such a person in a situation to experience many different manifestations of the divine, including music (see Merriam 1967:3–9). The Romani Pentecostal composers as well as new converts sometimes endured conditions similar to initiatory ordeals, where physical suffering, isolation, and reversals of the normal social order mark the initiand's transition from one societal group to another. Songs often came at night; Brother Miklós had recalled being awakened by musical sounds, and the relatives of another composer said that most of his songs came to him during the night. Sister

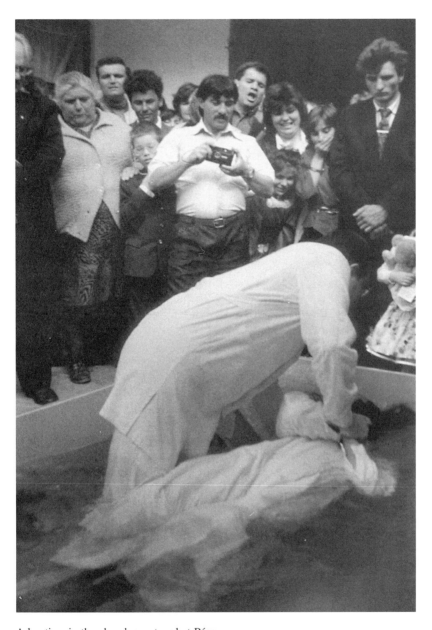

A baptism in the church courtyard at Pécs.

Elza related with a sense of whimsy how her cousin, a prolific composer of over forty songs, got them while on his job as a night watchman at a livestock yard. Social isolation was also a factor; Sister Elza's cousin commented to the sociologist Magda Matolay that his night job had provided the opportunity for intensive Bible study, praying, and getting songs from God, but his subsequent activity as a preacher for three separate congregations did not allow such private communion. Brother Miklós related that he had felt alone and "had no one" during the time he had gotten the song "O Precious Jesus."

Most of the composers had leadership roles in their congregations, but others had a feature of special license that is found crossculturally among musicians: they were persistently on the margins of their particular communities (see Merriam 1964:133–40). Sister Elza's cousin had been a lay leader in the Free Christian church. By 1990 when I was researching in Hungary, her cousin had stopped attending its meetings—although Romani congregations all over Hungary still remembered and sang his songs. Another prolific composer, Gusztáv Váradi, from Ózd, had tried Pentecostalism briefly before deciding that its behavioral strictures were too severe. Váradi's connection with the Pentecostal religion was common in Romani communities; he did not attend church, but some of his immediate relatives were staunch believers. Although he did not use the believer's lexicon, he characterized his compositional activities as religious experiences.

> GV: One thing is certain, that when I came into connection [*kapcsolatba kerültem*] with the Holy Spirit—well, it did not go like I would sit down and write a spiritual song [*szent ének*], not that way. It was such an inner awareness, and I had to pray, pray to God. So much in the spirit, in the heart. I had to be in sympathy [*együttérezni*] with God, for him to help me. And somehow this little inner freshness, that outer contact, that state of calm. I had to completely live the fact that I would unite [*egyesül*] with the melody that is somewhere in I don't know what layer of my heart. When these melodies came into existence, unequivocally they always brought such a moving emotion [*meghatódottság*]. Not just then, but now.

> BRL: What did it bring?

> GV: A moving emotion. In a certain way I could say, I don't know, that I cry along with my song. It affects me.

> BRL: This is a kind of sympathy?

> GV: Of course. I don't know exactly. That God utilizes me is a marvel to me. Because I must tell you that I do not live like a believer, as a believer lives, because I have many other things in my life that I must complete. And I can't properly live in that lifestyle. But in spite of this God utilizes me in some way; with my inner spirit, I'm always with God.

Rather than "getting" the songs, as believers termed it, Váradi said that the songs "got written" (*íródtak*) or "come into existence" (*megszületik*). His statements were ambivalent; he referred to feeling deep emotions in connection with these sacred songs but spoke in a rather detached way of "coming into connection with the Holy Spirit" rather than experiencing dramatic physical and emotional sensations. Although Váradi resolutely maintained a nonchurchgoing stance, he let the believers' songs affect him deeply. In commenting on his determination not to attend church, Váradi utilized ideas similar those of Brothers Babos and Gál about their own conversions. The idea that one would be compelled to convert by a strong impulse was prevalent in a community that extended beyond the believers themselves.

> BRL: Isn't it a bit lonely for you that . . . a song comes and you can't stand up in the congregation and sing it? Do you ever go to church and [sing] your own music?
>
> GV: There have been opportunities for that, and not just one. But God has not made me ready to go to church. And until something drives me or I feel an inner feeling, I won't go until that happens. So for me to go for that reason, that would be strange, it would make me feel strange. . . . The desire is not burning in me, it's missing. I do not know what God's goal or plan is for me.

In spite of this nonbelieving stance, Váradi was affected by his songs. On one occasion when he, a number of his relatives, and I were playing his songs together he abruptly stopped and rushed from the room. His sister Kati explained that the songs could "influence" (*meghatódik*) him so much that he would begin to cry. When I went out to the porch where Váradi had lit a cigarette, he commented that he was "weakhearted." When Kati commented about her brother's emotionality on another occasion, Sister Annus asserted that the Holy Spirit was bringing him to the point of conversion. For most believers Váradi's marginal position did not affect the power of his songs; they were popular in Romani communities all over Hungary. Some knew that these songs had come from a person who was not a convert, and in fact, one Romani leader said that something was not quite right about the process. But it was not important to most believers; Sister Annus articulated their views when she asserted that because he was so emotionally affected by these songs the Holy Spirit was manifesting through him despite the fact that he was not converted.

Magyar Expressive Forms

Music composition was associated with Romani believers, whereas many Magyars valued spoken expression. Elderly believers found meaning in the poetry and spontaneous exclamations that were thought to come from the Holy Spirit. A focus on speech is particular to the culture of Protestantism in Hungary. Possibly in a continuation of their religion's historical involvement with Hungarian as a literary language, the Calvinist ministers I became acquainted with spoke in a refined and elaborate way. The autodidact preachers who had flourished in Hungary's impoverished Alföld region are an alternate example of the emphasis on speech. As Hungary's indigenous offshoot of Pentecostalism, the prophet movement established apocalyptic speech as an important Holy Spirit manifestation. I visited a meeting of the movement's institutionalized group, the Church of Ancient Christians. During an extremely long prayer session the tone of several speakers became slightly rhythmic and increased in volume, possibly indicating prophetic messages from the Holy Spirit. The congregation was otherwise quite reserved, thus not enabling me to understand with just one observation what levels of significance these utterances might have had.[9]

To church members, the liberated way they could worship in the IG was such an important distinction that they commented on it both humorously and angrily. One of the church members asked if I had visited another Pentecostal church in the area, commenting with a half-smile that the atmosphere was "like death." Sister Herceg said that except for the first short period of time when she had gotten the Holy Spirit, it was expected for members to be silent in the Church of Ancient Christians: "There, you know, the leader is very sad in the Spirit. It wasn't allowed to even say a 'Halleluia.'" But after getting the Holy Spirit she felt spontaneously compelled to *hallelujáz* during worship services. Believers used the verb *hallelujáz* to mean that they loudly interjected the phrases "Halleluia," "Praise the Lord," or "Gloria" into any part of the worship service, including silent prayers or sermons. One reason for Sister Herceg to switch her allegiance to the IG was so that she could be free to *hallelujáz*.

> Here there is more *erő*, you know? Here the *testvérek* are more zealous [*buzgóbb*], yes more zealous. Here we can be joyful according to the Spirit, as we want. We can *hallelujáz* and praise the Lord but there it was not possible. There they really forbade halleluias, praise, [saying] that it's not necessary, you must be slow, silent, you know? Halleluia and praise toward the Lord Jesus, that was not possible. Well I suppressed my depths but then it would break out. I wasn't supposed to let it out of myself, that *erő*, that joy, you know?

To *hallelujáz* represented a radical departure in behavioral norms for most Magyars. Even secular Hungarian society stressed quiet, polite speech. The mainstream and the fundamentalist religions in Hungary required absolute silence during worship services, except for murmured prayers and congregational singing. This came from a view that God should be humbly revered, rather than enthusiastically celebrated. The Pentecostal missionaries probably brought a more expressive style of worship to Hungary from the United States in the 1920s, and the presence of Roma in the IG might have helped revive such enthusiastic practices. The term *hallelujáz*, possibly from early Pentecostal expressions like "get the halleluias," may even derive from the first Hungarian missionaries. IG members did not have an equivalent for the term "shouting," used now for such exclamations in some small U.S. churches. To *hallelujáz* was comfortable and natural for the IG's Romani members, since in the secular context, they cultivated many different ways of augmenting and emphasizing speech, but it remained culturally alien to most Magyar converts. Brother Horváth emphatically demonstrated interethnic tolerance when he allowed free rein for this expressive style of worship. He attributed iconic properties to *hallelujázás* ("halleluia-ing"), telling the congregation that the words "Halleluia" and "Gloria" were literal representations of heaven because these words occurred in biblical passages describing what the angels said. Magyars who like Sister Herceg said they felt so much joy after getting the Holy Spirit that they simply had to *hallelujáz* joined the IG, where they were free to practice their more enthusiastic worship style. There did seem to be a point at which Brother Horváth felt these interjections to be disruptive. On one occasion, I did an on-the-spot translation for a visiting American while Brother Horváth was preaching. She loudly interjected "Praise the Lord" or "Amen" in English after each phrase. Brother Horváth at first smiled but then became more tense as he paused after each exclamation.

Poetry recitation was one favorite testimony activity for elderly Magyar women, including Mrs. Horváth. Every week at Sunday afternoon services, they recited or read poems from tattered personal manuscript books. Most of the poems came from old books of religious verse that had been available before World War II. Some church members got poems from God, just as others had gotten songs. The young Magyar Sister Gyöngyi mentioned that she had received a poem from God in a dream that answered another poem she had written while not yet a convert. The seventy-six-year old Sister Herceg recited her own poetry. She reported praying at night and then getting poems, most of them within a few years of having first gotten the Holy Spirit. Sister Herceg's challenges as a believer were typical of those faced by elderly Magyars and quite different from those of the Romani converts. She had easily followed behavioral strictures. But she told me that her neighbors mocked her after her Holy

Sister Herceg giving testimony. She stood at the front of the church next to the anteroom and recited poetry that she "got from the Lord."

Spirit experiences, and family members cut off contact with her. The texts of her poems demonstrate how the Holy Spirit made this ostracism bearable. Like many other IG members, Sister Herceg said that for several years she was in regular connection with the Holy Spirit. While this appears to have been an ecstatic state, it did not generate the expressions of liminality characteristic of some Romani believer's songs. Her poem texts expressed a mixture of certainty and pain as she recited them in a fervent way. Their two primary subjects were events in the Bible and the wonders of heaven. Her favorite poem, "Jób élete" (Job's Life), takes that biblical character's persona to explore his condition at length.

Job's Life

I am Job, man of the lord
he judged me worthy of this place
I got wealth from him
and [my] matchless, beautiful dear family
He gave me beauty, much good
but already he has taken it away
my vast treasures are missing

I am a beggar, poor without a homeland
My seven fine sons and my three daughters
are no more. Oh, what pain! Death, death,
why did you seize them? Where is the heart that can
endure this? satan envies my life
and the lord has given me over [to him].
What a great trial! help me, my lord
To resist and bear it out

evil, you knew what would hurt me
you robbed me of my ten fair children
The wealth, I don't care about
but I will mourn them as long as I live
I will not open my lips to happiness
but because there is so great a cross upon me
I have come to despise my own life
Cursed is the event of my birth!
I wonder, when will the lord look upon me?

Jób élete

Jób vagyok én az Úr embere,
ő méltatott engem e helyre
Tőle kaptam a gazdagságot
s páratlan szép kedves családot
Adott szépséget, sok javakat
s ím már el is vette azokat
rengeteg kincsem mind oda van

Koldus vagyok, szegény, hontalan
Hét szép fím három lányom
nincsen többé, oh mily fájdalom! Halál, halál,
miért ragadtad el? Hol a szív, mely ily kint

elvisel? irigyli a sátán életem
és átadott az úr engemet.
Mily nagy próba! segíts meg uram
Hogy megálljak, végig kibírjam

tudtad gonosz mi fáj majd nekem
elraboltad tíz szép gyermekem
A nagy vagyont sohsem sajnálom
de őket míg élek gyászolom
boldogságra nem nyitom ajkam
de mert ily nagy kereszt van rajtam
Megutáltam saját életem
Átkozott legyen a születésem!
vajon az úr rám mikor tekint?[10]

The attention to the special language of prophecy in the Church of Ancient Christians may have helped generate Sister Herceg's poetry, even if the church had not tolerated her exclamations during sermons or her general religious enthusiasm. This poem's adoption of a biblical figure's persona makes it very different from the Romani *hívő énekek*. Sister Herceg never revised these poems since in her view they came from the Holy Spirit. Another key gift from the Holy Spirit, she believed, was the ability to memorize and recite these poems. She had only completed the fifth grade, and, like the composers, she did not view her human intelligence as capable of such things.

JH: I completed five grades, five. I couldn't memorize even a poem of even two stanzas, you know. Even if I said it a hundred times, I couldn't learn it.

BRL: So you have only recited in church.

JH: Only in church. The Lord Jesus taught me, you know, that intelligence. In school I didn't have it. Not by choice but that's the way it was. You know what I always wanted to learn? In our reader when I was a schoolgirl, there was the poem "The Beautiful Border of My Homeland."[11] I couldn't memorize it, only the first verse. There are four verses. I couldn't memorize it.

BRL: Even though you wanted to.

JH: I really wanted to. But it was human, human intelligence, you know. Now the Lord Jesus has given his own intelligence into my mind and my heart. That's why I could memorize [my own poems].

Sister Herceg's comments reflect a general opinion in Hungary that to memorize verse is a basic mark of refinement (*műveltség*). Poetry recitation is an integral part of educational method; the Hungarian parents of young children I know consider it essential to teach their preschool children to recite verses, while they leave reading instruction to public school teachers. A child's cleverness is judged on the basis of how smoothly and accurately he or she can recite a memorized verse. Contests are a feature of later school life, where high school students can compete for prizes in the dramatic recitation of works by the distinguished Hungarian poets. Readings are not performed by poets themselves but by actors for whom the recitation of poetry is a key professional skill.

There is a tendency in Hungarian and other European cultures to treat songs as a type of verse as well as music. In the nineteenth century, folk songs and ballads were collected and first published sans melody as a means for those of populist sentiment to create vocabularies and syntaxes of individual "national" languages. In Hungary, many such volumes of *népköltészet* ("folk poetry") were published.[12] In the twentieth century, Hungarian folk songs received parallel analyses as verse and melody; the study of folk song as a type of verse was incorporated into the language curriculum of the Hungarian public school system. Sister Gyöngyi's perception of the songs in the IG demonstrates this privileging of the verbal over the musical. In her opinion, the *hívő énekek* were wonderful poems. She wrote down the song texts in her private manuscript book as verses, not as a memory aid for singing. For Magyar IG members, verse was thus an important manifestation of the Holy Spirit. There was a propensity in the Hungarian national institutions to privilege the verbal, both in secular literary culture and in other Protestant religions. The psychophysical experience of *erő* mentioned by many Magyar believers in connection with the Holy Spirit is not clearly connected to poetry composition; more Magyar believers felt the Holy Spirit as *erő* than as the discipline and formality of verse. In the IG, Magyar believers could openly express religious enthusiasm by being able to *hallelujáz*. Thus they felt that IG fostered an environment of expressive freedom by comparison with all other churches in Hungary.

Mutual Appreciation

Believers appreciated all the manifestations of the Holy Spirit, if they judged them to be genuine. Thus it was an elderly Magyar, Sister Borovics, who articulated to me why the songs that Romani believers got were special for the whole congregation. Conversely, some Romani believers loved hearing the elderly women recite poetry. Brother Bandi commented that these recitations demonstrated their long experience in the faith, the depth of their devotion, and the strength with which they had endured adversity because of their beliefs. Most Magyar members attended the IG specifically because the atmosphere allowed for much Holy Spirit manifestation. One couple who had switched allegiances commented about their previous congregation: "[It] wasn't as full of love—welcoming—as this community . . . here we always get more blessing from the Lord." The presence of the Holy Spirit generated communitas. Musical histories, stylistic codes, performance interpretations, and repertoires might diverge. However, when the Holy Spirit was felt to be present, differences within the group became insignificant as church members shared a common experience of divine energy.

5

Roma and the *hívő énekek*

One night when Brother Misi asked for song requests during the Szigetvár wor-ship meeting, Brother Gál's wife Anikó called out, "Viharos az élet [life is stormy]," a line from a song that I had only heard a month before on a trip north to Ózd. Brother Rudi played the descending pentachord that began the melody. Tap-ping his drumsticks together rhythmically, Brother Gál sang the first line under his breath. The church members began talking among themselves, and Gál said, "Con-gregation, be quiet, because we can't sing it . . . it's a new song." Some of the women started singing. They seemed uncertain about how long to pause between phrases and began the next lines hesitatingly, but their voices became louder during the chorus. An interesting point to me about this episode was how much the members of the con-gregation wanted to have a spirit-filled and smoothly proceeding performance of this song. Anikó had asked for the song before Brother Misi could even finish his state-ment. Some people started to sing before the orchestra had tried out the song. A whole experience of hearing and singing this song was apparent, one that had taken place before this formal meeting for worship. I witnessed how believers and nonbelievers enthusiastically learned these songs outside of church, thereby incorporating them into a larger frame of Rom-oriented popular culture.

Transmission of New Songs

The fact that the women in the congregation were among the strongest singers and advocates of new music indicates how the domestic setting was the most important place for songs to be accepted. Once a composer had gotten a song, a member of his extended family, usually his wife, wrote the text down in an *album*—a notebook with song texts, Bible verses, and illustrations.[1] Friends or family members performed the songs and made cassette recordings of them. The Romani church members then cir-culated the cassettes among households. They mailed them to each other if they lived far away. If they lived in the same neighborhood, when they visited each other they borrowed the latest cassettes from each other. A typical exchange occurred once when

I was spending the night at Brother Misi's house. His wife Erika's younger sister brought over a cassette she had borrowed from another family, who in turn had received it in the mail from some Ózd believers. One reason that cassette exchange worked effectively for song learning was that it supported ideals about sharing property. Michael Stewart observed in his work with Vlach Roma that an expectation to share resources issues from the egalitarian social ideal. Families might make the decision not to accumulate material goods because strains ensued if neighbors or relatives wanted to borrow expensive equipment (Stewart 1989:82). Cassettes were an ideal means of exchange since they were small and cheap but nonetheless contained something of value—new music performances. As electronic media, cassettes may also inherently have a democratizing tendency in that they allow the means for autodidact experimentation and are distributed by informal means (Enzensberger 1976[1970]:21–25, 31–33).

Actual visits that believers made from other parts of the country helped introduce the songs. IG members in southeast Hungary learned the songs of the Ózd church members but not those of Brother Miklós; the visits between Ózd and southeast Hungary were far more frequent and the relationships affectionate, whereas Brother Miklós maintained a connection primarily with Brother Horváth. The importance of personal interaction here affected cassette exchange. Some ethnographers have commented how Kalderash Roma in France and the United States utilize the most efficient means of technology available to maintain close contact, including telephones and airplane travel (Silverman 1988:270–71; Williams 1982:317, 336). In Hungary, the Romani believers made long train trips to visit one another.

Much exchange occurred in the households and neighborhoods where the Romani congregations were located, since some Romani church members lived together in multigenerational households, others resided near one another in the segregated housing areas called *cigánytelepek*, and most shopped at the same open-air market. At any given time, a household accommodated one or two guests. These guests were usually relatives, but a strong affinity also sprang up between various believers (I also gradually came to be included in these hospitality arrangements). Believers visited each other's houses almost daily to pray or talk together. They brought cassettes to each other or borrowed them during these visits. Once a cassette was at a given household the recording might be played constantly so that everyone in the household and neighbors who stopped by to visit could hear the music. This often provided an opportunity to proselytize. When Brother István brought a cassette to his home village, I was staying with his nonbeliever aunt. They asked him what the performers were singing about. Brother István came over, and while the recording played he transcribed some of the texts, explaining the biblical concepts and images in them.

The home as a location for learning songs was exemplified by the outstanding performances of four-year-old Renáta Kőhegyi. She knew song texts perfectly, kept a steady pulse, followed irregular forms, sang in tune, and smoothly negotiated large leaps in the melodies. She was a favorite performer during testimony periods, when one of her older sisters would lead her to the front of the congregation. The sisters stood by, and Brother Zoli accompanied softly on the organ as Renáta took the microphone and sang. Church members asserted that Renáta was talented. But when I visited the Kőhegyi family, it became apparent that her home environment contributed greatly to her successful performances. Two of her sisters were extremely shy; they attended church services but never gave testimony. But their religious belief was very intense, as was reflected in how fervently they prayed during church services. They told me that they borrowed the Ózd tapes and listened to them while doing housework and taking care of their younger sisters. The eldest girl, Vali, knew all the songs by heart. She kept the value on having young children memorize, but she taught Renáta sacred material and music instead of the customary folk verses. Vali's involvement demonstrates how women played key roles in song learning.

Richard Bauman argues that the special structures and frames of performance enable verbal art to emerge (1977:38). In some contexts, rehearsal serves as a back-

Sister Vali, left, praying just before she was baptized. A devout believer, she taught many songs to her younger sisters.

ground structure. But here, when a congregation performed a song during a formal worship meeting, it had emerged from casual interactions, unframed singing in the domestic setting, and performances recorded on electronic media. By the time IG members sang a new song together as a group, it had already been communicated in their social networks. In the process of adoption as congregational music, songs were transformed from private messages of the Holy Spirit into a venue for shared experience. This process involved attaching significance mostly of a spiritual but also of an ethnic nature to the songs through multiple mediations and the participation of key individuals. These individuals were not only male leaders but also women, who might be in the background during formal performances of songs at worship events. Many among the Romani believers had already learned the songs by the time they reached the point where they were sung regularly at services.

The Style of *hívő énekek*

Church members were verbally articulate about only a few formal components of the *hívő énekek*. But the structures of the songs did provide places to locate details of expression. I related earlier how church members interpreted emotional expression, including my own, as signaling the presence of the Holy Spirit. In singing, this expression sometimes attached directly to textual meaning; that was the case for the way IG members sang the translated gospel hymns discussed in the next chapter. But in the *hívő énekek*, expressive details were also linked to the songs' structures, to the overall message of the text, or to a general sentimental ethos in the popular song idiom called "Gypsy *nóta*" that *hívő énekek* resemble.

Repetition, line length, and ending pitches are all irregular in the *hívő énekek*. The chorus serves predominately as a refrain, but other song forms resemble those of American musical theatre or European *couplet*, where the verse serves as a prelude to a chorus with several sequences of text. The chorus is often in a higher tessitura than the verse. There are many elements of line-pair construction in the songs, ranging from repeated sets of two lines to overlapping text and music. A preponderance of aeolian mode in the *hívő énekek* provides a striking contrast to the major tonality that dominates other repertoires of gospel hymns and Christian pop.[2] The *hívő énekek* in a major key are simply constructed, whereas the aeolian and minor-key songs include many variations. Performances of some aeolian melodies emphasized the low seventh scale degree. Other melodies include modulations to the relative major key. In one of these songs, "Názáreti, názáreti Jézusom" (My Jesus of Nazareth), the melody moves primarily stepwise, and the range of the song stays within a minor seventh. A number of motives stress a minor sixth interval and the half step between scale degrees 5 and 6. The final is emphasized through reiteration. Repeated lines of narrow range give the melody a chantlike character (ex. 5.1).

> My Jesus of Nazareth, of Nazareth
> So wondrous and beautiful for me to hear
> Don't abandon me, don't abandon me,
> My Jesus, my Jesus, don't abandon me.
>
> > *Názáreti, názáreti Jézusom,*
> > *Oly csodás, szépséges hallanom,*

EXAMPLE 5.1. "Názáreti, názáreti Jézusom" (My Jesus of Nazareth). IG congregation, Szigetvár, December 1990.

Hogy ne hagyj el, hogy ne hagyj el,
Jézusom, Jézusom, ne hagyj el.

People, people, come.
This name has redeemed you.

Emberek, emberek jöjjetek,
Ez a név megváltott bennetek.

Chorus 1:
Come, come, come, do not fear
Precious good Jesus awaits you.

Jöjjetek, jöjjetek, jöjjetek, ne féljetek,
A drága jó Jézus vár bennetek.

Chorus 2:
Come, come, come while you can
He awaits you until the last day.

Jöjjetek, jöjjetek, jöjjetek míg jöhettek,
Az utolsó napig vár bennetek.

Chorus 3:
   Halleluia, my Jesus (2x)
   Halleluia, halleluia my Jesus.

   Halleluja Jézusom (2x)
   Halleluja, halleluja Jézusom!

The modal writing of the *hívő énekek* expresses musical tension in a different way than tonally structured melodies. Reiterations give modal melody its impact, whereas the purpose of functional harmony is to provide a forward momentum by exciting and channeling desire (McClary 1991:36). The aeolian melodies in the *hívő énekek* were usually accompanied with a harmonic minor chord series so that these two ways of pacing energy were mixed together. When the believers sang "My Jesus of Nazareth" a cappella, the stepwise motives returning to the first scale degree and the high held note of the verse's second line were prominent. When there was a guitar accompaniment, the church members used snappy rhythms and sang loudly at the middle and ends of lines where the guitar played dominant chords that were then resolved to the tonic.

By using motives from popular music idioms of previous eras, the *hívő énekek* do link melody with functional harmony in ways that are familiar to Magyars and Roma. The instrumental *verbunkos* idiom from the turn of the nineteenth century, *magyar nóta*, and Hungary's urban popular song from the first part of the twentieth century all share motivic material that derives from harmonically functional music. The Romani believers, particularly those from the Romungro ethnic group, were thoroughly familiar with the sounds of *verbunkos* and *magyar nóta* as the repertoire of their families' former music professions. Cadence patterns of three held notes, augmented seconds, and the use of many ornaments are characteristic of *verbunkos* itself and the accompaniment style for *magyar nóta* (see Sárosi 1978[1971]:158–61; Szabolcsi 1964[1955]:56). Motives from *magyar nóta* also appeared in pop song during the 1930s and 1940s: sequences, narrow-range motives, question-answer motives, first and second endings, varied leaps, and half-step upper and lower neighbor tones. All of these idioms, as popular song, exploit the changing moods of triadic outlines that are linked through common tones (Lévai and Vitányi 1973:19–21, 62–66).

In his study of Venda children's songs in south Africa, John Blacking described how they recombine elements from the sound environment of other Venda musics (1973:96–100). A similar process of internalizing and transforming stylistic elements from *magyar nóta*, *verbunkos*, and early twentieth-century popular music is evident in the *hívő énekek*. Roughly one-third of the songs contain melodic movement that outlines chords. This type of movement does not pervade the songs, as in *verbunkos* or early twentieth-century Hungarian pop, but instead occurs in the chorus or in a single phrase. Turns are a common feature. Rather than ornamenting a pitch, they are metricized and each pitch is set to the text syllabically. Upper- and lower-neighbor tones are also set syllabically. Some songs have actual sequences that repeat three or more times at different pitch levels, whereas others repeat them only twice (see ex. 5.1, chorus).

A basic feature of song is that sensual qualities like repetition, rhyme, pitch, or duration are augmented to transform the intonation and rhythms of speech into melody (see Roseman 1991:148). The *hívő énekek* mix elements of enhanced speech with *magyar nóta* and *verbunkos* motives. Some *hívő énekek* use speech rhythms and repeat notes within the interval of a minor third. Others mix steps and small leaps, some of which serve as appogiaturas. Motives associated with instrumental music like the *verbunkos* idiom are often difficult to execute vocally, but the entire congregation seemed to perform the *hívő énekek* with ease.[3] Occasionally the melody lines of the songs incorporate large leaps ranging from a fifth to an octave. Because these are rare, they carry more expressive valence; the singers usually gave additional energy to the leaps, manifesting as an increase in volume. Some of the large leaps are part of harmonically functional cadence patterns. The combination of speech qualities and *magyar nóta*/*verbunkos* motives could deeply involve a congregation in a song performance. Once when he was evangelizing Brother Gál sang "Egy nap az égboltra felnéz mindenki" (One Day Everyone Will Look up into the Heavens), a song by Váradi (ex. 5.2). In Gál's rendition the verse lines are modal and the chorus lines are in minor tonality. The first four lines of the verse are declamatory in character, winding around narrow intervals. Brother Gál emphasized this by singing in speech rhythms. The chorus, beginning at a higher pitch range, includes a diminished triad and other chord outlines. The last two lines of the verse and of the chorus are musically identical. They are comprised of a cadential pattern incorporating a turn figure and outlining a first-inversion dominant chord. This set of motives evokes *magyar nóta* and confirms a harmonic basis for this portion of the melody. Even though they did not know the song, the audience began singing along with these lines after the

EXAMPLE 5.2. "Egy nap az égboltra felnéz mindenki" (One Day Everyone Will Look up into the Heavens). Verse 2 and chorus. Brother Gál and assembly, Berettyóújfalu, January 1991.

first repetition. The participants were Romungre, but their singing resembled a Vlach Rom style, where the group participates by joining in at the ends of musical phrases (see Kovalcsik 1981).

One day everyone will look up to the heavens
One day when he comes.
One day they will recognize his holy face
That he is the great savior.
One day he will judge like a true judge
The humble, dear, faithful redeemer.

> *Egy nap az égboltra felnéz mindenki,*
> *Egy nap mikor jönni fog Ő.*
> *Egy nap a szent arcát meg fogják ismerni,*
> *Hogy Ő a nagy üdvözítő.*
> *Egy napon ítél majd, mint igaz bíró,*
> *A szelíd, kedves, hű Megváltó.*

Sometime in your life he will come too.
You might have been happy until now.
He who calls through the blue clouds
Will be your redeemer, yours.
If you can cry one day, in tears
Peace [will] move into your heart.

> *Egy nap az életedben is majd eljön,*
> *Oly boldog lehetsz ideig.*
> *Aki átszól a kék felhőn,*
> *Megváltód lesz, a tiéd.*
> *Ha egy nap sírni tudsz, könnyek között,*
> *Béke a szívedbe költözött.*

One day everyone will look up to the heavens
One day when he comes.
One day they will recognize his holy face
That he is the great savior.
One day if the last hour comes
If the trumpet sounds.

> *Egy nap az égboltra felnéz mindenki,*
> *Egy nap mikor jönni fog Ő.*
> *Egy nap a szent arcát meg fogják ismerni,*
> *Hogy Ő a nagy üdvözítő.*
> *Egy nap, ha eljön az utolsó óra,*
> *Ha megszólal a trombita.*

One day everyone will look up to the heavens
One day when he comes.
One day they will recognize his holy face
That he is the great savior.
And the dead will rise at the sound of the call,
If the Lord calls: "Come home."

> *Egy nap az égboltra felnéz mindenki,*
> *Egy nap mikor jönni fog Ő.*

> *Egy nap a szent arcát meg fogják ismerni,*
> *Hogy Ő a nagy üdvözítő.*
> *A holtak is fölkelnek a hívó szóra,*
> *Ha hív' az Úr: „Jöjj haza!"*

Chorus:
> All, all the many stars will fall from the sky
> Everything beautiful will pass from the earth
> If the last hour comes one day,
> If the trumpet sounds.

> *Az égről a sok csillag mind, mind lehull,*
> *Földön mi szép volt, minden elmúl,*
> *Egy nap, ha eljön az utolsó óra,*
> *Ha megszólal a trombita.*

Emotional and Spiritual Intensity

Believers evaluated singing primarily in terms of whether it was *áldásos* (having blessing); that is, to what degree it brought down the Holy Spirit. There were additional markers of this feeling besides speaking in tongues. When I remarked that everyone seemed to sing very emotionally, a young believer explained to me that some situations related in the songs were important because the members of the congregation had experienced (*átélt*) them. Nuances of this intensity were apparent one Sunday morning during the prayer hour when the believers sang one of the songs by Gusztáv Váradi, "Kopogtat egy hang" (A Voice Is Knocking). This song includes several properties of Hungarian popular music. A minor sixth just before the tonic note at the end of the verse outlines a first-inversion dominant chord. The descending tetrachord that begins and concludes the song is a motive that permeates Hungarian popular song (see Sárosi 1978[1971]:151–88). The congregation started singing somewhat softly but in moderately strong chest voices. With succeeding held notes and then the chorus's movement to an upper register and a change of key, many members of the congregation sang in a more open and ringing vocal tone. On the chorus lines, Sister Annus and other women began to deliver some words as a combination of singing and outcry. When the chorus repeated, the singers slid downward through small leaps in the melody on such phrases as "to sing with joy" (*örömmel énekelni*). When they repeated the verse, some singers emphasized the word *Jézus* with an extra push of air from the diaphragm. The congregation repeated the song a number of times and stopped singing after they reached a second ending to the chorus, which they had sung softly and with a dark tone (ex. 5.3).

> A voice is knocking on the door of your heart
> And it says, "You are already mine."
> My Jesus Christ, redeemer king,
> Who has already stepped into your heart.

> *Kopogtat egy hang a szíved ajtaján,*
> *És így szól: „Te az enyém vagy már."*
> *Jézus Krisztusom, a megváltó király,*
> *Aki szívedbe lépett már.*

EXAMPLE 5.3. "Kopogtat egy hang" (A Voice Is Knocking). IG congregation, Szigetvár, December 1990.

Chorus:

>   He knows every thought, he knows every pain
>   Because he loves you, just pay attention to him
>   He teaches whoever has accepted him like a child
>   It is a pleasure for you to serve the Lord, the redeemer king.
>   To sing with joy, I thank him for everything,
>   I am thankful that the redeemer king discovered me.

>>   *Ő tudja minden gondolatot, Ő tudja minden fájdalmat* [sic],
>>   *Mert szeret Ő, csak figyelj rá!*
>>   *Aki Őt elfogadta, gyermekként így tanítja*
>>   *Szeretni szolgáld az Urat, a megváltó király*
>>   *Örömmel énekelni! Köszönök mindent neki.*
>>   *Köszönöm azt, hogy rámtalált a megváltó király.*

This song performance illustrates how a variety of vocal tones could indicate emotional and spiritual intensity, correlating sometimes to points of musical structure. This was not due to technical demands; it occurred in some songs with less than an octave range. Congregation members frequently sang parts of songs with a full or open vocal tone. This could occur not only on held notes, in the chorus, and high notes but also when a section was repeated. In addition to the open tone, there were several other ways of producing sound in a high tessitura; all seemed to indicate added spiritual energy. Congregation members used an intense forced tone with some notes high in their vocal ranges. This did not always correspond with a song's technical difficulty but rather indicated the situation of sensory bombardment that seemed to help the Holy Spirit to come down on the congregation. The forced tone was one of the qualities that caused sound waves to reverberate, intensify, and bombard our senses in the small worship halls. In semiprivate contexts, some men employed a contrasting light tenor voice. Gál demonstrated a song using this vocal tone when he once discussed with me how he would persuade other Roma to convert by evoking the sadness of their outcast condition.

Many congregation members incorporated elements of speech in their singing. Women sometimes uttered the highest pitches with a tone that was like an outcry. Accents from the diaphragm gave words like *Jézus* a sobbing sound. The singers used crisp pronunciation in parts of songs that were significant, either from the point of view of the text or the musical structure. A line of the song "My Jesus of Nazareth" addresses the listeners: "Come, come come, do not fear." The congregations crisply enunciated the [y] sounds that began the first two syllables of the word *jöjjetek* (come)—adding a sort of pleading intensity to the word and thereby emphasizing the dotted rhythms of the melody (ex. 5.1, chorus). Speechlike sounds intensified elements of the songs that resembled prayers or sermons. In his performance of "One Day Everyone Will Look up into the Heavens" Gál began to speak several words in the text as the themes progressed in intensity from a general statement about the Last Judgment to the rising of the dead. On a return to the first verse of the song, Gál interspersed speech tones and then moved into a formal prayer sequence that expanded on the ideas of the song, pausing between each sentence:

>   Praise to you, Jesus.
>   Thank you for coming on the clouds of the sky, Jesus of Nazareth.

You will take your people with you out of misery, out of sin.
So we bless your precious works.
We praise your holy name, my Lord. Thank you, wondrous Jesus.
Halleluia, halleluia, halleluia.[4]

This style of enhanced speech is in reverse sequence from one customarily employed by African-American preachers, where preaching moves first into chantlike utterances and then into song (see Rosenberg 1970). Gál's rendition reflects the logocentric orientation of Pentecostalism in Hungary, where music is an adjunct to preaching.

The believers altered pitches in many ways at textual and structural points of importance in the songs. Some pitch glides occurred on meaningful words like "Jesus" or "heart." Others correlated to motivic material. In "A Voice Is Knocking" some congregation members added a pitch slide on a descending third where the word was simply "to sing." They anticipated stepwise motion with slides that used extra breath and diaphragm support (ex. 5.3, m.19). Other shifts of pitch created from the diaphragm resembled sobbing. Some occurred as free tones before the main pitch; others were placed after the main pitch with a light glottal stop that resembled the soblike *krekhts* of east European Jewish cantillation. In her performance of the last verse of "One Day Everyone Will Look up into the Heavens," Gusztáv Váradi's sister Kati sang the line "If you can cry one day" (*Ha egy nap sírni tudsz*) straightforwardly, but then on the next line she added soblike sounds to the words "into your heart" (*szívedbe*) and "has moved" (*költözött*). The singers often added upper neighbor ornaments to held notes. Sometimes this ornament followed melodic movement that resembled it; in "A Voice Is Knocking," church members placed upper neighbor ornaments immediately after a suspension in the first line of the verse (ex. 5.3, m. 2). Another technique added a sense of drama. The singers changed registers in what Hungarian folk song scholars have called an "octave break" (*oktávtörés*), a common technique in Romani secular music (Kovalcsik 1985:30–32).[5] Brother Gál included octave breaks in the chorus of "One Day Everyone Will Look up to the Heavens" so that the resulting melodic line had large leaps and an angular contour. The Romani singers often sang the initial version of a melody line with octave leaps and used a more consistent low register for later verses.

The episodic pacing given by these register changes, like the cyclical flow of energy emanating from modal structure in the *hívő énekek*, is an alternative to functional harmony's procedure of tension and release. In art music, register change is a device to add drama. The octave breaks as used by these singers provided surges of tension rather than a gradual buildup. Pitch slides or changes in vocal tone also injected waves of expression. The songs lacked the deliberate lead to climax and denouement that is associated with art music or commercial popular song. They may have included motives associated with instrumental music, but the many elements of speech in the *hívő énekek*, aided by modal writing, intuitively followed an ebb and flow of emotion.

Romani Elements in the *hívő énekek*

Since most of the new songs that the church members favored as a congregation had been composed by Roma and it was they who performed the music most often, I asked several composers in what way their songs might be related to their ethnic background. Brother Gál explained that his songs were part of the mandate from God to evangelize to fellow Roma. But other composers saw a more tenuous connection between their songs and secular Romani music. In an interview with Brother Rokkó, the guitar player and preacher from Ózd, I asked about the respect Roma have for music. Did this make it significant that leaders in the Ózd congregation were also instrumental musicians? In his answer, Brother Rokkó reacted to my ethnic reference rather than to the topic of music. He defined himself and his family as Gypsies but not with any unique characteristics.

> R: I'm a little bit troubled because I have never looked at racial [*faji*] differences of Gypsy and Hungarian—never. Only at people. We have a very good saying that the person who is Gypsy by birth is not a Gypsy; a Gypsy is also a person who behaves like one. I don't know if you understand that.

> BRL: So you would not accept being called a Gypsy because this means something bad.

> R: No . . . I too am a Gypsy by birth, but by that fact itself neither my parents nor I were raised in a way that we would know that we are Gypsies. Do you understand? So we don't speak the Gypsy language . . . we don't even know the Gypsy language. Another thing is that we went to school properly, we work properly, we work the proper way, we have an orderly home. I have only seen the backward Gypsy peoples who live in *putrik* on TV—do you know what a *putri* is? With those people the Gypsy tradition still lives, you know the language and different customs of a Gypsy nature. I am completely withdrawn from these, but not because I deny my nationality, but because I didn't grow up in this. I was born in a city, I grew up in a city, and no one put me down as a Gypsy. It's precisely my conduct, my nature, and the fact that we—already my parents—could integrate.

At this point, I apologized for having offended him, and Brother Rokkó explained his point further.

> R: I don't deny my ancestry. On the other hand I don't like the general problem that people assert and generalize about people who are no longer in that circle that they are backward Gypsy people. They might have more education, work properly, and from a material standpoint have everything they need, that is, they don't live in the *putri*. But it must be said that those people who are in the situation of not having integrated to this society are the greater proportion of Gypsies. That's why they condemn the Gypsies. They put the more proper Gypsies under the same umbrella [*egy kalap alá*]. Do you understand? I'm not offended, but because of this I do withdraw myself from this a bit.

Brother Rokkó's reaction showed several understandings and uses of the word *cigány*. One is based on ancestry, another on behavior, and another on language, and a fourth is a generalization by outsiders that combines all these properties. When speaking with Roma in Hungary during the early 1990s, I tried to employ the most common expression to identify them—that is, the word *cigány* with a neutral tone of voice and relaxed expression. In an interview with the composer Gusztáv Váradi I used the word *cigány*. But I was not completely at ease in Hungarian, so this gave the word a tone that was not casual enough. I learned over the course of the following months that I could modify my tone with a compound form. In an interview with József Gál that I completed toward the end of fieldwork, I used the term *cigány nemzetiség* (Gypsy nationality), a designation that was overly polite but at least did not have pejorative connotations. In Váradi's reply to my much earlier question, he politely voiced impatience with the differentiation it seemed I had made.

BRL: In your opinion, do you think there is a special Hungarian or Gypsy style in your songs?

GV: No, I don't think that it's possible to know in this if a Gypsy or a Hungarian wrote this song. I think that the stylistic characteristics that are characteristic of the Gypsies were lacking from them. Perhaps it resembles them in one way that, what do I know, it would be possible to conclude that a Gypsy wrote and composed this. Perhaps just its meaning [*értelmesség*] (*sic*). Because I do feel somehow that, what do I know, it is possible, if I'm correct, that the Gypsies have more spirit and heart with regard to music. So if we hear nonprofessionals sing, Gypsies and separately Hungarians, but not musicians, I would emphasize that with Gypsies perhaps the only difference is that they sing from their heart, and the others just sing. . . . These melodies didn't get written concretely for Gypsies. Not for skin [color]. The person is most important. I absolutely reject finding differences between races. Because if everyone really, in truth, loved God as they should, they would not differentiate between human beings, because we all come from God. That is, we are one. We're human.

These observations demonstrate something about the conditions of the early 1990s. Whereas many Roma, like Brother Rokkó's family, were integrated to some degree into the economy, both he and Váradi commented on how the media made negative judgments about Roma. Brother Rokkó's remarks show a sense of Romness in family orientation. He differentiated between this and a set of negatively valenced "Gypsy" traits, whereas for Brother Gál obvious Gypsy characteristics could be positive as a means of drawing a community of potential converts. Váradi's comments indicate that it might be possible to discern a particular intensity of feeling in the music. Sister Annus, who had chaperoned me to his interview, concurred by interjecting "Amen" in response to his comment about spirit and heart.

Hívő énekek belong to a style of music that some Roma call Gypsy *nóta* (*cigánynóta*). Gypsy *nóta* includes both secular music and *hívő énekek*, and it resembles Hungarian popular song.[6] Ferenc Csók, a Magyar who worked as a village disc jockey, was familiar with the *hívő énekek* and thought that they were virtually the same as *presszó rock* (coffee-bar rock), music that was played in local village and town bars for listening (see Lange 1996b). But I had become aware that Gypsy *nóta* was subtly different from such Hungarian popular music. A circular definition reflected this; one acquaintance defined *cigánynóta* as "the *nóta* of the Gypsy people." *Nóta* was the most casual of the Hungarian terms for song, and when used alone applied to music that people sang and heard in domestic or neighborhood contexts.[7]

As Romungre, the composers of *hívő énekek* and the greatest proportion of the church members had orientations as Roma that were not always obvious. Whereas the more culturally separate Vlach and Boyash Roma often identified with music in their home languages, Romungre saw a range of music as having to do with them. Most of this music was marked as "Gypsy" for non-Rom audiences. One such genre, *cigánydal* ("Gypsy song"), was related to *magyar nóta* and was recorded by professional singers with stereotypes of Gypsy vocal tone, dress, and movement. It had *csárdás*-like motives, rhythms, and structure and often included textual references to Gypsies. Romungre appreciated, learned, and performed *folklór* songs in the Boyash or Romani languages that were accompanied by acoustic guitar, water jug percussion, spoons, and vocables (Lange 1997a). Framing marks violin music, *folklór* music, and *cigánydal* as something "Gypsy" for outsiders. Framing draws the attention of the audience to a performance through metacommunicative features (Bauman 1977). Elements like virtuoso playing, extreme rubato, and the harmonic minor scale communicated an exotic or flamboyant-seeming "Gypsiness" (see Kodály 1960:6; Sárosi 1986:153).

Gypsy *nóta* is somewhat different from these musics. Its performance is often unframed. A typical occasion when I heard Gypsy *nóta* occurred once when I was waiting for the bus by the side of the road with some Romani acquaintances. A young man began singing a song I had heard echoing from cassette players in a number of courtyards, "Jaj, de *shukar* ez a cigánylány" (Oh, This Gypsy Girl Is Pretty). Several other young men joined in during the third and fourth lines. But no one, not even they, paid much attention; instead people rapidly shifted their attention from me to a baby that one of the women was carrying and then to an elderly man who asked what they were going to do in town. Where Gypsy *nóta* recordings were played for sale, they were also unframed, forming part of the general soundscape of open-air marketplaces. Cassette sellers played this music alongside *presszó* rock, "wedding rock" favored by the Hungarian working class, and other kinds of popular music that came from the mainstream media. Gypsy *nóta* melodies also were not identified as such in the formal church setting. When believers sang versions of these songs with sacred texts in church, they commented only on the nature of the texts, leaving many Magyar believers unaware of the secular analogs.[8]

Roma identified with various signs in Gypsy *nóta*. In response to my queries about whether a given song could be considered Gypsy *nóta*, the most frequent observation was that the text was about a Gypsy girl. Sometimes the reference was explicit, as in a line from the popular song "Sosana": "You left me long ago, Gypsy girl." The songs sporadically included Romani loan words. "Oh, This Gypsy Girl Is Pretty" used the Romani word for pretty, *shukar*. Other Romani acquaintances were sensitive to the pronunciation styles that they heard from some performers. Brother Babos explained that they heard singers' Gypsy backgrounds in their speech. Although this was a positive value in Gypsy *nóta*, the Romani believers judged what they heard as "Gypsy" characteristics in their own speech quite negatively. They criticized the style of one of the most inspired Romani preachers because in their view his voice was hoarse and his pronunciation unclear. One young believer, Rózsi, said that she wished she could pronounce words as clearly as I could.[9] Whether negatively or positively valenced, these readings by Roma demonstrated how with interpretive acts they constituted themselves as a community (Fish 1976).

Gypsy *nóta* melodies mostly use the minor key, although in vernacular performance sometimes the sixth and seventh scale degrees are lowered to aeolian mode. Some songs consist of verse only, often with recurring musical lines, and others utilize the *couplet*-chorus structure. Most songs utilize first and second endings. Many melodies outline chords. They include more motivic material from *magyar nóta* than contemporary Hungarian popular song, with metricized turns and versions of the three-note cadence. Other standard components include metricized upper and lower neighbor tones and sequencelike motive series. "Őrülten szeretlek téged" (I Love You Madly), sung for me by several adolescent girls, uses the aeolian pitch set except for cadences, where the sixth and seventh step are raised to create melodic minor. The verse structure includes an internal repeat. There are metrical turns on most lines, and a cadence figure is stretched out rhythmically. The girls rendered the song partly in parlando style rather than with a regular rhythmic pulse (ex. 5.4).

> I love you madly
> I can't live without you.
> I don't know what tomorrow will bring
> I believe you will always wait for me.
>
> > *Őrülten szeretlek téged,*
> > *Nem tudok élni nélküled.*
> > *Nem tudom, mit hoz majd a holnap,*
> > *Hiszem, hogy mindig vársz még rám.*

Gypsy *nóta* singers used fewer details of expression than did the singers of *hívő énekek*. Male performers sang in a high, husky tenor voice. The singers swooped up to pitches from below and interjected gasplike breaks (both techniques were used by the girls in "I Love You Madly"). The accompaniment on Gypsy *nóta* recordings was more complicated than that for *hívő énekek*. It was functionally harmonic and utilized many of the Latin rhythm options and special effects available on synthesizers. The forms and motives of *hívő énekek* are more varied and irregular than in Gypsy *nóta*. The Gypsy *nóták* (pl.) and the *hívő énekek* have similar ranges, but the Gypsy *nóták* do not use a high tessitura for choruses. Use of major keys and high-tessitura choruses may show the effects of gospel hymnody on the *hívő énekek*. Both Gypsy *nóták* and *hívő énekek* include motives from *magyar nóta/verbunkos* to an approximately equal degree. Chord outlines and prima volta–secunda volta forms are more

EXAMPLE 5.4. "Őrülten szeretlek téged" (I Love You Madly). Kati Orsós and friends, Hetvehely (recorded in Szolnok), May 1991.

common in the Gypsy *nóták* than in *hívő énekek*, possibly indicating that *magyar nóta* has greater influence in the secular genre. The *hívő énekek* include far more speechlike motives and large leaps than do Gypsy *nóták*.

Since Gypsy *nóták* sound so similar to Hungarian popular song, their musical markers may signify an orientation toward Roma simply in a tendency to include more *magyar nóta* and *verbunkos* motives. The texts are more clearly marked. A particular quality of sadness and nostalgia permeates the texts of Gypsy *nóta*, perhaps reflecting the intensity of feeling to which Gusztáv Váradi referred. The recordings of one southwest Hungarian group, the Csóré Duó, were very popular with young Roma. None of their songs with which I was familiar made any overt reference to Roma. However, on their recordings the group included occasional cafe standards, like a *csárdás* by the *verbunkos* composer Márk Rózsavölgyi, for electric guitar. A large number of Gypsy *nóta* songs, including those by the Csóré Duó, are about failed relationships. The Csóré Duó songs include nostalgic lyrics like "Yesterday . . . We gazed at the falling snow / [Now] everything has become empty." Such lines parallel the ethos in other popular songs that Roma identified as Gypsy *nóta*, including a statement in the song "Sosana": "You left me a long time ago now, Gypsy girl / Since then it is bleak everywhere." This quality of emotion moved Roma even to hear internationally famous pop songs as speaking to them. The first time I heard the Gypsy *nóta* term I was traveling by bus with some Roma on an excursion to a folk festival. My seatmate, a Boyash from a small town near Pécs, sang a number of Boyash songs and other music from the stereotyped *cigánydal* genre. Then he sang a Hungarian translation of "Those Were the Days, My Friend," and many other people on the bus joined in. As we finished, a woman exclaimed, "You sang a Gypsy *nóta*! Really!" The most common themes in Gypsy *nóta* of failed romantic love or the dead mother have an unreal and sentimental quality. But as the narratives of Brother Gál and other musicians related in previous chapters illustrate, Roma had experienced many real disruptions since World War II. By dwelling on broken relationships, Gypsy *nóták* seemed to bring up more emotion for my Romani acquaintances than the idealizations of life in nature, uninhibited celebration, or brotherhood that dominate their genres for outsiders.

The believers' song texts often responded to Gypsy *nóták*, thus sanctifying the secular texts in the church members' view. A small number of *hívő énekek* consisted of sacred texts set to actual Gypsy *nóta* melodies. In some cases, these texts were completely different. Others were rejoinders to Gypsy *nóták*. The secular text of a Csóré Duó song begins "Why couldn't I meet with you?" The *hívő ének* (sing.) to the same melody asserts "It's so good that I met you [Jesus]." These texts substitute certainty for the ruptured relationships in the secular texts. This optimism may come from U.S. religious influence; Peter Stromberg has argued that upon conversion U.S. Evangelicals begin to construct positive knowledge from contradictory and disturbing modes of communication (1993:120–21). A version of this strategy is evident in the Roma's rejoinders to Gypsy *nóta* texts.

Many of the *hívő énekek* utilize the phraseology of romantic love not in relationship to a human, as in Gypsy *nóta*, but in relationship to God. With Victorian imagery and phraseology, this is already present in gospel hymn translations and is not unusual in Christian pop translations. The *hívő énekek* often mix romantic love language with biblical motifs. One of Gusztáv Váradi's songs begins with a stock phrase from secular pop by implying a lover's relation to Jesus. An elision of the lost sheep and prodigal son parables from the Gospel of Luke follows. The song's chorus mixes standard expressions from Hungarian love songs with motifs of the last judgment.

> I think of you with longing
> My loving good Father
> Your lost sheep
> Has found its way back to you.
>
>> *Vágyakozva gondolok reád,*
>> *Szerető jó Atyám,*
>> *Egy eltévedt bárányod*
>> *Hozzád visszatalált.*
>
> Every candle has burned down
> My Jesus, we await you
> Send your blessing from heaven
> Look down upon us.
>
>> *(ha) Minden gyertya csonkig égett már,*
>> *Jézusom, várunk rád.*
>> *Áldásod küldjed a mennyből,*
>> *(és) Tekints le ránk!*

Chorus:
> Think of me, think of me
> My savior God
> Trumpets and heavenly wonders
> Signal your return.
>
>> *Gondolj majd rám, gondolj majd rám,*
>> *Én megváltó Istenem.*
>> *A harsonák, az égi csodák,*
>> *(hogy) Jelzik a jöveteled.*

The *hívő énekek* do not dwell on failed relationships as do the Gypsy *nóta* texts, but they do voice uncertainty in a subtle way. The romantic love sentiment, as the preceding song text illustrates, does not culminate in a stable relationship to God. A number of song texts express fear about really having a permanent relationship with Jesus. The speaker in "My Jesus of Nazareth" pleads "My Jesus, my Jesus, don't abandon me." One of Miklós Lukács' songs asks: "Don't leave me down in the deep / Because I have lost you." Gusztáv Váradi's song "One Day Everyone Will Look up into the Heavens" evokes the greatest degree of uncertainty about the day of judgment. Some songs from the U.S. gospel tradition, like "John the Revelator," discuss those events from a detached third-person point of view. Váradi's song takes the view of people on earth. Through the use of litany, the song's verses move from a general depiction of the day of judgment to direct address, reminding the listener about the personal accounting that Pentecostals believe will occur (ex. 5.2). In principle, conversion and sanctification guarantee a place in heaven. In fact, one of the best-known *hívő énekek* asserts: "I am a Gypsy, it doesn't bother me / Jesus is coming for me." But many Romani believers were in doubt as to whether God would truly judge them worthy of heaven. Brother István encouraged the people he had personally persuaded to convert to follow behavioral codes that were more strict than those advocated by the IG, explaining to me that he wanted to be absolutely sure that they got into heaven.

The *hívő énekek* include more speech conventions common among Roma than do Gypsy *nóták*. One of Váradi's songs, "I Saw Him in Light," mixes happy and sorrowful emotions with references to a vision, conversion, the crucifixion, and the power of Jesus' name. This mixture of themes resembles the folk song texts of Vlach Roma in its loose construction. László Szegő, one of the first scholars to examine the latter texts in depth, commented that lines, periods, and stanzas seem to be connected by chance (Szegő 1977:294). The mixture of references allows listeners and performers to construct a flexible taste horizon by emphasizing different themes that are present in a song. When Váradi and his sister sang "I Saw Him in Light" during his interview with me, they emphasized certainty and happiness with a light vocal tone, lilting tempo, slight rubato, and pitch slides in the chorus. Brother Misi suggested that the Szigetvár congregation sing the same song on Maundy Thursday, probably because of its references to the crucifixion. On that occasion, the congregation sang at a slow parlando tempo with subdued vocal delivery.

> I saw him in light, his beautiful glance
> And I saw that he was very sad.
> At that time I didn't know why blood flowed from his heart
> And why there were wounds on his holy hands.
>
> > *Fényben láttam meg Őt, gyönyörű szép tekintetét,*
> > *S láttam, hogy nagyon szomorú.*
> > *Akkor nem tudtam szívéből miért folyik vér,*
> > *S miért van seb szent kezén.*
>
> Jesus is his holy name, I can't exist without him anymore
> I owe him eternal thanks.
> There is no word that is more beautiful, Jesus is so good
> He loves me and expects me to come.
>
> > *Jézus a szent neve, nélküle már nem létezem,*
> > *Örök hálával tartozom.*
> > *Nincs is szebb szó, Jézus oly jó,*
> > *Szeret és vár nagyon.*

The audience or the composer can also construct an autobiographical narrative with cryptic references. The organ player Brother Rudi had gotten one song; although its text was comprised of standard phrases I heard in preaching and testimony, he said it was about his past as a nonbeliever and what he felt God had done for him.

RA: Once I was at home, and as I was reading the Holy Word, every word came automatically, entirely out of thought, into my ears. At that time, it wasn't apparent that it would become a song.

BRL: I see. So it happened suddenly?

RA: Suddenly into my thoughts. I don't know from where, because I am not a composer, that is, I got it completely from God. I wrote it down and afterward it was my project that that we should present this text that I got, my spirit, in some sort of melody and sing it in the congregation. Let me tell you this part of the text about my repentance, when I would have liked to repent and accept God, how I wanted to stand before God. When I took the pencil and the pen it came into my mind that I would like to have been delivered, and I asked God, "Free me of my sins, Jesus, because my sins have swept me into the depths, which is darkness." And then I got a further thought, "I plunged into great darkness / Jesus Christ, you save me." And then afterward, I waited a bit, and again came "I don't want to live for the world," because at that time I was young, twenty-eight years old. But nevertheless the thoughts came that "I want to be the child of Jesus Christ, I want to leave off my sins, I want to start with a pure heart. When Jesus comes for us, let us not be afraid, because joy will take us away where Jesus will be with us forever."

Brother Rudi's autobiographical interpretation resembles the way Vlach Roma composed and read meaning into songs. Songs had the most meaning for the community that knew the singer's personal history (Kertész-Wilkinson 1992; Kovalcsik 1991:46–52); similarly, the many audience members who knew Brother Rudi's personal history could impute a deep meaning to his text's formulaic statements and recall his dramatic conversion.

The *hívő ének* texts reveal a blurred boundary between self and group that is characteristic of many Roma I know. This sense was reflected in everyday speech; Éva, wife of Brother Babos, often started a sentence by stating her individual opinion but concluded it with reference to a group action. Many *hívő énekek* contain shifts in midsentence, as with Váradi's line "My Jesus, we await you." A single verse of a song by Miklós Lukács switches several times between the first person plural and singular, mostly with the use of possessives.

> My Lord Jesus, you are the Messiah
> O my precious Jesus, oh do not leave me
> If our end comes, save our lives
> So that we can live with you forever.
>
> > *Úr Jézus Krisztusom, te vagy a Messiás,*
> > *Ó, drága Jézusom, ó, ne hagyj el!*
> > *Ha jön a végünk, mentsd meg az életünk,*
> > *Hogy örökké veled élhetünk* [sic].

Even as believers attributed the composing of songs to the Holy Spirit, their Romani cultural background also played a part. Improvisation and formulaic construction, two processes in Romani secular music, are paralleled in divine song composition. Romungro instrumentalists had traditionally improvised to a limited degree (Sárosi 1986:152–54); improvisational skills were honed to the greatest degree in everyday speech contexts. Michael Stewart's comment that Vlach Roma "who talk well and amusingly, and can fire back wit quicker than they receive joking insults are more widely respected than quiet, withdrawn figures" is equally true for the other Roma I know (Stewart 1989:94). I found it remarkable how early people developed this skill. The Boyash Rom neighbor of Sister Éva had a series of teasing sessions with her eleven-year old daughter Moni, insisting that she was ready to be his bride. In a series of challenges where each response augmented the tension and emotion of the previous statement, Moni asked whether he had the right clothes and told him to name the date and place of the wedding. Éva left Moni to fend for herself and was amused by the whole proceeding.

Hívő énekek as Religious Language

Enthusiastic Christian speech forms, because they rely on spontaneous inspiration in the form of the Holy Spirit, have many improvisational characteristics. Some follow the strict oral-formulaic style outlined for epic poetry by Albert Lord and Milman Parry. African Americans' chanted sermons use the regular meter and stock expressions of oral formulas (Rosenberg 1970:5). The *hívő énekek* and other speech forms in the IG did not have this degree of regularity. They had been influenced not by African Americans but by white Evangelicals, whose speech utilizes many stock expressions and sometimes resembles metrical chant but cannot be said to achieve the consistency of oral formula (see Titon 1988:278–88). The *hívő énekek* used the stock phrases from other forms of religious language in the congregation that were linked closely with U.S. styles.[10]

The Bible is a primary source of phraseology for the songs, as it is for enthusiastic Christian speech forms in the United States. Sacred song texts, ranging from the gospel hymns through other *hívő énekek*, provide only a minor source of expressions.[11] Most of the biblical motifs in the *hívő énekek* come from the Psalms, the Gospel of Matthew, and the book of Revelation. One song explores the metaphor of the "narrow way" in Matthew 7:14 that church leaders exhorted believers to follow. Several of József Gál's songs include the image of the kingdom of God. Although most of Váradi's song "One Day Everyone Will Look up into the Heavens" is expressed in everyday language, it includes words like "firmament" (*égbolt*) and the chorus line "when the trumpet sounds" (*ha megszólal a trombita*), which clearly reference the book of Revelation. These elements also echo the language of the Hungarian Pentecostals' version of the Bible in a situation analogous to that of the King James Bible for many American believers. Church members often asserted that the seventeenth-century Károlyi translation they used was more authentic and more beautiful than the newer Hungarian Bible translations of the mainstream denominations—an opinion shared in fact by a number of Hungarian Protestants, since over one hundred editions of the Károlyi Bible had been issued (Bucsay 1985:94). The most common theme for paraphrase in the songs is the idea that Jesus died so that man could have eternal life. A number of lines in the songs personalize the metaphor of being cleansed by Jesus' blood that appears in Revelation: "His precious blood has cleansed me"; "Purify me with your precious blood." The idea of the cleansed heart, important to believers because of Jesus' words in Matthew 5:8 assuring that the "pure in heart" will "see God," also occurs regularly; one song by Váradi says: "O precious Jesus, you are everything to me / You love me so much that with you the sinful heart is cleansed."

Group prayer, as one of the defining Pentecostal devotions in Hungary is another source of phraseology for songs. The believers began prayer sessions by murmuring. Heard outwardly, the collective sound became cacophonous as each person spoke in a progressively more emotional way. When believers prayed passionately, the pitch of their voices became perceptibly higher. They cried out such expressions as "my Lord," often pausing to weep. Some prayer interludes were rather formal. The head preacher invited another man or woman to lead the praying, although only some of what this individual said could be heard above the group. Many *hívő énekek* include stock phrases used by prayer leaders and thus have the character of formal praying. Prayer leaders seldom used biblical language but instead tended to repeat expressions like "Halleluia" and "Thank you Jesus." These simple phrases had the effect of increasing the feeling of spiritual intensity. At one point, after some American missionaries had visited the congregation, Brother Gál began to repeat "Halleluia" as they did, in sets of three with descending intonation. I felt frustrated with what seemed to me like a mindless imitation, but when I queried him about this, Gál replied that it seemed to give more power when he spoke the words in this way. Similarly a number of songs use the single phrase "Halleluia, my Jesus," as a chorus. Many song phrases also parallel the prayer leader's speech by speaking for the group. Váradi's song "I Think of You with Longing" utilizes two prayer leader expressions when it asks "Send your blessing from heaven / Look down on us."

The prayers that I witnessed in semiprivate contexts were more emotional, intensely felt, and irregular in phraseology than the speech of prayer leaders. The song that believers attempted to perform as I described at the beginning of this chapter has references to suffering that give it an ethos of private prayer. However, it uses a public speech style. Its first line evokes sermon, with the metaphor of the "narrow way" from Matthew 7:14. The second line then moves into prayer language. In the IG, formal prayer utilized expressions like "we ask you to lead us" and "make our spirits pure." This song restates such phrases from a first-person standpoint.

> Narrow is the way that leads to you
> I ask you to reshape me.
> Cleanse my heart,
> Cleanse my soul.
>
> *Keskeny az az út, amely hozzád vezet,*
> *Formálj meg, kérlek, engemet!*
> *Tedd tisztára a lelkemet,*
> *Tedd tisztára a szívemet!*
>
> Life is stormy if you are not with me
> [Since] people always attack me.
> I just cry out to you from my heart
> And I know that you will forgive me.
>
> *Viharos az élet, ha nem vagy velem,*
> *Támadnak mindig az emberek.*
> *Szívemből csak hozzád kiáltok,*
> *S tudom azt, hogy te megbocsájtol.*

Chorus:
> I cry out to you, my Lord
> Show me the way toward you.
>
> *Kiáltok én hozzád, Uram,*
> *Mutasd meg feléd az utat!*

The plaintive tone of this song's second stanza is characteristic of prayer in a semi-private context. The comment that "people attack me" was something I heard from church members both in prayers and in everyday conversation, since nonbelievers frequently challenged their assertions of faith and their ability to follow behavioral restrictions. The line to which singers gave the most energy had performative language: "I cry out to you, my Lord." Singers evoked actual crying on this line with soblike diaphragm accents, appogiaturas, and pitch glides. This statement was doubly inscribed when it was sung rather than just spoken, revealing a correspondence to the augmented level of expression in semiprivate prayer.

Preaching and Testimony Style in the *hívő énekek*

Many *hívő énekek* shift from a personal orientation in their initial stanzas to a more general tone. Speech styles from preaching and testimony appear in these later stanzas. They include didactic language, stock phrases derived from the biblical text, exhortations, and especially references to testimony narratives. The testimony in the IG spanned many themes. In their accounts the church members described visions, encounters with nonbelievers, dreams, and healings; they also recited poetry or gave song performances. These performances were important not only for the events they related; in addition, they demonstrated the workings of divine energy. Stories about song composition served as forms of testimony. Since the Romani believers read narratives into brief references, they perceived a metacommentary about Holy Spirit experience when a *hívő ének* was performed in the context of testimony. Váradi's phrase "I saw him in light" might refer to the fact that Váradi actually did see a vision of Jesus on the cross. Another song by Váradi begins "I dreamed of the heavenly world," evoking the many dreams that believers told during testimony and interpreted as messages from the Holy Spirit.

The *hívő ének* could reinscribe the testimony event at multiple levels. "Szolgálni jöttem" (I Came to Serve), by an Ózd believer, includes in the text itself the framing statements of testimony.

I came to serve you, my Lord
To create joy in converting hearts
It is great happiness for me to serve my God
[Because] God, the certain victory, is with you.

> *Szolgálni jöttem téged, Uram,*
> *Örömet szerezni a megtérő szíveken.*
> *Nékem nagy boldogság szolgálni Istenem,*
> *[Mert] véled az Úr, a biztos győzelem.*

I came to serve because desire drove me
To pass on my beautiful song.
He loves everyone so, no matter if they have sinned,
If you sincerely repent, victory is certain.

> *Szolgálni jöttem, mert hajtott a vágy,*
> *Gyönyörű énekem adjam tovább.*
> *Ő mindenkit úgy szeret, nem baj, ha vétkezett,*
> *Ha őszintén bánod, biztos a győzelem.*

The speaker in this song text intends that her service—that is, her testimony—will have the effect of converting listeners. The audience can infer from the second verse that "my beautiful song" refers to the experience of being given a song by the Holy Spirit.

Although preaching was the major activity in the IG's services, the *hívő énekek* make the least reference to it. The IG's leaders used a variety of preaching styles, all variations on a basic sequence identified by Bruce Rosenberg for American folk preaching of citing biblical text, contextualization, and application of doctrine to the everyday situation (Rosenberg 1970:14). A standard conclusion to evangelical sermons is an exhortation to convert. The IG's preachers did not often make exhortations, but they are a consistent feature in the *hívő ének* texts. After its first stanza of prayerlike language, one variant of "My Jesus of Nazareth" is a simple exhortation: "People, people come / This name can redeem you." The song "I Came to Serve" addresses nonconverts with its last two lines about love and repentance obviating sin. Váradi's song "A Voice Is Knocking" centers on a figure of speech from preachers' exhortations, that of God knocking at the nonbeliever's heart. Like a sermon, this song elaborates on that image, explaining who knocks and that he is all-knowing.

In using formulaic language from preaching and sacred music, the *hívő énekek* follow conventions of evangelical religious speech. But this phraseology is not nearly as pervasive or emotion-filled as the language from prayer, testimony, and secular song that reflects a doubt-filled relationship with God. Sandra Sizer has shown how the Anglo-American gospel hymns incorporated a language of intimacy, arguing that this could occur because the songs gained popularity in tandem with the rise of an idealized domestic sphere (Sizer 1978:33–39, 107–10). The language of romantic love and commentary to listeners in *hívő énekek* are similar in that they come out of a familylike congregation. Studies of religious speech in the United States emphasize how they address local communities like working-class women or Appalachian residents (Lawless 1988a; Patterson 1995; Peacock and Tyson 1989; Titon 1988). *Hívő énekek* addressed the immediate community of Roma. The expressive performance of the songs emerged from an atmosphere of fervor and a feeling that the Holy Spirit was present.

6

The Politics of Nineteenth-Century Gospel Hymns

B elievers requested the song "Föl, barátim!" (Forward, My Friends) at almost every midweek service of the IG that I attended in Pécs, where many elderly Magyars were present. It is a translation of Philip Bliss's "Hold the Fort." Although no one used a musical score, the singers interspersed dotted and even rhythms in a way that was nearly congruent with Bliss's original.[1] They used heavy accents and handclaps, emphasizing many consonants and alliterative "z" sounds in the refrain line. Even though the believers sang at a very slow tempo ($\downarrow$ = 84–92), the accented words gave the song a vigorous quality that reinforced the song's dominant metaphor of faith as a military battle. At midweek meetings, I heard a large number of tunes like this that were familiar to me as nineteenth-century gospel hymns.

With their prodigious outputs, formulaic composition of both text and melody, use of advertising, and repackaging in numerous editions, the nineteenth-century gospel hymns are a form of "mass art" that predated electronic mediation (Adorno and Horkheimer 1972[1944]:124–28). They were distributed worldwide, to areas like Polynesia as well as Eastern Europe (Stillman 1993). Translated from English into numerous other languages, they became one of the first examples of "glocalization," a marketing technique whereby a product is targeted to specific populations around the world (Robertson 1992:173–74). Such a uniform style can compress disparate peoples into constituencies that cross national or ethnic boundaries. But local appropriations also occur. In Polynesia a genre of part-singing, *himeni*, resulted. Once received in Hungary, the reproduction politics of the gospel hymns was also unique to time and place. The features of the Hungarian language, the different class backgrounds of believers, censorship, and the use of religion as a means of resistance all affected the style of the gospel hymns in Hungary.

Sister Borovics once explained to me with a twist of southwest Hungarian dialect that the songs in their hymnbook were ones that "somebody got sometime [from God]" (*valaki kapta valamikor*). Indeed, most of the song texts that the older members used from a blue chapbook entitled *Hitünk énekei* (Songs of Our Faith) were printed without author attribution. Only the texts of a few other "written songs" (*írott énekek*) were typed into notebooks, contrasting with the *hívő énekek* in manuscript books. Sister Borovics's comments illustrate how for IG members the gospel hymns operated like "traces" or signifiers in a chain of reference without origin; the believers were almost completely unaware of the history of their older songs (see Derrida 1976[1967]:60). The ethnographic context thus would not seem to mandate an exhaustive investigation into the songs that I recognized as being Anglo-American gospel hymns. But a number of offhand comments and small gestures motivated me to examine their history in Hungary. With obvious care and emotion, several elderly believers showed me old hymnbooks that they kept at home and still used by themselves. Occasionally when the congregation was preparing to sing a song, Brother Horváth advised them, "This is the new text." During sermons, he sometimes said a few song lines that differed from what was in the songbook. Was he paraphrasing, or was he quoting an old text?

Jeff Titon has suggested that to analyze hymnbook contents from an ethnographic standpoint, a song's actual performance is an important guide (Titon 1988:223–24). This idea could be extended to include performance style as well as the repertoire choice to which Titon referred. The accents, volume, rubato, and pitch slides that IG members used in singing their hymnbook songs might at first seem to be related purely to the meanings of the texts, but they also had a quality of overemphasis. Writing in the 1950s, a Calvinist hymnologist, Kálmán Csomasz Tóth, advised that congregations should "free ourselves from the lisping manner of the half steps from Gypsy music and the markets" (1950:238). "Gypsy music" here refers to the *magyar nóta* accompanied by Romani string bands. These comments in no way reflect the musical styles of actual Romani believers, because churches did not accept them until the 1980s; they imply that believers were infusing sentimentality into their songs from secular music. However, I believe that IG members' performance energies also correlate with historical changes in Hungary's religious popular music. Even the fact that gospel hymns predominated in the older IG members' repertoire indicates their strong connection to the particular period of the 1920s when Pentecostalism came to Hungary.

Several factors affected how the gospel hymns and other foreign Protestant songs were received in Hungary. One is a linguistic problem identified by Bartók, Kodály, and other Hungarian folk song scholars: since the Hungarian language is accented differently from other European languages, Hungarian texts are not congruent with the rhythms and contours of non-Hungarian melodies (see Erdely 1965). As well as being introduced because of contact with the British Isles and the United States, the gospel hymns were mediated through the German-speaking areas of Europe. In England and the United States, the gospel hymns resembled secular commercial song in that melody and text had a one-to-one correspondence. However, in the first years of translation both Hungarian and German writers applied a previous Protestant music practice of using tunes as contrafacta. These openings for slippage in the text contrast with the situation for scores. Nearly all the Hungarian and German score publications replicated the four-part scores of the English-language gospel hymn publications. These scores seemed to be a small factor in the musical life of the IG because other Protestant groups with which IG had little contact had published them. The IG members had changed the gospel hymn melodies to a slight yet significant degree.

Home Mission Literature in the IG Repertoire

The translation of "Hold the Fort" came out of the home mission revival in the late nineteenth century. "Föl, barátim" was among the very first translations of gospel hymns to appear as verses in *Keresztyén*, a periodical that the Calvinist clergymen who had visited Scotland compiled in the style of Victorian evangelistic tracts (Murányi 1970). Issues of *Keresztyén* contained translations of Robert Lowry's "Shall We Gather at the River," George F. Root's "Come to the Savior, Make No Delay," and others. Over a century later, IG members were still singing some of these songs and reciting poems that originally appeared in *Keresztyén*. The historian Imre Révész comments that the style of these gospel hymns was new to East Europeans: "they created an exceptional impression with their novelties, their catchy nature, and the decidedly rousing content of their texts" (Révész 1943:24). On one occasion, the Scottish evangelist A. N. Somerville, during his only trip to Hungary, had dictated "Hold the Fort" in translation to an ad hoc choir. The local pastor reported that "after church, our believers deluged me, asking for the *English songs*" (Kálmán 1888:216, italics in original). Home mission advocates published musical booklets and two large songbooks. One of these—*Hallelujah!*—included many gospel hymn translations, original compositions, and songs designed for Sunday school and some translations of European pietist songs. At least fifteen score and text editions appeared between 1905 and 1948. One indication of this popularity was that although the Horváths had given away all of their other songbooks, Mrs. Horváth still kept her copy of *Hallelujah*.[2]

The home mission translators often came from families with a history of respected leadership within the Calvinist church. They served as pastors, bishops, or theology teachers, and as revivalists, they worked to establish religious societies, foster ecumenicism, translate tracts, and revise the Hungarian Bible. The translator of "Hold the Fort," Béla Szász, was the son of a university teacher and theologist. Mrs. Gyula Varga, also a prolific translator, was from the Szász family. Aladár Szabó, translator of Jones's "Power in the Blood" (*SSS* no. 145), founded the Bethany Society in Hungary, translated and wrote numerous tracts, and even encouraged the Hungarian Protestants to do missionary outreach. Nearly all of the home mission advocates had studied abroad and were conversant in both English and German. This training is reflected in the translations; many of them are faithful to the ideas, rhythms, and even poetic devices of the originals, while the settings match the cadences of Hungarian speech. Szabó's translation of "Power in the Blood" (mentioned in chapter 4) uses dactylic feet that in many spots correspond with a long-short-short rhythm in Jones's melody. Szász's translation of "Hold the Fort" retains the narrative direction in Bliss's song, describing an army in the midst of a battle, the struggle against Satan's forces, and a vision of ultimate triumph.[3] The Hungarian text even fits with the melodic contour. In the first verse, for example, the word "precious" (*drága*) is set so that it falls on the highest pitches and the stressed part of the beat. IG members augmented such text points with extra volume and accents (ex. 6.1).

> Forward, my friends, under the banner of precious Jesus!
> Be brave, be brave, his help gives victory!
> Trust, for Jesus is coming, he is the commander-in-chief.
> Let our lips sing: We implore you for help!

EXAMPLE 6.1. "Föl, barátim!" (Forward, My Friends). IG congregation, Pécs, November 1990.

> *Föl, barátim, drága Jézus zászlaja alatt!*
> *Bátran, bátran segedelme diadalmat ad!*
> *Bízzatok, mert Jézus eljön, Ő a Fővezér,*
> *Zengje ajkunk: hozzád esdünk segedelemért!*

Lo, Satan will break out in opposition with great rage
He faces the bravest fighters.
Trust, for Jesus is coming, he is the commander-in-chief.
Let our lips sing: We implore you for brave hearts!

> *Lám a Sátán nagy haraggal szembetörni kész!*
> *A legbátrabb harcosoknak is szemébe néz.*
> *Bízzatok, mert Jézus eljön, Ő a Fővezér,*
> *Zengje ajkunk: hozzád esdünk bátor szívekért!*

In the midst of the battle's noise our savior stands guard
Courage! He is ready to help in the battle of our hearts.
Trust, for Jesus is coming, he is the commander-in-chief.
Let our lips sing: We implore you for victory!

> *Harci zajnak közepette mentőnk résen áll!*
> *Bátorság! Ő áll segélyül szívünk harcinál!*
> *Bízzatok, mert Jézus eljön, Ő a Fővezér,*
> *Zengje ajkunk: hozzád esdünk győzedelemért.*[4]

The activities of the home mission advocates were controversial, primarily because they challenged rationalist aspects of the Calvinist religion that in Hungary were allied with national sentiment. All the way until midcentury, while the home mission advocates were promoting and publishing the gospel hymns, other clergy attacked them for introducing facile melodies and dance rhythms. One critic objected that the home mission songbooks were establishing a "superficial, sentimental religiosity." Their popularity was precisely the threat: "It is a fact that over thousands of years of church history every useless and false teaching, error and sectarianism most easily and preferably relies on the wings of catchy songs" (Sebestyén 1923:270). Such statements did not recognize the effective settings and poetic devices in the translations. However, it was possibly these elements that made the home mission songs compelling to believers. As a form of civil society, the home mission was targeted for elimination during the socialist period (see Horváth and Matolay 1980). But the IG members' energetic performances attest to how effectively the sentiments of the gospel hymns had been mediated through the home mission.

Baptist Songs

In their objections to the melodies and texts of the gospel hymns, critics had ignored another activity: some leaders were writing new texts. When I visited the IG's Romani congregation in Ózd they interspersed between *hívő énekek* a melody that I recognized as S. F. Bennett and J. P. Webster's "Sweet By-and-By" (*GH* no. 110). I was surprised at how subdued this performance was, even when the chorus rose in tessitura. There are many dotted rhythms in the Webster score, but singing by ear, the congregation utilized straight rhythms as the synthesizer and guitar played continuous eighth notes. On translating the song into English, I realized that their text differed radically from the original. The Hungarian text praises struggle and suffering, asserting the necessity for strength on the narrow way of the believer. Bennett's verses and chorus describe existence in heaven (ex. 6.2).

> There is no comfort on the pilgrim's way.
> On it are many lumps and thorns.
> It is narrow, straight, steep,
> Ah, but good, since it leads to salvation!

> *Jámborok útján nincs kényelem,*
> *Sok azon a göröngy, a tövis!*
> *Keskeny az, egyenes, meredek,*
> *Ah, de jó, hiszen az üdvre visz!*

> Your life is short in this body
> Therefore don't let it be useless!
> If you step on the true way
> Then there will be a single goal of your heart.

> *Rövid e testben az életed,*
> *Épp' azért ne legyen hasztalan!*
> *Ha igaz útra lépsz, akkoron*
> *Szívednek csakis egy célja van.*

Chorus (2x):
> Forward to heaven, straight ahead!
> Oh, it is worthwhile to struggle for it!

> *Mennybe fel egyenest!*
> *Ó! azért küzdeni érdemes!*[5]

EXAMPLE 6.2. "Jámborok útján nincs kényelem" (There Is No Comfort on the Pilgrim's Way). IG congregation, Ózd, November 1990.

This text dates from one of the first Baptist songbooks to contain gospel hymn translations, *Sion énekei* (Songs of Zion) ([Csopják] 1900 [1896]). Since the Baptist evangelizers worked first among German ethnic minorities in Hungary and then among Hungarian speakers, they had initially utilized German-language publications and Hungarian psalters. By the 1870s they began producing tracts, periodicals, and song literature in Hungarian (Bányai 1996:13–16). In the earliest Hungarian Baptist songbooks to contain gospel hymns, the tunes are treated as contrafacta; *Sion énekei* includes not only translations of the gospel hymns but more original texts written by Hungarians.[6] The practice had precedents in the Genevan psalter, which had been available in Hungarian from the beginning of the seventeenth century, and in some of the first gospel hymn treatments in German (Blankenburg 1974:517–28; Csomasz Tóth 1990:202–7).[7] In *Sion énekei* the text that the Ózd congregation sang, "Jámborok útján nincs kényelem" (There Is No Comfort on the Pilgrim's Way), appears on facing pages with the translation and score of "Sweet By-and-By," the latter designated as a contrafactum. Additional texts in this publication convey an ethos of martyrdom with lines like "To follow Jesus here, you must suffer and strive; / I feel—with the cross on my shoulders / The bumps in the road" ([Csopják] 1900(1896): no. 29). The author of these texts is not identified but probably is Attila Csopják, the chief editor. Csopják had more education than the very first Baptists and worked in Hungarian government service. Besides translating and composing song verses he edited the periodical *Békehírnök* (Peace Herald), wrote books on the history of the church, served as vice president to the national organization, and led one of the country's major congregations (Bányai 1996:52–60; Bereczki 1996:138–39). Originally composed texts like "Jámborok útján nincs kényelem" tended to be congruent with the rhythms of Hungarian speech and with melodic lines, whereas the translations were not always so. Gyula Bernhardt, an organist with a large Pentecostal church in Budapest, commented that they "come out Schwabian-like" (*svábosan jön ki*). Many

Hungarians use the word *sváb* (Schwabian) to refer generally to ethnic Germans. Here Bernhardt meant that accented notes in the melody fall on unstressed syllables and sound like German inflections to a native speaker of Hungarian.

The IG congregation and other Pentecostals drew the bulk of their song literature from two Baptist publications that were dominant at the time Pentecostalism was established in the 1920s and 1930s—*A hit hangjai* (Voices of Faith), a Baptist congregational songbook, and *Evangéliumi karénekek* (Evangelical Choir Songs), designed for choral and youth activities. These publications appear not to have been generally available like the home mission songbook *Hallelujah*, but they were important to all of the small churches in Hungary because of their close affinity with the Baptists. Both had four-voice scores; they contained many gospel hymn translations, as well as German songs in the style of gospel hymns and original compositions by Hungarians (Bányai 1996:303–4). Pentecostals also used Hungarian-American Baptist publications, reflecting how their first missionaries interacted with Baptists in the United States.[8] IG members still sang songs that bore traces of the earliest Baptists' work with uneven translations or a puritan ethos. But even by the 1890s, Baptist leaders in Hungary advocated choral training, music reading, the use of orchestral instruments, and revision of their hymnbooks. In Hungary, they are now admired for their music education system and polished choirs.

The home mission and Baptist revival activities were separated to some extent by ethnic constituency and class orientation, and so their versions of the same gospel hymn frequently diverge. The Pentecostals potentially could sing coexisting variants, since they drew from the literatures of both movements. Only one example of this occurred in the IG, with Elizabeth Prentiss and William H. Doane's "More Love to Thee, O Christ" (*GH* no. 61). At least four melodies and three different texts for this song existed in Hungary. On the most serious of occasions, like Easter week, IG members tended to sing the translation most faithful to the English, but it was unattributed and set to another melody in a minor key. At many prayer meetings, they sang a different translation crossreferenced to the Baptist hymnbook that used Doane's melody. Delinked from their corresponding melodies, such texts now seemed to be vehicles for the ethos pertaining to different religious trends. In German-speaking countries, the one-to-one correspondence of tune and text was restored with an authorized edition of the gospel hymns (Rauschenbusch and Sankey 1921[1910]). But such editions were not made for the countries on the margins of Europe, so that radically different texts became attached to melodies even as the translations of the English texts faded out of use.

The Pentecostals' Music Literature

Besides relying on music from other evangelical groups in Hungary, the Pentecostals incorporated additional gospel hymns. IG members also sang a number of original melodies that blended elements of the gospel hymns with Hungarian vernacular music. In this, their practices are similar to those of U.S. Pentecostals. From their beginnings in the United States, Pentecostals often used the song literatures of other evangelicals and set a trend of accepting popular culture that is continued in large institutions like the Assemblies of God (Larsen 1987; Duncan 1987). Delton Alford argues that Pentecostal music differs from other Christian genres because it is "emphatically spirited and spiritual in its attitude of performance. . . . The very nature of the Pentecostal outreach and ministry has lent itself to an emphasis on the gospel hymn" (Alford 1967:18,49). In the American context, early Pentecostal singing, like other aspects of worship, was fervent. This is also true for Hungary, but there such emotion resisted the rationalism of religious elites and the socialist state.

Brother Horváth recalls that the first Pentecostal songbook contained texts only. Within the first few years that Dezső Rároha and his wife worked as Assembly of God missionaries in Hungary, they reported publishing a songbook. The information in an expanded version of this songbook, *Üdvözítőnk dicséretei* (Hymns of Our Savior), dates it from preschism years of the late 1920s or early 1930s while Rároha was still working in Hungary. This songbook has 113 songs, approximately half in score, and contains almost entirely gospel hymns. Texts only are supplied for such gospel hymns as "Higher Ground," "Oh Happy Day," and "When the Roll Is Called up Yonder," implying that they were well known in Hungary at this point. The songbook utilizes varied score typefaces and tune references, demonstrating that the literature was drawn from a broad range of available publications. These included Baptist songbooks, the home mission songbooks, and at least one English-language source, *Pentecostal Power*. Many of the texts address Jesus directly, some mention the Holy Spirit, and none express a puritan sensibility. The tone of these songs certainly remained in the IG repertoire, but church members sang only a few of the texts that appear to have been the original Pentecostal contributions. There is a gap between this songbook and subsequent publications that corresponds with the World War II years.

Zengő harangok (Ringing Bells) and Sentimentality

IG members performed some gospel hymns with striking rhythmic variety and sentiment. "Bűnömet elvette Jézus" (Jesus Has Taken away My Sins), a paraphrase of the Paul Rader gospel hymn "Go!" was one such song (exs. 6.3 and 6.4).

> Jesus has taken away my sins, he died on Golgotha
> So I could win salvation with him and be his only.
>
>> *Bűnömet elvette Jézus, meghalt a Golgotán,*
>> *Hogy üdvöt nyerhessek nála s Övé legyek csupán.*
>
> His bloody struggle was hard, torture and death awaited him.
> He passed down his thorny road, knowing he would find me.
>
>> *Nehéz volt véres tusája, várt reá kín s halál,*
>> *Végigment tövises útján, tudva, hogy rám talál.*
>
> Since he opened his two pierced hands to me,
> I happily sing the song of new life to the Lord.
>
>> *Mióta felém kitárta átszegzett két kezét,*
>> *Boldogan zengem az Úrhoz új élet énekét.*
>
> When my last hour strikes and the heavenly hymn calls me,
> My body will rest silently, the tired heart will cool.
>
>> *Hogyha üt a végső órám s mennyei szózat hív,*
>> *Testem majd elpihen némán, kihűl a fáradt szív.*

EXAMPLE 6.3. "Go!" *Spiritual Songs* no. 15 (notation style replicated).

Chorus:
> I am coming to you and I'll be immersed in you,
> Precious Jesus, who brings happiness, be mine forever!

> *Jövök hozzád s elmerülök benned én,*
> *Boldogító drága Jézus, örökre maradj enyém!*[9]

IG members freely modified the song's 6/8 rhythm between verses (ex. 6.4, verses 1 and 2) and within measures. They did this by using both parlando and rubato. Parlando, or speech rhythm, is linked to the structure of the Hungarian language. Some syllables in Hungarian can be lengthened for grammatical purposes because they have long vowels or suffixes that receive doubled consonants. In the first verse and chorus

EXAMPLE 6.4. "Bűnömet elvette Jézus" (Jesus Has Taken away My Sins). Verse 1, chorus, and verse 2 line 1. IG congregation, Pécs, 1990.

of this song, the singers paused on several words with a long [æ] sound, designated in Hungarian orthography with "á." They also paused on words like "he took away" (*elvette*) that have doubled consonants.

The singers also used rubato for the sake of emotional emphasis. They lengthened words and phrases that emphasize intense communion with God: the name of Jesus, his death on Golgotha (*meghalt a Golgotán*), and a wish "that I be only his" (*Övé legyek csupán*). The chorus of the Hungarian text, "I am coming to you, I immerse myself in you," reflects a relationship with Christ that Mary De Jong, in describing the gospel hymns, has characterized as "intimate [and] subtly erotic" (1986:471). The congregation members used pitch glides at the most climactic moments of this chorus. The rubato treatment in this section clearly occurs out of sentiment. The word "I immerse myself" (*elmerülök*), for example, has no lengthened vowels or consonants. But the singers paused on the word's first syllable, as well as bending its pitch, rushed through the next two syllables, and paused again. With such rhythmic inflections, the result was a mixed sense of forward motion and pauses. This is an example of the style that the hymnologist Csomasz Tóth decried. In this he followed folk song scholars who drew a distinction between the types of rhythmic variety in Hungarian folk song and in popular songs. Bartók found a positive value in old-style Hungarian folk song. Much of it was sung parlando, in speech rhythms. He condemned the more exaggerated rubato, as well as the pitch slides of *magyar nóta*, like Csomasz Tóth attributing it to Gypsy bands; they "deformed the parlando-rubato melodies with excessive rubato and with florid, superimposed embellishments" (Bartók 1992[1921]:70).

This song comes from *Zengő harangok* (Ringing Bells), one of the two songbooks that Pentecostals published in the years immediately after World War II. A score publication of thirty-five songs, it is undated, but according to Gyula Bernhardt, it was published in approximately 1945. It is entirely in score, and the editors write in a short preface that the booklet is primarily meant for youth orchestras and choirs. Many of the scores have chord designations, indicating how guitars, mandolin orchestras, or accordions were at that time accompanying the congregations. Nearly all of the songs are urban gospel hymns. István Siroky, the leader of a large Pentecostal group at the time, indicated to me that he had written many of the texts, which are attributed with initials. One feature that distinguishes the music in this booklet from other gospel hymns in Hungary is its text paraphrases and loose translations. The texts are extremely sentimental. Attila Fábián, the current president of the Evangelical Pentecostal Fellowship, sees these as bearing the stamp of popular culture from the 1930s, contemporaneous with early Pentecostal activity in Hungary. Indeed, the style of the particular gospel hymns like "Go!" that were paraphrased reflects a parallel ethos in the United States. Copyrighted in 1918, with its reductionist chorus line, "Go!" comes from a period of gospel hymnody that used "enjoyable" melodies, stressing "lighter, optimistic" themes (Eskew and Downey 1986:251). These may have been features that originally distinguished Pentecostals' music from that of other revivalists in Hungary. At the same time, their sentimentality both in singing style and in textual content was part of the Hungarian secular popular culture of the day.

A different Pentecostal group published a far larger compilation of 546 songs in 1948. Entitled *Dicsőitlek Uram!* (I Praise You, My Lord), it contains primarily texts with crossreferences to scores in other publications—a pattern that the succeeding Pentecostal songbooks then followed.[10] This compilation draws primarily from Baptist songbooks but also from the home mission literature and references many texts directly to English hymnbook titles, among them *Elim Choruses*, *Pentecostal Power*, *Tabernacle Hymns*, and *Spiritual Songs*, indicating that a variety of gospel hymn publications had by then become available to the compilers. These were also a likely source for the melodies and text paraphrases in the *Zengő harangok* booklet. The repertoire for IG members was solidified in the 1948 edition of *DU* until the church began to attract Romani members and younger Magyars in the late 1980s. Although most of the IG's hymnbook songs can be found in *DU*, the congregation did not use it. At least one person, Sister Borovics, still kept a tattered copy and read the texts because she said it reminded her of her days as a young believer. Her relationship with *DU* was similar to how a member of the Nazarene church in Hungary would treasure his hymnbook: "This book is daily reading that he not only regards as inspired but as a certain and direct document of true faith" (Szigeti 1981:53). For many revivalists in Hungary songbooks were a focus for such private devotion. The sentimentality of the 1930s texts came to serve as a defense against repressions and rationalism.

Hymnbook Reform and Censorship

From the 1950s through the 1980s the private devotionalism in the Pentecostals' songbooks was subject to outside pressure, affected by the socialist state's efforts to rationalize the citizenry and to suppress indications that all was not well in society. In his conversations with me, Gyula Bernhardt humorously identified Pentecostal hymnbook editions from 1959 and 1965 as the "Rákosi-type" and the "Kádár-type," referring to two Hungarian heads of state. Censorship was severe and repression violent under Rákosi, the Stalinist dictator of Hungary until 1956; a milder suppression prevailed under János Kádár from the 1960s until 1988. The hymnbook at issue was *Hitünk énekei* (Songs of Our Faith), first published in 1959 to replace the previous hymnbook, *DU*.[11] The state supervised many forms of publication by subjecting them to a reading process (*lektorálás*) that combined aspects of academic review and political censorship. The outside readers saw themselves as representing the modernizing spirit of church institutions. One of their other projects had been to revise the Nazarenes' hymnbook, "demonstrating the cooperative points of view, the book's high standards, the filtering out of the dissonant sounds of the old songbook," but many of the Nazarenes resisted such changes (see Kardos and Szigeti 1988:336–38; Szigeti 1981:51). The texts had to be changed to conform to the philosophies and policies of the government. Fábián and Bernhardt indicated in their conversations with me that unlike the Nazarenes, the Pentecostal editors were willing to change some texts on the direction of these readers. They also made many changes themselves to forestall the possibility that an entire publication would be rejected for its content. In this they followed a general trend of self-censorship in Eastern Europe (see Schöpflin 1979), but Bernhardt recalled the process with irony.

> There were texts in it [*DU*] that did not please the Rákosi order. . . . Because of these matters of principle, when our songbook ran out—*Dicsőitlek Uram!*— *Hitünk énekei* was published. We had to "democratize" the whole *Hitünk énekei* songbook. Not only democratize, but fix it up according to the order's taste. . . . [The editors] stewed their heads for weeks and months over how they should change these with different wording.

Bernhardt pointed out to me that the theme of suffering was meaningful to the many believers who endured privations after World War II and repression in the 1950s. However, the songs could not imply that conditions were bad under socialism. Bernhardt recalled this by taking on the voice of socialist rhetoric: "There is a song, 'Itt a földön nagyon sok a szenvedés' [Here on Earth There Is Great Suffering]— Now what is this about there being great suffering here on earth? Suffering, in socialism? This is not a problem, now revise it." Bernhardt remembered that such text lines and titles would have been changed to become general statements like "Here on Earth There Is Often Suffering" (Itt a földön gyakori a szenvedés). The texts of songs that referred to the end of the world were changed to evoke the death of the individual believer.

Mobilizing language was also changed. The first line of Fanny Crosby's "Jesus Will Give You Rest" was translated in the 1948 edition of *DU* as "Battle with faithfulness [*hűség*] the good fight of faith"; the 1959 version advises: "Always fight truthfully [*híven*] against your sins." The translation of Bliss's "Hold the Fort" was altered drastically. All the military metaphors are missing in the 1959 version, as is the direct mode of address; instead, the song becomes a very general statement about continually worshiping in order to reach heaven.

"Föl, menny felé" (Upward to Heaven)

Upward to heaven, dear brother, Jesus is calling.
Awake, awake, start away, his Holy Spirit is leading you.
Just trust in him, he will come for you and lead you up to heaven.
So place your trembling hand in his holy hand.

> *Föl, menny felé, drága Testvér, Jézus szól neked.*
> *Ébredj, ébredj, indulj már el, Szentlelke vezet.*
> *Bízz csak Benne, eljön érted s mennybe felvezet.*
> *Helyezd tehát szent kezébe reszkető kezed!*

The tempter never sleeps, he is preparing to break upon you.
Cleverness and intelligence will not succeed opposite him.
Trust in Jesus, he will come for you, he gives new strength,
So that you can always defeat sin, the tempter.

> *A kísértő sosem alszik, reád törni kész.*
> *Vele szemben nem segíthet ügyesség s az ész.*
> *Jézusban bízz, eljön hozzád, Ő ad új erőt,*
> *Hogy legyőzzed mindenkor a bűnt, a kísértőt.*

When Jesus calls you home, it will not happen unexpectedly
If on earth you do not become tired in your worship.
So let us always be with him in good and bad
And then in heavenly beauty he will help us to salvation.

> *Mikor Jézus hazaszólít, nem ér váratlan,*
> *Ha e földön el nem fáradsz az imádatban.*
> *Legyünk tehát mindig Véle jóban, rosszban itt*
> *S egykor mennyei szépségbe: üdvre elsegít.*[12]

This song text is antithetical to the communitas that opposes a socialist "unity"; the believers' mobilization toward future ecstasy contradicts the idea of material progress. In making the theme of this song an individual crisis, the 1959 text change reflects how socialist rulers atomized Hungarian society in general so that the alienation and isolation that sociologists saw by the late 1980s in turn caused more Magyars to join small, close groups like the IG (see Hankiss 1989).[13]

Restrictions on publication were subtler during the early 1960s, when the Pentecostals prepared the next edition of *HÉ*. It is a thin chapbook whose blue cover is embossed with a symbol of cross and crown and the date 1926—the year Pentecostalism was established in Hungary.[14] In it, most of the 1959 text changes are reversed. Its preface refers to this in a cryptic fashion, remarking, "we have restored the original texts of a few songs that were changed in the previous editions" (*HÉ* 1965). There is even a reference guide to many of the text reversals in the front of the 1965 edition. But in this hymnbook, the editors actually revised the texts again, explaining that "taking into account comprehensibility, Hungarianness, accent, correct rhyme scheme, and primarily biblical requirements it was necessary to modify the texts of a good many songs" (*HÉ* 1965). Fábián explained that the editors, leaders by this time of the Evangéliumi Pünkösdi Közösség (Evangelical Pentecostal Fellowship), the organization from which Brother Horváth had split, changed some texts for the third edition because they were not very developed from a theological standpoint. Bernhardt believed that many of the changes were helpful because they made the language of the texts and their musical settings more natural to the Hungarian ear. This was the hymnbook edition that IG members used.

Whereas Pentecostal editors changed some texts on their own, others were changed under the recommendation of the outside readers. The Baptist readers aimed more toward institution-building than the other small churches in Hungary. In discussing the changes they made to the 1957/1960 edition of their own hymnbook *A hit hangjai* (Voices of Faith), one of the Baptist editors commented to me that the goal was to emphasize songs that were directed to God; the editors eliminated songs with very simple melodies and texts with a pervasive first-person viewpoint. On the other hand, Pentecostal editors retained numerous such songs in the 1965 edition of their hymnbook, *HÉ*. The Pentecostal editors did change a number of texts so that they were congruent with those of the Baptists, writing tactfully in their own preface "we have substituted about one hundred songs; we took them partly from the modified texts of *A hit hangjai*, with the gracious permission of the Baptist *testvérek*" (*HÉ* 1965). But Bernhardt exclaimed that as "protected song" (*védett ének*), the Hungarian versions of "Safe in the Arms of Jesus," "Pass Me Not," "Teach Me Thy Way, O Lord" and others had sustained the believers through many years. This made it difficult to accept the changes made by the church council readers.

Even though Pentecostals adopted the revised texts, they retained many of the songs in their 1965 publication of *HÉ* that the Baptists had eliminated from their own hymnbook. Some of these songs indeed have simple melodies, take a first-person point of view, and depart from biblical imagery, as the Baptist editor objected. In this, they show parallels with other European Pentecostal hymnbooks (see Bloch-Hoell 1964:60). Extreme emotions are expressed in many of the songs that the Hungarian Pentecostals kept: dependence on Jesus, the ecstasy of sanctification, despair and fear of the earthly existence paired with the anticipated beauty in heaven. They continue and reshape the ethos of revivalism from the English-speaking countries, as found in the gospel hymn publications, tracts, and religious fiction of the Victorian era. The domestic orientation, personal viewpoint, and melodramatic character that inflect all of these genres are also emphasized in the song translations that IG members favored (see Sizer 1978). Myriad changes and political tumults were what lay behind Brother Horváth's occasional variations in the song texts he quoted or his remarks that a given song had a new text. Even the most recent text changes seemed to be erased from ordinary church members' memories. The IG members sang the most recently revised versions of songs. I did not hear objections to them, although when the 1965 edition of *HÉ* appeared it might well have caused controversy. IG members did not seem to be consciously aware of the historical sources, mediations, and alterations that their songs had undergone. Traces of intellectual involvement, German language, puritan ethos, and church institutions emerged variously in performance as denatured qualities or, conversely, tendencies toward spiritual power.

This was evident in how Pentecostals changed rhythm, added accents, and, more indirectly, altered melodies.

Melodic and Rhythmic Changes

At the meetings of the IG I heard church members singing the gospel hymns only a cappella or to drone-style accompaniment. But one Wednesday an elderly man appeared at church, sat at the organ, and opened a very large score bound in black. As the church members requested songs, he played the melodic line accompanied by functional harmony. Brother Horváth and his wife had told me that this score existed but seemed reluctant to help me find it. It turned out that the elderly man was the organist at the Pentecostal church in Pécs that had expelled Brother Horváth in the early 1960s. He was using a score edition of *HÉ*, one of the few available in the entire country and the only copy in Pécs. This was one of the occasions that Brother Horváth used to advocate for the authority of the score. As the organist played a melody for a song that was different from the one the believers were singing, Brother Horváth told the congregation to learn the new melody. I lost control at this point and exclaimed: "But you have a nice tradition here of using your own melodies!" I then realized that I had begun to idealize how the believers had gone their own way in religion and musical style. I did not need to worry about change, though, because the force of habit prevailed, and after following the organist's rendition for that evening, the church members reverted to their previous melody.

Gyula Bernhardt later explained to me that the scorebook had been issued in 1964 without official permission almost as an item of samizdat. This was not because it seemed politically confrontational but because the readers judged its quality to be inferior. When publication of the score edition was refused, one of the Pentecostal leaders painstakingly set the scores using a music typewriter, and a small number of duplicates were then made. The book contained four-part scores for the approximately three hundred songs that could not be referenced to any other Hungarian-language song publications. They were in an almost manuscriptlike hand with typed text underlay, and the pages seemed to have been duplicated from an old-fashioned ditto machine.[15] As the incident with the guest organist illustrates, neither the *HÉ* score edition nor the many Baptist and home mission scores that *HÉ* referenced had an effect on how IG members sang. One reason is that they had stayed somewhat separate from other believers. Another related reason might be that the orally transmitted versions of the songs had changed to correspond with the pace of religious experience and types of emotions that the believers felt. A folklorizing process thus occurred; IG members sang versions of the songs that were different from score editions in rhythm, melody, and sometimes form. Without functional harmonic underpinnings and with an emphasis on song as speech, the congregation changed intervals that followed from harmonic complexity. The IG performances often eliminated the buildup of tension and subsequent release in many of the gospel hymns that move to the dominant and back to the tonic. Similarly to the way they sang *hívő énekek*, the congregation retained and sometimes even added large leaps to melodies. They included fanfare motives, especially fourth leaps, in a number of songs with mobilizing language. In "On the Pilgrim's Way," the congregation simplified Webster's melody by substituting the last melodic line of the chorus for the last verse phrase. The melodic movement of the chorus phrase dramatically repeats the interval of a fourth and corresponds with the sense of the verse lines in the Hungarian text (ex. 6.2). The IG members' melodic leaps often simplified the harmonies of the scores, for example substituting a minor sixth for a diminished fifth. They sometimes increased melodic momentum with stepwise movement where the gospel hymn scores utilize small leaps.

Believers varied rhythm from the score editions. They used irregular and complex rhythmic values when they performed gospel hymns with text settings that diverged greatly from the score rhythms, when they were expressing emotion, and when score versions were in compound meter (see exs. 6.3 and 6.4). They utilized an entire range of long-short rhythmic patterns, including the heterorhythmy of parlando, the lilting sensation of "swung" rhythms, and rhythms that in their crisp articulation and contrasting durations could be characterized as "dotted" although not mathematically precise. Hungarian Sunday school songs supplied another rhythmic influence. Composed by home mission revivalists, they utilized straight rhythms, narrow ranges, stepwise movement, and motivic material from *magyar nóta*. (Orthodox Calvinists criticized the songs for just these characteristics.) Whereas the score versions of many gospel hymns mix halved time values with related dotted rhythms, IG members often sang virtually entire melodies in straight rhythmic divisions so that they resembled the Sunday school songs (see ex. 6.2). This is possibly because the gospel hymns appeared in the home mission and Baptist publications together with the Sunday school songs. Where they occurred, often in celebratory songs, dotted rhythms thus had greater prominence. They even carried a new vernacular inflection with lower neighbor tones reminiscent of the *verbunkos* style. In the translation of George C. Stebbins's "Come to the Fountain" (*GH* no. 274), entitled "Jövel az élet vízéhez" (Come to the Water of Life), which the congregation sang before water baptisms, the singers used straight rhythms rather than the dotted ones printed in Stebbins's verse. But with words of inspiration in the chorus, they retained some dotted rhythms and added lower neighbor alternations at two points where Stebbins's score repeats pitches (exs. 6.5 and 6.6).

> Then come here, do not delay
> Here you find heavenly salvation and tranquility!
>
> *Jöjj hát ide, ne tétovázz!*
> *Itt égi üdvöt és nyugtot találsz!*[16]

EXAMPLE 6.5. "Jövel az élet vízéhez" (Come to the Water of Life). Chorus mm. 1–4. *Evangéliumi karénekek* no. 83.

♩ = *92 - 96*

Jöjj hát i- de, ne té - to - vázz! Itt é - gi üd - vöt és nyug - tot ta - lálsz!

EXAMPLE 6.6. "Jövel az élet vízéhez" (Come to the Water of Life). Chorus mm. 1–4. IG congregation, Pécs, November 1990.

Some of the Pentecostals' older songs incorporate the fifth shift, an important structural feature of *magyar nóta* and Hungarian folk song where a phrase is repeated at the interval of a fourth or fifth. Some Hungarian folk songs in fact consist of only one transposed phrase (Manga 1969:12–13). New-style folk songs frequently have what Bálint Sárosi and others term "closed architectonic" structure: "In the four-phrase melodic stanza the first and last phrases are identical musically, while as regards the melodic contours, the second and third phrases, or at least the third, lie exactly or approximately a fifth higher than the first and last" (Sárosi 1986:52). Songs with the fifth shift demonstrate how the IG members were still connected with the popular culture of the early part of the twentieth century. Some of these had been included in the Pentecostal songbooks. Others were in the oral tradition as a folk repertoire that the Pentecostals shared with rural Baptists (see Bányai 1996:74–78). Although they all included elements of the fifth shift, the songs had many different connections to Hungarian vernacular music. One that IG members sang was set to an actual folk melody; another was sung with the dotted rhythms and neighbor tones that characterize *verbunkos*. Another used a *csárdás* melody, and yet another modified the fifth shift by eliding two phrases.

Bartók believed that Hungarian folk songs had undergone centuries of subtle shaping according to the peasants' sense of what was suitable musically, so that uniform style elements resulted (1952[1934]:3). The assessment of Gyula Bernhardt about how the Pentecostals mixed Hungarian and Western sensibilities contrasts with this theory. He explained that American melodies were more comfortable to believers than their own folk idiom: "If an original Hungarian song appears that is from the pentatonic world—well, the whole thing seems unfamiliar. . . . English music, that is, the music which comes from that part [of the world], has its own special features. It is pleasant. People accept it faster." This attraction may have led to syncretism; some songs combined the fifth shift with the stepwise melodic motion and major tonality of the gospel hymn repertoire. One such song, "Elédbe borulok, Jézusom" (I Throw Myself at Your Feet, My Jesus), had a fifth-shifting structure common in the Hungarian folk idiom, aa^{5}a^{5}a. However, the song was not constructed with a pentatonic pitch set; it used stepwise motion within a major tetrachord. In performance, the pervading straight rhythmic pattern also made the song seem related to the gospel hymns and Sunday school songs. Some of the songs with fifth-shifting melodies had texts that emphasized repentance and martyrdom.[17] The congregation members sang those with a wailing tone and many pitch slides. But IG members sang "I Throw Myself at Your Feet" in a sprightly way and requested it often (ex. 6.7).

EXAMPLE 6.7. "Elédbe borulok, Jézusom" (I Throw Myself at Your Feet, My Jesus). IG congregation, Pécs, December 1990.

I throw myself at your feet, my Jesus,
Be my solace always!

> *Elédbe borulok, Jézusom,*
> *Mindenkor Te légy a vigaszom!*

You steer my life
Lead me with your Holy Spirit!

> *Te kormányozod életemet,*
> *Vezess Szentlelkeddel engemet!*

Chorus:
Come, come, my soul awaits you!
Jesus, be king in my heart!

> *Jövel, már, jövel már, lelkem vár!*
> *Jézus, légy szívemben a király!*[18]

Melodic, formal, and rhythmic changes, as well as the particular song preferences of IG members, constitute what might be termed a "native hymnology" in paraphrase of Anthony Seeger. He proposed that examining the relationships between different forms of performance might yield an understanding of the expressive structures that give a genre of music its particular style (Seeger 1987:138). The impact of different agents of revival in Hungary is present in the ways that IG members performed the gospel hymns. They adjusted Anglo-American melodies to Hungarian rhythms and combined the major-key constructions of the gospel hymns with the structures of Hungarian vernacular song. In Hungary and other parts of Eastern Europe, religious revivals were repressed, blunting the force of the gospel hymns as mass culture. The hymns' musical formulae were thus reshaped by the contrasting dynamic of marginalization.[19] Delinked from musical notation and affected by the ways that Hungarian speakers express emotion through rhythm and pitch, the gospel hymns developed a wide rhythmic variety and diversified somewhat in melody, at one point even adding Hungarian folk characteristics. Censorship and secularism may have erased this music from mainstream religious practice, but with their rubato singing of some songs and vigorous accentuation of others, elderly believers still took pleasure in singing the nineteenth-century gospel hymns.

7

Stigma and Stereotype

M any small congregations like the IG operate with a sense of egalitarianism aris-
ing out of their structure as folk churches where their sense of communicating
with God and each other is immediate. They resemble the early Pentecostals in
America, who characterized their community as one "body of Christ." IG members
even used the phrase "we are one body" (*egy test vagyunk*) at times when they were
explaining their ethnic mixture to outsiders. Writers in the early issues of the American Pentecostal movement's periodical *Apostolic Faith* used images of melting and
of multitudes gathering (MacRobert 1988:55–56). This fervent unity was one generation removed by the time missionaries went to Hungary. Within the complex
hierarchies of the large Pentecostal institutions that have subsequently emerged in
the United States, leadership committees and councils utilize the idea of spiritual brotherhood. Their missionary literature contains frequent references to foreign adherents
as brothers. There are many opportunities to demonstrate unity in the highly stylized
format of bylaws, periodicals, and church services. By contrast, IG members put their
version of spiritual brotherhood into action face to face. In this context, the differences between Magyars, Roma, and missionaries were often foregrounded.

The IG members' term *szent testvériség* (holy brotherhood), with the meaning
of sanctification they attributed to the word *szent*, indicates one way that the IG
members bridged differences. They viewed themselves not just as contradicting but
as actually having transformed some of the tensions that occurred in secular society
between Roma, Magyars, and people from different social strata. When explaining
how they regarded each other as *testvérek*, Magyar and Romani church members both
gave the believer's greeting as an example. They gave solid handshakes, made clear
eye contact, used a very energetic tone of voice, and smacked each other vigorously
on the cheek. This contrasted with how Magyars and Roma often approached each
other in the secular world. For Romani church members, the greeting could also
symbolize the egalitarian ideal. Michael Stewart commented about Vlach Roma that
"the correct use of greetings was emblematic of a willingness to engage in a relationship of mutual respect" (Stewart 1997:44). The church greeting demonstrates how

Sister Horváth, left, with Sister and Brother Borovics before a church service. Behind them, Brother István reached out to exchange a handshake of greeting with another church member.

believers captured local gestures and changed them to add a sacred meaning. Their scrupulous attention to this activity foregrounded its importance as a contradiction to how much tension there could be between Magyars and Roma.

Musical Compromises

Another way that congregation members demonstrated acceptance of each other was to accommodate the contrasting repertoires of *hívő énekek* and old hymnbook music, including the gospel hymn translations. However different the melodies and textual themes, the songs sounded similar in performance. They were nearly always mono-phonic. They were often sung rubato; if the music had a regular beat the tempo was ponderously slow. This style was striking when applied to the *hívő énekek* that had originated with Roma. In southwestern Hungary the *hívő ének* "Szolgálni jöttem" (I Came to Serve) was performed at a tempo of approximately ♩ = 100–104. In Ózd, where the converts were nearly all young Roma and did not mix much with Magyars, the congregation sang the same song at ♩ = 112–118 and included many syncopations. In southwest Hungary the *hívő énekek* were sometimes sung in parlando-rubato. In Ózd, the rhythms of the songs accommodated speech patterns within a regular rhyth-mic pulse, as the singers placed syllables with long vowels on long note values. These contrasts indicate how the newer church members in southwest Hungary had assimi-lated the elderly believers' style of singing. As I discussed in chapter 6, the parlando-rubato style was common for hymnbook songs. The slow tempo came from Calvinist psalmody. To outside ears the difference between Calvinist and Pentecostal singing could seem negligible, although believers from the revivalist religions generally asserted that they sang with much more spirit (see Szigeti 1981:60–62). All over Hungary, the elderly Pentecostals shared a tense bodily posture, slow tempo, and heavy accents with Calvinist singers. A pastor's description of rural Calvinists during the interwar period resembles what I witnessed with the elderly Pentecostals:

> When the Hungarian peasant sings with a truly full heart and lungs, he grips the bench. His eyes bulge and the veins stand out on his forehead. Besides spiritual work, he does real bodily work, as he pours the feelings of his heart into swelling waves of sound with great, slow dignity. (Illyés 1931:39–40)

This combination of force and restraint depicts how the elderly believers could mix devotion and asceticism. The situation was slightly different for Roma. They spoke of replacing the *testi* (bodily) with the *lelki* (spiritual). One aspect of this was to inhibit ways that they might have expressed musical pleasure in the secular context.

The communitas that church members experienced during worship paralleled a basic aspect of Romani verbal and musical performance—group participation. Katalin Kovalcsik has reported how Vlach Rom performers experience the contributions of many others as helpful and invigorating; at storytelling sessions, listeners interrupt the storyteller constantly with questions and exclamations (see Kovalcsik 1988:32).[1] Group participation is facilitated with vocables in several different kinds of Romani secular music. Vlach Roma sing the melody of dance songs with vocables called *pergetés*. They accompany the same dance songs with other vocables called "oral bassing," versions of the accompaniment parts from string bands that add percussive sounds, replicate instrument timbres, and utilize pitch hierarchies. All the Roma I knew were familiar with this style because it was used in *folklór* music. A stereotyped version delivered at a manic tempo with less syllable variation was quite familiar to Romungre, since it came from the commercial *cigánydal* genre.[2] Vocables connoted chaos to some Roma, who possibly had internalized the perception from peasant society that Roma lead disorderly lives. On the occasion when I traveled to a festival with some Roma, Romungre who had formed a *folklór* group were on the bus. They began singing, and the string bass player, who did not have his instrument, started oral bassing. The group's director stopped him and told the ensemble that they should rehearse with more precision.

There was a general experience among the Roma of my acquaintance that singing in vocables carried a stigma. In principle, there is a parallel between tongue-speaking and vocables. Some American Pentecostals and charismatics chant and sing in tongues, an activity that is sometimes called "singing in the spirit." IG members expressed a general Pentecostal belief by asserting that tongues were messages in translatable but unknown languages (see Samarin 1972a:143–73). Whereas church members explained that tongue-speaking imparts divine intelligence, many had an opposite interpretation of vocable singing. Once Gusztáv Váradi's relatives gathered to sing as many of his songs for me as they could remember. His mother began singing one of the melodies in vocables rather than text. His sister Kati quickly interrupted her. "Stop," she urged. "There's no sense [*értelem*] in it." Another fear was ridicule. Even though József Gál and several other men enjoyed singing *szájtrombita* during casual music sessions at church, he avoided vocables during services, telling me that he feared others would make fun of him. Some church members reconciled pleasure that they felt in vocable singing with a sanctification process. Sister Elza sometimes proselytized to fellow Roma with her husband. She said that on those occasions she sang melodies in *pergetés* so she could gain rapport with nonconverted Roma, since it meant happiness to them. But she asserted that after conversion *pergetés* would lose its appeal because then Jesus was a source of happiness. Thus, some Romani believers were willing to risk shame in order to get the pleasure they felt in singing vocables, whereas others relocated the good feelings into sanctification.

The group ethos manifested in other ways that were unacceptable. Once when Renáta was singing at testimony, many members of the IG congregation were so charmed by the little girl that they started to sing along and it became difficult to hear her. Brother Horváth exclaimed to the congregation in a somewhat angry tone of voice that they did not know how to behave properly and that they should be silent. At this implication that they were *egyszerű*, the church members seemed ashamed, many of them looking down at the floor, and immediately stopped singing. For several months afterward their singing, outcries, and episodes of speaking in tongues were more subdued. In doing this, Romani church members exhibited the extra sensitivity of stigmatized people who are highly aware that they might need to change their behavior in order to be accepted by the mainstream (Goffman 1963:111).[3] For example, Brother Misi told me that the Romani believers were careful to suppress almost all kinds of behavior marked as Gypsy-like in order to be sure that elderly Magyar church members would not condemn them, whether it was for engaging in bodily pleasure or for being uncultured.

Members of different Romani ethnic groups mutually condemn each other for being uncouth or immoral, possibly as a way to establish ethnic boundaries. In the IG, as in other parts of Europe, Pentecostalism brought the Romani ethnic groups together with a feeling of spiritual brotherhood. Preachers of different Romani ethnicities welcomed each other as guests at their houses, and by the mid-1990s some church members from different Romani ethnic groups had married. But views of acceptable participation nonetheless divided the Romani ethnic groups. Brother Gál sometimes led services for a small group of about twenty Boyash Roma in a village near his home town. Once during his sermon the congregation passed glasses of water to each other. Brother Gál told them in a friendly tone that the devil was taking away their concentration. But Boyashes have a very strong tradition of focusing their attention at funeral ceremonies (see Szapu 1985:14–20). During all-night vigils, they tell stories continuously in the Boyash language. In describing these, one acquaintance said, "there has to be *néma csend* [deaf silence]. " On an occasion when I actually attended a Boyash vigil, it became evident that *néma csend* was relative rather than absolute. The audience was focused on one person, the storyteller, something that contrasted greatly with their group contributions in everyday settings. But this did not mean complete acoustic silence or physical stillness. They asked the storyteller to clarify points in the narrative or to explain the meanings of words; they whispered to one another occasionally, scolded others outside the room for being too loud, and passed glasses of wine around the room. Thus when Boyash church members passed a glass of water during church services, they were completely within their own highest standards of decorum—only having substituted water for wine. As

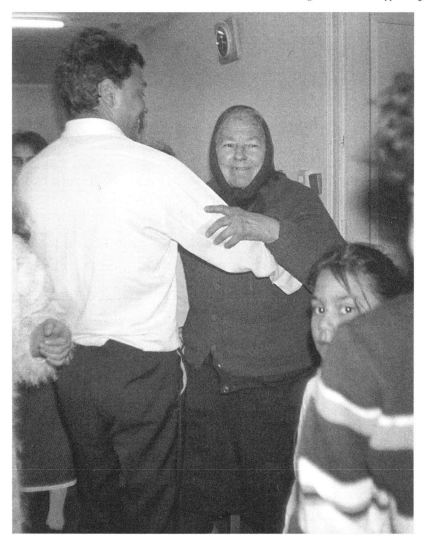

Brother Gál dancing with Sister Herceg at a marriage celebration.

a member of the Romungro ethnic group with very different funeral customs, Brother Gál had no frame of reference for this and interpreted the behavior as disruptive.

Ordinary Magyar believers enjoyed group participation. During prayer, if anyone, Magyar or Rom, cried out loudly or began speaking in tongues, this seemed to give the other church members more energy. Everyone responded "Halleluia" at various times during sermons. The elderly Magyar church members characterized this behavior as *buzgó* (zealous). They seemed to regard group participation in music as a similar type of zealousness. A few weeks after Brother Horváth reprimanded the congregation for singing along with Renáta, a young Romani man who was a recent convert began clapping rhythmically, saying "Halleluia," and singing along with someone else's testimony. I asked Sister Herceg what she thought of his behavior, and she replied that she appreciated it very much and contrasted it with the lack of interest her own grandchildren had for religious things: "We can't keep them by force. I'm happy that they come; it's a stroke of luck. I wish my own [children] would come. There is no desire for it yet in their hearts. . . . It's a joy to see and hear them. It's a joy to me to listen to them." In contrast to church leaders, Sister Herceg's comments reflect a consensus among church members that group singing during testimony was like other engagements with the Holy Spirit.

The effects of the suppressions were usually to reinforce a hierarchy. Brother Gál's and Brother Horváth's comments both indicated an ideal separation of subject and object. Whereas Brother Gál's comments seemed to be designed simply to generate some sense of a group being led by an individual, Brother Horváth's high art model required aesthetic distancing, where an audience should silently absorb and reflect on an object. His admonition to the congregation was forceful simply because he had far higher status than the church members did. Sometimes stratification was reinforced more obviously and phrased in terms of sanctification. On a few occasions during midweek services the members of the Szigetvár congregation voiced some critiques to the musicians, asking them to change the tempo, tune, or beat configuration. Once the officiating Romani preacher told the congregation just to think of God and not distract themselves. Then he himself told the musicians to change several aspects of their playing. These sorts of actions led congregation members to observe about more than one of their Romani leaders that they "beat up on the congregation" (*megveri a gyülekezetet*). Brother Gál illustrated his capacities as a charismatic leader by giving very mild instructions and thus possibly circumventing the sense of shame. At one of the evangelizations I attended in eastern Hungary, a woman gave testimony while others exclaimed "It was that way for me too" and "That is true" so loudly that they drowned her out. With the everyday tone used in domestic repartee, and with vernacular phrasing, Brother Gál said, "*Testvérek*, stay quiet so we can hear her!"

Even though the regulation of congregational behavior within the IG was very mild compared to those of major denominations, the church leaders found various forms of group participation beyond praying or saying "Halleluia" to be unacceptable. Brother Horváth's comments appeared to indicate that he saw group participation with soloists as uncultured. The comments of the Romani leaders classified it in the more serious area of unsanctified behavior. In both cases, the leaders may have been reacting to how communitas leaked beyond limits that the leaders could control. Their unease highlights the intermediate structuring of the IG between a charismatically led group and an institution. Where Brother Horváth saw a lack of education or socialization to mainstream behavior standards, the Romani leaders saw resistance. Shaming, Brother Horváth's method of enforcement, was effective to some degree, whereas the Romani leaders were not very effective. The drastic language of some Romani leaders points out how much more force they may have thought they needed to use to attempt to change ordinary church members' behavior.

Ethnicity and social stratification thus intersected in the IG around aspects of group participation. The emergence of group participation under the varied leadership styles and worship environments just within this small church resembles the kinds of interactions that Gerald Berreman identified in a north Indian city. Symbols of identity could be manipulated in the urban context that offered somewhat more flexibility than village society. But Berreman's co-respondents also feared that dramatic or violent mobilizations would soon occur. Berreman identified this pressure as coming from such forces as Westernization, industrialization, and modernity—factors now reframed as aspects of globalization (Berreman 1975:98–100; Robertson 1992).

Missionaries

The collapse of socialism was an event that verified globalization of the cultures associated with capitalism. As such, globalization impinged upon the IG at the end of the socialist period. My initial attempts to work with the congregation's instrumental musicians illustrate a situation similar to the one Berreman identified: by being open to an interest from the outside, my own, the congregation allowed the pressures of ethnic and gender stratification to increase. American missionaries, though, represented a far greater force. Acting to assimilate the IG to their institutions, they added a completely different sense of hierarchy that seemed to denature how Magyars and Roma worked through their differences. Brother Horváth had hosted foreign evangelists throughout his life, but they could not have much effect under socialism since their visits had to be clandestine. By the mid-1980s, state surveillance was less severe and missionaries were visiting small churches all over the country. In the early 1990s, Brother Horváth began to scale back his connections with independent evangelists in order to officially affiliate with one U.S. denomination. Many of the visits I witnessed were from these denominational missionaries, who came to the IG almost on a bimonthly basis. Although I frequently interpreted for them and had conversations with them, the missionaries were extremely suspicious of me as a nonbeliever. The comments on missionaries here are thus of a somewhat general nature. No missionary will be identified by name or denomination.

A philosophy of manifest destiny appeared to inform much of what the missionaries did. Manifest destiny's goal "to establish on earth the moral dignity and salvation of man" had a strongly religious cast (O'Sullivan 1839:430). Although manifest destiny was associated with the nineteenth century and U.S. territorial expansion, at the end of the twentieth century, the Evangelical missionaries I met still seemed to follow its precepts. Under what they see as divine sanction, Evangelical missionaries have had the goal to gain converts in particular geographic areas and assimilate them to their U.S. churches. This was apparent as they flooded Eastern Europe after the fall of socialism. The missionaries with whom I spoke made remarks that revealed that they (along with U.S. businessmen and teachers I met) thought of Eastern Europe as a frightening and uncivilized place. Unaware that open-air produce markets were held in every large town, one commented that she could not get vegetarian food in Hungary. Missionaries tended to see the region not as a set of separate countries but as a vast area that God had not touched. One evangelist related testimony to the IG about his trips to Romania and Russia, the thousands of people to whom he had preached, and miracles of healing that had occurred, although the congregation did not respond in an enthusiastic way. Similar to conquering a geographic territory, baptism was symbolically the most important of the activities that missionaries engaged in since it demonstrated that they had won permanent adherents. The missionaries conducted the baptisms personally, recorded the events with photographs or video, and mentioned to me how they publicized baptisms in their sermons and publications back in the United States.

Missionaries did not view the preexisting religious practices in Eastern Europe as valid from a theological standpoint. The behavioral practices of the IG members were somewhat more in flux than those of the missionaries, based on their understanding that the Holy Spirit could guide them spontaneously. Possibly because they extrapolated behavioral and organizational principles from the Bible in a more detailed way, the missionaries appeared to see their doctrines as superior to East European ones. One missionary's wife said to me that their goal was to "uplift" the Hungarian believers: "It's our job to strengthen them in the Word. Some pastors don't have very much knowledge." The knowledge that U.S. Evangelicals have is a system of references that are made to be internally consistent to the point of tautology. To Evangelicals this is a positive attribute, as Vincent Crapanzano has pointed out (2000:153–60). Missionaries could tie specific behavioral restrictions and worship practices to a web of biblical text elements as a form of literalism that extended to almost every area of life, all leading to the first and second coming of Christ. Missionary "B.," who was fluent in Hungarian, once demonstrated this interpretive method in a sermon to the IG congregation. The theme was praising God. He read from approximately ten different Bible verses on the subject, reconciling Hebrew, English, and Hungarian usages of the verbs meaning "to praise." He cited the number of times that the word appears in the Bible. He extended the theme of praising God from the Psalms to the twelve tribes of Israel and then to the Messiah. In between, he interspersed short anecdotes about salvation, feeling the Holy Spirit, and personal misfortune. Periodically some markers of United States–style preaching "in the Spirit" became apparent (see DeShane 1996; Rosenberg 1970; Titon 1988). His phrases shortened, the syllable "uh" appeared at the end of them, and his voice took on a slight chanting tone. His Hungarian even began to include diphthongs as though it were inflected with a southeastern American regional accent. The missionary concluded his sermon with an altar call.

At the time B. delivered this sermon in 1990, IG members, besides being unfamiliar with the way American preachers moved around the worship hall, were not used to this Holy Spirit style, the detailed textual exegesis, the references to original languages, or the connecting of Old Testament events in such a specific way to those of the New Testament. They responded "Halleluia" when B. mentioned conversion, salvation, or miracles worked by God, that is, at points where they would have responded to a Hungarian sermon. They liked B. for reasons rooted in the local. Sister Zsuzsa once observed, "the common people really love him" (*nagyon szereti a nép*). Some of B.'s conduct fit in well with the ideal of warmhearted relationships that IG members tried to follow among themselves. At the time I was doing fieldwork, nearly all foreign missionaries were working in Budapest and other cities, occasionally making day visits to other locations. By contrast, B. traveled to remote corners of the country, slept at the houses of elderly believers and Roma, ate the food they offered with gusto, and humorously related aspects of his personal devotion and home church in the United States. Once after completing a sermon and altar call in a tiny village, he chatted with the believers and sang his favorite praise choruses for them.

Although the believers seemed to appreciate how B. was unlike other missionaries, B. nevertheless had the goal of establishing his denomination's organizational structure. This was an additional sense of the "strengthening" that the other missionary had mentioned: to reshape existing church structures, doctrines, and practices. At the time I was working with the IG, B. was simply introducing ideas as well as the general evangelical culture of the United States. By the end of my fieldwork, he was beginning to make specific actions to establish his denomination's authority structure, recruitment system, and dogma. One way that B. was similar to other missionaries was that his economic standing pertained to the West, not to Hungary, and therefore was vastly better than that of the IG members. Missionaries exhibited material wealth ostentatiously. When they came to visit the congregations they drove large West European automobiles. They documented their visits with cameras and video recorders, which in the early 1990s were unusual; IG members frequently commented on the comparative expense and high quality of this equipment (including my own). B.'s house in a Hungarian city included amenities like a copier, a VCR, and West European cooking appliances that at the time I did not see even in wealthy Hungarian homes or offices. A different missionary commented to the congregation that God had blessed Americans materially because they had freedom of religion. This shows how to some missionaries the differences between their wealth and their audiences' poverty proved the superiority of their doctrines and reinforced the sense that evangelical Christianity is destined to spread. Some IG members pointed out the ironies of the great income difference between themselves and the missionaries. One leader observed wryly that the denominational missionary received a salary for his work, but he and his fellow leaders all had to get their income from manual labor instead of being able to devote their time to winning converts.

Sometimes when missionaries distributed some of their wealth, the donations simply had no effect. The console organ in the Pécs worship hall was a recent gift from some missionaries. But few of the skilled musicians showed any interest in the instrument and instead brought their own synthesizers. Brother Zoli emphasized that they needed a sound system. But amplifiers, mixers, and microphones do not symbolize sacredness in the way that the organ apparently did for the missionaries. In 1999 when I visited the IG, the organ had disappeared and been replaced by an expensive synthesizer with a piano-sized keyboard and a new sound system. Instead of merely being unimportant, other gifts had the potential to agitate and disrupt the group. A missionary once suggested buying a car for the Romani congregation in Szigetvár. In several serious discussions members and leaders voiced fears that resentment would develop over who could ride in the car and that their tithes would not cover maintenance expenses. The Romani church members were bothered the most by these contrasts in wealth. Although they framed issues in terms of their immediate community, they were very aware of global consumer goods, including expensive and effective musical technologies, media, or household items. This awareness indicates that their ideas were partly congruent with one of the U.S. Evangelical values, that material wealth and believerhood are compatible. By contrast, the elderly Magyar believers had almost all spent their lives being *alázatos* (meek) and living on small amounts of money. The worried reactions to the possibility of a car demonstrate the limits on the egalitarian ideals in the church community for Roma. The Romani members of the IG recognized how donation of a car for collective use might cause divisions and resentments within the group.

Another way that B. resembled other American missionaries was in his preference for Christian pop music. He played this music in his car and brought videos to the IG congregation of huge U.S. convocations where Christian pop was performed. The church members had witnessed some of these performances themselves at European conferences of B.'s denomination that they had attended. But these are just a few of the ways IG members knew about Christian pop. With multiple availabilities and versions emerging from many directions, Christian pop exhibited a rhizomelike quality that Gilles Deleuze and Félix Guattari have characterized as pertaining to global culture (Deleuze and Guattari 1987[1980]:3–25). Some Christian pop was plainly from the foreign missionaries, since it was in English. Brother Horváth and his wife had heard Christian pop on their trip to the United States. There were also translations of Christian pop songs that church members sang regularly. Like the gospel hymns, these operated as traces that had slipped from their origins; church members only knew this music as coming into the IG from the Free Christians in Hungary, not from U.S. sources.

Christian pop is connected with the music industry in the United States and even has a *Billboard* magazine designation as Contemporary Christian Music. It is also the style of music predominating in large U.S. Evangelical churches. It developed there as part of a general infusion of pop music into churches starting in the 1960s (Price 1993:15). The genre encompasses music in pop styles from the 1970s through the present, in solos, small groups, and large ensembles. IG members mostly heard the large ensemble style, which until the late 1980s utilized rock band instruments, orchestra, choir, and soloists. This music has a uniform texture, lightly syncopated rhythms, and a bel canto style of vocal delivery. In the 1980s it relied on many devices of musical climax that could be created by a full orchestra, but that may also have been translated from gospel piano style: fast scalar and chromatic runs, upward key modulations, fanfare motifs from brass instruments, and high-pitched violins.[4] The lyrics of Christian pop were very different from the IG congregation's other music. The song texts often reflected the same detailed derivations from the Bible that U.S. Evangelicals use in sermons and daily life. Whereas other IG repertoires borrowed ideas and short phrases from the Bible, many Christian pop texts in English are "praise choruses" with longer passages taken directly from the Bible. The Christian pop songs translated into Hungarian did not address God as intimately as did the IG genres. Nonetheless, the congregations found the translations of such songs as Scott Wesley Brown's "He Will Carry You" extremely moving and performed them at events like the Sunday prayer hour.

Brother Horváth and his wife had been delighted with the music they had heard at large Pentecostal churches when they visited their son in the United States. They were overwhelmed by the polished character of the music at the first U.S. service they had attended. Mrs. Horváth recalled seeing how the large choir, dressed in uniform, had entered the worship hall. She and Brother Horváth commented to each other that they must be in heaven, since the musical ensemble was like a band of angels. Brother Horváth confirmed that the music heard on several videos of large evangelizations and that B. played in his car was the type that he had heard during his visit. Brother Horváth and his wife were impressed by Christian pop's production values.

Whereas the extremely polished and smooth character of Christian pop results from its commercial environment in the United States, Brother Horváth associated the same qualities with art music.

> SH: They cultivate the music to a high level [*magasan művelik*] over there. Beautiful chorus, orchestra, why, they play from a score. . . . You know, the beautiful music and the orchestras really captivated me in the churches. For example, in Portland, an orchestra of about 100–150 members. A chorus of 100–150 members at David Wilkinson's [church] too. . . . So it was enormous, beautiful. It is the purity of the world of music. That is musical art; in other words, they play at the level of art. It's beautiful, it overwhelms you. There was much I didn't understand, but music is international. There's no Babel [*bábeli zavar*] there.

Brother Horváth's comments demonstrate how in Christian pop he found an ideal that encompassed musical training, score-reading, large ensembles, uniformity, and a high level of musical *műveltség*. There was even a military implication in his thinking, reflected in a Biblical analogy he made between heaven and the Christian pop choirs. Brother Horváth and his wife commented that the choirs were like the "heavenly hosts" (*mennyei seregek*). In Hungarian, the word *sereg* (host) has the connotations of protective defense, and it also refers to a military battalion (*hadsereg*). In his sermons, Brother Horváth sometimes described heaven as a place where large hosts of angels moved in perfect order.

The reactions of the IG's Romani converts and many of the church's Magyar members to Christian pop were very different from Brother Horváth's. In contrast to the Horváths, most church members identified it as popular, not "cultured" music. Brother Zoli referred to Christian pop as "rock." Upon seeing one missionary video, Sister Annus smiled and exclaimed, "It's holy disco [*szent diszkó*]!" There was a detached quality in these believers' reactions. For example, when I asked Brother Misi about the potential for incorporating the pop style of B.'s denomination, he commented in a very abstract fashion that this type of music was something that a convert who had been a pop musician in his secular life might continue to perform as a believer. Some of the singers on video recordings used a gritty vocal tone derived in the U.S. context from expressive codes in African-American gospel music that connote suffering and spiritual strength (Burnim 1985). IG members' only point of reference for these vocal styles was the secular idiom of Hungarian hard rock. The urban churches in Hungary where Christian pop was translated tended to accompany it with guitar styles that are taken from Hungarian rock, blues, or country. The Romani church members' lukewarm reaction to this music seems to have come from these stylistic codes, since they perceived much rock music as alien and artificial. Church members did not perceive Christian pop performances on cassette or video as having much immediacy. There were many translations available. But except for adolescent girls, the IG congregations did not learn much of this music, focusing instead on the *hívő énekek* and their performance by musicians whom they knew.

The commercial source and orientation of Christian pop were thus erased in the Hungarian context. Church members did not buy Christian pop recordings. They received very few of them from missionaries as gifts, and then they simply made copies of these recordings to give to other believers. Neither missionaries nor congregations sold Christian pop recordings. The only exception was some original music in the Romani language by a Budapest ensemble that I only heard in the capital city's markets. It was precisely the commercial and thus nondenominational origin of Christian pop that caused the missionaries not to disseminate many cassettes of the music. Missionaries were far freer in giving out videos and books associated with their specific denominations. Many slippages of meaning resulted, not necessarily due to the polysemic properties of music. The rhizomic infusion of Christian pop made it pertain to a spectrum of disparate values, from art music to what church members saw as artificial rock performances to the biblical applications of the missionaries.

B. may have been aware that the IG members found large-ensemble Christian pop alien. He mentioned to me that he would like to liven up the singing of the IG members but that he wanted to be very cautious in introducing American music. He appreciated the revival-style singing of Carman, a white evangelist who uses some African-American gospel singing techniques, but he believed that the congregations were not ready for the wild enthusiasm of the audiences on the Carman recordings. Like many other observers of Hungarian Protestants, B. may have been reacting to the slow and heavy singing he heard in the IG. He might not have been aware of the lively ways the Holy Spirit could manifest, since the congregation members deployed their strategy of suppression to act very conservatively when missionaries visited. B. also might not have witnessed the intimate prayer meetings where believers expressed much sentiment with rubato and pitch slides; on his visits he controlled the format and held evangelizations. Possibly as a trial step toward change, B. described to the church leaders a common method of song selection and leadership in the United States, using overhead projectors for the song texts. He asserted that it would deepen spiritual involvement because then church members would be free to raise their hands when singing. The use of projectors exemplifies the approach of the institution; since songs have to be selected in advance, it privileges the choices of a few people. The overhead system could prevent ordinary believers from introducing new songs or ones that they might find meaningful at that moment. I witnessed a possible occurrence of this with a congregation in Budapest that used projectors and sang Christian pop. After the service a small group of women clustered in the courtyard, listened intently to a Romani woman sing, and then attempted to sing along with her.

Music was an important communicative device when the American missionaries held evangelizations at the IG. When foreigners were present, Brother Horváth always directed the congregation to sing the hymnbook song "Nagy Istenem" (My Great God), a translation of "How Great Thou Art," and the praise chorus "Halleluia." He and the congregation members understood these songs to be popular with Americans because they had been used in the Billy Graham crusades.[5] Church members usually sang them in a very subdued way. It is not clear whether this is because they didn't find the songs conducive for getting the Holy Spirit or because they were making an effort to behave decorously for the foreign guests. The missionaries indicated to me that they were familiar with the translations of Christian pop that the church members sang. But these songs, like the translation of "He Will Carry You" or Les Garrett's "This Is the Day the Lord Hath Made," were included on a random basis, since Brother Horváth and the other church members thought of them as coming from the Free Christians and not the United States.

In addition to singing what they knew to be a nearly universal evangelical repertoire, the IG leaders used music to communicate the unique qualities of the church membership to missionaries. Once at an evangelization Brother Horváth introduced Brother Gál to the foreign missionary. As I interpreted, Brother Gál began with a set of themes that he often used in talking to outsiders about Roma. He described the general poverty that they endured as well as saying that they had been sinful before converting. He then announced a song that he said God had given to him, thus demonstrating that God had mercy for the Roma. Gál did not mention to the missionary or to the Magyar believers something that was well known to the Roma in the congregation: the text of this song was set to the Gypsy *nóta* "Oh, This Gypsy Girl Is Pretty." In describing to me how he got the song, Brother Gál had extended his interpretation of the divine mandate he felt to evangelize to Roma. Just as in one of his dreams he had seen the leavings after a harvest as Roma who could be gathered up for God, he saw the secular song as something that had the potential to be sanctified. Gál related to me that the original text described a promiscuous girl. When I interviewed him Brother Gál described to me how he had prayed for a new text.

> At the time [this song] was a hit . . . and it was a nice Gypsy song with a good rhythm, and in my thoughts I said, "Dear God, this nice melody! Why can't it praise you with a wondrous text?" And I asked the good God, dear God, I can't write, I'm not a composer of music or a novelist or a poet. Give me thoughts so that I can give this wondrous melody to my *testvérek* with a different text . . . and all the way home I prayed and my first song was born.

The secular song had been recorded in *folklór* style, with spoons, guitar, waterjug, oral bassing, and *pergetés*. Some syllables were added and others dropped, giving the pronunciation a Gypsified effect (ex. 7.1).

> Oh, this Gypsy girl is pretty
> She stands in [front] of the mirror and shakes herself
> She shows herself off to everyone
> Just grab her if you want a piece of ass.
>
> *Jaj, de shukar ez a cigánylány,*
> *Tükörben áll és úgy [ʃɛ] rázza magát.*
> *Mindenkinek [ɛ] kelleti magát,*
> *Az fogja meg, aki nem akarja farát.*

In Gál's version, the melody is altered slightly so that its first notes follow the contours of a folk song about Lajos Kossuth, a man who led Hungary's War of Independence from Austria in 1848 (Lázár 1989:145–63). The fact that many song texts mention his name in conjunction with patriotic sentiments or the soldier's life indicates his status as a folk hero (Kerényi 1961:47, 213). In the IG, these associations appear to have carried over to Gál's song only in the fact that the folk song's melody was very well known. On the few occasions when the congregation sang this song with no guests except me in attendance, it resembled much of their other rhythmically regular music with slow tempo, synthesizer accompaniment, and occasional percussion strokes. When they sang this song for the missionary, though, the believers included much more percussion throughout, clapping their hands on each beat. One

EXAMPLE 7.1. "Jaj, de *shukar* ez a cigánylány" (Oh, This Gypsy Girl Is Pretty). Sátoral-jaújhely Gypsy Folklore Ensemble, *Fekete lábú menyecske*, Koncert Kiadó B7, 1989.

person shook the tambourine at a rhythmic density equivalent to a steady series of sixteenth notes (ex. 7.2).

Once out in the wide world
We lived in sin, serving Satan.
We looked for love
But they hated us for our sins.

> *Valamikor, kint a nagy világban,*
> *Bűnben éltünk a Sátánnak szolgálva.*
> *Kerestük mi a szeretetet,*
> *De bűneinkért gyűlöltek bennünket.*

Our brown skin and our ragged clothes
The whole world looks down on us.
Where can we go? Where do we find comfort?
I wonder, is there truth at all?

> *Barna bőrünk meg a rongyos ruhánk,*
> *Lenéz minket már az egész világ.*
> *Hova menjünk, és hol találjunk vigaszt?*
> *Vajon, valahol lehet-e egy igaz?*

Jesus spoke in a wondrous voice.
"My children, I wonder where you are?
I love you very much.
Come, I give new life."

> *Jézus szólt egy csodálatos hangon:*
> *„Gyermekeim, vajon, ti hol vagytok?*
> *Szeretlek én benneteket nagyon,*
> *Jöjjetek, én új életet adok.*

EXAMPLE 7.2. "Valamikor, kint a nagyvilágban" (Once Out in the Wide World). Verse 2. IG congregation, Szigetvár, October 1990.

"So come, poor Gypsies,
Today the road leads up to Golgotha.
Confess your sins
And I will forgive you everything."

Jöjjetek hát, ti, szegény cigányok,
Vezet út ma fel a Golgotára.
Bánjátok meg ti a bűneitek
És megbocsájtok mindent én tinéktek."

So thank you, Lord Jesus
For your wondrous holy blood
That cleanses us of every sin
And leads us to the eternal praise.

Köszönjük hát, Úr Jézusom, neked,
A te csodás drága szent véredet,
Amely megtisztít minden bűntől minket,
És elvezet az örök dicsőségre.

Praise, praise, praise, halleluia!
Jesus Christ is returning soon.
He will take us to a wondrous, beautiful land
Where we will live with him always in joy.

Hála, hála, hála, halleluja!
Jézus Krisztus visszajön már hamar,
Elvisz minket egy csodás szép országba,
Hol mindig vele élünk boldogságban.

When singing for the missionary, the Romani church members altered the melody. In both the secular original and in the ordinary sacred context, the melody was aeolian. However, as they sang for the missionary, they interjected a half step into the song's second phrase. With this inflection they transformed it into what Kodály and others termed "Gypsy minor," a set of pitches that incorporates augmented seconds and raises the fourth and seventh scale degrees (Kodály 1960:6–7). Thus they added two aspects of stereotype—pitches that people have identified as pertaining to the "Gypsy scale" and dense percussive sounds that highlighted the rhythm.

In his verbal introduction to the missionary, Brother Gál stressed that Roma suffer extremes of the ordinary conditions of poverty and sinfulness. With this song performance, the Romani believers stressed exceptionality in an additional way, by miming the exotic. The song's text is oriented first to Roma and then possibly to Magyar listeners. It exhorts a Romani audience to convert by evoking misery and anger at the outcast state and then presenting a solution in Jesus' acceptance with a future life in heaven. But the missionaries did not hear detailed translations of song texts. It is the mimetic qualities of a musical performance that made impressions on them. The Gypsy minor inflections in this performance contrasted drastically with the major mode of the songs familiar to the missionaries. The performance was very effective; along with his wife the missionary responded enthusiastically to the performance, even exclaiming "*Jó!*" (good) in an American accent at the end. The changes in performance for the missionary appear to have been intuitive modifications. But Brother Gál confirmed that he thought it effective to stress "Gypsiness" in performance for foreigners. He once said to me that he thought it was important for those Romani believers who dressed in a traditional fashion to adopt standard Hungarian dress once they converted because their clothing was associated with what he thought of as Roma's sinful aspects and also with Vlach Roma, the least assimilated ethnic group. However, he said he envisioned one situation where it would be acceptable to wear these pleated skirts, flowered scarves, and fedoras: as costumes for the Romani believers when they were introduced formally at international Christian conferences. He pictured them dancing onto the stage and snapping their fingers in accompaniment as they sang one of the *hívő énekek.*

In one of his discussions about how truth can be controlled through discourse, Foucault suggests "detaching" its power from that of dominant institutions (1980:133). Gál's comments and the practice of the congregation demonstrate how miming the exotic can be an effective way to do this, if only on a temporary basis. Since missionaries have the goal of assimilating local congregations, combining markers of difference with the basic evangelical message is possibly the only way for those believers to communicate that they already have valid religious commitments. Evangelizers conducted events where they and their institutions mediated the Holy Spirit. But in folk churches like the IG, the divine is experienced in a relatively direct way. When applied to a vision of world Christianity, the sacred brotherhood ideology restructures the attempts that people like the IG members are already making to accommodate each other. Affiliation with the wealthy and well-organized institutions of Evangelical Christianity has advantages. But for believers on the margins it can have the effect of attenuating the experience of the Holy Spirit and of altering spiritual community.

Conclusion

As the IG congregations were meeting in the 1990s, an atmosphere of conflict permeated society. The violence in the Balkans to the south caused Hungarians to worry about ethnic tensions in their own country. Introducing a free market had drastic effects; when Roma became unemployed, some Magyars, impoverished themselves, objected to the fact that they got welfare payments from the government. The sociologist Zsuzsa Ferge warned that Hungary could become like the United States, where "society eventually divides in two. Hate and opposition within the majority against the 'lower class,' mostly consisting of Blacks, is much greater than ever before." She warned against the possibility that an ideology like fascism would pit poor people against those who were yet poorer (Kertész 1992:17). In fact, some hate crimes were committed against Roma in Hungary, and police harassed them consistently (Human Rights Watch 1996). But even major critics of intolerance pointed out that the Hungarians were difficult to provoke. Aladár Horváth, one of three Romani MPs, observed, "this country is not mean to the core." He asserted that the media and the government could successfully put a stop to anti-Rom actions and sentiments "if they implemented laws and policies that equalized the treatment of Roma" (Lázár 1992). Zsuzsa Ferge qualified her own warnings with the comment that "the Hungarian people to their credit are calm and do not allow themselves to jump into every kind of hysteria" (Kertész 1992:17). IG members were unusual by contrast with other Hungarians because rather than staying passive, they willed themselves to change. Brother Horváth not only objected to past injustices like Roma's mistreatment in the educational system, he made small steps to remedy them in the church context. By praising the congregation generally, and through physical gestures, Magyar believers demonstrated a willingness to be close with Roma. Romani converts tolerated misconceptions of themselves and changed some of the behavior that they thought would disturb the elderly believers.

From an outsider's point of view, aspects of secular life like intermarrying, living together, or sharing work might directly demonstrate that church members were close. Not much of this activity occurred in the IG. Hardly any Magyars and Roma shared work; this may have been partly due to the difference in their ages but was also because everyone in Hungary I knew turned to their family members first to complete work projects. Of the new marriages that took place in the IG during the early 1990s, I have mentioned that several were between members of different Romani ethnic groups. Another important marriage was between a Magyar girl and a Romani preacher, and more such unions were discussed. Marriage meant much closer ties between the families involved, as these young couples usually lived with their relatives. But it is also my sense that most of the believers felt closest when they were communing with each other at the time of church services. To them Bible study, praying, giving testimony, or singing were just as meaningful and virtually as intimate as everyday life could be. The believers had plenty of close exchanges with each other in and around the church environment. The group of young men who studied the Bible together at the back of the worship hall before and between Sunday services included Magyars and Roma of at least two different ethnic groups; a few Roma were among the elderly women who clustered around the heating stove to warm themselves and gossip about spiritual matters.

The intense experiences the believers had as members of an enthusiastic group provided extra strength to overcome suspicions they had about each other. Victor Turner argued that the activation of symbols and the special ordeals entailed in ritual provide a means for communities to resolve conflict (Turner 1986:39–44). The doctor of the Ndembu in Africa must "tap the various streams of affect associated with these conflicts . . . [and] channel them in a socially positive direction" (Turner 1967:392). The IG's worship did not have the spectacular visual or movement symbology found in many rituals. But the essence of Pentecostal experience, the descent of the Holy Spirit, channeled affect in a unifying direction. The Holy Spirit obviated differences of all kinds and replaced them with ecstasy. After feeling the Holy Spirit, the believers were affectionate, open, and welcoming to nearly everyone who had participated in an event; this positive feeling even extended to people like me who simply observed. The Holy Spirit experience did seem to need reinforcement. This may explain how some church events were oriented toward getting the Holy Spirit, through praying, singing, and short exhortations. Some of the changes to the gospel hymn melodies reflect this orientation. As originally written, the gospel hymns utilize standard phrase structures that build harmonic tension and then resolve to the tonic. In the cyclical versions that IG members had shaped through singing by ear rather than to a score, the gospel hymns evoked a series of dramatic moments rather than having just one climax.

The music in the IG also generated a kind of righteous pleasure for church members; they saw themselves recapturing part of the secular world in order to sanctify it. They sometimes verbalized this transformation of popular music with references to evil songs made *szent*. Other times this victorious sense was implied as the believers poured extra energy into hand clapping, rhythmic pauses, or register changes. Elderly Magyars and Romani converts both added popular music inflections of rubato and pitch slides to the translated gospel hymns, something that was easy since the high level of sentiment in their texts resembled that of secular Hungarian music. Charles Keil has proposed that pleasure happens with a groove, when the performers deliberately deviate from a musical standard (Keil and Feld 1994:96–108). In jazz and salsa, the pull occurs with rhythm or between members of an ensemble, whereas in the IG the contrast was between sacred and secular. The *hívő énekek* derived their energy from borrowing on the polysemic properties of music to mediate between secular and sacred.

Many Hungarian intellectuals believe that the IG and other small churches in Eastern Europe encourage Romani converts as an attempt to increase their membership and thus become less marginal. Church members, by contrast, said they were motivated by feelings of joy and love. My intellectual acquaintances took into account the way that the European nation-states formulate political representation. These societies reward cultural autonomy, so it does not seem to make sense for Roma to join organizations like Evangelical churches with global systems of belief and expression. In Europe, essentializing has been one of the most effective ways for subaltern groups to interrupt discourses about themselves (Smith 1994). Nicolae Gheorghe and Thomas Acton point out that in order to gain credibility within the ethnically constituted nation-states of Europe, Roma have to emphasize objective characteristics even if their inventions of tradition are just as transparent as those of the nation-states (Gheorghe and Acton 1992:32–35).

Utilizing a language and musical sound that identified them as culturally separate, some Vlach Roma were religious in a way that is congruent with the model of cultural autonomy. In northeast Hungary, they attended the Eastern Rite (*görög*) Catholic Church, whose priest conducted masses in the Romani language and invited folk ensembles to perform at masses. The Eastern Rite version of Catholicism has not spread among other Roma because of the concept that one is born into such a religion. Unlike in the IG, Roma did not become clergymen; the Catholic Church has not made changes to the requirements of formal education and celibacy that qualify people to enter its authority structure. But in the 1970s, young Vlach Roma who had participated in these masses became leaders nationally in establishing *folklór* groups, working with other young people, and pursuing high school and college educations. They were among the first Roma who were hired into the government administrative structure as social workers and who first negotiated with the state about equal treatment (Diósi 1990b:143–77). Religiosity was probably not the main element in this trajectory toward obtaining power in the mainstream society, but it was at least adjunct to the process.

Unlike the Vlach Roma's religiosity, Pentecostal conversions seem like assimilation. Michael Banton has pointed out that as a dynamic of ethnic change, assimilation is a process of multiple steps. Outsiders first join "the ethnic groups and social strata that are closest to them in the situation in which they find themselves," and these may actually be in opposition to the main trends or values of a given society (Banton 1981:43–46). Nicole Toulis sees such a pattern in England, where Pentecostal churches appeal to Jamaican immigrants of all income and status levels (Toulis 1997:120). Their dogmas may orient them away from secular society, but Evangelical groups like the IG and the Jamaican Pentecostal churches follow some conventions of the mainstream. Converting to Evangelical religion is a way that Roma can be included in at least one segment of Hungarian society.

Assimilation does not have to mean erasure. In the IG, the Roma's strategies for accommodating mainstream expectations were contingent. They suppressed some aspects of group participation on occasions when Magyars were present but resumed them when they were not. Similarly, they mimed stereotypes of Gypsiness on those occasions when it was the most effective way of communicating to missionaries their unique value as converts. Musical performance was particularly suited to such flexible strategies because it was ephemeral. A given song could be rendered in different styles, depending on the ethnic balance of a particular gathering. Musical eclecticism was a relatively straightforward way to harmonize the different age and ethnic orientations in the IG. The nineteenth-century gospel hymns evoked suffering from the past and sentimental attachment to Jesus. The stylistic codes in *hívő énekek* demonstrated how authentic was the Roma's religious experience. Since Roma could interpret the music as one of their own popular forms, Gypsy *nóta*, they could invest it with the same emotionality. Thus, the *hívő énekek* could appeal to potential converts at the same time that they gave expression to some of the difficulties of believerhood. When *hívő énekek* were performed at church events, it demonstrated to Roma that the Pentecostal religion includes them not just as converts but also as Roma. At the time I conducted fieldwork, the sacred texts of the *hívő énekek* in some cases also appealed to elderly Magyar believers. When it was sung in a multiethnic setting and combined with the drawn-out style of old Protestant singing as well as the rubato style of *magyar nóta*, the music could speak to both constituencies. To Magyars the songs connoted God's grace toward Romani converts and probably thus toward sinful Gypsies as well. To missionaries a Gypsified style hinted at the alien territory they could conquer for God.

The attitude of reform with which the IG's head pastor approached his congregation and its music was similar to the stance taken by mainstream church authorities in Hungary. For at least a century, these reformers had designed and instituted plans to change their parishioners' customs, including their singing. Such plans applied to people of many ethnic backgrounds whom church authorities thought of as needing education. When the Catholic Church issued a new songbook just before World War I, it was designed in part to weed out the popular music that Hungarians sang on pilgrimages. In the IG the head pastor chose to exert his power more flexibly than in the mainstream churches. His strategies support the idea that hegemony is an incomplete exercise of power (Femia 1975:34); such leakiness may actually enable reforms to be effective. At the time of my fieldwork, although he had affiliated with a United States–based mission, an indigenous Romani leadership flourished under him that did not conform to the mission's finely graded structure. Brother Horváth exerted his power quite strongly where behavioral strictures were concerned. In the area of music, he had goals for reform, but he advocated them only intermittently. This may have been an intuitive strategy, since music was such an important means for Roma to learn about and to maintain commitment to the Pentecostal religion at the time.

Many leaders of secular movements for change have come out of Protestant revival churches. Gerlach and Hine suggest that because it changes an individual radically, Pentecostal belief can give rise to social action (1970:xix). This was the case with some of the IG's Romani converts, who began to express altruistic feelings in response to the misery that all the unemployment in their region caused. A number of them crossed into secular domains to assume political leadership. They took jobs as social workers in towns and villages or became minority representatives to their local governments. This was true not only of Romungre but also of the Vlach Rom believers, who often have had lower status in Hungarian society. Roma's actual participation in local and national administrations reflects the pragmatic approach of much government in postsocialist Hungary. Before the end of socialism, intellectuals in the East European countries had power because they could claim a defense of the "authentic" with regard to culture (see Verdery 1991:94). Thus, it was Roma with university educations whom Magyars were likely to recognize as leaders, if at all. But in the 1990s, local governments ignored this and simply began to rely on those people who might be most effective in coping with the problems of overcrowded housing, population movement, or unemployment. One strategy was to return to a historical pattern in Eastern Europe of treating pastors as political leaders. The Pentecostal religion might have been reviled and even viewed as subversive, but the skills that the IG's Romani leaders gained there were similar enough to those of the intelligentsia, and their religion was close enough to Calvinism that local governments began to rely on them as social workers, negotiators, and planners. Local governments in southwestern and northern Hungary recruited, among others, Brother Gál, Brother István, and Brother Rokkó for social work and for positions as representatives to communicate between the Roma at large and the city governments.

One necessary attribute for mediating with governments was that the Romani representative should have some sort of basis in leadership of fellow Roma. No Roma of my acquaintance trusted government and school institutions; instead, they placed faith in other people's personal integrity. The Pentecostal preachers demonstrated honesty and consistency in their views and actions, something for which nonbeliever Roma did respect them. Their competence in maintaining the egalitarian ethos also helped. Brother István was so skilled at repartee and he took such care to observe the values on mutual respect with his fellow Vlach Rom neighbors and family members that they eventually recognized him as a leader. He parried mockery and at the same time advocated for Pentecostal values so persistently that by the late 1990s he had a considerable following of believers in his own village. At the same time, he became part of the local minority government. In several families, the converts were first viewed with scorn, but then a gradual reacceptance between converts and nonconverts took place. Pentecostal values were a matter of much debate; nonetheless, nonreligious people spent a fair amount of time in the kitchens of their religious relatives, chatting, participating in or organizing work, and in the end attending services regularly.

Some Roma converted authority they gained from leadership in the IG to power that extended far outside their towns and neighborhoods. József Gál was an outstanding example of this. In 1993, Hungary passed a law on minority representation (Schafft and Brown 2000). Roma were elected to local ombudsman positions and then voted for a national council. They demonstrated a value on practical knowledge by only electing one prominent Romani intellectual to this body, while they elected József Gál first to their national council in 1994 and then to the vice presidency of this council in 1998. Gál's method of demonstrating respect for local leaders while articulating an evangelical message thus did convert to political credibility. But the IG's members and leaders accommodated these secular crossovers only to a limited degree. Since they had previously experienced government as oppressive and corrupt, the older generation of Magyars and some Romani believers continued to define Holiness with decisive boundaries. After Brother Gál was elected to his positions in the ethnic minority government, Brother Horváth asked him to give up his IG affiliation, and he indeed did so for several years.

The IG, along with other groups in Eastern Europe, was drastically changed by organizations with a global reach after socialism dissolved and political systems became open. The universalist ideas of Christian evangelism correspond with globality or the tendency to see the world as a unit (Robertson 1992:132). Nonetheless, IG members had until the early 1990s struggled with inequalities and oppressions that correspond with the dynamics of regional systems. Historically Hungary was on the geographic and economic margin of Western Europe. György Konrád and Iván Szelényi believe that for this reason Hungary developed stratified class relations that were nearly feudal and that referred more to "Asiatic" modes of exchange than to capitalist modes of production (Konrád and Szelényi 1979[1974]:87–88). Such differences were clearly present with the distinctions between "refined" and "simple" people that the IG members felt so keenly. Stratification remained constant, even as the United States and West European countries spread their systems of organization into Eastern Europe. One flood of information, money, and ideas from the United States came via missionaries. Sabrina Ramet has observed that in the 1990s some people in the former Soviet Union and Eastern Europe adopted American Evangelical practices wholesale (1998:268). The IG followed this pattern; after it affiliated with the Oneness mission, the IG began to follow the mission's model of recruitment, financing, doctrine, and institutional structure.[1]

In the early 1990s, the U.S. missionary to the IG began to buy buildings in various parts of the country and to conduct a centralized Bible course on a regular basis for the church leaders. Roland Robertson has observed that global organizations may substitute for the state in constructing the individual according to an institutionalized pattern (1992:104–5). The U.S. mission did this with its Bible classes and building purchases. The mission's purpose of designating its own leaders became clear to me when a missionary mentioned why he bought a new building in another part of Hungary: he wanted to make sure the existing pastor would not control the congregation. The Bible classes taught the exegetical style and details of dogma espoused by the mission. In order to advance within the mission's leadership structure, men had to complete these Bible courses. Thus the mission replaced the IG's somewhat informal framework of leadership with a detailed program.

There were Roma who wouldn't be constructed according to the mission's system. Some refused to attend the classes. At least one appeared to have done this because of the negative association with schooling; in line with the value on divinely revealed learning, he reportedly asserted that he had more biblical knowledge than any teacher. The families who hosted the congregations at existing meeting places had been among the most important leaders. The Romani proprietors of the house churches that the mission replaced were offended. In several towns, they and their families stopped attending church regularly, and when I visited them in the late 1990s they had turned their energy to building up secular businesses. In one case the congregation continued, but there was bad feeling between the members, who had split between the two churches. Other congregations simply stopped having close or frequent communication with the national leadership of the IG and the mission. Following its historical pattern of periodically reconstituting its membership, the constituency of the IG changed by the late 1990s. The church continued to have a large number of Romani members, but it included many more Magyars from the middle classes and from urban areas than previously. The Romani congregations that had become independent were small neighborhood groups. They seemed to be liberalizing; church members wore shorts and dyed their hair. Networking took place only between Romani leaders with no American or Magyar intermediaries.

Music had changed in all the congregations when I visited them in the late 1990s. The repertoire in the IG congregation continued to include gospel hymns, but the church members were now singing a number of songs that had come from the large Evangelical church, the Hit Gyülekezet. These were original to Hungary, but they used the melodic style and rhythms of U.S. Christian pop. In the independent congregations, I was surprised to hear members sing the *hívő énekek* I knew from ten years previously. I had expected that there would be a completely new set of the songs, since in 1990 the believers added them at the rate of one or more a month. The number of instrumentalists was also much smaller, and the synthesizer dominated. The tempo of the singing was very slow; the synthesizer added melody, chord patterns, rhythm options, and special effects so loudly that I, at least, could not hear the words. But the believers seemed deeply involved in singing as they closed their eyes, sang very loudly, and raised their hands up. There was a sense of immersion into feeling that seemed more intense to me on these visits than in the early 1990s.

The IG's adherents now have a range of ways in which they practice their beliefs. Some stay within the missionized church, accepting and even rising within its authority structure. The IG's integration into this structure was so successful that at the end of the 1990s, Brother Horváth was named to the mission's international leadership council. While the IG is now part of a global organization, the dropouts from the IG are autonomous from a religious standpoint. In these independent Romani congregations, formalized elements that inspire a feeling of group cohesion may be superfluous. In the early 1990s, Romani converts to Pentecostalism may have needed to create songs almost out of uncertainty that God or Magyar sponsors would accept them. Now that they have refused patronage, the independent believers seem introverted. When I visited them they did not speak about holy brotherhood or emphasize the greeting between believers or even ask people from the congregation to lead prayers. But singing and praying as intensely as ever, they continued a major quality that has defined Pentecostalism and its music in Hungary. They contradicted dominant modes of interaction and experience, while at the same time they recaptured these modes for a purpose they found spiritually compelling.

Recordings, Interviews, and Personal Communications

UWEA number indicates that tape recordings of interviews and church services are located at the University of Washington Ethnomusicology Archives, Seattle. All recordings are of Isten Gyülekezet congregations unless otherwise noted.

Events

Baptism (Sunday afternoon service). Pécs, November 11, 1990. UWEA 94-27.13.

Christmas service. Pécs, December 25, 1990. UWEA 94-27.28.

Easter service. Pécs, April 2, 1991. UWEA 94-27.51.

Evangelization with American missionary, Pécs and Szigetvár, October 13–14, 1990. UWEA 94-27.3–4.

Evangelization with József Gál. Berettyóújfalu, January 20, 1991. UWEA 94-27.37–38.

Excursion of the Mohács Cigány Hagyományőrző Táncegyüttes to the Nemzeti és Etnikai Kisebbségek Fiataljainak Találkozója, Szolnok/Zagyvarekas, May 31–June 2, 1991. UWEA 94-27.61.

Preworship prayer hour. Pécs, November 25, 1990. UWEA 94-27.18.

Services/evangelizations. Ózd, November 13, 1990; January 22–24, 1991. UWEA 94-27.14, UWEA 94-27.41–42.

Sunday services. Pécs, December 23, 1990. UWEA 94-27.27.

Thursday worship meetings. Szigetvár, December 6 and 20, 1990; May 28, 1991. UWEA 94-27.23, UWEA 94-27.27, UWEA 94-27.50.

Váradi/Nyiri/Gallyas family music session. Ózd, May 1991. UWEA 94-27.59.

Wedding of Géza Kovács. Szigetvár, November 10, 1990. UWEA 94-27.9–10.

Wednesday and Friday Bible hour/services. Pécs, November 7, 16, and 23, 1990; January 4, 1991. UWEA 94-27.4–5, UWEA 94-27.17, UWEA 94-27.45.

Other worship services, midweek meetings, and special events of the IG recorded in Barcs, Csillabérc, Budapest, Kispalád, Laskod, Mátészalka, Ózd, Pécs, and Szigetvár: UWEA 94-27.1–59.

Interviews

Almási, Rudolf. Pécs, January 6, 1991. UWEA 94-27.35.
Babos, József. Szigetvár, February 6, 1991. UWEA 94-27.35.
Berki, Béla. Csillabérc, October 26, 1991. UWEA 94-27.66–67.
Berki, József "Rokkó." Csillabérc, October 26, 1991. UWEA 94-27.66–67.
Bernhardt, Gyula. Budapest, May 12, 1992. UWEA 94-27.90.
Borovics, Mrs. József. Kacsota, October 24, 1990. UWEA 94-27.5.
Bogdán, István. Szigetvár, December 13, 1990. UWEA 94-27.25.
Gál, József. Szigetvár, June 15, 1991, UWEA 94-27.102; Szigetvár, May 1991. (uncat.)
Herceg, Mrs. Sándor (Juliska). Pécs, April 2, 1991. UWEA 94-27.51.
Horváth, Sándor. Pécs, June 6, 1991. UWEA 94-27.103.
Kenesei, Zoltán. Pécs, March 2, 1991. UWEA 94-27.44.
Kovács, Mihály. Szigetvár, December 27, 1990. UWEA 94-27.31.
Kocé, József. Uszka, April 13, 1980. Interview conducted by Magda Matolay. (uncat.)
Lukács, Miklós. Pécs, May 16, 1991. UWEA 94-27.58.
Márton, Illyés and Erzsébet. Pécs, February 1991.
Siroky, István. Inarcs, May 1991. (uncat.)
Váradi, Gusztáv. Ózd, January 24, 1991. UWEA 94-27.43.

Commercial Recordings

13+1 Zenekar. 1988. *Folytassa Cirmos*. Qualiton MK 16754.
Csóré Duó. 1989. *Nem tudni mit hoz majd a holnap*. Kaleidoszkóp/Aréna. no number.
Sátoraljaújhely Cigányegyüttes. 1989. *Fekete lábú menyecske*. Koncert Kiadó B7.

Personal Communications

Beharka, Pál. Budapest, July 1999.
Bernhardt, Gyula. Budapest, July 1999.
Bohn, Gyöngyi. Pécs, April 2, 1991.
Bogdán, István. Various locations, 1990–92.
Csók, Ferenc. Molványhidpuszta, 1991.
Fábián, Attila. Budapest, July 1999.
Gál, József. Various locations, 1990–91.
Gallyas, Mrs. Bertalan "Hajni." Ózd, August 22, 2000.
Horváth, Sándor. Various locations, 1990–91.
Horváth, Mrs. Sándor. Pécs, November 1990.
Kálmár, Mrs. Ferenc (Rózsa Kőhegyi). Pécs, 1990.
Kőhegyi, Vali. Darány, December 1990.
Kovács, Mihály. Various locations, 1990–91.
Krasznai, Bandi. Szigetvár, May 1, 1991.
Lukács, Mrs. Miklós (Zsuzsa). Kispalád, August 17, 2000.
Missionary "A" and Mrs. "A." October 1990.
Missionary "B" and Mrs. "B." November 1990, May 1991.
Pfeifer, Elza. Komló, December 1990.
Siroky, István. Inarcs, May 1991.
Ungváry, Mrs. Sándor. Szigetvár, May 1992.
Varga, Ilona. Budapest, May 1994.

All recordings and personal communications took place in Hungary.

Glossary

Rm: Romani
Engl.: English

áldás (adj. *áldásos*)   lit. "blessing"; a feeling that the Holy Spirit has descended

bizonyság   testimony, a period during a worship service when believers stand in front of the congregation, sing solo or in small groups, recite poetry, or relate personal histories, all to signify the work of God in their lives

Boyash   a Rom who is bilingual in Romanian and Hungarian

buzgó   zealous

cigány   Gypsy

cigánydal   lit. "Gypsy song"; a style of song that is related to *magyar nóta* and recorded by professional singers with stereotypes of Gypsy vocal tone, dress, and movement

cigánynóta (pl. *cigánynóták*)   Gypsy *nóta*; popular song that Roma identify as theirs

csárdás   couple dance of Hungary

dal   song; with prefixes may connote folk song, composed song, or popular dance song

egyház (pl. *egyházak*)   church

egyszerű   lit. "simple"; having little education and unrefined behavior

ének   song (usually religious)

engedelmeskedni   lit. "to obey"; in Isten Gyülekezet usage, to be in a condition of spontaneously following what God tells one to do

erő   power or strength

folklór songs   songs in the Boyash or Romani languages accompanied by acoustic guitar, water jug percussion, spoons, and vocables

gyülekezet   congregation

hallelujáz   to loudly interject the phrase "Halleluia," "Praise the Lord," or "Gloria" into part of the worship service (Isten Gyülekezet usage) *hívő ének* (pl. *hívő énekek*)   lit. "believers' songs"; original songs that Hungarian Pentecostals believe are composed by the Holy Spirit

hívők lit.   "believers," devout people

imaóra   lit. "prayer hour", a period of singing and prayer that precedes a worship service

írott ének lit. "written song"; song whose text is found in a manuscript notebook

isteni   divine

kisegyházak   lit. "small churches"; Christian religions that came relatively recently to Hungary and are not affiliated with the state

magyar   "Hungarian"; the majority group in Hungary constituting a nationality as the group with which the country of Hungary has historically been identified

magyar nóta   a genre of popular song from the nineteenth and early twentieth centuries, composed in a folklike style and identified with the Hungarian nation

művelt (n. *műveltség*)   lit. "cultured"; having formal education and refined manners

muzsikus   musician; connotes the musician trade

muzsikus cigányok   lit. "musician Gypsies"; Romungre

nóta (pl. *nóták*)   the most casual of the Hungarian terms for song

nővér   sister

paráznaság   lit. "fornication"; the activity forbidden by the Bible's seventh commandment. Also, among Isten Gyülekezet members, public interactions between men and women outside of the family context that implied closeness or sexuality

pergetés   lit. "rolling"; rendition of a melody in vocables

prédikátor (Engl. *preacher*)   general designation for an ordained minister in the Isten Gyülekezet

próféta mozgalom   lit. "prophet movement"; a religion native to Hungary that focuses on prophecy as a Holy Spirit gift and dispenses with adult baptism

pünkösdi (n. *pünkösdista*)   Pentecostal

református (Engl. *Reformed*)   Calvinist church in Hungary

Rom (Rm.; pl. *Roma* adj. *Romani*)   term of self-identification for Gypsies

Romungro (Rm.; pl. *Romungre*)   a Rom who speaks Hungarian with Romani loan words. Historically Romungre worked as professional musicians in Hungary

szájtrombita   lit. "mouth trumpet"; imitation of a trumpet sound with vocables

szent   holy; in Isten Gyülekezet usage, the completed process of being sanctified

szentelt   sanctified or consecrated

Szentlélek   Holy Spirit

Szentszellem   Holy Ghost

szent testvériség   lit. "holy brotherhood," the ideal relationship between Pentecostal believers

szolgálat (inf. *szolgálni*)   service; term used in the Isten Gyülekezet for general leadership of the congregation, including music-making, short exhortations, and sermons

testvér (pl. *testvérek*)   sibling or brother; term of address and reference for fellow believers

verbunkos   style of Hungarian instrumental music dating from the turn of the nineteenth century and the style of accompaniment for *magyar nóta*

világ (adj. *világi*)   lit. "world/worldly"; in Pentecostal usage, the secular world

Vlach Roma   Roma who are bilingual in Hungarian and Romani

zenész   instrumental performer, usually of art music

zene   instrumental art music

Notes

Acknowledgments

The funds of the IREX grants for my research were provided by the National Endowment for the Humanities and the United States Information Agency. None of these organizations is responsible for the views expressed.

Introduction

1. At the beginning of migration from India, Roma may have come from several different strata (including nobility) to join military activity in the region (see Hancock 1995). Records documenting their first appearance in Eastern Europe also show them in military specializations (Crowe 1994).

2. László Karsai estimates that 5,000 Roma died as a result of the *porrajmos* in Hungary (Karsai 1992). This figure has been challenged; Ágnes Diósi observed that many more deaths could have gone unregistered, due to the attitude of casual cruelty toward Roma (Diósi 1991). Donald Kenrick and Grattan Puxon (1972) provided the first summarization of *porrajmos* casualties in Europe. Guenter Lewy (2000) documents Nazi holocaust operations concerning Roma.

3. Péter Szuhay points out that the idea that Roma have "no culture" is analogous to the "culture of poverty" concept that Oscar Lewis delineated in his study of the urban poor in Mexico City (Lewis 1961; Szuhay 1999:11–15). Vekerdi's arguments were thoroughly refuted by the late 1980s (see Réger 1988), but a major debate raged among dissidents in Hungary over policy applications. Some were concerned with general problems of the poor in Hungary, a great many of whom were Roma. Others, including Roma advocated recognition as an ethnic minority with the educational programs, cultural funding, and government representation this could entail (see Diósi 1990b; Szuhay 1999:11–15).

4. Conventions for religious writing vary in Hungarian. The major churches capitalize pronouns that refer to God, thereby indicating respect. The published songbooks of the small churches tend not to capitalize such pronouns, perhaps signaling a close relationship with the divinity. Capitalization practices varied over time and even within songbooks themselves. When discussing published texts here, I use the versions from the most recent edition of the Pentecostal publication in which they appear. In transcribing unpublished song texts, I apply

a style from church members' manuscript books of capitalizing the personal pronoun only in the third person. This style may reflect the combination of awe and intimate love that believers felt toward God.

5. As of the mid-1980s, data mostly derived from baptism registries revealed membership proportions of Catholic, 62 percent; Calvinist, 18 percent; Lutheran, 3.3 percent; Eastern Rite Catholic, 2 percent; other, including Pentecostals, .5 percent; and no religion, 14–15 percent (Walters 1988).

6. Elaine Lawless (1988a:25) believes that the terms "enthusiasm" and "Holiness" should be restricted to Wesleyan groups, whereas I. M. Lewis (1989), Peter W. Williams (1989 [1980]), and Benton Johnson (1961) apply them more broadly.

7. Jeff Titon, along with the head pastor of an independent Baptist church, found a number of parallels and possible interchanges between that congregation and neighboring Pentecostals (Titon 1988:57, 143–44, 260–61, 269, 341).

8. This figure is congruent with my observations and queries to IG believers from around the country. Walters (1988) says that there are 3,000 members.

9. Like most Protestants, IG members did not believe in transubstantiation or consubstantiation.

1. The Isten Gyülekezet in Hungarian Society

1. Published sources on the history of Pentecostalism in Hungary vary in accuracy and depth. A history by one of Hungary's largest Pentecostal churches, the Evangelical Pentecostal Fellowship (Evangéliumi Pünkösdi Közösség), draws from personal recollections, interviews, letters, church publications, and organizational records (Tóth et al. 1998[1978]). One government document ignored or gave inaccurate accounts of groups like the IG whose existence was not officially recognized (Fodor 1984). Hungarian social scientists and religion scholars researched small congregations using qualitative methods. As dissident writing, these studies had a limited circulation (Horváth 1977, 1984; Horváth and Matolay 1980; Kardos 1969; Schöpflin 1979). In the 1980s, publishers released several histories of religion that had long been in preparation (Bucsay 1985; Kardos and Szigeti 1988; Szigeti 1987).

2. Eric Wolf identifies three different waves of labor migration, linking them all to "capitalist development: from European villages to cities, from Europe to the United States, and to the Third World (Wolf 1982:361–66).

3. Hungarian congregations in Cleveland, Flint, South Bend, Detroit, Milwaukee, Freemansburg, and elsewhere in the Midwest gained branch status with the Assemblies of God, for which they had to authorize pastors and demonstrate links to the cities' larger English-speaking congregations.

4. The extreme expressions that characterized Lenten processionals in other parts of Europe were not present in Hungary, although before the world wars many Hungarians made pilgrimages to local shrines.

5. In his overview of Hungarian religious organizations, Philip Walters translates the group's name as the Ancient Christian Apostolic Church and lists the national membership at 2,200 in the late 1980s (Walters 1988:162).

6. Removing occupational designations from passports was part of a general strategy by the government to harass dissidents and deprive them of occupations as writers, researchers, or teachers.

7. Oneness was not a completely new idea in Hungary; Transylvanian principalities had provided refuge to Unitarians in the sixteenth century (Bucsay 1985:76–81).

8. A paraphrase of Luke 14:23.

9. During the time that Roma were converting to the Free Christian religion, a group of sociologists conducted an innovative study with Roma in Hungary. As part of this study, they recorded personal narratives from many Roma, including Free Christians (see Kemény 1974). Social and political criticism was implicit in these narratives since they covered topics like the Romani holocaust, religiosity, or the destructive effects of state policy on Romani family life (see Csalog 1976). Because of the death of the main researcher on Free Christian religion, Magda Matolay, only a small excerpt of the interview material was ever published (Diósi 1988:65–75).

10. This figure represents my estimate from personal attendance at services and conversations with Roma from different regions of Hungary.

11. Kovács underwent several trials, and a parliamentary hearing was held on his book; it was suppressed and only reprinted in 1989. The tone of sociography was often quasi-dissident (Schöpflin 1979:151–52).

12. Since Troeltsch introduced his ideas, many other writers have observed that sects can have churchlike characteristics. The binary distinction still has currency in Hungary, where ideas on religion did not receive a full airing under socialism.

13. In Eastern Europe both before and during the socialist period, culturedness, as a type of intellectual capital, had a hyperimportant yet in many ways illusory value (Bourdieu 1984[1979]; Szelényi and Szelényi 1991; Verdery 1991).

14. Olga Nagy (1986) and Gábor Tüskés (1987) noted that peasant folk beliefs and customs in the Calvinist areas of Hungary were greatly reduced, by comparison with Catholic communities, and were restricted to specific arenas like funerals and death rituals.

2. *Instrumental Music, Charisma, and Church Leadership*

1. I believe that the many studies on cultural appropriation in Africa and the African diaspora can only be applied to Roma in a limited way. Carol Silverman has pointed out that Roma and Blacks in diaspora both utilize popular culture to test the limits imposed by marginality (Silverman 1996:235–37). Paul Gilroy, Coco Fusco, and others have demonstrated how the bricolages of the African diaspora interrupt dominant discourses (Fusco 1995; Gilroy 1993). In Africa and the African diaspora, the shifting perceptions of a common racial identity give rise to multiple layerings of signification in music and to dynamic musical bricolages (see Erlmann 1999; Guilbault 1993). Patrick Williams argues that Roma are not like people of African descent in the Americas and Europe, because they do not feel linked to a distant home. Their connection to India is centuries removed (Williams 1991a:16–20). I believe that Roma do comment on their subaltern position through music but in an indirect way that could also be read as a replication of basic pop thematics (see Lange 1997b and chapter 5).

2. The major source on Romungro music, Bálint Sárosi's *Gypsy Music*, summarizes the content of historical documents that mention Romani instrumental musicians in Austria-Hungary (1978[1971]). Sárosi has also provided an ethnographic description of Romungro musicians and their patrons in the cafe environment (1966). His surveys of Hungarian instrumental music include explanations of terminology and sound aesthetics that Romungro string musicians utilize (1967, 1996). László Lajtha also described aesthetics and playing techniques used by Romani instrumentalists in villages (Lajtha 1953, 1988).

3. Bartók's famous polemic against "Gypsy music" (1947[1931]) is actually a critical review of a *magyar nóta* publication. His comments on rhythm and intonation apply to the effects that he believed Romani instrumentalists were having on the singing style of Hungarians. But his comments on authenticity apply to the *magyar nóták* and to the Magyars who composed them. Judit Frigyesi argues that these cricitisms could not help but be seen as ob-

jections to the rigid class structure in Hungary, since *magyar nóta* was a product of the gentry (1998:56–60, 78–80). But in the twentieth century, *magyar nóta* singing spread to nearly all Hungarian-speaking areas and became a symbol of Hungarian national identity in general. By the late twentieth century, accompanied on synthesizers, it was a genre favored by peasants and working-class people (Lange 1996b).

4. Diósi's work on Roma is in the sociography genre. Besides implicitly criticizing the socialist government's policies toward Roma, her essays are of interest from an ethnographic standpoint because they include excerpts of interviews with Romani musicians. She reports on Romungro musicians since 1949 (Diósi 1988). Tivadar Fátyol (1986) briefly mentions the licensing systems and official orchestras that were established under socialism.

5. An important aspect of Romani political activity was to restore knowledge about the instrumental tradition. One of the first activities by Romungre after the end of the socialist period was to publish books and articles on famous Romungro musicians. Activist periodicals regularly included short articles on the subject, for example, József Lévai's occasional series "A cigány zenészek historiájából" (From the History of the Gypsy Musicians) in *Amaro Drom*, the magazine of the Hungarian Roma Parliament, a self-advocacy group.

6. I once attended a service commemorating the Calvinist leaders of a rural area in southwest Hungary that had gone into decline under socialism. During a service in an unheated church that lasted nearly two hours, the elderly parishioners were completely still, even as snow drifted in on them from several broken windows.

7. The IG and many other similar churches view themselves as continuing the activities of the Apostles as described in Bible passages like Acts 8:17–18 and 9:17. In the IG, the laying on of hands is reserved for male leaders only.

3. Mediating Moralities

1. An earlier article focused on the gender-related aspects of my fieldwork (Lange 1996a).

2. *Dicsérjétek őt kürt-zengéssel . . . Dicsérjétek őt dobbal és tánczczal, dicsérjétek őt hegedűkkel és fuvolával; Dicserjétek őt hangos czimbalommal* ("Praise him with the ringing of horns; praise him with drum and dance; praise him with fiddles and flute; praise him with loud zithers"). In the seventeenth-century translation of the Bible by Gáspár Károlyi that IG members used, the word *dob* may be understood literally as "drum" but also as the crashing noise made by drums and other percussion instruments.

3. Marilyn Strathern has noted that the female domain of activity in many societies can be particularist, whereas men have general interests. These can contradict each other (Strathern 1981:187). In the IG, gossip, as a particularistic concern, could affect activities that were for the whole congregation. Women, the primary exponents of gossip, helped restrict public musical performance to men.

4. Feminist theorists argue that subjective and objective approaches should be combined when examining how structures of dominance affect women (Mascia-Lees et al. 1989:28; Code 1991:43–48). Micaela di Leonardo identifies "agency and value judgements" as the central themes of feminist anthropology. The ethnographer must explain particular cultural determinants of action with regard to gender and acknowledge aspects of her own social or economic position that shape her assessment of them (di Leonardo 1991:140–154). It was my own cultural background, as well as the standards of Western anthropology, that led me to believe that it might be acceptable to contradict the gender-oriented practices of the IG members.

5. Many female ethnographers with a Euro-American background are interested in "the tension between identification and distance" and therefore find value in such broad forms of participation (Chodorow 1978:176). A concern with relationship informs ethnographic projects

like Elaine Lawless's with female preachers, who have to balance family and ministerial responsibilities (1988b).

4. The Holy Spirit and Song Composition

1. This chapter is based on many informal discussions and formal interviews I had with Romani believers all over Hungary who experienced divine song composition. Magda Matolay conducted other unpublished interviews in 1979 with Romani members of the Free Christian Church in northeast Hungary.

2. A two-word form, *Szent Lélek*, appears in older Bible versions. United States Pentecostals often use the term "Holy Ghost." IG members only used the analogous Hungarian term, *Szentszellem*, in formalized speech situations like song texts, public prayer, or interviews.

3. According to the IG's interpretation of Acts 2:41, the three thousand believers were baptized both in water and "in the Holy Spirit," that is, they were filled with the Holy Spirit.

4. *Térjetek meg és keresztelkedjetek meg mindnyájan a Jézus Krisztusnak nevében a bűnöknek bocsánatjára; és veszitek a Szent Lélek ajándékát* (Károlyi translation, 1590). Walter Hollenweger comments that the American Pentecostals' first two stages of repentance and sanctification resemble the doctrine of the Nazarenes (1972:24–26). After the first years of the twentieth century, American Pentecostals collapsed the first two stages into one. IG members viewed and treated these two stages separately, possibly due to the Nazarenes' influence as Hungary's first Holiness church.

5. Church members commented that their glossolalia was "like Italian" (*olaszos*), since it included many labials and the vowels [o] and [a]. William Samarin gives glossolalia a close relationship to language, noting the similarity of different tongue-speaking styles to other religious speech forms (1972b:124–27).

6. Jones's text reads: "Would you be free from your burden of sin? / There's power in the blood, power in the blood; / Would you o'er evil a victory win? / There's wonderful power in the blood. / There is power, wonder-working power in the blood of the Lamb."

7. The IG, according to Brother Gál, held that there were nine Holy Spirit gifts articulated in scripture.

8. The Károlyi translation as quoted by Gál differs considerably from English versions of this passage; the King James Bible refers to the "fruit of the Spirit."

9. Because of strained relations, ranging from bitter rivalry to tenuous cordiality, between most fundamentalist and Pentecostalist churches in the area, I could make only limited observations of congregations like the Ancient Christians who were not affiliated with the IG.

10. This is an excerpt of the poem. It is presented and translated with the original spelling, capitalization, and punctuation of Sister Herceg's manuscript.

11. Károly Kisfaludi, "Szülőföldem szép határa."

12. The first song text publications in Hungary paralleled Herder-inspired European folk song scholarship. The first important volume of folk song texts, entitled *Vadrózsák* (Wild Roses), was published in 1842. János Kriza, a Unitarian bishop, had assembled the material in Transylvania.

5. Roma and the hívő énekek

1. Manuscript notebooks continue a tradition in Hungary of "folk literacy" (*népi írásbeliség*) dating at least back to the sixteenth century. Religious songs and poetry were important components. Some notebooks kept by members of the Hungarian nobility included musical notation. The inclusion of particular songs probably indicated how popular they were at a given time (see Dégh 1948; Ujváry 1980:425–556).

2. Roughly two-thirds of the *hívő énekek* are in aeolian mode or minor keys.

3. *Magyar nóta* is considered to have style elements that come from instrumental music, specifically *verbunkos*. Folk song analysis in Hungary and elsewhere in East-Central Europe makes a distinction between vocally and instrumentally oriented song. The analyses focus on vocally oriented song; they evaluate proportionality and organicism by tabulating melodic contours, forms, and line length in syllables (see Bartók 1981[1924]; Kodály 1960).

4. Line breaks indicate pauses. This method of notating paralinguistic features is based on Dennis Tedlock's model (1983:45–51).

5. Katalin Kovalcsik suggested that among Vlach Roma, widespread use of the octave break might indicate changes in their sense of melodic contour (Kovalcsik 1985:30–32). In the study of Hungarian folk song, octave breaks are criticized for obscuring the formal properties of the melody and thought to result from a deterioration of the singer's ability (Járdányi 1961:7–8). Hungarian researchers' notes also reveal a concern with how intentionally a singer varies his performance. If a singer seems to be adding style elements like octave breaks that are associated with urban popular song, his performance is frequently described as *modoros* (mannered).

6. Some of my comments on Gypsy *nóta* appeared in an earlier article (Lange 1997b).

7. The term *ének* is used by ordinary people and scholars for all types of religious song, including the *hívő énekek*. Another term for song, *dal*, is used mostly by the intelligentsia and with added prefixes can mean folk song (*népdal*), song as a compositional work (*műdal*), or popular dance song (*táncdal*).

8. Investigating Gypsy *nóta* required me to cultivate the casual style of communication that prevailed in semiprivate environments. As Thomas Turino has pointed out, signification in the domestic setting often has a shorthand character, entailing fewer mediational levels than performances that refer to overt, intellectually articulated identificatory categories (Turino 1999:237–38). I had to utilize an allusive and shorthand style of speech in order to find out about this music. If I asked about Gypsy *nóta* or Romani musical elements in a direct way, then my co-respondents immediately began to describe and explain the more clearly marked kinds of Gypsy music.

9. These reactions might have been partly due to the negative stereotypes of Gypsy speech in 1930s Hungarian films and to accents that Roma actually used in some villages, although not generally in southwestern Hungary.

10. Whereas the believers did not use oral formulas, in Hungary the Vlach Roma improvised slow songs (*loki gilyi*) on secular topics that utilized formulaic language and consistent line length (Kovalcsik 1985:38–39). The sense of regular line length and standard phraseology seemed to come about through consistent practice; for example, the Vlach singer János Balogh noticed irregularities in a child's Romani version of the Hungarian Gypsy anthem on the soundtrack of the film *Latcho Drom* (Lange 1999:44). In the 1990s it became fashionable to hire professional singers at events where the participants used to improvise songs; thus, fewer Vlach Roma now are skilled at *loki gilyi*.

11. One of the couplets from the *hívő ének* "I Am a Gypsy," for example, states *Jézus ölébe vágyom* (I desire to be in the embrace of Jesus), paralleling the first line of Fanny Crosby's hymn "Safe in the Arms of Jesus" (Jézus ölébe bizton).

6. The Politics of Nineteenth-Century Gospel Hymns

1. Nearly all the English language gospel hymns referenced in this chapter appear in the main publications compiled by Ira Sankey and his successors: in the United States, *Gospel Hymns Nos. 1–6 (GH)*, and in Great Britain, *Sacred Songs and Solos (SSS)*. The Hungarian versions of the gospel hymns appear in many different publications; except where noted, the first known source and the IG members' source will be referenced here. "Hold the Fort" is

GH no. 11. The hymnbooks referenced in this chapter are in uncataloged collections. In many cases, first editions were not available (see bibliography).

2. The first major home mission publication was *Hozsanna* (Viktor 1908). Its two editions in 1901 and 1908 were notable for their four-voice scores and their credits of many authors, composers, or translators. The songs from *Keresztyén* and other translations of gospel hymns were a significant component. Popularity of gospel hymns in English can be inferred from their inclusions in the many social hymnbooks of the early twentieth century. In Hungary, this method cannot apply for specific songs, since by comparison with English- or German-speaking areas, few songbooks containing gospel hymns were published.

3. While the gospel hymns included much phraseology from the Bible, the Hungarian translations did not. One possible reason for this was that the home mission advocates and many other urban Calvinist leaders considered the Károlyi Bible to be in great need of reform; a new translation was one of the mission's goals (Forgács 1925:404). "Föl, barátim" includes some lexical and syntactical archaisms reminiscent of seventeenth-century psalm translations into Hungarian.

4. *Keresztyén* 1894 (June 1); *HÉ* no. 150. (*HÉ* 1965 unless otherwise noted.)

5. *Sion énekei* ([Csopják] 1900 [1896]) no. 19; *HÉ* no. 248.

6. The inclusion of gospel hymns in these books, in addition to being an acknowledgement of their popularity, represented part of an effort to become institutionally independent from the German Baptists (Bányai 1996:67).

7. Two such publications, *Frohe Botschaft* ([Gebhardt] 1875) and *Reichs-Lieder* (1897), use gospel hymn tunes as contrafacta.

8. *A hit hangjai* (1918); *Dicséretek* (1927).

9. *Zengő harangok* no. 1; *HÉ* no. 71.

10. In *DU*, a designation of initial chord and starting pitch follows each song title in the table of contents; *DU* also includes a supplement of single-line score notations in manuscript for songs without cross-references. Some of the melodies notated in score are folklike.

11. One result of the restrictions on information during the socialist period is that not every publication includes information on publishers, presses, or editions. An abridged edition of *DU* published in 1955 may have counted as the first edition of *HÉ*. The *DU* edition of 1955 lists a permit number from the Baptist church as its only publishing credit.

12. *HÉ* 1959 no. 150.

13. Ironically, Bliss's melody may also have had some exposure in Hungary as a state-sanctioned song of the masses (*tömegdal*) because it had been set to a British labor text (see Murányi 1970:316; Rothenbusch 1991).

14. According to Fábián, the second and the third editions of *HÉ* were identical; they were prepared in the early 1960s (a copy of the second edition was not available). There were two printings of the third edition. The first was printed outside the country and brought in clandestinely. Bernhardt recalls that a bargain also had to be made with the state for the second printing; Swedish believers supplied high-quality paper, part of which went to the state and part of which was used for the hymnbook.

15. Bernhardt, along with another elderly leader of the Evangéliumi Pünkösdi Közösség, gathered all available scores together from the other Hungarian songbooks to publish a comprehensive score edition of *HÉ* in 1996 (Lázár and Bernhardt 1996). Much of the harmonization in the original *HÉ* scores utilized chorale-prelude techniques of secondary chords, seventh chords, passing tones, and movement to the subdominant. In Bernhardt's view this occurred because a *nem hívő* (nonbeliever) was hired to do the arranging who did not understand the directions and nuances of the melodies. Neither Bernhardt nor the organist who had visited the IG played exactly what was in the score. Many U.S. publications, including the one replicated in ex. 6.3, also used nonstandard notation.

16. *Evangéliumi karénekek* (1928) no. 83; *HÉ* no. 285.

17. One of these songs, "Mennyei jó Atyám" (My Good Heavenly Father), set to a folk song melody (Bányai 1996:78), has melodic and textual parallels to the believers' song "Halleluja néked!"

18. *HÉ* no. 118.

19. When Protestant singers were isolated for long periods of time in North America, they developed melismatic and heterophonic styles of singing (Berg 1996; Nettl 1957). This did not occurr in Hungaran Protestant singing, although both styles may demonstrate musical independence.

7. Stigma and Stereotype

1. Kovalcsik refers to these sessions as having "the conspicuous character of a communal rite" (1988:31–32).

2. Both vocable styles give the impression of having an element of conscious construction. Vlach Roma speak specifically of imitating instruments (Kovalcsik 1987). The *cigánydal* vocables give an effect of uninhibited celebration that can excite the audience. At a 1994 concert I observed the primary exponent of *cigánydal*, Margit Bangó. During one episode of vocable singing she tossed her shoes off her feet and began dancing barefoot. This caused a stir among the mostly Magyar audience members, who began to clap and gesture in the air like Gypsy dancers.

3. Stigmatized groups may also protect themselves by rejecting the mainstream. Erving Goffman even cites such a practice among Roma as an example (1963:6). Many Vlach Roma in Hungary did this (see Stewart 1997).

4. Large-ensemble Christian pop resembles African-American gospel music in the use of mass choirs and pop instrumentation. In the latter, however, there are many changes in texture, and the primary focus is on the spiritual experience symbolized in a solo singer's virtuosic delivery (see Burnim 1985). Electronic sampling replaced the large-ensemble format of Contemporary Christian Music in the 1990s. The music then used percussive timbres characteristic of 1990s secular dance music in the United States. The brass timbre was reduced in variety, and the parts sounded in ranges where actual instruments are incapable of producing a pitch. Similarly, the synthesized string sounds in 1990s Christian pop had less variety of articulation than actual stringed instruments. The choral sound still appeared to be produced predominately by groups of singers rather than by multitracking. Milburn Price describes an example of small-ensemble Christian pop that incorporates congregational singing (1993:11).

5. Billy Graham's activities were very well known in Hungary, although his crusade was first held there only in the late 1980s.

Conclusion

1. Fundamentalism often appears to be an effective means to resist the relativism that accompanies globalization (Robertson 1992:69). Nationalism may be considered the dominant style of fundamentalist thinking in Eastern Europe.

Bibliography

Hymnbooks

Locations
EPK Evangéliumi Pünkösdi Közösség, central office. Uncataloged collection. Budapest.
BE Baptista Egyház Szövetségi Iroda. Archives, uncataloged collection. Budapest.
RR Református Ráday Kollégium Könyvtára. Budapest.
P Private ownership.

Cs. A. [Csopják, Attila], comp. 1900 (1896). *Sion énekei* (Songs of Zion). Budapest: n.p. 2nd ed., enl. Score. BE..
Dicséretek (Hymns). 1927. New York: Amerikai Magyar Baptista Szövetség. Score. BE.
Dicsőitlek Uram! (I Praise You, My Lord). 1948. Budapest: Tomi József. P.
————. 1955. Budapest: A Baptista Hitközség. Permit no. 4136. EPK.
Evangéliumi karénekek (Evangelical Choir Songs). 1928. Oradea-Nagyvárad, Romania: Romániai Baptista Szövetség. Score. BE.
[Gebhardt, G., comp.] 1875. *Frohe Botschaft*. Basel: Spittler. Score. RR.
Glaubenstimme. 1907. Hamburg: J. G. Oncken. 11th ed. BE.
A hit hangjai (Voices of Faith). 1905. Budapest: Magyar Baptisták Szövetkezete. 1st ed. Score. BE.
————. 1918. Cleveland: n.p. American ed. Score. EPK.
————. 1987 (1960, 9th ed.). Budapest: Magyarországi Baptista Egyház. 13th ed. BE.
Hitünk énekei (Songs of Our Faith). 1959. Budapest: Magyarországi Szabadegyházak Tanácsa. P.
————. 1964. Budapest: Evangéliumi Keresztyének Központja. Score. EPK.
————. 1965. Budapest: Evangéliumi Keresztyének (Pünkösdiek). 3rd ed. EPK.
Kováts, Lajos, ed. 1914. *Hallelujah!* Budapest: n.p. Dist. by Bethánia. Score. RR.
————. 1944. *Hallelujah!* Budapest: n.p. Score. P.
Lázár, István, and Gyula Bernhardt, eds. 1996. *Hitünk Énekei Evangéliumi Ének Gyűjteménye III. kiadása alapján összeállított kottás énekeskönyv* (Score Songbook Compiled for the Third Edition of Songs of Our Faith Collection of Evangelical Songs). Budapest: Evangéliumi Pünkösdi Közösség. Score. EPK.
Rároha, Dezső (Dávid) F., and Mrs. Dezső Rároha, comps. n.d. *Üdvözítőnk dicséretei* (Hymns

of Our Savior). Kispest, Hungary: A Magyarországi Istengyülekezetek Központja. Score. EPK.

Rauschenbusch, Walter, and Ira D. Sankey, comps. and eds. 1921 (1910). *Evangeliums-Sänger. Autorisierte Ausgabe der Gospel Hymns.* Vols. 1–3. Kassel: J. G. Oncken. 16th ed. RR.

Reichs-Lieder. 1897. Neumünster, Germany: G. Shloff. 3rd ed. RR.

Sankey, Ira, comp. 1921 (repr. 1972). *Sacred Songs and Solos. 1200 Pieces.* London: Marshall, Morgan, and Scott.

Sankey, Ira, James McGranahan, and George C. Stebbins, comps. 1895. *Gospel Hymns Nos. 1–6.* New York: Biglow and Main. Facsimile ed. New York: Da Capo Press, 1972.

Spiritual Songs. 1930. Springfield, MO: Gospel.

Viktor, János, comp. 1908. *Hozsanna!* Budapest: Londoni Traktátus Társulat (Religious Tract Society of London). Score. P.

Zengő harangok (Ringing Bells). n.d. Budapest: Tomi József. Score. P. Also in László Fortin, ed., *A bárány dicsérete* (Praise of the Lamb). 1990. Budapest: Primó Kiadó. P.

Secondary Sources

Acton, Thomas. 1974. *Gypsy Politics and Social Change.* London: Routledge and Kegan Paul.

[———]. 1979. "The Gypsy Evangelical Church." *Ecumenical Review* 31(3):289–95.

Adorno, Theodor W., and Max Horkheimer. 1972 (1944). *Dialectic of Enlightenment.* New York: Seabury Press.

Alford, Delton L. 1967. *Music in the Pentecostal Church.* Cleveland, TN: Pathway.

Anderson, Robert Mapes. 1987. "Pentecostal and Charismatic Christianity." In *Encyclopedia of Religion,* vol. 11, edited by Mircea Eliade, 229–35. New York: Macmillan.

Banton, Michael. 1981. "The Direction and Speed of Ethnic Change." In *Ethnic Change,* edited by Charles Keyes, 31–52. Seattle: University of Washington Press.

Bányai, Jenő. 1996. *A magyarországi baptista egyházzene története* (The History of Hungarian Baptist Music). Budapest: Baptista Kiadó.

Bartók, Béla. 1947 (1931). "Gypsy Music or Hungarian Music?" *Musical Quarterly* 33(2):240–57.

———. 1952 (1934). *Népzenénk és a szomszéd népek népzenéje* (Our Folk Music and the Folk Music of Neighboring Peoples). Budapest: Zeneműkiadó Vállalat.

———. 1981 (1924). *Hungarian Folk Music.* Albany: State University of New York Press.

———. 1992 (1921). "Hungarian Folk Music." In *Essays,* 58–70. Lincoln: University of Nebraska Press.

Bateson, Gregory. 1972. "A Theory of Play and Fantasy." In *Steps to an Ecology of Mind,* 177–93. New York: Ballantine.

Bauman, Richard. 1977. *Verbal Art as Performance.* Prospect Heights, IL: Waveland Press.

Beck, Sam. 1985. "The Romanian Gypsy Problem." In *Papers from the Fourth and Fifth Annual Meetings, Gypsy Lore Society, North American Chapter,* edited by Joanne Grumet, 100–109. New York: Gypsy Lore Society.

Bencze, János. 1989. "Jézus Krisztus postása" (Messenger of Jesus Christ). *Helyzet,* July 14, 1989, p. 16.

Bereczki, Lajos, ed. 1996. *Krisztusért járva követségben* (Going in Mission for Christ). Budapest: Baptista Kiadó.

Berg, Wesley. 1996. "Hymns of the Old Colony Mennonites and the Old Way of Singing." *Musical Quarterly* 80(1):77–117.

Berliner, Paul. 1978. *The Soul of Mbira.* Berkeley: University of California Press.

Berreman, Gerald. 1962. *Behind Many Masks: Ethnography and Impression Management in a Himalayan Village.* Ithaca, NY: Society for Applied Anthropology.

————. 1975. "Bazar Behavior: Social Identity and Social Interaction in Urban India." In *Ethnic Identity: Cultural Continuities and Change*, edited by George de Vos and Lola Romanucci-Ross, 71–105. Palo Alto, CA: Mayfield.

Biernaczky, Szilárd. 1982 (1970). "Abszurditások, avagy a beatről" (Absurdities, or On Beat Music). In *Zenekultúránkról* (On Our Musical Culture), edited by István Balázs, 117–20. Budapest: Kossuth Könyvkiadó.

Blacking, John. 1973. *How Musical Is Man?* Seattle: University of Washington Press.

Blankenburg, Walter. 1974. "Church Music in Reformed Europe." In *Protestant Church Music: A History*, edited by Friedrich Blume, 507–90. New York: Norton.

Bloch-Hoell, Nils. 1964. *The Pentecostal Movement: Its Origin, Development, and Distinctive Character*. Oslo: Universitetforlaget.

Blumhofer, Edith. 1993. *Restoring the Faith: The Assemblies of God, Pentecostalism, and American Culture*. Urbana: University of Illinois Press.

Bourdieu, Pierre. 1984 (1979). *Distinction: A Social Critique of the Judgement of Taste*. London: Routledge and Kegan Paul.

Brumback, Carl. 1961. *Suddenly . . . from Heaven: A History of the Assemblies of God*. Springfield, MO: Gospel.

Bucsay, Mihály. 1985. *A protestantizmus története Magyarországon 1521–1945* (The History of Protestantism in Hungary, 1521–1945). Budapest: Gondolat.

Burnim, Mellonee. 1985. "The Black Gospel Music Tradition: A Complex of Ideology, Aesthetic, and Behavior." In *More Than Dancing*, edited by Irene V. Jackson, 147–67. Westport, CT: Greenwood Press.

Búth, Ottó. 1991. "A gyülekezet zenekari élete" (The Orchestral Life of the Congregation). *Élő Víz* 6:13–15.

de Certeau, Michel, Dominique Julia, and Jacques Revel. 1986 [1980]. "The Beauty of the Dead: Nisard." In *Heterologies: Discourse on the Other*, 119–36. Minneapolis: University of Minnesota Press.

Chodorow, Nancy. 1978. *The Reproduction of Mothering: Psychoanalysis and the Sociology of Gender*. Berkeley: University of California Press.

Clements, William. 1976. "Conversion and Communitas." *Western Folklore* 35(1):35–45.

Clifford, James. 1986. "Introduction: Partial Truths." In *Writing Culture*, edited by James Clifford and George Marcus, 1–26. Chicago: University of Chicago Press.

Code, Lorraine. 1991. *What Can She Know? Feminist Theory and the Construction of Knowledge*. Ithaca, NY: Cornell University Press.

Crapanzano, Vincent. 1980. *Tuhami: Portrait of a Moroccan*. Chicago: University of Chicago Press.

————. 1987. "Spirit Possession." In *Encyclopedia of Religion*, edited by Mircea Eliade, vol. 14, 12–18. New York: Macmillan.

————. 2000. *Serving the Word*. New York: New Press.

Crowe, David M. 1994. *A History of the Gypsies of Eastern Europe and Russia*. New York: St. Martin's Press.

Csalog, Zsolt. 1976. *Kilenc cigány* (Nine Gypsies). Budapest: Kozmosz Könyvek.

————. 1984. "Jegyzetek a cigányság támogatásának kérdéseiről" (Notes on Questions of Assisting the Gypsy People). *Szociálpolitikai Értesítő* 2:36–79.

Csohány, János. 1974. "A puritán paraszti közösségek válsága Magyarországon a kapitalizmus kialakulásának korában" (The Crisis of the Puritan Peasant Communities in Hungary during the Time of Capitalism's Development). *Theologiai Szemle* 1–2:36–39.

Csomasz Tóth, Kálmán. 1990. "Egyházi zenéélet. Protestáns egyházak" (Church Musical Life: Protestant Churches). In *Magyarország zenetörténete 2. 1541–1686* (Hungarian Music History 2. 1541–1686), edited by Kornél Bárdos, 186–213. Budapest: Akadémiai Kiadó.

————. 1950. *A református gyülekezeti éneklés* (Reformed [Calvinist] Congregational Singing). Budapest: Magyar Református Egyház.

Dearman, Marion. 1974. "Christ and Conformity: A Study of Pentecostal Values." *Journal for the Scientific Study of Religion* 13(4):437–53.

Dégh, Linda. 1948. "Adatok a magyar parasztság irodalmi életéhez" (Additional Data on the Literary Life of the Hungarian Peasantry). *Magyar Századok*, 299–315.

————. 1990. "Are Sectarian Miracle Stories Contemporary American Folk Legends? A Preliminary Consideration." In *Storytelling in Contemporary Societies*, edited by Lutz Rörich and Sabine Wienker-Piepho, 71–89. Tübingen: Gunter Narr.

————. 1994. "Tape-Recording Miracles for Everyday Living: The Ethnography of a Pentecostal Community." In *American Folklore and the Mass Media*, 110–52. Bloomington: Indiana University Press.

Deiros, Pablo. 1991. "Protestant Fundamentalism in Latin America." In *Fundamentalisms Observed*, edited by Martin Marty and Scott Appleby, 142–96. Chicago: University of Chicago Press.

De Jong, Mary. 1986. "'I Want to Be Like Jesus': The Self-Defining Power of Evangelical Hymnody." *Journal of the American Academy of Religion* 54(3):461–93.

Deleuze, Gilles, and Félix Guattari. 1987 (1980). *A Thousand Plateaus: Capitalism and Schizophrenia*. Minneapolis: University of Minnesota Press.

Derrida, Jacques. 1976 (1967). *Of Grammatology*. Baltimore: Johns Hopkins University Press.

DeShane, Kenneth R. 1996. "'Sometimes It Takes Experts to Tell the Difference': A Believer's Perspective on Pentecostal Sermons." *Southern Folklore* 53(2):91–111.

di Leonardo, Micaela. 1991. "Contingencies of Value in Feminist Anthropology." In *(En)gendering Knowledge: Feminists in Academe*, edited by Joan E. Hartman and Ellen Messer-Davidow, 140–58. Knoxville: University of Tennessee Press.

Diósi, Ágnes. 1988. *Cigányút* (Gypsy Road). Budapest: Szépirodalmi Könyvkiadó.

————. 1990a. "A cigányok vallási világa" (The Religious World of the Gypsies). *Egyház és Világ* 1:18–20.

————. 1990b. *Szűz Mária zsebkendője* (The Virgin Mary's Handkerchief). Budapest: Kozmosz Könyvek.

————. 1991. "Meditáció a legnagyobb szenvedés kiváltságáról" (Meditation on the Prerogative of Greatest Suffering). *Amaro Drom* 1(7):4–7.

Dobos, László Gábor. 1987. "Belmissziói és szociális irányzatok a protestáns egyházakban és vallásos szervezetekben" (Social and Home Mission Directions in the Protestant Churches and Religious Organizations). In *A magyar protestantizmus, 1918–1948* (Hungarian Protestantism, 1918–1948), edited by Ferenc Lendvai, 263–313. Budapest: Kossuth Könyvkiadó.

Dumont, Jean-Paul. 1978. *The Headman and I*. Austin: University of Texas Press.

Duncan, Larry. 1987. "Music among Early Pentecostals." *Hymn* 38(1):11–15.

Enzensberger, Hans Magnus. 1976 (1970). "Constituents of a Theory of the Media." In *Raids and Reconstructions*, 20–53. London: Pluto Press.

Erdely, Stephen. 1965. *Methods and Principles of Hungarian Ethnomusicology*. Bloomington: Indiana University Publications.

Erdős, József, Endre Kozma, Csilla Prileszky, and György Uhrmann. 1986. *Hungarian in Words and Pictures*. Budapest: Tankönyvkiadó.

Erdős, Kamill. 1960. "A Classification of Gypsies in Hungary." *Acta Orientalia* 10(1):79–82.

Erlmann, Veit. 1999. *Music, Modernity, and the Global Imagination*. New York: Oxford University Press.

Eskew, Harry, and James Downey. 1986. "Gospel Music." Part 1. "White Gospel Music." In *The New Grove Dictionary of American Music*, vol. 2, edited by Stanley Sadie, 249–54. New York: Macmillan.

Fabian, Johannes. 1983. *Time and the Other.* New York: Columbia University Press.

Fátyol, Tivadar. 1986. "Gondolatforgácsok a cigányzenéről" (Kindlings of Thought on Gypsy Music). In *Egyszer karolj át egy fát! Cigányalmanach* (Embrace a Tree Once! Gypsy Almanac), edited by Gábor Murányi, 156–59. Budapest: TIT Országos Központja, Cigány Ismeretterjesztő Bizottsága.

Fél, Edit, and Tamás Hofer. 1969. *Proper Peasants.* Chicago: Aldine.

Feld, Steven. 1982. *Sound and Sentiment.* Philadelphia: University of Pennsylvania Press.

Femia, Joseph. 1975. "Hegemony and Consciousness in the Thought of Antonio Gramsci." *Political Studies* 23(1):29–48.

Fish, Stanley. 1976. "Interpreting the *Variorum.*" *Critical Inquiry* 2(spring):465–85.

Fodor, József. 1984. *A magyarországi kisegyházak története, elterjedtségük és befolyási övezetük, hitéletük és szociáletikai tanításaik főbb jellemzői* (The History, Distribution and Zones of Influence, Beliefs, and Main Characteristics of the Ethical Teachings of Hungary's Small Churches). Budapest: Művelődési Minisztérium Marxizmus-Leninizmus Oktatási Főosztálya.

Forgács, Gyula. 1925. *A belmisszió és cura pastoralis kézikönyve* (Manual of the Home Mission and *cura pastoralis*). Pápa, Hungary: Magyar Református Egyház.

Foucault, Michel. 1980. *Power/Knowledge.* New York: Pantheon.

———. 1990 (1976). *The History of Sexuality: An Introduction.* Vol 1. New York: Vintage Books.

Friedl, Ernestine. 1986. "Field Work in a Greek Village." In *Women in the Field: Anthropological Experiences,* edited by Peggy Gold, 194–217. Berkeley: University of California Press.

Friedson, Stephen. 1996. *Dancing Prophets.* Chicago: University of Chicago Press.

Frigyesi, Judit. 1998. *Béla Bartók and Turn-of-the-Century Budapest.* Berkeley: University of California Press.

Fusco, Coco. 1995. *English Is Broken Here: Notes on Cultural Fusion in the Americas.* New York: New City Press.

Gay y Blasco, Paloma. 1999. *Gypsies in Madrid.* Oxford: Berg.

Geertz, Clifford. 1973. *The Interpretation of Cultures.* New York: Basic Books.

Genovese, Eugene. 1974. *Roll, Jordan, Roll: The World the Slaves Made.* New York: Pantheon.

Gerlach, Luther P., and Virginia H. Hine. 1970. *People, Power, Change: Movements of Social Transformation.* New York: Bobbs-Merrill.

Gheorghe, Nicolae, and Thomas Acton. 1992. "Dealing with Multiculturality: Minority, Ethnic, National and Human Rights." *OSCE ODIHR Bulletin* (Organization for Security and Cooperation in Europe. Office for Democratic Institutions and Human Rights) 3(1):28–40.

Ghezzo, Márta A. 1989. *Epic Songs of Sixteenth-Century Hungary: History and Style.* Budapest: Akadémiai Kiadó.

Gilroy, Paul. 1993. *The Black Atlantic.* Cambridge: Harvard University Press.

Glock, Charles. 1973 (1964). "On the Origin and Evolution of Religious Groups." In *Religion in Sociological Perspective,* edited by Charles Glock, 207–20. Belmont, CA: Wadsworth.

Goffman, Erving. 1959. *The Presentation of Self in Everyday Life.* New York: Doubleday.

———. 1963. *Stigma.* Englewood Cliffs, NJ: Prentice-Hall.

Goodman, Felicitas. 1972. *Speaking in Tongues.* Chicago: University of Chicago Press.

———. 1987. "Glossolalia." In *Encyclopedia of Religion,* vol. 5, edited by Mircea Eliade, 562–66. New York: Macmillan.

Gronemeyer, Reimer. 1981. "Unaufgeräumte Hinterzimmer." In *Kumpania und Kontrolle: moderne Behinderungen zigeunerischen Lebens,* edited by Mark Münzel and Bernhard Streck, 193–224. Giessen, Germany: Focus.

Guilbault, Jocelyne. 1993. *Zouk: World Music in the West Indies.* Chicago: University of Chicago Press.

Gyurkovics, Mária S. 1981. "A hodászi cigánytelep" (The Gypsy District of Hodász). *Vigilia* 10:680–83.

Hadházy, Antal. 1983. "A cigány-misszió területén szerzett tapasztalatokról" (On Experiences from the Field of the Gypsy Mission). *Theologiai Szemle* 26(3):177–79.

Hancock, Ian. 1987. *The Pariah Syndrome*. Ann Arbor: Karoma.

———. 1995. *A Handbook of Vlax-Romani*. Columbus, OH: Slavica Press.

Hankiss, Elemér. 1989. *Kelet-európai alternatívák* (East European Alternatives). Budapest: Közgazdasági és Jogi Könyvkiadó.

Havas, Gábor, Gábor Kertesi, and István Kemény. 1995. "The Statistics of Deprivation: The Roma in Hungary." *Hungarian Quarterly* 36:67–80.

Hegedüs, T. András. 1989. "A cigányság képe a magyar sajtóban (1985–1986)" (The Picture of Gypsies in the Hungarian Press, 1985–1986). *Kultúra és Közösség* 1:68–79.

Hegyi, Imre, and Márta Kovalik. 1981. "Kreol mise" (Creole Mass). *Vigilia* 10:685–95.

Hollenweger, Walter. 1972. *The Pentecostals*. Minneapolis: Augsburg.

Horváth, Zsuzsa. 1977. "Megteltek mind Szentlélekkel. Az evangéliumi pünkösdi közösség egy gyülekezetéről" (They Were All Filled with the Holy Spirit: On a Congregation of the Evangelical Pentecostal Fellowship). *Világosság* 19(6):380–86.

———. 1984. "Sects in Hungary." *Religion in Communist Lands* 12:4–10.

———. 1990. "Az állami egyházpolitika és a kisegyházak 1945 után" (The Church Politics of the State and the Small Churches after 1945). Unpublished essay, Sociology Institute, Hungarian Academy of Sciences, Budapest.

———. 1992. "A Hit Gyülekezetének szociológiai sajátosságai." (The Sociological Characteristics of the Congregation of Faith). Unpublished essay, Sociology Institute, Hungarian Academy of Sciences, Budapest.

Horváth, Zsuzsa, and Magda Matolay. 1980. "Egy szabadkeresztyén gyülekezet. Kutatási jelentés" (A Free Christian Church: Scholarly Report). Unpublished monograph, Department of Philosophy, Hungarian Academy of Sciences, Budapest.

Human Rights Watch. 1996. *Rights Denied: The Roma of Hungary*. New York: Human Rights Watch.

Huseby-Darvas, Éva. 1989. "Migration and Gender: Perspectives from Rural Hungary." *East European Quarterly* 23(4):487–98.

Hustad, Donald. 1982. "The Explosion of Popular Hymnody." *Hymn* 33:159–67.

Illyés, Endre. 1931. *A magyar református földmivelő nép lelki élete* (The Spiritual Life of the Hungarian Agricultural People). Szeged, Hungary: n.p.

Járdányi, Pál. 1961. *Magyar népdaltípusok* (Hungarian Folk Song Types). Budapest: Akadémiai Kiadó.

Jaulin, Robert. 1970. *La paix blanche: Introduction a l'ethnocide*. Paris: Éditions du Seul.

Johnson, Benton. 1961. "Do Holiness Sects Socialize in Dominant Values?" *Social Forces* 39(1961):309–16.

Kálmán, Farkas. 1888. "Somerville az Alföldön" (Somerville in the Alföld). *Protestáns Egyházi és Iskolai Lap* 31(8):245–46.

Kardos, László. 1969. *Egyház és vallásos élet egy mai faluban* (Church and Religious Life in a Modern Village). Budapest: Kossuth Kiadó.

Kardos, László, and Jenő Szigeti. 1988. *Boldog emberek közössége. A magyarországi nazarénusok* (The Community of Joyful People: The Hungarian Nazarenes). Budapest: Magvető Könyvkiadó.

Karsai, László. 1992. *A cigánykérdés Magyarországon 1919–1945* (The Gypsy Question in Hungary 1919–1945). Budapest: Cserépfalvi Könyvkiadó.

Keil, Charles, and Steven Feld. 1994. *Music Grooves*. Chicago: University of Chicago Press.

Kemény, István. 1974. "A magyarországi cigány lakosság" (The Hungarian Gypsy Population). *Valóság* 1:63–72.

———. 1997. "A magyarországi roma (cigány) népességről" (On the Hungarian Roma [Gypsy] Population). *Magyar Tudomány* 42(6):644–55.

Kenrick, Donald, and Gratton Puxon. 1972. *The Destiny of Europe's Gypsies*. New York: Basic Books.

Kerényi, György. 1961. *Népies dalok* (Folklike Songs). Budapest: Akadémiai Kiadó.

Kertész, Péter. 1992. "Ferge Zsuzsa: A nép nem hagy magából csőcseléket csinálni" (Zsuzsa Ferge: The People Do Not Form a Mob by Themselves). *Népszabadság*, January 18, p. 17.

Kertész-Wilkinson, Irén. 1992. "Genuine and Adopted Songs in the Vlach Gypsy Repertoire: A Controversy Re-Examined." *British Journal of Ethnomusicology* 1:111–36.

———. 1997. *Vásár van előttem. Egyéni alkotások és társadalmi kontextusok egy dél-magyarországi oláhcigány lassú dalban. The Fair Is Ahead of Me: Individual Creativity and Social Contexts in the Performances of a Southern Hungarian Vlach Gypsy Slow Song*. Budapest: Institute for Musicology of the Hungarian Academy of Sciences.

Kodály, Zoltán. 1960. *Folk Music of Hungary*. Budapest: Corvina Kiadó.

Konrád, György, and Iván Szelényi. 1979 (1974). *The Intellectuals on the Road to Class Power*. New York: Harcourt Brace.

Koskoff, Ellen. 1989 (1987). An Introduction to Women, Music and Culture. In *Women and Music in Cross-Cultural Perspective*, edited by Ellen Koskoff, 1–24. Urbana: University of Illinois Press.

Kovács, Imre. 1989 (1937). *A néma forradalom* (The Silent Revolution). Budapest: Cserépfalvi Kiadó.

Kovács, János. 1975. "Szekták a Duna-Tisza közén" (Sects between the Danube and the Tisza). *Forrás* 3:140–55.

Kovalcsik, Katalin. 1981. "A szatmár megyei oláh cigányok lassú dalainak többszólamúsága (Polyphony in the Slow Songs of Szatmár County Vlach Gypsies)." *Zenetudományi dolgozatok*, 261–71.

———. 1985. *Szlovákiai oláhcigány népdalok. Vlach Gypsy Songs in Slovakia*. Budapest: Institute for Musicology of the Hungarian Academy of Sciences.

———. 1987. "Popular Dance Music Elements in the Folk Music of Gypsies in Hungary." *Popular Music* 6(1):45–65.

———. 1988. Introduction to Katalin Kovalcsik and Gábor Grabocz, *A mesemondó Rostás Mihály. Mihály Rostás, a Gypsy Story-Teller*. 25–41. Budapest: MTA Néprajzi Kutató Csoport.

———. 1991. "Chansons tsiganes lentes sur des experiences personnelles. L'écart entre le chanteur et le groupe." *Cahiers de Littérature Orale* 30:45–64.

Lajtha, László. 1953. "Egy 'hamis' zenekar" (An "Out-of-Tune" Orchestra). In *Emlékkönyv Kodály Zoltán 70. születésnapjára* (Festschrift in Honor of the Seventieth Birthday of Zoltán Kodály), edited by Bence Szabolcsi and Dénes Bartha, 169–98. Budapest: Akadémiai Kiadó.

———. 1988. *Instrumental Music from Western Hungary*. Budapest: Akadémiai Kiadó.

Lange, Barbara Rose. 1996a. "Gender Politics and Musical Performers in the Isten Gyülekezet: A Fieldwork Account." *Journal of American Folklore* 109(431):60–76.

———. 1996b. "*Lakodalmas* Rock and the Rejection of Popular Culture in Post-Socialist Hungary." In *Retuning Culture: Musical Changes in Eastern Europe*, edited by Mark Slobin, 76–91. Durham, NC: Duke University Press.

———. 1997a. "Hungarian Rom (Gypsy) Political Activism and the Development of *Folklór* Ensemble Music." *World of Music* 39(3):5–30.

————. 1997b. "'What Was That Conquering Magic . . . ': The Power of Discontinuity in Hungarian Gypsy *Nóta.*" *Ethnomusicology* 41(3):517–537.

————. 1999. "Political Consciousness in the Vernacular: Versions and Variants of the Hungarian *Cigányhimnusz* (Gypsy Anthem)." *Journal of the Gypsy Lore Society* 5, 9(1):29–54.

Larsen, L. B. 1987. "We Have Come a Long Way . . ." *Hymn* 38(1):16–18.

Lawless, Elaine J. 1988a. *God's Peculiar People: Women's Voices and Folk Tradition in a Pentecostal Church.* Lexington: University Press of Kentucky.

————. 1988b. *Handmaidens of the Lord.* Philadelphia: University of Pennsylvania Press.

Lázár, Ildikó. 1992. "Trading Stereotypes for Self-Reliance." Interview with Aladár Horváth. *Budapest Week,* February 20–26, p. 7.

Lázár, István. 1989. *Hungary: A Brief History.* Budapest: Corvina.

Lederman, Rena. 1986. "The Return of Redwoman: Field Work in Highland New Guinea." In *Women in the Field: Anthropological Experiences,* edited by Peggy Golde, 359–88. Berkeley: University of California Press.

Lee, Ken. 2000. "Orientalism and Gypsylorism." *Social Analysis* 44(2):129–56.

Lemon, Alaina. 2000. *Between Two Fires: Gypsy Performance and Romani Memory from Pushkin to Postsocialism.* Durham, NC: Duke University Press.

Lévai, Júlia, and Iván Vitányi. 1973. *Miből lesz a sláger* (What Makes a Hit Song)? Budapest: Zeneműkiadó.

Lewis, I. M. 1989. *Ecstatic Religion.* London: Routledge. 2nd edition.

Lewis, Oscar. 1961. *Children of Sanchez.* New York: Vintage Books.

Lewy, Guenter. 2000. *The Nazi Persecution of the Gypsies.* New York: Oxford University Press.

Liégeois, Jean-Pierre. 1994. *Roma, Gypsies, Travellers.* Strasbourg: Council of Europe.

Linton, Ralph. 1943. "Nativistic Movements." *American Anthropologist* 45:230–40.

Liszt, Franz. 1881 (1859). *The Gipsy in Music.* London: William Reeves.

Lortat-Jacob, Bernard. 1995. *Sardinian Chronicles.* Chicago: University of Chicago Press.

MacRobert, Iain. 1988. *The Black Roots and White Racism of Early Pentecostalism in the USA.* New York: St. Martin's Press.

Magay, Tamás, and László Országh. 1990. *A Concise Hungarian-English Dictionary. Magyar-angol kéziszótár.* Budapest: Akadémiai Kiadó.

Manga, János. 1969. *Hungarian Folk Songs and Folk Instruments.* Budapest: Corvina.

Mascia-Lees, Frances E., Patricia Sharpe, and Colleen Ballerine Cohen. 1989. "The Postmodernist Turn in Anthropology: Cautions from a Feminist Perspective." *Signs* 15:7–33.

McClary, Susan. 1991. *Feminine Endings: Music, Gender, and Sexuality.* Minneapolis: University of Minnesota Press.

Menzies, William. 1971. *Anointed to Serve: The Story of the Assemblies of God.* Springfield, MO: Gospel.

Merriam, Alan. 1964. *The Anthropology of Music.* Chicago: Northwestern University Press.

————. 1967. *Ethnomusicology of the Flathead Indians.* Chicago: Aldine.

Mezey, Barna. 1986. *A cigánykérdés dokumentumokban, 1422–1985* (The Gypsy Question in Documents, 1422–1985). Budapest: Kossuth Könyvkiadó.

Murányi, Róbert. 1970. "The First Appearance of the Gospel Hymns in Hungary." *Studia Musicologica* 12:311–17.

Nagy, Olga. 1986. "Vallásos élet Havadon" (Religious Life in Havad). In *Mert ezt Isten hagyta. Tanulmányok a népi vallásosság köréből* (Because God Left This to Us: Studies from the Area of Folk Religiosity), edited by Gábor Tüskés, 496–515. Budapest: Magvető.

Némedi, Dénes. 1985. *A népi szociográfia 1930–1938* (Folk Sociography 1930–1938). Budapest: Gondolat.

Neményi, Mária. 1991. "'Végül is mindannyian cigányok vagyunk!'" (In the End, We Are All Gypsies). *Phralipe* 7:23–25.

Nettl, Bruno. 1957. "The Hymns of the Amish: An Example of Marginal Survival." *Journal of American Folklore* 70:323–28.

———. 1983. *The Study of Ethnomusicology*. Urbana: University of Illinois Press.

Niebuhr, Richard. 1929. *The Social Sources of Denominationalism*. New York: Holt.

Ortner, Sherry. 1989–90. "Gender Hegemonies." *Cultural Critique* 14:35–80.

O'Sullivan, John L. 1839. "The Great Nation of Futurity." *Democratic Review* 6(23):426–30.

Pákozdy, László Márton. 1972. "Glossolália—egykor és ma" (Glossolalia—Then and Now). *Theologiai Szemle* 1–2:10–15.

Patterson, Beverly Bush. 1995. *The Sound of the Dove: Singing in Appalachian Primitive Baptist Churches*. Urbana: University of Illinois Press.

Peacock, James L., and Ruel W. Tyson, Jr. 1989. *Pilgrims of Paradox: Calvinism and Experience among the Primitive Baptists of the Blue Ridge*. Washington, DC: Smithsonian Institution Press.

Pitts, Walter. 1991. "Like a Tree Planted by the Water: The Musical Cycle in the African-American Baptist Ritual." *Journal of American Folklore* 104(413):318–40.

Polanyi, Karl. 1944. *The Great Transformation*. Boston: Beacon Press.

Polgar, Steven. 1984. "A Summary of the Situation of the Hungarian Catholic Church." *Religion in Communist Lands* 12:11–38.

Pope, Liston. 1942. *Millhands and Preachers*. New York: Yale University Press.

Price, Milburn. 1993. "The Impact of Popular Culture on Congregational Song." *Hymn* 44(1):11–19.

Rabinow, Paul. 1977. *Reflections on Fieldwork in Morocco*. Berkeley: University of California Press.

Ramet, Sabrina. 1998. *Nihil Obstat: Religion, Politics, and Social Change in East-Central Europe and Russia*. Durham, NC: Duke University Press.

Réger, Zita. 1988. "A cigány nyelv: kutatások és vitapontok" (The Gypsy Language: Scholarship and Points of Debate). *Műhelymunkák a nyelvészet és társtudományai köréből* 4:155–78.

Réger, Zita, and Joan Berko Gleason. 1991. "Romani Child-Directed Speech and Children's Language among Gypsies in Hungary." *Language in Society* 20:601–17.

Révész, Imre. 1943. "Egy fejezet a magyar református ébredés történetéből" (A Chapter from the History of the Hungarian Reformed [Church] Revival). *Theologiai Szemle* 19(1):10–45.

Robertson, Roland. 1992. *Globalization*. London: Sage.

Rogers, Susan Carol. 1975. "Female Forms of Power and the Myth of Male Dominance." *American Ethnologist* 2(4):727–57.

Roseman, Marina. 1991. *Healing Sounds from the Malaysian Rainforest: Temiar Music and Medicine*. Berkeley: University of California Press.

Rosenberg, Bruce. 1970. *The Art of the American Folk Preacher*. New York: Oxford University Press.

Rothenbusch, Esther. 1991. "The Role of *Gospel Hymns Nos. 1 to 6 (1875–1894)* in American Revivalism." Ph.D diss., University of Michigan.

Rouget, Gerard. 1985 (1980). *Music and Trance*. Chicago: University of Chicago Press.

Samarin, William J. 1972a. *Tongues of Men and Angels*. New York: MacMillan.

———. 1972b. "Variation and Variables in Religious Glossolalia." *Language in Society* 1(1):121–30.

Sanday, Peggy Reeves. 1981. *Female Power and Male Dominance: On the Origins of Social Inequality*. New York: Cambridge University Press.

Sárosi, Bálint. 1966. "Étterem-monográfia" (Restaurant Monograph). *Magyar Zene* 6:587–98.
———. 1967. *Die Volksmusikinstrumente Ungarns*. Handbuch der europäischen Volksmusikinstrumente, series 1, vol. 1. Leipzig: VEB Deutscher Verlag für Musik.
———. 1978 (1971). *Gypsy Music*. Budapest: Corvina.
———. 1986. *Folk Music: Hungarian Musical Idiom*. Budapest: Corvina.
———. 1996. *A hangszeres magyar népzene* (Hungarian Instrumental Folk Music). Budapest: Püski Kiadó.
Sato, Ellen B. L. 1988. "The Social Impact of the Rise of Pentecostal Evangelism among American Rom." In *Papers from the Eighth and Ninth Annual Meetings*, edited by Cara De Silva, Joanne Grumet, and David Nemeth, 69–94. New York: Gypsy Lore Society.
Schafft, Kai, and David L. Brown. 2000. "Social Capital and Grassroots Development: The Case of Roma Self-Governance in Hungary." *Social Problems* 47(2):201–19.
Schöpflin, George. 1979. "Opposition and Para-Opposition: Critical Currents in Hungary, 1968–78." In *Opposition in Eastern Europe*, edited by Rudolf Tőkés, 142–86. London: MacMillan.
Sebestyén, Jenő. 1923. "Zsoltárok és hozsannák" (Psalms and Hosannas). *Kálvinista Szemle* 4(31):270.
Seeger, Anthony. 1987. *Why Suyá Sing*. Cambridge, UK: Cambridge University Press.
Shelemay, Kay Kaufman. 1997. "The Ethnomusicologist, Ethnographic Method, and the Transmission of Tradition." In *Shadows in the Field*, edited by Gregory E. Barz and Timothy J. Cooley, 189–204. New York: Oxford University Press.
Silverman, Carol. 1982. "Everyday Drama: Impression Management of Urban Gypsies." *Urban Anthropology* 111(3–4):377–98.
———. 1988. "Negotiating 'Gypsiness': Strategy in Context." *Journal of American Folklore* 101:261–75.
———. 1996. "Music and Marginality: *Roma* (Gypsies) of Bulgaria and Macedonia." In *Retuning Culture*, edited by Mark Slobin, 231–53. Durham, NC: Duke University Press.
Sizer, Sandra. 1978. *Gospel Hymns and Social Religion*. Philadelphia: Temple University Press.
Smith, Anna Marie. 1994. "Rastafari as Resistance and the Ambiguities of Essentialism in the 'New Social Movements.'" In *The Making of Political Identities*, edited by Ernesto Laclau, 171–204. London: Verso.
Stewart, Michael. 1989. "'True Speech': Song and the Moral Order of a Hungarian Vlach Gypsy Community." *Man* 24(1):79–102.
———. 1997. *The Time of the Gypsies*. Boulder, CO: Westview Press.
Stillman, Amy Ku'uleialoha. 1993. "Prelude to a Comparative Investigation of Protestant Hymnody in Polynesia." *Yearbook for Traditional Music* 25:89–99.
Strathern, Marilyn. 1981. "Self-Interest and the Social Good: Some Implications of Hagen Gender Imagery." In *Sexual Meanings: The Cultural Construction of Gender and Sexuality*, edited by Sherry Ortner and Harriet Whitehead, 166–91. Cambridge, UK: Cambridge University Press.
Street, Brian V. 1984. *Literacy in Theory and Practice*. Cambridge, UK: Cambridge University Press.
Stromberg, Peter. 1993. *Language and Self-Transformation: A Study of the Christian Conversion Narrative*. Cambridge, UK: Cambridge University Press.
Sugar, Peter F. 1990. "The Principality of Transylvania." In *A History of Hungary*, edited by Peter Sugar, 121–27. Bloomington: Indiana University Press.
Sugarman, Jane. 1997. *Engendering Song: Singing and Subjectivity at Prespa Albanian Weddings*. Chicago: University of Chicago Press.
Sutherland, Anne. 1975. *Gypsies: The Hidden Americans*. New York: Free Press.
Szabolcsi, Bence. 1964 (1955). *A Concise History of Hungarian Music*. Budapest: Zeneműkiadó.

Szakály, Ferenc. 1990. "The Early Ottoman Period, Including Royal Hungary, 1526–1606." In *A History of Hungary*, edited by Peter Sugar, 83–99. Bloomington: Indiana University Press.

Szapu, Magda. 1985. *Mesemondó és közössége Kaposszentjakabon* (The Storyteller and his Community in Kaposszentjakab). Budapest: MTA Néprajzi Kutató Csoport.

Szegő, László. 1977. *Csikóink kényesek. Magyarországi cigány népköltészet* (We Have Fine Colts: Hungarian Gypsy Folk Poetry). Budapest: Európa Könyvkiadó.

Szelényi, Iván, and Szonja Szelényi. 1991. "Az elit cirkulációja" (Circulation of the Elite)? *Kritika*, October: 8–10.

Szigeti, Jenő. 1981. *És emlékezzél meg az útról . . . tanulmányok a magyarországi szabadegyházak történetéből* (Remember the Journey . . . Studies on the History of the Hungarian Free Churches). Budapest: Szabadegyházak Tanácsa.

———. 1987. "A kisebb magyarországi egyházak" (The Smaller Hungarian Churches). In *A magyar protestantizmus, 1918–1948* (Hungarian Protestantism, 1918–1948), edited by Ferenc Lendvai, 188–262. Budapest: Kossuth Könyvkiadó.

Szuhay, Péter. 1999. *A magyarországi cigányok kultúrája. Etnikus kultúra vagy a szegénység kultúrája* (The Culture of Hungarian Gypsies: Ethnic Culture or Culture of Poverty). Budapest: Panoráma.

Tedlock, Dennis. 1983. *The Spoken Word and the Work of Interpretation*. Philadelphia: University of Pennsylvania Press.

Thompson, E. P. 1963. *The Making of the English Working Class*. New York: Vintage.

———. 1991. *Customs in Common*. New York: New Press.

Titon, Jeff. 1985. "Stance, Role, and Identity in Fieldwork among Folk Baptists and Pentecostals in the United States." *American Music* 3:16–24.

———. 1988. *Powerhouse for God*. Austin: University of Texas Press.

Tóth, László, János Makovei, Béla Kovács, and Albert Pataky, eds. 1998 (1978). *A pünkösdi mozgalom Magyarországon*. Budapest: Evangéliumi Pünkösdi Közösség.

Toulis, Nicole Rodriguez. 1997. *Believing Identity*. Oxford: Berg.

Troeltsch, Ernst. 1931. *The Social Teaching of the Christian Churches*. Vol. 2. New York: Macmillan.

Turino, Thomas. 1999. "Signs of Imagination, Identity, and Experience: A Peircian Semiotic Theory for Music." *Ethnomusicology* 43(2):221–25.

Turner, Victor. 1967. *The Forest of Symbols*. Ithaca, NY: Cornell University Press.

———. 1969. *The Ritual Process: Structure and Anti-Structure*. Chicago: Aldine.

———. 1986. "Dewey, Dilthey, and Drama: An Essay in the Anthropology of Experience." In *The Anthropology of Experience*, edited by Victor Turner and Edward Bruner, 33–44. Urbana: University of Illinois Press.

Tüskés, Gábor. 1987. "A protestáns közösségek népi kultúrájának néhány kérdése" (A Few Questions on the Folk Culture of Protestant Communities). *Népi Kultúra—Népi Társadalom* 14:215–33.

Tyler, Stephen A. 1986. "Post-Modern Ethnography: From Document of the Occult to Occult Document." In *Writing Culture*, edited by James Clifford and George E. Marcus, 122–40. Berkeley: Univerisity of California Press.

Ujváry, Zoltán. 1980. *Népszokás és népköltészet* (Folk Custom and Folk Poetry). Debrecen, Hungary: Hajdú-Bihar Megyei Múzeum.

Vargyas, Lajos. 1981. *A magyarság népzenéje* (The Folk Music of the Hungarian People). Budapest: Zeneműkiadó.

Vekerdi, József. 1988. "The Gypsies and the Gypsy Problem in Hungary." *Hungarian Studies Review* 15(2):13–26.

Verdery, Katherine. 1991. *National Ideology under Socialism*. Berkeley: University of California Press.

Wallace, Anthony F. C. 1956. "Revitalization Movements." *American Anthropologist* 58:264–81.

Walters, Philip, ed. 1988. *World Christianity: Eastern Europe.* Monrovia, CA: Missions Advanced Research and Communications Center.

Wang, Kirsten. 1989. "Le mouvement Pentecôtiste chez les Gitans espagnols." In *Tsiganes: identité, évolution,* edited by Patrick Williams, 423–32. Paris: Syros Alternatives.

Weber, Max. 1947. *The Theory of Social and Economic Organization.* Glencoe, IL: Free Press.

———. 1958 (1920). *The Protestant Ethic and the Spirit of Capitalism.* New York: Scribners.

Williams, Patrick. 1982. "The Invisibility of the Kalderash of Paris: Some Aspects of the Economic Activity and Settlement Patterns of the Kalderash Rom of the Paris Suburbs." *Urban Anthropology* 11(3–4):315–46.

———. 1984. "Pour une approche du phenomene pentecôtiste chez les Tsiganes." *Etudes Tsiganes* 2:49–51.

———. 1987. "Le developpement du pentecôtisme chez les tsiganes en France: mouvement messianique, stereotypes et affirmation d'identité." In *Vers des sociétés pluriculturelles: études comparatives et situation en France,* Actes du Colloque International de l'AFA (Association Française des Anthropologues), Paris, January 9–11, 1986, 325–31. Paris: Éditions de l'ORSTOM.

———. 1991a. *Django.* Montpellier: Editions du Limon.

———. 1991b. "Le miracle et la nécessité: A propos du développement du pentecôtisme chez les tsiganes." *Archives de Sciences Sociales des Religions* 73(January–March):81–98.

———. 1993. *Nous, on n'en parle pas. Les vivants et les morts chez les Manouches.* Paris: Maison des sciences de l'homme.

Williams, Peter W. 1989 (1980). *Popular Religion in America.* Urbana: University of Illinois Press.

Wilson, Bryan. 1970. *Religious Sects: A Sociological Study.* London: World University Library.

———. 1975. "American Religious Sects in Europe." In *Superculture: American Popular Culture in Europe,* edited by C. W. E. Bigsby, 107–22. Bowling Green, OH: Bowling Green University Popular Press.

Wolf, Eric. 1982. *Europe and the People without History.* Berkeley: University of California Press.

Yoder, Don. 1974. "Toward a Definition of Folk Religion." *Western Folklore* 33:2–12.

Žižek, Slavoj. 1989. *The Sublime Object of Ideology.* London: Verso.

Index

Song titles and most names of organizations are listed under their English translation.

199